CETTIA'S SHADOW

Cettia's Shadow

OLIVA AND WILSON

CONTENTS

For Kira, Colt, Aria and Christopher.

We'd like to thank our close friends and family for supporting us. We battled 2020, loss, a house fire, and devastation throughout this journey, and we couldn't have finished it without your patience. We love you all.

First Printing, 2021

MAP OF ATHOZE

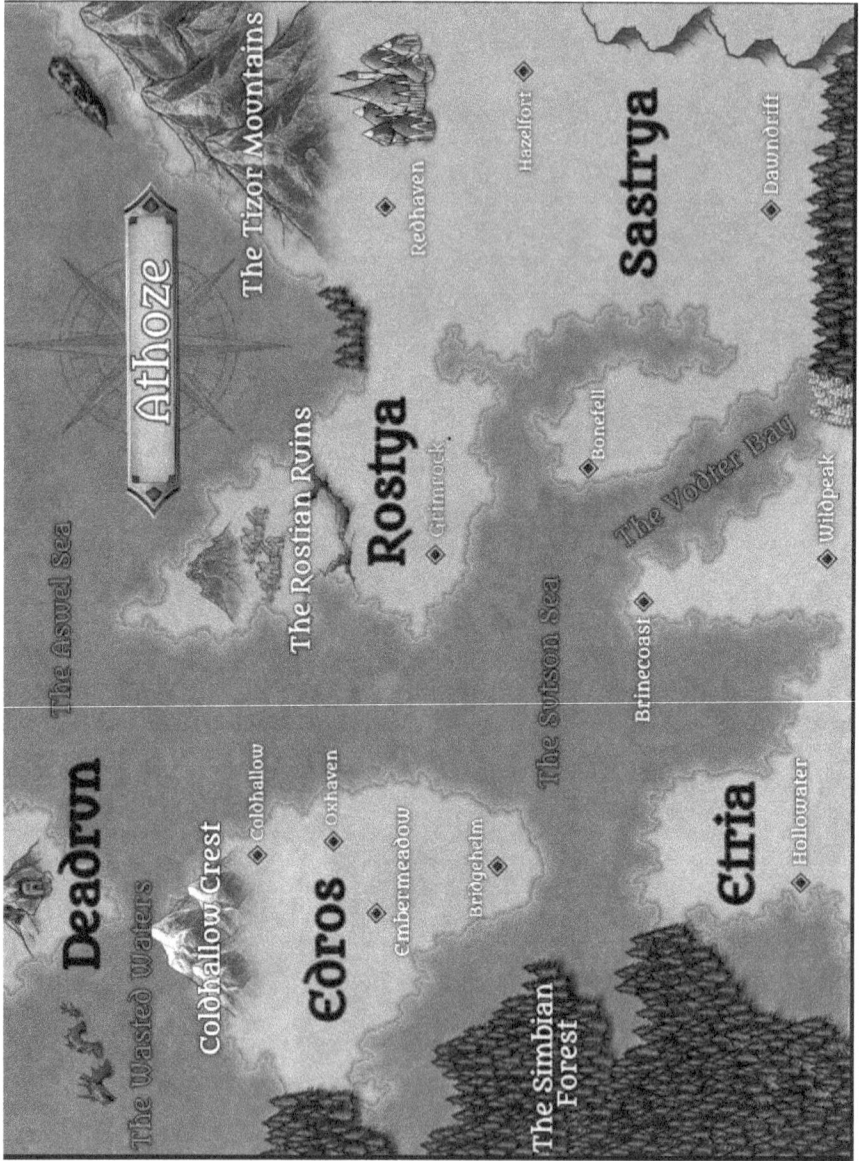

~ I ~

THE FIRE

"What are you staring at?"

Azrian drops his eyes and lets a soft chuckle past his lips. "Nothing, Rhix. Sorry. Just don't get how you can do that, is all."

A heavy hammer swings again with a force that shouldn't be possible from a human — but, then again, Rhix isn't exactly human. "You've been around Praediti for how long? Our gifts should no longer come as a surprise to you, and jealousy will get you nowhere, Az. It certainly won't help you sharpen that Hokrine knife. Tuyon will be coming back for that soon."

"You're right, boss. As always." He focuses once more on angling the blade right as he slides it across the oiled stone. The tips of his fingers are scarred and calloused from one too many slips, and the last thing he wants to do is to add yet another. But he *is* distracted, he's always distracted. Working for a blacksmith that also happens to be a ridiculously strong Viribus is a fairly distracting thing — he can hardly blame himself for focusing on the unnatural way Rhix pounds the Hokrine into submission. It's not attractive, not really. It's just... powerful. The sort of thing that makes mere humans wish they were *more*.

As the sunlight starts to fade, Azrian works a little faster. No less carefully, to be sure... but quicker, more urgently. When the night comes, it's best for folks like him to be tucked away somewhere safe. "Tuyon wants this in the morning, right?" he asks.

Rhix twirls the hammer in his hand like it's little more than a feather. "Yes. Will that be a problem?"

"Nope. I'll be back before the sun peeks over Coldhallow Crest." He starts packing his things as Rhix moves his large body closer to inspect his work. Azrian watches him with apprehension; it's hard to tell on any given day what kind of a mood his boss is really in. When he offers him a nod in acknowledgment, Az takes it without questioning him further.

He barely makes it home before the last of the light fades. When he walks in, his mother is huddling around a small fire, but Azrian shakes his head at its inadequacy. It's going to be cold overnight and that flame won't heat more than a few square feet. "Unless you want to freeze to death in your sleep, I suggest you move so I can feed it."

Roe glares at him. "I did the best I could, and unless *you* want to starve to death, you need to go to the market. I thought you'd be home by now."

The smell coating him from hours of sweat and coal dust catches up to him now that he's no longer in the open air. He needs to *bathe;* not worry about something she could've handled during the day. "It's not safe, Mother. You know this. It'll have to wait until morning. I'll fix the fire, go clean up and run first thing to... *shadows.*"

"Azrian?"

He narrows his eyes. "I can't go in the morning, I have to finish something at work, and it can't wait. If I leave you some money, will you go?"

The rumbling of an empty stomach answers his question. Azrian isn't even sure if it was his or his mother's, but it matters little. He knows they can't wait and he's already wasted enough time arguing about it. "I'm sorry, Az," she says. "I'll be fine with the fire like this until you get back. Take one of the torches. You'll be okay... you might not be as strong as Rhix, but you're no weakling." Her voice is filled with pride, and it makes him soften. She's right; he may not be a Viribus born with supreme physical prowess, but he's capable of holding his own... against other humans, anyway. Praediti are a different story entirely.

"I'll be back as soon as I can. Bolt the door behind me this time and don't open it until you hear our knock." He tosses another log on the fire before lighting his torch and checking for his knife, then waits on their small porch until he hears the bar snap in place behind him.

The air seems thicker, darker, more dangerous now. He ignores the pull in his chest telling him to go back and forces his feet to move. One after the other, left and then right until the uneasiness creeping down his spine manages to work all the way down to his toes.

The torchlight doesn't do much to illuminate his path and he finds himself jealous once again — this time of the Igneme. If he had fire-starting abilities like they did, not only would the thing in his hand be more effective, but he'd also be able to burn anything or anyone that crossed him to a crisp.

If only.

The market is unusually empty as he finally approaches with cautious, light steps. Thankfully, some of the small shops are still open and he's able to trade a handful of coins for some bread and a few ears of corn. There's no one left that late in the day that still has meat, but he's hopeful one of the traps he'd set earlier in the week finally caught something worth cooking.

He focuses on putting one foot in front of the other, but it takes too long to double back. He knows he has to do it; knows he can't risk being followed... but that doesn't stop his fear from rising as his torch burns out halfway home. Not for the first time, he wishes they could live somewhere less dangerous — if such a place even exists for people like them.

When a twig snaps nearby, Azrian nearly jumps out of his skin. He stays silent, letting the scream manifest as a full body shiver and an adrenaline spike instead of actual noise. Immediately, he scolds himself for it. He's a quarter of a century old, he shouldn't be this scared of the dark. And maybe he wouldn't be if the dark hadn't taken so many of his friends.

The knife at his side is a comfort. While it's not a failsafe method of protection, even the precious, gifted Praediti bleed like humans do. He just has to be faster than they are, so he lets Cettia guide him as he moves like a shadow through the trees. Sometimes, he thinks that star is the only thing shielding them from total, unrelenting hell... and maybe it is. Either way, it never fails to lead him home.

He knocks three times in quick succession then twice more with a long pause between. Silence greets him, so he knocks again. Finally, he hears the creaking of the bar and the door opens.

"Were you followed?"

Azrian bites back his retort that she should know better and simply shakes his head. "Here, eat a little and get some sleep. I'll check the traps after work tomorrow, maybe the gods will take pity on us." After taking a moment to scarf down some bread himself, he feeds the fire and strips off his dirty, tattered tunic. Rhix likely won't be happy that he didn't get a chance to bathe, but if he's lucky, he'll be able to keep his distance.

Yeah right, he thinks to himself. *When am I ever lucky?*

~

The next morning, Azrian shows up to work exhausted and dirty. Rhix gracefully doesn't comment on his appearance, and neither does Tuyon — he's actually so pleased with the work Az did on the Hokrine knife that he gives him a monetary tip instead of a verbal one to take a bath.

Az counts that as a win. He pockets the coins and carries on, standing up a little straighter now that he's proven himself again. Rhix waits until Tuyon is far out of earshot and comes over to nudge him. "You know your way around a blade. Now if only you had the same skill with partners."

Scowling, Azrian ducks under his meaty arm and swats him. "Sweet *shadows*, Rhix. Do you ever stop? I do just fine."

"She's coming in tomorrow, you know," he teases. "Those door handles her father commissioned are done, I sent word out to them just before you got here."

The rag he'd been holding falls uselessly to the ground. Morella is arguably one of the most gorgeous people he's ever seen, and the thought of seeing her again makes his pulse quicken. "Rella? You're sure?"

"He won't be coming down to get them himself, so... yeah, I'm sure."

The lump in his throat grows a little more. "Oh."

Rhix eyes him with amusement and walks over to ruffle his long, dark hair. "Just tell her how you feel. What's the worst that could happen? She tells you to shove off?"

Under his breath, Azrian mumbles something about *Rhix* shoving off, which earns him a sharp flick to the forehead. Coming from anyone else, it would've been little more than an annoyance... but from someone like him? Azrian felt the reverberation down to his heels. "That was uncalled for, Giant."

"It's not my fault you're puny. Now go, if you don't get yourself cleaned up, she'll laugh herself silly before you even get a chance to tell her she's cute."

Az rubs the spot on his forehead and grabs his bag. He knows better than to argue — he might only be a few inches shy of six feet, but Rhix is at least a half foot taller. "I'm going. I'll see you in the morning."

For once, he makes it home well before sundown which gives him time to check the traps and find a dorscuir. Its long, wiry tail sticks out through the wooden bars and for a moment, Azrian feels bad for it. It would barely give them enough meat to last two days, and somehow, that doesn't seem worth the cost.

He fishes the furry creature out of its cage and kills it quickly. Roe already has a fire going in the back, so Az prepares the beast and gets it cooking before finally making his way to the river. He takes his time, stripping down and scrubbing his body with the little bit of soap they managed to make from the last animal they'd trapped. His hair and short beard are a little harder to get clean, but he manages, then spends a few minutes just floating in the water.

Unbidden, Rhix's advice comes back to him. He *could* tell Morella how he feels, or... he could not. The second option sounds better, safer, and infinitely more likely — but he can't put it off forever. If he waits until she finds someone else, he'll regret it and he knows it. But trying to convince a Praediti that a human is worth their time is practically impossible. Why would they ever choose to be with someone mundane when there are alternatives? Someone that can manipulate elements, move objects with their minds, or travel through space and time itself? Azrian certainly wouldn't choose a human if he weren't one himself, so why should she?

Sufficiently grumpy, Az drags himself out of the river and fetches the small pile of clothes he'd left on the bank. Water drips down his back from his unruly mop of hair, and the temperature contrast makes him shiver now that he's no longer fully submerged. Getting dressed helps, but not much. He carefully washes the clothes he'd taken off in the measly leftover suds then trudges back to the fire.

The dorscuir looks done enough to be edible, which is more than sufficient for Azrian. He yells for his mother as he pulls the meat off the spit and sections it off, then smiles as he sees her come out carrying a steaming pot. "Corn?"

She nods, and for once, they eat a full meal. Things could be worse.

~

All morning, Azrian looks for her. He waits, knicking his fingers on too-sharp blades more than once when someone passes by that resembles her. The third time it happens, Rhix throws a stone at him that he barely dodges in time. "You're going to cut your damn fingers off and then you won't be any good to me," he scolds.

"It's fine. It's only bleeding a... lot." He winces, wiping off the blood on the underside of his tunic. It stains through, but he doesn't mind; the leather apron he's wearing mostly covers the spot.

Rhix rolls his eyes so heavily that Az has to wonder if that's a Praediti talent, too. He helps him bandage his fingers anyway, and Azrian is just about to thank him for it when he finally spots her — the *real* her, not one of the many imposters he's already seen. "Sweet shadows, she's here!" He knocks his knee off the smithing table and grunts but plasters a smile on his face as she approaches. "Miss Morella, it's a pleasure, as always."

"Hello, Mr. Mihr. I — is that blood?" She looks closer with wide eyes. "Do you have a healer on hand?"

He blushes but furrows his brows. "Does *anyone* have a Sana on hand? That's — no, I'm fine. It's just a cut... or three. I've had worse." Instantly, he regrets saying it. He watches the way her face changes and tries to switch the subject. "So, door handles, huh?"

"Yes. Father is very picky, he said no one but Rhix could pull it off. I'll be the judge of that." She winks playfully at Rhix. "Let's see them."

Azrian turns betrayed eyes on his boss and mentor. Naturally, she's choosing him... of course. He clears his throat. "Rhix is busy."

"I am *not* busy," he says, stepping closer to Morella with a smirk. "I'd be happy to show you. Right this way." Rhix extends one arm out as the other finds its way to the small of her back, and Az watches helplessly as he leads her away.

When they return, Azrian has his apron off and tunic unbuttoned at the top. "Do you need help taking them home, Miss Morella?"

"Quite the gentleman." She waves her hand with a chuckle, sending a blast of wind that knocks Azrian back into the wooden bannister. "I think I got it. Sun will be going down soon; you shouldn't be out any longer than necessary. See you around, boys."

"Yeah." Azrian rubs his chest where the air hit him and tries not to let his face betray his feelings. When she's out of earshot, he turns to Rhix. "Fine. Say it. I was an idiot to think she'd even look twice at me... but shadows, did she need to go all Caelim on me? We get it, she makes the air around us her servant, no need to prove it. I didn't stand a chance."

"You're not an idiot, Azrian. She's just... spoiled. You don't want one of those girls. Plenty more craivil in the sea. I saw Wayke checking you out the day before last. He's Praediti, but... hardly. Oculare have very little uses, so he's on the outside, too."

That sounds like a nice way of saying Az was useless, but it's yet another thing he can't argue with. "Yeah? He's not so bad... though I don't know how I'd handle him trying to talk to ghosts while we're getting it on." He shudders, then realizes Morella hadn't been kidding. "Mean or not, she's right. I don't have a lot of time to get home."

"As long as you don't 'get it on' in my shop, get who you wanna get. Go on now, don't want another bathless night."

"Right." Without another word — especially about his lack of a sex life — Az ducks out of the shop. He's already in a sour mood, but the rain that immediately smacks him in the face just makes it worse. It's coming down so hard it's difficult to see more than a few paces in front of him. All that does is prolong his journey to the point that he loses all daylight, but he huffs a bitter laugh when he realizes a rain bath is better than nothing at all.

He barely makes it through the front door before Roe's yelling at him about a leak in the roof. The sound makes it obvious enough, the heavy droplets smacking against the metal pail are so loud and tinny they make him blink involuntarily. "When in the shadows did that happen?"

"It's the first real rain of the season, Azrian. I came in from the garden and grabbed a bucket as fast as I could. You have to go up and fix it, the entire roof could buckle."

Ignoring her absolute lack of understanding, he blinks at her. "You want me to go up there... in the *dark*... in the middle of a downpour? Where a torch will be utterly and completely useless?"

"I'm sorry, Az. But what other choice do we have? I'll be right below if you need me." Roe sighs and touches his face. "I don't know what I would do without you."

For a moment, he leans into her touch. What he wouldn't give to be a child again, back before his father ran out and his biggest concern was how muddy he could get on the riverbank. "I'll try. I won't be able to fix it properly until tomorrow, but I'll do my best." He cups her hand and slowly pulls it away, then glances up at the ceiling. "Here goes nothing."

Ten minutes later, he's soaked to the bone and barely balancing on the slippery roof. He can't see a damned thing and his hair keeps falling into his eyes to further obscure his vision. Frustration builds in his gut until he thinks it'll boil over and swallow him whole, but still... he tries.

When the hammer slips and nearly breaks his thumb, his yell is lost to the sound of the rain. It's hard to remember a time when he felt quite like this, all lost and disappointed and scared. He feels around mindlessly in an attempt to locate the extra nails he brought, but all his fist closes around is damp, splintered wood. He slams his palm down on the mess and bows his head, shaking from the cold and consequences of a hard day, a hard life. A life he tries desperately every day to survive, even improve. "I just need to *see* it! I can't fix it if I can't faeching *see* it!"

Abruptly, his hand flies upward as a ball of silver... *something* drives it up from the wood. It illuminates the area around him brighter than Cettia itself, and the suddenness of it has him losing his precarious footing. With a startled cry, he topples backward until he hits the ground below him, and the world goes dark once more.

~

Muffled voices pull him from sleep. He opens his eyes slowly, carefully, like he's sure he won't like what awaits him. Sure enough, one of his bones snaps painfully into place thanks to a Sana. "Wh — ow," he whispers. "Aren't you supposed to be a healer?"

She chuckles and rubs the spot firmly. "Yes. Even healing isn't painless. Would you like to go back to sleep? I'm not quite done."

His healthy distrust of Praediti has him shaking his head. "No, no. I'll stay awake." But this time, she has to re-break one of his fingers to get it to set the right way and he deeply regrets that decision. "I'm fine, you can just leave the rest of them."

"There are only two more. On the count of three; one... tw—" *Crack, crack!* "All done. Breathe. We'll have to keep you here for an hour to monitor you, but you'll be back home in a bit. How's your head?"

It's pounding, but at the moment, his focus is fixed on his hand. "I'll live. Have I done anything... weird since I got here?" *Like started glowing silver,* he adds silently.

She tilts her head. "Weird? What do you mean?" Her face is etched with suspicion, which makes Az immediately backtrack.

"You asked about my head. Don't people with head injuries sometimes act... strange? I was just wondering if I'd... never mind." He flashes her a dimpled smile before remembering she's Praediti. The last one wouldn't give him the time of day, so it's unlikely he'll be able to charm his way out of this one. "Where's my mom?"

"In the waiting room. I'll go get her." She turns to leave and glances back when she reaches the door, pausing for a beat before exiting.

Once he's alone, he pushes himself up and takes stock of his body. He's bruised and a little bloody, but she seems to have done a decent job mending his bones. His hand shakes slightly as he raises it to his face and inspects the lines on his palms. *I know what I saw,* he tells himself. *I know what I did.*

Azrian tries several times to make that silver light appear again, but nothing happens. No Praediti he's ever heard of has that kind of power, so maybe he *is* crazy, or maybe it was all just a side effect of falling off the roof. Irritation builds inside of him and there — just briefly — he thinks he sees his skin glow.

He's interrupted by the door swinging open and his mother rushes into the room. "Azrian." She cups his chin to check him out. "I'm sorry I had you on that roof. It was foolish. I was so worried. Rhix had to come carry you here."

"Sweet shadows, *Rhix* carried me? I'm never going to live that one down." He chuckles quietly, laying back again just to escape his mother's grip. "I'm okay. I'm assuming this little trip is going to cost me my entire life savings, though. How many broken bones did I have?"

"Seven." She looks down. "We have a little savings, we'll make do. The garden made a lot of tomatoes this season, we'll sell some. Let's go home, Az. I don't trust these places." Roe doesn't explain any further... she rarely ever does.

Defying reason, the prospect of staying for a while and actually getting some sleep sounds enticing. There aren't many better excuses to skip work than a hospital stay, but something about his Sana is freaking him out and he's actually a little eager to get out of there. "Right, okay. Let me just..." He swings his legs over the side of the soft bed and forces himself to stand.

The world around him sways as he readjusts to being upright, and his mom is there in an instant to help, but they barely make it three steps out into the hallway before his Sana is rushing over to stop him from leaving. "I told you, we need to keep you for observation."

"I'll come back if there's an issue," he assures her. "I still have a roof to fix, and if I don't show up to work tomorrow, head trauma will be the *least* of my concerns."

The Sana narrows her gaze but nods. She has no right to keep him. "Very well. If you lose consciousness at any point, come back as soon as possible." Hesitating, she stands in their way a moment longer before stepping aside.

"I'll make sure to walk my unconscious-self right back here." He salutes her, ignoring the look on her face as they walk out. The moment they're free, he tugs his mother along a little faster. "We need to talk."

Roe looks worried but doesn't push until they finally close the door behind them at home. "Azrian, you're scaring me."

"Something happened on the roof, Ma. I didn't just lose my balance, I... ahh, shadows, you're never gonna believe me." Azrian bolts the door behind them and peeks through the curtains. "I *did* something. Some kind of... I don't know, energy? Light? Fire?"

Roe covers her mouth with her hand and backpedals into her favorite chair. "You... no... what happened exactly?"

"I don't know!" he whispers harshly. "One minute I was screaming to Cettia that I couldn't see anything, and the next thing I knew, there was some silver blob coming out of my hand and I lost my balance. It sort of happened again in the hospital."

Roe gasps and reaches him in a few short strides, gripping his face to meet his gray eyes. "Never tell a soul. Forget it ever happened Az, and for the love of Athoze... *never* tap that darkness again. Do you hear me?" She's whispering, but the words are sharp with no trace of self-doubt.

A little stunned, Az just blinks. "I don't even know how I did it. Or if it even happened, that's not a thing. Strength, mind control, element manipulation, telekinesis... those are Praediti powers. This... whatever this was, I've never seen it before. How can I stop it if I don't know how I did it?"

"Oh, Az. I've never heard of such power, so we just have to move along as if it never happened. I told you what that... *Cogitare* did to me. Never go near the Praediti," she spits harshly before returning to her chair.

He should know better than to bring up mind control around his mother. Apologetic, he makes sure she's comfortable before making his way back up to the roof to fix the leak.

Now that he can see, it doesn't take him long to do the job, and he's back down in the kitchen making dinner before dark. If he's being honest, he still doesn't feel quite right — but he's also never broken so many bones in one fell swoop before, either. Maybe it's just a side effect.

Dinner passes in awkward silence. As they light the candles to prepare for the coming night, he finally speaks. "I'm sorry, Ma. I shouldn't have even said anything, I'm sure it was nothing."

"You don't have anything to apologize for, Son. Whatever this miserable galaxy throws our way, we'll deal with it... together." She takes his hand, smiling at him sadly. "Sweet shadows, I love you. I still see my wide-eyed little boy, climbing all the trees and causing me more stress than the soil gods."

The memory only makes him think of his father. He hugs Roe tightly, willing himself not to ask the questions still burning in his mind, like why his father left them or what he was really like. It's hard to gauge a man through the eyes of a child. "I love you too, Ma. Now get some sleep, I'll make you breakfast before I go to work in the morning."

"My boy. You get some good sleep, and if you aren't feeling well tomorrow, Rhix will understand. Stay home one more day if you have to, Azrian." Roe stands and grabs her candle. "See you in the morning sun."

"The morning sun," he echoes, then huffs a quiet laugh as she disappears into her room.

The thought of Rhix letting him sleep all day is amusing. He's had more broken bones than days off in the time he's been the man's apprentice, and there's a good reason for that. Getting a job is hard enough for a human, but a manual job like that? He'd had to prove to a *Viribus* when he was just fourteen years old that he was strong enough to wield a hammer... and he hadn't been.

That day, he'd used trickery to get the job. Rhix's apprentice at the time was an Igneme, and if Azrian knew anything about firestarters, it was how easily distracted they were. He'd kept the man talking until the blade he'd been sharpening was too thin, and when he'd tested it out, it had shattered. Azrian had made sure to tell him exactly why, and that alone gave him his position.

He's had to fight to keep it every day since. No way an accident screws that up, not after he's come so far. But curiosity eats at him; he can't help it. He coaxes the energy he *knows* must be bubbling just under the surface of his skin, calls to it, begs it to come out. A warning rings out in his mind — his mother had just told it to him minutes before, he shouldn't mess with the darkness — but if this silvery glow can drive *away* the darkness... he won't have to be so afraid of the night anymore.

It's faint, but it comes. He sits up excitedly as his palm starts to glow, and the light brightens as his pulse quickens. Slowly, it takes shape in his hand. It's not a perfect circle by anyone's estimation — it's just as jagged and rough as he is — but it's *there*. It's *real*. And Azrian can't believe his eyes.

He blinks and it disappears. Desperately, he tries to summon it again... but it's gone. Sighing in disappointment that shouldn't be as strong as it is, he lays down and pulls his thin blanket high up on his shoulders. *I knew I wasn't crazy;* he tells himself. *I'm Praediti, I have to be. But what... what kind? And why hasn't this happened until now?*

Explanations come and go like the craivil floating through the river. They travel to the surface in search of food but disappear before you can even be sure you've laid eyes on them, lost to the ever-changing current. He can't seem to settle on one before it vanishes again.

Sleep finds him that way, half lost in thought. He dreams of power, of light, of finally showing the Praediti what it's like to be kind. The last bit startles him even in the thick of the dream. He wants revenge on the Praediti for all they've put him through, put his mother through... but more than that, he just wants humans to not have to live in fear.

A high-pitched scream pulls him back to consciousness and he's on his feet with a blade clutched tightly in his hand in single breath. Briefly, he thinks he imagined it. That it was little more than the brutal edge of a strange dream, but the crackle of fire tells him otherwise. Azrian tears open his bedroom door and is met with a wall of flame so hot it knocks him backward, but he doesn't hit the ground — rough, burning hands hold him steady, but they're not hands he recognizes.

Terror spikes through him as he thrashes and screams for Roe, but he's being dragged backward by someone even larger than Rhix. "Get... *off!* Who are you? *Mom!*"

"She can't hear you, Azrian. Be a good lad and come with us," his captor grunts out.

Az manages to knock him back a few paces and wrenches free, but the fire is blocking his exit. He looks around wildly and grabs a blanket, then wraps himself up and hurls himself through the flames. When he lands, he lands hard, and a boot stomps down on his throat.

Struggling only makes it worse, and all Azrian can see before he's passing out for the second time in as many days... are blood-red eyes and a cold, wicked smile.

~ II ~

THE CELL

The chill in the air soaks Azrian to his bones. He sits up gingerly, wincing from the soreness... well, everywhere, and the first thing he notices is that he's on the floor. A *concrete* floor. His house in Edros doesn't have concrete floors. "What...?"

A quick glance around tells him he's in some sort of a cell. There's a bed, a small desk, and a round, metallic bowl in the corner with some sort of a handle on it. The only light filtering in is coming from the ceiling at least ten feet above his head. If he squints, he can make out the outline of a window.

Scared all over again, he pushes himself to his feet and heads for the door. Part of him knows nothing will happen, that the door will be locked and he'll be stuck there... but the truth of it stings all the same. He pounds on the door with his fists and screams, "Let me out! Open the damn door!"

Silence.

He tries harder, aiming a kick at the bottom a split second too soon — he watches in horror as his bare foot slams into the metal and a new wave of pain washes through him. *Where are my boots?*

Another quick assessment finds him in some sort of uniform. It's baggy and dull, and the material scratches at his skin where it touches. He hates it already. "Hello?" he calls out again, quieter this time. The word — all of his words, really — are coming out in raspy, forced bursts, likely a side effect of having someone attempt to crush his windpipe. He rubs the spot as he sits on the bed in a heap.

The walls are bare, smooth, and tall, which tells him he won't be climbing out through the window above him. No, the only way out is through the door, and someone *has* to open it eventually, right? They can't keep him locked up forever.

It would help if he knew who "they" even were. All he remembers about being taken are red eyes, hands too hot to have not burned his skin, and his mom's scream.

Mom. His adrenaline spikes and he tries again to get out, to rip the door off its hinges if he has to. It doesn't budge, but Azrian doesn't stop. He *can't* stop, not until he gets to her — confirms she's safe somewhere and not held captive like he is.

He's nearly out of energy when the door swings open, making him stumble and grip the frame to steady himself as he blinks at the sudden influx of light. It's hard to make much of anything out, but as his eyes adjust, he takes a step *back* — not forward, not out like he'd planned.

There's a man in front of him, not much older or younger that he is, holding a tray full of food. Arguably, it's more food than Azrian has seen in years. Sheer hunger overpowers any longing for freedom or escape he might have, and he reaches out for it, snatching it up eagerly.

If I don't have any energy, I won't be able to run, he reasons with himself as he takes the first bite. It's bland, even by Edrosi standards, but it's *food*.

His captor says nothing as he eats, just stands guard like a creepy sentry. Azrian watches him and hurls unanswered questions at him every few moments as he takes in his features. He's handsome, to be sure... but there are scars on both sides of his head that disappear around the back under partially shaved hair. The top of his head is a mess; the brown locks fall whichever way they please and dip down over his eyes. His very *golden* eyes.

"Where am I?" Azrian asks for a second time, but still gets no answer. The food is half gone, so he slows — afraid that when he finishes, the man will leave and he'll never get answers. "Who are you, and why am I here?"

Nothing.

"Nice stubble, but I'm really starting to think you need a new barber," he jokes, trying a different tactic. The bread he shoves into his mouth after makes it hard to speak for a moment, but he talks around it anyway. "Are you mute?"

"No," the man finally replies. His hands are clasped behind his back and his brows furrow together as he tilts his head.

It might actually be endearing if it wasn't so frustrating. "Great," Az sighs as he sets his tray down. "Now that you've admitted you can understand me, how about you tell me what in the shadows I'm doing here?"

"Shadows?" he asks curiously as he looks around the room. "I don't see shadows."

Azrian snorts. "Shadows. Hell. It's a figure of speech, you're telling me you've never heard it?"

"No." His eyes dart to Azrian's tray. "You need to eat, Azrian."

Uneasiness takes his appetite away. "That's not really fair. You know my name, yet I don't know yours." He stands up and takes a few steps forward, noting for the first time how much taller his captor is. "You won't answer my questions, yet you're telling me what to do."

"My name?" He unclasps his hands and shows Az his knuckles. "This is what they call me... and I don't *have* answers for your questions yet."

Azrian's eyes widen as he takes in the four marks on his knuckles: K8.0. "Kay eight point zero? That's your name? Seriously?"

"Yes." He looks confused again. "Where are you from? They... never tell me."

He shakes his head quickly and backs up toward the bed again. "No way. You refuse to answer my questions, I'm not answering yours. Find me someone who can tell me why I'm here and let me out," Az says firmly. Now that the initial shock of meeting K8.0 is over, his mind travels back to his mother. *Is she here? Is she safe?*

He frowns and stares at Az intently. "Who's Roe? Your... mother?"

Suddenly, the way he's been acting makes sense. The unanswered questions, the secrecy... the golden eyes. He doesn't care about what Azrian is saying out loud, he cares about what he's *thinking,* and Az was an idiot for not realizing it straight away. He grabs his tray and swings it wide, causing the remnants of the food to fly off and splatter against the wall as he backs up, feeling caged. *"Cogitare!"*

K8.0 looks completely shocked as he backs away, his hands held out in front of him. "Don't! Put the tray down, Azrian. I'm not here to hurt you... or anyone." Az can practically feel the man searching his thoughts and when he speaks again, Azrian just wants to hit him. "I would never do that to your mother."

"You don't get to talk about her. Get out of my head... and let me *go."* He stalks forward, no longer as afraid as he should be. There's nothing more important to him than getting free and finding his mom, and he'll be stoned if he lets a Cogitare — or *any* Praediti — stop him.

"Stop!" K8.0 commands, rooting Azrian to the spot. "I didn't want to do that." He snatches the tray away and leaves the room, but even after he's gone, it takes several seconds before Azrian is able to move his own body again.

He pounds uselessly on the door as tears prick his eyes. Nothing he can say or do will make a difference. With K8.0 being a Cogitare, his thoughts aren't even his own — he'll be manipulated at every step; his plans discovered the moment he thinks of them.

Wherever he is... he's trapped.

~

K8.0 stands outside of Azrian's cell until he stops pounding. If one of the guards hears, they'll go inside and *make* him stop, so it's better that he waits him out instead of letting that happen. The amount of time it takes shows him just how strong-willed the man really is, and he can't help but smile because of it. He'd learned the hard way in there that Azrian is more difficult than most to manipulate — not that K8.0 *likes* manipulating people. He hates it. Reading minds is one thing, he can't help it. He isn't even allowed in the meetings because he can't stand all of their voices at once. But manipulation... that's something else entirely.

By the time K8.0 enters Melior's office to check in, he's full of questions he instantly starts rattling off. "Why is Azrian Mihr so much older than the others? Why is he worried about his mother... why did she scream?"

His boss simply chuckles softly. His sleek, graying hair is pulled back today which makes the scar down his face more prominent, and K8.0 nearly shivers when those endless black eyes lock on him. "It's not like you to be so inquisitive, K8.0. Let's see... he's older because it took his gifts longer than most Videre to present... and what was your other question? Ahh, yes. The scream. I wasn't there myself, but their home caught fire, did it not? I imagine that would make anyone scream. We arrived just in time to save them from dying in the flames."

"Oh. Okay. Well, that's all he's thinking about. He's worried about his mother. As far as the others, nothing new to report, Sir. Ronan has finally stopped crying. I think he is ready for a stroll in the courtyard," he says as he attempts to read Melior's mind again. Unsurprisingly, he fails. He might get a glimpse into his thoughts every so often, but even those are muted as if they're underwater.

Melior nods. "That's good news. Ronan will likely have to teach Azrian how to use his considerable gifts and it's better if he's not sobbing during the process. You may go, I don't need anything further. I'll see you soon."

K8.0 takes Melior's wave as a dismissal and glances at Adeinde on his way out. As always, he gets nothing but deafening silence from the guard's mind. She's the only person who has ever been able to completely block him out and he has no idea how she does it, nor what kind of Praediti she is. It's infuriating.

He goes back to his day, but the boredom is starting to creep in. It's always the same — observe and report, serve food, make his rounds. Occasionally he'll be tasked with getting a new resident settled in, but that's the only thing that ever changes about his routine. He feels bad for new residents when they take their relocations poorly, but he knows they're in a better place and just need time. He's only seen flashes of the outside world and from what he has seen, it's ugly. Why would anyone want to be out there? When he'd met Azrian, he'd heard his thoughts about how he's never seen so much food. Why would he ever want to be hungry again?

He makes himself comfortable and checks out the screens, then reaches out into their minds to see how they're all doing. Ronan looks sad again, but K8.0 believes he just needs some sunlight. It always makes him feel better even if he only gets to spend a few moments a day outside.

When he turns his attention to Azrian's quarters, he isn't surprised to find him pacing. He stares at the toilet like it's strange, and when K8.0 looks into his mind, he chuckles. Azrian has no clue what it is. K8.0 closes his eyes and pushes the toilet's function into his mind. Based on his reaction, he definitely heard him because he begins spinning around like he's looking for him. The feed is grainy, but Azrian's mouth moves as if he's talking so K8.0 reaches into his mind to listen.

"Get outta my head!"

He flinches from the force of it but doesn't listen. *"I was just trying to help. It's for urine and feces, move the handle after and it will disappear."*

"And what? You want to watch?"

"No. I will turn away of course. Why would I want to watch?" K8.0 knows he's neglecting his duties by talking to Azrian so much, but he can't help it, he finds him fascinating. Especially for a Videre.

"Unless you're going to tell me where I am, shove off."

K8.0 sits up straighter and tries to think of how to respond, but before he can, Az thinks something else: *"That's what I thought."*

The disappointment Azrian feels seeps its way into K8.0's skin, and he shifts uncomfortably. He doesn't know why, but he wants to comfort him. He just doesn't know how.

To keep from talking to the new guy, K8.0 busies himself with the other residents and is only interrupted once when Belua comes in to check on him. He stands there, staring at the screens behind K8.0 to get his *own* assessment of Azrian, and the second he considers paying him a visit, K8.0 feels the need to distract him. "Is there something I can help you with?"

Belua grunts and continues staring intently. His thoughts are filled with flames — which isn't surprising for an Igneme — but K8.0 once again hears Azrian's mother's scream. He reaches in further to try and see exactly what happened to her, but Belua jerks his head toward him as if he can feel it. "Stop it."

"Stop what? What happened with the fire?" Belua isn't known to lose control of his fire, he's been trained longer than K8.0's been alive. How could a fire in Azrian's house even happen?

"Dammit, K8.0! This is why no one comes to see you. Stay out of people's heads or they might just crush yours."

K8.0 tilts his head again in an attempt to gauge if that was a warning or a threat, but Belua straightens quickly and turns on his heels. "Time for lunch. Let us know what that Videre is thinking when you are finished." He leaves the room, his mind clouded with heated whispers that make it impossible for K8.0 to dig any further. *He always does that;* he thinks to himself. *What is he hiding?*

K8.0 doesn't dwell any further. He was raised to obey and to stay out of the elders' minds, and if he doesn't push again, maybe Belua won't tell Melior he tried.

He *is* hungry, and they always get a cookie for lunch, so he focuses on that and makes his way to scarf down his own food before feeding the residents. This time, he saves Azrian for last. He hopes they can talk a little more this round but based on his prejudices against Cogitare... he knows it isn't likely.

He takes a breath before entering and Azrian jumps to his feet when he closes the door behind him. "Don't throw this food. They won't give more," K8.0 advises.

Azrian takes the tray carefully and watches him intently. "You really do like to *watch,* don't you?"

"Like to? Not really. It's very boring, but it's my job. You'll have a job soon," he states matter-of-factly. "Eat. They ran out of cookies, but I can split mine with you." K8.0 pulls one out wrapped in a napkin, then breaks it in half and reaches his hand out for Azrian to take it.

"Are you going to answer any of my questions yet?" Azrian asks, not making a move to take the cookie. "If not, then I don't want *anything* from you, and you can go."

"I..." K8.0 frowns and lowers his hand as he glances up at where he knows the camera is. Belua is the one watching now, and he's annoyingly curious as to how K8.0 will handle this situation because he isn't allowed to give any information. That's Melior's job. K8.0 is just meant to observe.

The sadness he feels when he looks down at the broken cookie is unexpected, but he gives Azrian what he wants and opens the metal door. "I have to take the tray back. Knock when you finish."

Azrian stands and hurries toward him, food forgotten. "Wait! Wait... can you just... one question. Answer one question for me."

K8.0 steps back inside and closes the door behind him. It isn't supposed to be open under any circumstances, and if Azrian makes a run for it... well, he doesn't want to see Belua lose his temper, especially on someone as confused as Azrian. "Possibly..." His eyes dart back to the camera, and for once, he's grateful no one can hear them.

"The... light. Where does it come from? I can see it every time you open the door." Az walks closer, then looks directly up at the ceiling. "And that's not the sun or Cettia. How is it so bright in here?"

This is something he *can* explain. "It's the Videre. Their energy — sorry, *your* energy — can light up a room... not just the small ball you've accomplished. You'll get there with training, probably sooner than most. I can see how badly you want it. You're far more powerful than you realize, Azrian."

It's abundantly clear that he doesn't believe him. "Look, I don't know who told you what, exactly... but there's no such thing as what you're saying. I've been to a lot of places, and this —" he waves his arm toward the door and roof — "doesn't exist anywhere else."

"What do y—" K8.0 focuses on Azrian's mind and sees nothing but darkness. If the light doesn't come from the sun or stars, it comes from sticks with small flames on the end. "That's not enough... what are those flame sticks you carry around your old home?"

Azrian blinks, then cracks a smile for the first time since he'd arrived. "Flame sticks? *Torches?* How do you not know what a torch is?"

"Torch." He tests the word and licks his lips. "I've never left here. I've always been around the Videre. You've never met another like you? What about your father?"

The smile disappears instantly. "My father ran out when I was a kid. I barely knew him." Az flicks his eyes to the camera and squints like he's not sure what it is. "What exactly are these *Videre?*"

"They bring light. They can even use the energy in an attack if needed, but long periods of time making the energy can be draining. You have to pace yourself, but that's how it is with all Praediti. When I was little, I couldn't leave my room without getting a migraine, but now I just avoid large groups of people. I'm the only Cogitare here now and I've only met a few others like me." He frowns and scratches the top of his messy hair. "I don't know what happened to them. They must have left."

Azrian's face changes to something decidedly unhappier. "Yeah, I've only met a few and they've all been terrible. Just because you *can* mess with people's minds doesn't mean you *should.*" He finally sits again and picks at his food. "I can't do that light/energy thing you're talking about. Let me go home, I need to make sure my mom's okay. She won't be able to eat without me."

"Why lie? You know I can see it." K8.0 walks closer and *almost* sits next to him on the bed but decides not to. "Why would you want to go home? We have food here, and toilets. They'll take care of you. They've taken care of me."

"Maybe because I don't want to be a prisoner? And did you not hear me? My mom will die without me. She'll starve, she's already probably homeless thanks to the fire. I have to go back to her, so... thanks but no thanks on the toilets, just tell me how to leave."

K8.0 backs away again, unsure of how to respond. "I can ask about your mother. I've never seen a mother here... but maybe they can send for her." He wants to help the transition as much as possible but letting Azrian leave seems dangerous. "What if bad people take you? That's why you're here with the Venandi. They'll keep you safe. Videre don't live long on the outside."

"I've lived twenty-five years just fine on my own, and I'm *not* a Videre. I'm a human, I've always been a human. So, I hallucinated a couple of times — so what? I fell off a roof, it's not surprising." Az starts to panic again and his thoughts start to come through a little muddled. "Who in the shadows are the Venandi? Where am I?"

"You're home." Someone bangs on the door three times, making K8.0 flinch. His head swivels toward the noise and then back on Azrian before he takes two steps forward and grabs the tray. With hurried movements, he sets the food on the bed next to Azrian and rushes to the door. "See you for dinner."

"Wait!" Azrian yells again, but this time, K8.0 swings the door shut in his face. He listens as Azrian's palm smacks repeatedly on the door, and it shakes under the strain but doesn't budge.

He turns to see Belua standing there. "What were you doing in there for so long, K8.0?"

"Observing," he states and turns to walk down to return the tray. "He's struggling. He wants his mother." K8.0 places the tray on the trolly and spins quickly to meet Belua's red eyes. "Where is she?"

Belua regards him for a moment with his chin raised. "She's no longer in danger, and that's all that should concern either one of you. He belongs to the Venandi now, and like all others before him, his life before he came to us no longer exists."

He searches Belua's mind for more information and all his thoughts run together again. "Well then, that will take time. He's still holding on because he worries for her. I'm trying to help him see reason, but all I have are half-truths. I need to see Melior." K8.0 turns to push the trolly back to the kitchens, knowing his questions are angering Belua... but he hardly ever questions anyone. He's entitled to answers.

"You'll see Melior when you're *scheduled* to see Melior, and not a moment sooner. In the meantime, Azrian is not your concern. I'll handle whatever lingering questions the boy has when *I* take him dinner tonight." Belua's eyes flash a little brighter. "Run along now, K8.0. You're late for your security detail."

After searching for a tiny kink in his armor and coming up short, he returns the trolly and walks toward security. He naturally seeks out Azrian. It's clear quickly that he hasn't eaten any more food, so he once again goes against his rules and reaches out. "*They said your mother is safe.*"

"*You'll forgive me if I don't believe that. I was kidnapped and my house was set on fire... why would I believe that she's miraculously okay?*"

K8.0 runs a hand through his hair and frowns. He wishes it weren't against the rules to show Azrian how he knows and what he saw in Belua's mind. Yes, they were broken thoughts, but he couldn't lie to him. He'd know. "*So, you think they can lie to me?*"

"*In my experience, Praediti are cunning and selfish. So yeah, the fact that you're not concerned at all that I'm telling you I was attacked and taken from my home tells me they're either lying to you, or you're just as bad as the rest of them.*"

K8.0 stops communicating and pointedly looks at the other residents. He's not in the mood to argue and he also doesn't have a clue how to respond. How could they lie to him? He's caught them in lies before, so he believes they would try, but he *always* catches them and realizes it was done for his own good. But he's much older now... why keep secrets?

The day drags on, especially knowing he won't get to speak to Azrian face-to-face again until tomorrow. He waits until he sees Belua enter Azrian's cell and watches. He can't help it. He can't hear them, and he can only get bits and pieces from their minds — but as soon as he is able to siphon out Belua's swirling, overlapping thoughts to home in on Azrian's, the door to security flies open and a security guard kicks him out of the room. K8.0 was supposed to leave a while ago, and most people don't particularly like being around a Cogitare, so he isn't surprised... even if the dismissal stings.

~

Azrian eyes the newcomer apprehensively. He's much less scarred up than K8.0 but looks a hell of a lot meaner. "Who are you?"

"I'm Belua. What questions do you have, Azrian? K8.0 has new questions every time he leaves here so... ask away." He sets the tray down and crosses his arms.

"Where am I? Why am I here? Where's my *mom?*" Azrian wastes no time, barely even glancing at the food on the tray despite how good it smells.

"You are in Deadrun, your new home. And your mother... is not a concern. You never have to worry about her again. For food... shelter... anything. She is taken care of, as you will be, provided you can adjust to your new life here."

Azrian can't stop the foreboding shiver that races down his spine. "I want to see her. I want to go home, take me back to her."

"We can't do that. You are in danger now that your powers have awoken. We don't know why they took so long to manifest, but we would like to run tests when you agree to comply."

His mother's words ring through his mind. *Never tap that darkness again.* "I don't have powers, you're wrong. I'm a human. Can I go now?" Az stands and heads for the door. "I don't want your protection. I've never needed it before, and I don't need it now."

"You *do* need protection. You were spotted using your powers in the hospital, and we arrived just in time. Humans set fire to your home... do you not remember the flames?"

He'll remember those flames until he dies. Humans hadn't even crossed his mind — but now that he thinks about it, it makes sense. It hurts, but it makes sense. "I don't care. I want to go home. We'll move to Etria or Sastrya, somewhere they don't know us."

"We lost a man rescuing you and ensuring your mother's safety. The least you could do is be thankful and accommodating, Azrian." Belua takes a step forward and takes the tray of food back. "We don't waste food here."

I'm a prisoner. I can't leave, they didn't save us, and I... Azrian swallows and holds his hands out for the tray. "I'll eat it."

"Good. Any other questions? Or will you let K8.0 do his job tomorrow without issues?"

"Yes. But... what do you want from me?" he asks carefully. "There's no way I'm here for free."

"We want to help you learn and understand your powers. I think you'll find you like it here, just give it a chance." Belua clears off Azrian's tray and leaves the food on the bed, then goes to leave.

"Sleep well, you won't have to be *here* —" he waves at the small cell — "long. This is just until you accept our help."

Deep down, Azrian knows something isn't right, and that accepting their help means he'll never go home. "And what happens if I don't accept your help?"

"You will." He leaves without another word and the door seals shut behind him with a deafening sound.

Azrian's hopes fall straight through the floor. He's mindful of the strange-looking thing in the corner as he turns his back on it, pulling the food a little closer and taking a bite just to distract himself. He hates how alone he is, how unknown all of it is, how badly he longs for a place he used to loathe.

His skin crawls with the desire to use his powers, but he won't. He won't give them the satisfaction of getting what they want, not after what they did. If he really is one of these secret Praediti, one of these *Videre* — they don't get to reap the benefits.

The hours pass slowly as he paces, waits, tugs on his long hair. He's still filthy from the fire and stares at the small basin next to the toilet. He'd discovered earlier that water comes out if he twists the knob, and even though he has no soap, he definitely needs a bath badly enough that he's willing to use what he's got. Stripping down, he wonders if they're somehow using the box in the corner to spy on him. It seemed like that's what K8.0 had been doing, and he certainly seemed interested in it when he'd been there. *K8.0... never thought I'd miss him, but that new guy is an ass. Maybe now that I know more, he'll talk to me.*

Once he's naked, he uses his hands to rub the cold water over his body and scrub off the ash and dirt. He has no clean clothes, and it's much too chilly in the room to put on wet ones, so he assumes he'll have to wear the tattered ones he came in with or put his dirty uniform back on. Unless... *"Kato, can you hear me? How does this even work?"*

"Kato? It's a zero, Azrian, not an O."

"Okay, well, Kay-eight-point-zero sounds stupid, so I'm calling you Kato. I... I need some clothes. Maybe a blanket... do you have any soap?" Azrian cringes, hating having to ask for a favor already. But the blanket isn't all that negotiable, and if he has to ask for one, he might as well go the distance.

"Yes. I can get those things. The rooms are locked but... I know how to open them. Anything else? I still have your half of our cookie."

Of all the things to make Azrian soften, he hadn't been expecting that to be it. "I'll take the cookie. But no, I just need those things... maybe some water, too?"

"Okay... don't drink the toilet water. It's unsanitary. I'll be there soon."

Azrian screws up his face and glares at the toilet. He'd sooner drink from the basin, but even then, he's not sure where the water is coming from and therefore doesn't trust it.

When Kato finally arrives, Az is still naked. He covers his crotch with his balled-up tunic as the door swings open, then grins apologetically. "Sorry, I'm gonna clean up... didn't want to put these clothes back on."

"It's okay." Kato walks in and looks at him, not shying away in the slightest. "You're very firm. What did you do before here?"

Az straightens up a little bit. It's been so long since anyone's looked at him like that, he almost forgets Kato's the enemy. "I'm a blacksmith. Or, an apprentice, anyway. I won't really be one for a couple more years." He chooses not to point out he won't be one at all if he can't go home, and instead takes the soap from Kato and heads back to the basin. He realizes his body is fully on display now, but if he has to choose between exposure and solitude, he's picking exposure.

Kato sits on his bed. "You... like that work? It seems... dirty."

"Yeah, I love it. Sure, it's hard and I don't get a lot of sleep, but... I make things that matter to people. I help, and it gives me enough money to take care of my mom." The water warms up slightly and Azrian lets out a satisfied sigh, cleaning a little lower on his body. He can't see Kato, but assumes he's not looking and doesn't want to prove himself wrong. "It's hell on the fingers if you don't pay attention, though."

"I..." He's quiet for a few seconds and then he huffs a laugh. "You just recently cut your finger. I see a woman. And... doorknobs? Who is she? We don't have many women here."

Azrian squeezes the soap in his hand and bows his head slightly — between his current physical state and Kato digging through his thoughts, he feels raw. "Her name is Morella. She didn't feel the same, end of story. Get out of my head."

"Okay, sorry." Kato stands again and walks toward the door. "I didn't mean to that time."

The worst part of all of it is that Azrian actually believes him. It's like he can't help himself. He nods. "Thanks for the stuff... just curious, though. I thought you said I'd be treated well here. You just had to steal me a bar of soap so I could rinse off in a... whatever this is. Basin. It's not even a real bath."

Kato turns back with a small frown. "They didn't tell me I couldn't. It's a sink... and I can take you for a real shower tomorrow, I'm sure... I..." He looks as if he's never considered another way of life. "Is it different out there? Who makes your rules?"

"I do. The Regnum make the rules for all of Athoze, but day to day? We make our own. Human, Praediti... it's not perfect, but it's better than this." Azrian doesn't bother asking what a shower is — he has no intention of still being there the following day. "You've really never been out of here? Not even to Rostya or Edros?"

Kato tilts his head in confusion. "Athoze was taken by humans and all the Praediti were killed. I've only been to the courtyard. It's the only place the sun shines here."

"Whoa," Az says quietly. He drops the soap in the sink and walks over to Kato, dripping all over the floor. "No... you've got it backward. The Praediti stole the world from *humans*... and we pay for it every single day. Guess that answers your question about whether or not you're being lied to."

Kato stares into Azrian's eyes as if he's searching for a lie. "Can I see?" He slowly reaches out a hand.

"If it means you'll stop being so gullible, then yeah. Just none of that control stuff, all you're doing is looking, right?" Az asks, suddenly skeptical.

Kato nods and touches Az's temple, closing his eyes to see. "I can see it... it's so clear... normally it's fuzzy but now it's like I'm truly there."

Azrian shifts uncomfortably and tries to steer him through the streets of Embermeadow, showing how the Praediti reign supreme over the humans. He doesn't want to give away any specific information about his home or mom, Rhix... With a sinking feeling, he remembers he didn't show up for work. "You have to let me leave, Kato."

Kato flinches and back peddles until he hits the door. "All of that was real? And I'm supposed to believe I've been lied to all my life? Melior wouldn't... he..." He suddenly looks pained as he reaches up to squeeze his temples.

Not knowing what else to do, Azrian grabs him to steady him. "Hey, you should sit, come on." He leads him down to the bed and hands him the water, then gets up to pull the clean clothes on.

"This is yours." He holds it out for Azrian again and when their eyes meet, he opens up a line of communication. "*No wonder you hate me.*" His eyes widen as he jumps up from the bed. "I have to go." Kato sets the cup on the floor and rushes to the door without a look back.

~ III ~

THE TRUTH

Nightmares plague him. Bright, burning flames, the sound of the wood splintering around him, and his mother's scream. The boot that cut off what little air he had. Red eyes that looked all too similar to Belua's.

Azrian wakes with a jolt, glancing quickly around the room and letting out a breath. He takes a moment to wipe the sweat from his face before getting up and standing directly under the window. *Cettia, where are you?*

Disappointment and fear take hold again as he remembers that light isn't natural — it's coming from Videre, people like *him* — and he can't help but wonder if they're there by choice, or if they were kidnapped, too.

With no line of sight to the outside world, Azrian has no way to tell time. He hazards a guess that it's been several hours since Kato had run away from him, but whether or not it's time for breakfast, he's not sure. All he really knows is that his anxiety is coming alive under his skin and threatening to rip right out of him if he doesn't get out of that room soon.

When the door opens, it's not Kato. It's a girl, younger than both of them, and the tray full of food is suspended in the air in front of her. "Caelim or Tactare?" he asks, not sure if her eyes are blue or purple in the low light. She simply urges him to take the plates off the tray and then leaves, throwing him into silence once again.

She comes back for lunch and again for dinner. Melior stops by after his last meal and asks if he's ready to accept their help yet — Azrian says no and spends the evening alone.

It continues like that. Silent girl, rejected request. By breakfast on the fourth day, Azrian is actually beginning to get worried. Have they punished Kato for helping him? He hadn't asked for much, or at least... he didn't *think* he'd asked for much... so why isn't he here? Is he mad at Azrian for asking too many questions, or for telling him the truth?

Is it all of the above?

Part of him knows he should stay out of it. He should be thankful that he's no longer coming face to face with a Cogitare every day, but he's not quite sure where Melior got that scar and Belua is likely the Igneme that burned Azrian's house down. It's better to stick with the enemy he knows.

The girl continues to say nothing, even when Az presses for information about Kato. After a full week passes, he reaches out. *"Kato? This thing on?"*

It takes so long that Azrian is convinced that Kato isn't going to answer, and when he finally does, his voice sounds far away. *"Are you okay?"*

"Funny, I was going to ask you the same question. Thought maybe they hurt you for being nice to me," Azrian tells him quietly.

"They did — no. I hurt myself, I guess. I get these migraines sometimes, and how long I'm down is based on how bad they are. That one was... bad. I'm in a room similar to yours, actually... they have to strap me down for my safety. I should be back tomorrow."

That sounds brutal to Azrian, and for a moment, he actually feels bad for him. It passes quickly. *"Guess you've been messing with too many people's brains, huh? I'd return the favor and watch you take a bath and bring you water, but... I'm kind of a prisoner. A real one, not just one strapped down because I overused my powers."*

Azrian can't hear him anymore, it feels as though the connection has been severed — but it only lasts a few moments. He hears Kato's voice again: *"You reached out to **me**, Azrian. I wasn't in your mind. Not since you gave me permission... shadowhead."*

The word makes him laugh; it's absurd, but he'll be lying to himself if he doesn't admit it's a little adorable. *"Maybe not now, but... you know what, never mind. Good luck getting better."*

He has no idea how to shut off the connection himself, so he squeezes his eyes shut and screams at himself to stop thinking about Kato. The problem is that just makes him think *harder* about Kato. His impressive height, the greenish ring around his stupidly gold eyes. The scars that he wishes he knew the cause of.

"Do you want me to go away, or do you want to just ask me about my scars?" Kato's voice interrupts his thoughts.

Azrian's entire upper body blushes, and he doesn't have it in him to ask Kato how much he heard. *"I didn't mean to ask that out loud. Wait... it wasn't out loud, I was thinking it, so it's not my fault you were still listening. But yeah, I know where all mine came from. Seems like yours aren't that old since your hair hasn't really grown back on the sides."*

"Brain surgery. A few of them. They want to know how my powers work, but they can't figure it out. I've never had hair on the sides because they always have to reopen it. I have another scheduled in a couple weeks. They almost did yesterday, but I started to feel better. You like my eyes?"

The absolute last thing Azrian needs is to get caught up with a Praediti... but having someone like Kato on his side could be very beneficial. *"They're good eyes. Don't read too much into it."* He walks over and leans forward against the door with his arm bracing his forehead. *"I need out, Kato. This room is driving me insane."*

"I'll see what I can do."

Azrian almost feels bad about asking him for another favor when he's clearly suffering himself, but at the end of the day... Az didn't ask to be here. He didn't ask to be ripped from his home and his mom, his job, his life. And he certainly didn't ask to be thrown in a cell and locked up.

He'll ask favors from whoever he pleases.

~

Kato takes another night to think of his approach with Melior. He *saw* the outside world from Azrian's eyes. He knows he's been lied to; he isn't denying that. But he wants to know *how* he's been lied to, and more importantly... what *else* he's been lied to about.

He recalls a moment from his childhood when he'd asked Melior about the outside. It was around the time he learned *not* to ask too many questions, but he had always been a curious one, so he couldn't help it. The picture he painted for young Kato was ugly, bloody, and enough to scare him from ever wanting to experience that firsthand. Melior only didn't tell him sooner to protect him — or at least that's what he's always been told.

Melior has only lost his patience with Kato a few times, but every time he does, he becomes completely cold. The disappointment he feels when he looks at Kato lingers for months, and Kato isn't sure he ever wants to live that way again. *Especially* after such a bad episode. The week he's been in isolation has been hard, harder than ever before, and he isn't sure if it has to do with his newly growing suspicions... or his new friend.

He knows "friend" is a stretch, but Azrian has already spoken to him more than some people he's been around for years. *No one wants a Cogitare swimming around in their heads,* he thinks to himself with a sigh. He meant what he told Azrian, he really *does* try not to use his powers. It's just nearly impossible to turn off.

The following morning, the Sana comes to release him bright and early, but he isn't permitted to work today. Melior has sent a message that he won't be able to meet with Kato until tomorrow, and that he should spend the day in the courtyard to regain his strength.

After a nice breakfast, he goes to see Ronan. "Hello, Ronan. Would you like to go to the courtyard?"

"K8.0! Where have you been?" Ronan strolls past him, looking much better than he had the previous week.

"I was with the Sana. I had another migraine, but I'm better. I have a nickname now; you can call me Kato." He smiles proudly, especially when Ronan smiles back.

"Awesome. I want a nickname!"

Kato chuckles and tosses a few options around in his head. "Rone? Roe? R?" He suddenly wonders if Azrian has a nickname and isn't sure why his mind drifted to him.

They reach the courtyard just as Kato turns his attention back on Ronan, and it's obvious which nickname he preferred. "Rone it is."

"Cool. Hey... did you read my mind?"

"I'm sorry. You were... kind of yelling it, though." Kato blushes as he walks to the center of the courtyard to lay down on the soft grass and stare up at the only piece of sky he can see.

"It's okay. But try not to... you just got over a migraine. You need to rest."

Kato offers him the ghost of a smile. "Thanks for worrying, but I'm really okay.

"Thank Cettia," he mumbles.

He can't help but feel bad for Ronan. He was only ten when he'd discovered he was a Videre, and his mother had tossed him out on the streets. Kato understands better than anyone what that feels like — his own mother was simply named "K" — and even in *her* eyes... 8.0 was an abomination. She never wanted much to do with him at all, and she disappeared a few years back. No one bothered to tell him where she went.

They spend an hour in the sun before Kato decides he wants to go see Azrian. He deserves some time outside, and instead of asking for permission to let him out, he decides he just... will.

As Kato approaches the holding cells, he feels something weird fluttering in his stomach. He doesn't understand why, but the feeling makes him hesitate at Azrian's door before he finally knocks twice and lets himself in. "Do you want to go on a walk?"

"Yes," Azrian says instantly. He looks around his room for a moment like he's searching for something but doesn't find it. There's nothing of his in the room at all. "Sweet shadows, let's get out of here."

"You have to stay close." Kato grabs his hand and forces him to meet his eyes. "Please." If Azrian runs off on his watch, Melior will never speak to him again — at least not kindly.

Azrian screws up his face, but nods. "I'll stay close."

Kato stares a second more, noting just how gorgeous Azrian's eyes are. They're gray, but they're anything *but* dull — truly the most beautiful shade of gray he's ever seen, and he's never wanted to draw someone's eyes so instantaneously before. They're warm, and he finds himself not wanting to look away... but that isn't why he is here. "Okay." Releasing Azrian's hand, he stands aside and lets him walk past, watching as he takes in the structure around them. "So... this is our home. This wing is for temporary lodging. I can show you mine so you can see what yours will look like when you get out of here. To the left is security, which is where I am most of the day. To the right is forbidden, if you even attempt to go that way, alarms will sound. Come this way." He leads Azrian forward where they can see the entrance to the courtyard, but he makes a sharp right toward the dorms.

Kato opens the third door to the right and waves Azrian inside. It's pretty bare, but his bed is bigger than Azrian's and he has a small collection of books on a shelf as well as a pile of parchment on his bed.

It's the pile that draws Azrian's attention. He shifts through it, his thoughts whirring from one to the next with words Kato's never heard before. When Azrian finally stops and holds one up in particular, Kato can read *that* thought loud and clear: "*Home.*"

"Home." He walks closer, taking the drawing from Azrian's hands slowly. "This was from Ronan's mind."

"Ronan?" Azrian blinks, stepping into Kato's space to get another look at it. "This is Edros. This is where I live... *lived.* Before I was taken."

Kato can feel Azrian's emotions; the heaviness of them is nearly crippling and he suddenly wants to wrap his arms around Az and pull him in... only he doesn't know why. Why would a person do that? Would Azrian find comfort in that? Probably not.

The silence stretches on while they stare at the parchment together, and when Azrian finally looks away, Kato gets that pesky urge to touch him again. "Y-You can have it."

"I don't want it," he rasps with tears in his eyes. "I want to *go* there."

Kato sets the parchment on the bed with a frown. "I can't do that. Everything you see in this room is all I have. All I've ever had. How am I supposed to get you home?" He doesn't understand why seeing Azrian sad makes him so angry, but then again, he doesn't understand a lot when it comes to him.

"You can let me out," Azrian counters. "You're a damn *Cogitare* for Cettia's sake... all it would take is one word from you and I walk right out of here and go home."

"I'm not allowed to use my gift against the Venandi. What part of that don't you understand? I've never disobeyed." Kato realizes that's a lie as it comes out of his mouth. He disobeyed as a child and someone lost their life... Melior didn't speak to him for a year. "I can't. Please understand."

Azrian studies him hard for a moment. His face changes slowly from anger to something colder. "Of course not. Let's just go... those drawings are really good." He exits the room without waiting, causing Kato to hurry after him.

"Wait!" Kato catches up and grabs his hand again. "Fine. We'll walk like this." He pulls Az along — ignoring his protests — and opens the foyer doors toward the courtyard. Only then does he release his hand. "Stop being a shadowhead. I told you to stay close."

"That's not a real word, and quit touching me." Az crosses his arms and looks around the courtyard with a sharp sigh. The moment he spots the ray of sunlight, he leaves Kato again to seek it out.

He follows closely and then sits down on the grass. "This is the only place we have sunlight. I was trying to be nice and bring you here for fresh air."

"I hate to break this to you... but this isn't sunlight. I don't know what the hell this is, but sunlight is warm... and seeps into your skin. This... this is shit." Az drops his eyes and toes the ground, his expression souring. "That's not real grass, either."

Kato looks up at the sky and then runs his hand through the grass. *Fake? Was this person sent here to ruin everything?* He stands up like the grass bit him and walks away to sit on a bench.

Not too long ago, he thought he understood everything around him and now... he just doesn't know anything anymore.

～

Azrian isn't sure what to make of Kato or his delusions. At first, they were almost endearing... but now they're just driving him insane. "How much more proof do you need, Kato? They're lying to you about *everything*."

"Shut up." Kato's eyes dart around the courtyard and then finally land on Az. "And you're not? If they're able to lie to me, so are you. Why do I even have this stupid power?" His hands slide up the sides of his head and pull at his messy hair in frustration.

The stupidity of that is almost too much. "What *possible* reason would I have to lie to you? I didn't come here on purpose. I don't want to stay; I don't want to ever see any of you again. I want to go home, back to my mom, my job, my *house.* Sweet shadows, Kato, I get the fact that you're sheltered, but you can't honestly be *that* dumb." He immediately regrets his words. Even though Kato isn't listening, he's been nothing but kind to Azrian since he was brought here. He reaches one hand out to touch his shoulder. "I didn't mean that."

Before Kato can answer, they're interrupted by a man Azrian hasn't seen much of. "What, exactly, are you two doing out here?"

Kato's eyes dart up and he stands instantly, running his hand through his hair to fix it. "Melior. I uh... I was showing him the... good things about our home. All he knows is a cell... I thought..."

Melior's eyes flash and for a moment, Azrian thinks there's going to be a fight. Instead, he plasters on a sleazy smile and extends his hand toward the opposite side of the courtyard. "That's a wonderful idea, K8.0. I'm sure he's quite hungry, should we adjourn for lunch?"

"I'm right here," Azrian points out. "And yeah, I'm hungry. The girl that took Kato's place is kinda skimpy with the sausage."

Melior's laugh is faker than the grass they're walking on and Kato instantly follows, waving a hand for Azrian to hurry up.

Rolling his eyes, Az keeps his distance and searches for an actual exit. In all his time here, he has yet to see one — or anything that resembled a door to the outside at all. *There has to be a way out,* he tells himself. *They came and got me somehow.*

"Azrian?"

He snaps his eyes toward Melior and clears his throat. "Sorry. First time out and about, I'm just taking in the sights." He realizes they're in some sort of a huge room with four rows of tables. "What's this?"

"This is the cafe. We get the food up there and sit here to eat." Kato stops talking and straightens as a tall woman walks in, standing across from them like a statue with her hands behind her back.

"K8.0," she says coldly as she turns to Melior. "Will you be joining them, Sir?"

Melior regards her with something that looks a lot like lust, and Azrian nearly laughs. He didn't think anyone in this place was capable of such a thing. "Yes, Adeinde," Melior says. "Stay close, I'll speak with you after."

As she nods and walks away, Azrian fights an eye roll. *These people really don't understand personal space.* "So, I can eat then? Is someone going to snatch my tray if I don't finish fast enough?"

"*Stop being so negative,*" Kato's voice cuts into his thoughts as they walk toward the front. "Just grab some food and eat so you'll stop talking," he says out loud as he grabs his tray.

Melior looks between them with a curious expression. "And here I thought you two were becoming friends. Was I mistaken?"

Az scowls at Kato's back. "Yeah, guess you were." He shoulder-checks the Cogitare as he pushes his way to the front, then loads up his tray with more food than he could possibly eat in one sitting. Melior tsks, but Az doesn't pay him any mind. "Do I have to sit with you?"

"Yes," Melior says quickly. "It's non-negotiable. I thought perhaps you'd want some of your questions answered, was I *also* mistaken about that?"

The promise of actual information is enough to make Azrian drop his attitude. "No, no... not mistaken. I'll sit with you."

The questions come too quickly to Azrian's mind once they're all seated. He has too many, and each one that pops into his mind spawns three more — he can't figure out where to start. "Why can't I leave?"

"You've already been told it isn't safe for you to go back home now that your powers have manifested," Melior explains calmly. "We're doing you a favor by keeping you here."

"Then why am I stuck in a room barely big enough for a bed?" he presses.

"Because you haven't accepted your place here. We don't waste valuable, precious resources on those that don't assimilate. I'm sure it's quite obvious that we don't have much."

Yeah, except fake light and energy that makes water come out of metal. "So, if I agree to whatever it is you want, I'll get a room like Kato's?"

"K8.0," Melior corrects. "Why do you insist on calling him a false name?"

"I like it," Kato spits out quickly, looking down a split second later with a blush.

"Because K8.0 is a stupid name," Az points out. "Almost everyone else I've met here as a normal name, why doesn't he?"

Melior sits back and folds his arms over his chest. "He was born here, one of few. The rest of us were all given our names in other parts of Athoze."

He's not sure why that bothers him, but it does. Everyone deserves a name... not just a mess of letters and numbers. "Right. Now, my other question? Will I get a room like his if I play along?" *More importantly, will I be able to move freely enough to find a way out?*

"Yes," Melior says with a nod. "Once you've accepted your role as your father did, you'll be moved to the dorms. You'll even meet some other Videre."

There's no way Azrian heard that correctly. He can't quite pinpoint the emotions that bubble up, but he *does* know he doesn't like any of them. "My father? The father that ran out on me and my mom when I was a kid? *That* father? Sorry, he was human."

"Your father wasn't running *from* you, Azrian. He was running *to* us. He believed in our mission, as will you once you've let go of your foolish attachment to the place you fear so much."

No. "Then why didn't he tell me? Huh? If he was really coming here to help you, why didn't he even say goodbye?" Traitorous tears threaten to spill from his eyes as the memory of that day comes back. His father had left late at night to get medicine from the market for Roe and never returned. Azrian had waited, watched, *searched* for his father for weeks... but he never came home.

Kato is frowning again, staring at Melior intently like he's searching his mind. "Ender... *that* was Azrian's father?"

"You know my dad?" Az asks, turning to face Kato fully for the first time since sitting down. "Where is he? Is he still here? Take me to him!" He stands, but Melior holds up his palm and shakes his head. Dread fills Azrian and he knows what's coming before the words even leave Melior's mouth.

"He died, Azrian. Some time ago. I'm sorry."

It's like losing him all over again. The grief pulses through him in a wave strong enough to make his body jerk. "What happened?"

Kato looks down and pushes his tray away. "I didn't know, Azrian. I was only twelve when he—"

"Your father believed in what we were doing here so much that he didn't know when to stop. Praediti powers are phenomenal and awe-inspiring, but they come at a cost. Most Praediti never know that cost. They sleep, access those great wells of power in moderation, and never push too hard. Your father forgot where his limits were... we tried to save him," Melior says quietly. "Our Sana at the time was fairly untrained. There was nothing we could do."

He doesn't speak right away. He can't, because every ounce of that sounds like a lie. From what he remembers, his father was lazy. Rarely worked, rarely did anything that wasn't an absolute necessity. He wasn't the type to overwork himself in any capacity, so why would this place be different? Not to mention, his father was painfully, obviously human. "I don't believe it."

Melior looks Kato's way and sits back, nodding toward him like Kato would give him answers that Melior couldn't.

"It's true, Azrian. I remember when they tried to save him. I'm... sorry."

That does little to convince Azrian. There are still a hundred explanations, and every single one of them makes more sense than the one he was just told. "Right." He sits again, staring at the tray full of untouched food. Now, more than ever, he just wants to go home and find his mom. "Well, then... if my father helped you, I will too." He doesn't even care what they're trying to accomplish — which is something he hasn't even been told yet. It doesn't matter, because whatever it is... he doesn't plan on being around long enough to find out.

"That's excellent news, Azrian," Melior says with a smile. "We'll begin your training tomorrow after breakfast. You'll understand, of course, that you won't be able to see anyone while we're assessing your strength and teaching you the basics of how to access your powers. It can be dangerous, and we wouldn't want anyone getting hurt if you lose control, would we?"

He silently shakes his head. Maybe this will be a blessing in disguise — if he can pick up a few tricks that help him deal with his gift before he goes, all the better.

"Not even me?" Kato asks. "Who will bring him his meals?"

"I will, or... if I'm busy, Rhinn can handle it." Melior wipes his mouth with a napkin despite not eating a single bite and stands up, motioning to Adeinde to come join them. "Don't be late to security, K8.0. And see to it that Azrian finds his way back to his cell... just until we prepare him another room. Come, Adeinde." He leads her out, and Azrian quickly realizes he's running out of time to actually eat.

He scarfs his food down like a starved animal, dreading the moment Kato actually starts talking again.

He doesn't, not until he's finished eating and they're making their way back across the courtyard. "I'm glad you decided to work with the Venandi, Azrian. I did know your father, but he didn't speak to people. He didn't seem to like Praediti, or the fact that he was one. Maybe he worked so hard so he could finish and get back to you?"

Or maybe he was forced to do it, like I am. "Yeah," Azrian agrees just to get off the subject. He stops outside of the door to his room and puts a hand on it. "Guess we won't see each other for a while, huh? Bet you'll be glad I'm finally gonna shut up."

Kato stares at him a moment like he doesn't know what to say and then backs away. "Right back at you, I guess."

Maybe if things were different, he and Kato could actually be friends. But he has no friends here, and he had no friends back home. "You told me to shut up twice, remember?" He pushes open his door and steps inside. "Go back to your precious Venandi and your stupid lie of a life." Energy sparks from his palms and it hits him just how badly that conversation had affected him. He's tired, so, *so* tired... and things are only going to get worse. "Go away."

With a wave of his hand, Azrian slams the door in Kato's face. He doesn't take the time to regret being so mean — instead, he focuses on the fact that he just shut the door without actually touching it. The silvery glow ebbs and wanes in his hands as blood pulses hard and fast through his veins, but as quickly as it appeared... it vanishes again. "What? No!" He shakes his hands out in front of him like he's going to snap that power back into place, but it doesn't come. In a rage, he slams his fist against the door and cries out when the impact rattles his bones.

He tries twice later that night to reach out to Kato. Twice, he's met with silence. Azrian knows he's being unfair to the boy with scars on his head, the boy who's being studied like some sort of sick experiment. He *knows* he is... so why can't he stop?

And more importantly... why has Kato?

~

Ignoring Azrian is one of the hardest things Kato has ever done. It isn't that he feels obligated to speak to him, he isn't, he just wants to yell at him. Az doesn't realize just how rare and powerful his gift is. He doesn't *treat* it like a gift, and neither had his father.

He thinks back to when Ender was alive. He'd treated Kato *so* poorly. Even as a child, he was used to being cast aside... but the way the man looked at him was pure hatred. Now that he knows what the other Cogitare did to Azrian's mother, it makes sense.

When he was young, he had even less control over his powers than he does now. He constantly heard everyone's thoughts around him, and he had no clue how to lower the volume, much less how to turn it off. He still struggles at times, but he's able to live a relatively normal life... or what he *thought* was normal, before Azrian showed him his life was nothing but a lie.

He can't even bring himself to visit the courtyard the following day. Finding out it's all fake had caught him by surprise, and he doesn't know if he'll ever look at that place — the place that used to be his safe haven — the same again.

Asking Melior for the truth is out of the question. It's clear that he's able to lie to Kato and manipulate his own thoughts to trick him, Kato just doesn't know how. Adeinde is always around when they speak, and even when Kato can't see her, he can feel her. She's always felt like a shadow, lingering just out of sight. A shadow of pitch black and silence. She's made Kato nervous ever since he was a child. Some part of him wonders whether or not she has anything to do with it.

When he lays down that next night, he fights the urge to reach out to Azrian. He's the only person who's ever communicated with him this way; everyone else has yelled at him to leave their minds and never once reached out to him. This is something he's only ever had with Azrian, and he's not even sure if it means anything — if they'd even be considered friends.

"Sweet shadows, K8.0."

Kato flinches at the voice surrounding him and sits up, frowning at the use of his assigned name. It makes him decide not to ignore Azrian any longer. *"Why did you call me that?"*

"You weren't answering to Kato. Figured maybe you'd answer to your weird name."

"I wasn't answering because you were rude. You told me to go away, so I did." Even as he says the words, he feels childish... but something about Azrian gets under his skin and he doesn't understand it.

"You told me to shut up. Guess that makes us even. I don't mean to bug you, but I don't know how to talk to anyone else right now and I'm losing my mind."

"Why? What happened?" Kato lays back on his bed and stares up at the ceiling.

"*You know what happened. I'm in training, so apparently, I'm unfit to be around other people. You're the only Cogitare around here, so... if I don't talk to you, I can't talk to anyone.*"

"Okay. So... we'll talk." Kato shifts a little uncomfortably, not sure what to even say. "*Shadowhead really isn't a word?*"

He can hear Azrian's laugh through their connection. "*No, it's not. At least not one I ever heard.*"

"*You don't know everything, you know. I say it's a word.*" Kato smiles for the first time in a day. "*Belua didn't like it, but it made me just like it more. He's worse than a shadowhead.*"

"*He's the one with the red eyes, right? I'm pretty sure he's the one that kidnapped me, so... yeah. He's worse than a shadowhead.*" Azrian pauses. "*Are you okay?*"

"Yes." Kato scratches his head and rolls on his side. "*No one's ever talked to me like this... or for any length of time.*"

"*What, in your mind? Or like you're a human and not just some experiment?*"

"Both... people hate Cogitare, like you do." He feels sad again and changes the subject. "*So, you're training... how does it feel to use your powers?*"

"*I hate it. I'm tired all the time and I suck at it. I feel like an imposter. But Kato... I don't hate you. I just hate it when Praediti use their powers to pick on people.*"

He doesn't know what to say to that. He's never picked on someone... at least, not on purpose. Sometimes, he just has a job to do. If he's honest, he'll tell Azrian he hates it, too... but he can't. Even the thought feels like a betrayal. "*You aren't an impostor... I've seen your power. Next time you try, take a deep breath and focus on your mission. Whatever that is.*"

"*They still haven't told me. They just have me trying to put my... whatever it is into these weird orb things. Like stationary, round torches without any fire. I only succeeded once, but the energy stayed for a while... longer than any torch. Brighter, too.*"

Kato bites his lip, hesitating for only a second. *"Not **their** mission Az. **Yours.**"*

"My mission is to go home and find my mom. I don't think this is going to help me, since I don't think this place even has an exit." Panic comes through the connection like Azrian hadn't meant to say all of that.

Kato knows where the exit is... but he won't say it. He can't. *"Then focus on that... you're the most powerful Praediti there is. Once you're trained, I don't believe anything could stand in your way."* Kato reaches out more, wanting to see exactly what Azrian is feeling... but he ultimately pulls back, knowing it isn't his business.

"I don't feel very powerful." Another pause. *"Goodnight, Kato. Maybe they'll let us have lunch again soon."*

"You are, Azrian. You'll feel it soon." He doesn't respond, and Kato makes sure to close the line of connection before saying "goodnight" out loud to himself.

Kato still feels bad for Az. He agreed to cooperate with the Venandi, but his mind — and his heart — are still back in Edros, and they probably always will be.

~ IV ~

THE LIE

Training gets easier the longer Azrian does it. Solitude, on the other hand, does not. He misses his mom, Rhix... even Morella. He'll give just about anything to see them again, but the longer he's stuck in Deadrun, the less likely that becomes.

Each time Melior or one of his goons makes Az do something, he does it with his mother in mind. They tell him she's still alive, and Kato would know if they were lying... but would Kato tell Azrian that? He's not so sure.

Brighter, stronger, *focus your mind.* The commands are on a loop in Azrian's head as over and over, he tries to replicate and expand on that silver light. Sometimes it works, and sometimes Az gets stuck so far in his own head that his hands barely do more than smoke. The first time *that* happens, he thinks maybe they've misunderstood his powers. Maybe he's Igneme, like Belua. Or maybe whatever graces the Praediti with their gifts decided to skimp out on Azrian's.

Either way, he's still pretty sure they've got it wrong.

Almost as often as he thinks of Roe, he thinks of Ender. The father that left him, abandoned him, and forced him to lie, cheat, and steal just to keep the family he left behind alive. But now, he's starting to wonder if maybe Ender didn't *leave* at all. Maybe he was taken like Azrian was. Or... maybe he hit his head a little *too* hard when he fell off that roof and this is all just some sort of dream.

Again, he thinks to himself, *when am I ever that lucky?*

"Repeat!" Melior barks, snapping Azrian back to what certainly *feels* like the present. "You're getting sloppy. Try it again."

"Alright, alright." *Shadowhead.* Azrian grins to himself when Kato's insult pops into his head. He closes his eyes as the thoughts all fade away and attempts to call on that inner energy. *Come on. Just one more time, then maybe he'll let me eat my damn dinner.* His eyelids light up red even before he opens them, and the elation he feels to see two perfectly round balls of silver heat almost makes him forget where and *what* he is.

"Excellent," Melior says quietly. "Keep it up. Can you bring them together?"

The request is new and knocks Azrian out of focus. They disappear, and he looks to Melior with wide eyes. "Together? Why?"

"If you can't control the totality of your power, you can't control it at all. Now bring them back, try again."

That seems incorrect at best, but Azrian sucks in a breath all the same. The faster he masters this, the faster he can come out of isolation. He needs to get to Kato in order to actually get out. "Understood. Okay." Az psychs himself up and tries again even as his bones start to protest the strain. One after the other, the orbs reappear and Azrian slowly brings his hands closer to each other. Anticipation and adrenaline course through him as the edges finally touch, and — with a burst that illuminates the entire room — actually come together.

It's nearly too much for Az to handle. They morph into something different, something strange, and the ringing in his ears drowns out the words Melior speaks. The light becomes a little wild, like it no longer wants to listen to Azrian and would much rather go somewhere else.

For a moment, he's tempted to let it. Maybe it would take his powers with it and he'd be allowed to go home again.

But that doesn't happen, nothing happens except the orbs abruptly disappear again. He feels drained, like he'd just worked all day in the heat of Rhix's shop and then walked clear from Edros to Etria. It's a struggle not to fall over, but Adeinde's cold hands grab a hold of him and hold him steady.

"Well done, Azrian," Melior praises. "Another few days of that and we might actually let you meet Ronan."

The name sounds familiar to him, but in that instant, he can't really place it. "Great. Can I get food now?"

"Of course. I have a meeting to get to, but Rhinn will be in shortly with your food. Adeinde, please escort him back to his room and meet me in my office."

She nods and steers Azrian out before he can find the words to protest. She's rough, which normally Azrian honestly wouldn't mind, but he's sore from the subpar bed and the constant workouts. "Easy, Addy."

"Don't call me that," she snaps. "I'm not your friend. Melior might need you, K8.0 might tolerate you, but I have no use for Videre."

They reach his door and Azrian reaches out to stop her from leaving. "What are you, anyway? I've never seen you do anything."

A sly smile creeps across her lips as she backpedals slowly. "That... is none of your concern. Have a pleasant evening, Azrian. I'm sure tomorrow will be an even *bigger* day for you."

"Right," he mutters to himself as he heads into the room and shuts the door. "Who cares if I'm tired and need a break, the weird wall globes need light."

He flops down on his bed and closes his eyes, wondering if he has time to take a nap before Rhinn arrives with his food. The answer comes rather quickly as she loudly knocks a moment later — but as always, she says nothing to him as she takes the tray and leaves. It suits him fine. He's used to being given the silent treatment... at least from people other than Kato.

"*Kato, you busy?*" he reaches out.

Unlike a lot of the other times, the response comes in instantly. *"Not really. Feeding the new residents. How's training?"*

"I think I'm getting better. Melior says he might let me out soon, so... I guess there's that. You need to teach Rhinn the value of meat." Azrian grins to himself as he picks at his food. *"She's not nearly as generous as you are."*

"I know you love meat and I like to share. Rhinn isn't very generous with anything, to be honest. Before I grew taller than her, she used to steal my pudding."

Az can't help but laugh out loud at the meat innuendo, but then immediately remembers how long it's been since he's had *that* kind of meat. Unbidden, he pictures Kato in his white tunic and gray softpants and wonders what's underneath. Afraid he might've thought that out loud, Az coughs loudly. *"Stealing pudding is mean."*

Kato doesn't speak right away, and Azrian is convinced he heard that embarrassing slip. He's about to say something else when Kato's voice returns. *"Yes, but she's mean, so... what did you just ask to see? The thoughts were muffled."*

Oh, thank Cettia, he thinks to himself. Or... at least he hopes he does. That is not something he wants to get involved with in any way, shape, or form. *"Sorry, I already forgot. Anyway, I should let you get back to it. See you soon... maybe."*

"Okay, Azrian. Make sure you rest." Kato's voice fades away and Az frowns deeply at the silence.

It might be his fault, but... still. He finishes his food and lays back to stare at the square hole on the ceiling. The light is a little brighter tonight thanks to him, and sleep comes easier because of it.

~

The next few days are decidedly not as easy. He gets better, but Kato stops responding almost entirely and Melior works Azrian until he has to be carried back to his room. Now, he's almost positive that his dad didn't die because he believed in the cause... he died because he was worked to death by the Venandi. It does little to change anything for him except to renew his urge to escape.

"*Kato?*" he tries, knowing there won't be an answer. "*Yeah, good talk.*"

He sleeps restlessly, tossing and turning from nightmares involving red eyes and disastrous flames. When he wakes, he's taken right back to the training room.

"Seriously? What time is it?"

"0500. You overslept," Melior scolds. "Perhaps you're not motivated enough. Would you like to know what you're doing here? Why we *really* brought you here?"

Azrian sways on his feet but nods. "Yes. I've been asking since the moment I woke up here."

"Sit. Have you ever heard of the Oculare?"

He eyes Melior with suspicion. "Of course I have. They're rare, but not as rare as Videre, apparently. They see things, right? Ghosts, auras, other things the rest of us can't."

"Exactly. Now, we're lucky enough to have two Oculare here. Together, we've managed to locate another world. One with contraptions that run on their own... *without* Videre or physical interaction of any kind. They have their own power. Great machines and wondrous things, Azrian. All we want... is for the Videre to open a doorway to this world, to Anzore."

That suspicion only grows. "Why, so you can steal their... contraptions?"

Melior shakes his head. "Of course not. We want to learn from them, that's all. To find out how they've become so advanced in a land that appears void of Praediti altogether."

The words settle in Azrian's chest like a beacon of hope. If there's a world without Praediti, it must be a world without fear. But letting the Venandi in sounds like a surefire way to *introduce* fear, and Azrian won't have any part of it. "You're all Praediti. What's to stop you from going over there and enslaving all of them? Tormenting and kidnapping them like you do here?"

"*You* are the very thing which you claim to hate, Azrian," Melior reminds him — as if that's something he needs reminding of. "You said you understood, that you were on our side."

"Well, I'm n—" Az stops, glancing between Melior and Adeinde. If he tells them he's not, they'll throw him back in his cell. They'll double his guard and he'll never get out. "I am."

Melior leans forward like he can smell the lie. "Adeinde, be a dear and collect K8.0 for me. We need to know if he's telling the truth or not."

She nods once and disappears. Dread pools in Azrian's gut — he's been steadily losing Kato, and for some reason, the guy seems irrevocably loyal to the people that routinely cut into his brain. If he tells on him...

Neither man says much until Adeinde returns with Kato. Melior stands, fixing his tunic and clearing his throat. "K8.0, I would like you to look into Azrian's mind. Find out his true intentions... is he with us, or not?"

Kato's eyebrows shoot up as he meets Az's gaze. "He's told me on multiple occasions not to read his mind," he starts, but as soon as Melior looks at him, he straightens and walks closer. "He's... with us." Kato turns like he's going to leave but Melior's continued stare stops him. "Is there something you want to know specifically, Sir?"

Azrian nearly kisses Kato for the outright, blatant lie. Melior on the other hand, has quite the opposite expression. "I want to know *exactly* what he thinks about our mission."

"*Kato, please,*" Azrian begs silently. He fixes his gray eyes on Kato but smooths his face over to hide the panic. "*Tell him... sweet shadows, anything you want, just not whatever it is you can see. Tell him I think it's great or something. Just... please.*"

There's more than extra meat on the line now. It quite possibly might be his life.

~

Kato sends back a silent *"shut up"* but it holds no bite. He walks back over, and before he can realize what he's saying, he speaks. "He thinks I have nice eyes."

Azrian looks like he's about to laugh as he purses his lips. "Well, I suppose the secret's out, then. Can we go?"

"No," Melior barks, much less amused. "That wasn't what I asked you to divulge for me, K8.0. You have one more chance."

Kato pinches his temples and grunts in frustration. *"I have to give him something."* He doesn't wait for Azrian to respond. "He is with us. But he is still worried about his mother, can you blame him?" Kato's powers focus on Melior, and though his thoughts are dark, it's clear that he's still not pleased.

"His mother is no longer his concern, she is safe from harm," Melior says coldly. "That still does not answer my question. Do we need to be concerned about *your* loyalties, K8.0?"

Panic filters in from Azrian. *"Kato, just tell him. It's fine, whatever happens to me... it's fine. I'll deal."*

"What do you want me to say, Melior? To lie? To say he isn't with us even though I'm saying he is? Do you think this Videre can deceive me? He can hardly use his own powers, let alone use mine against me. He is with us. He's just abrasive and doesn't do well with authority." It isn't an entire lie, but he's risking a lot by doing this. Luckily, he's the only Cogitare around and no one can prove he is lying but him.

Melior finally relaxes. "I can deal with abrasive. I *cannot* deal with disobedience. Very well. Adeinde, we have business elsewhere. Send Ronan in to assist him with his training today... if Azrian is truly on board, there's no reason to delay."

Azrian flashes Kato a smile as he's led out. Once the door swings shut, Melior lowers his voice and flicks his eyes toward the scars on Kato's head. "Tread carefully, K8.0. I'd hate to see you brought lower by someone of Azrian's... temperament. You know how fickle and unreliable the Videre are. He is no different."

"They say the same of me... and yet you keep me around." Kato tries again to search his mind, and still gets nothing.

"That's because you *are* fickle and unreliable, K8.0. Just look at what happened in there. I asked you a simple question, and you took the opportunity to flirt with him. But alas... you're the only one we have at the moment. So, I'll have to deal with you whether I want to or not." Melior folds his hands together behind his back and stands straighter as the corner of his mouth turns up. "Luckily for me... I have Adeinde."

One nod from him has her gripping Kato's arm and dragging him toward his least favorite place in all of Deadrun.

"Why! I did what you asked, Melior. Please... not there." He struggles against Adeinde's hold and uses all his strength to reach into her mind to force her to stop, but he's still completely blocked out.

"Call it a precaution," Melior yells after them. "It's nothing personal."

She drags him to where the Sana heal anyone hurt in training and gestures to the lone table, which is still adorned with straps from the last time he was disciplined. "Lay down, K8.0. Don't make this harder than it needs to be."

"I didn't do anything. I don't even have a migraine... the straps are unnecessary." He reaches out to Azrian without realizing, sending him a flash of the bed with straps before he climbs on it and lays down. He hates Adeinde. Ever since she showed up, this place has only gotten colder.

Carefully, she straps him down. With a tilt of her head, she smirks as she tests their strength. "Are you *sure* you don't have a migraine, K8.0?"

Pain travels up the back of his skull to his temples and he cries out at the suddenness of it. He's lightheaded from the pressure and feels like his brain might split open. "Ouch! Stop! Please!"

"I'm not doing anything," she says, and Kato can't sense a lie — he can't sense anything at all over the blinding pain growing more powerful by the second. "I'm just getting better at seeing the warning signs, that's all."

Tears prick his closed eyes as his body tenses against the restraints. "Please... call the Sana... something is wrong!"

"Where do your loyalties lie, K8.0? With Azrian Mihr... or with the Venandi, the ones who raised you, gave you life? Tell me, and I'll fetch the Sana."

"The Venandi! I've done everything you've asked... please." His sob echoes throughout the small room and when he meets her eyes, they're as dark as night. He doesn't need to be a Cogitare to know she's enjoying it. A mere human could see it.

Abruptly, the pain ceases completely. Adeinde grips Kato's chin and forces his face toward hers. "We've had an amicable relationship so far. You're allowed to roam free, do what you please... and all we ask in return is that you help control and point out our enemies. You will continue to do that, yes?"

"Yes," he agrees instantly as he starts to slip from consciousness. He's fading, but he's still able to make out the grin she plasters across her face before his world goes black.

When Kato wakes, the Sana is hovering over him checking his vitals. "What happened?" he croaks out.

His voice startles her, and she moves back a step. "You had another episode, K8.0. They moved your surgery up to today."

"Today? No... I..."

She shushes him and places her palm over his forehead. "Close your eyes. It will all be over soon."

He tries to protest, but he can already feel her powers coursing through his body as he slowly succumbs to the sedation.

This time, he wakes up in the surgery room, completely alone — and based on how badly his head hurts, they've already completed his twelfth surgery. He tries to sit up, but he's still restrained. "Hello? Anyone?"

The Sana eventually responds, "You're up much faster this time, K8.0."

"Can I have some water?"

She hums and walks over to undo his restraints, and when he sits up, the room spins around him. "Take it easy, Cogitare. Drink."

Kato hates being called that, but he's in no condition to argue. Plus, it wouldn't do any good. Talitha is nothing if not traditional. He takes the glass from her long, frail hand and chugs it in one go. "Thank you." Kato hands the empty cup back and touches along his raised scars. "Can I go now?"

Talitha shakes her head and tells him to stay sitting. "Melior will be in shortly."

Dread fills Kato's gut but he nods. There's nothing else for him to do but wait.

Time drags on for so long he lays back down, happy he isn't restrained. He attempts to reach out to Azrian to check on him, but all it does is cause an ache in his forehead, so he quits immediately. *How long have I been here?* he wonders to himself. *Hours...days?*

When he hears the lock on the outside door click, he sits up again to await Melior's entrance. Muffled voices creep under the door to his room and when the handle turns, Kato attempts to tame his messy auburn locks and then straightens. "Hello, Melior."

"K8.0, how are you feeling today?" he asks coldly.

"Like I got cut open. Wh—" Kato clears his throat again — "why did the surgery get moved up?"

Melior takes a seat, and although it's just the two of them in the room, he knows Adeinde is right outside. He can feel her. "You had another migraine. That's two in the last couple of weeks. We are trying to help you, K8.0. Can't you see that?"

If this is helping me, why am I now being treated like some new resident? He frowns at the floor, hating the way Melior is staring at him. It's like he's a stranger, not the man that had a hand in raising him. "Yes," he lies.

Melior clasps his hands together in his lap. "Good. Then I want you to rest. There's nothing more important to us than your continued health. Talitha informs me you did well this time, and she believes she's getting closer to figuring out what's triggering your migraines."

"Really?" he asks in a hopeful tone. If they could figure that out, he wouldn't be so afraid of digging deeper into people's minds... he wouldn't be afraid to search for the truth. "How long have I been here?"

"Five days," Melior says. "The surgery was a little more complicated this time around, but Talitha healed you. You shouldn't have any lingering effects from it. If you're feeling up to it, I don't see a reason why you can't return to your room now."

"Yes. Thank you." Kato stands up, bracing against the side of the bed and then forcing one foot in front of the other. "I'm hungry. Can I go to the kitchens first?"

Melior nods and steps out of the way. "Of course. It's the middle of the night, so not many people will be around. Just... exercise silence, yes?"

"Of course." Kato nods and makes his way toward the outside metal door, then waits for Melior to turn off the alarm and unlock the door.

Once he's far enough away from Melior and his shadowhead, he feels lighter. It's hard not to believe they're helping him when he feels better with each and every step, and by the time he reaches the kitchen, he's completely famished. He eats much too fast, then makes his way to his room to get some real sleep.

The second his eyes flutter open the next morning, he reaches out to Az. Instead of dwelling on the fact that he gets nothing in return like he wants to, he gets out of bed and makes his way to the showers. The warm water cascading down his body feels amazing, so he closes his eyes and lets the stench of surgery wash down the drain, hoping that things will get better.

~

Azrian stares at Ronan like he's an alien. "Okay, that was weird." He'd just watched the boy turn on some sort of... well, Azrian doesn't know how to explain it. It looks like a clunky box, but the front of it just changed. Instead of being the solid black it's always been, it had people on it. Three, to be exact. "How did you put them in there?"

Ronan giggles. "I don't know. It's been here longer than I have. I just know that when I put my power into it, this happens." The boy shrugs and does it again. "Now you try."

Blinking, Az lets out a breath. "How am I supposed to do that when I don't even know what it is?" Even still, he tries. He focuses his energy on the box and frowns deeply. "Okay, I still don't get it. What's it do?"

"It shows movies from another world. A world without Praediti. Movies are like... pictures that move and talk. But the box needs power and here, only we have power."

It's a lot for him to process, and he's not even sure what a "picture" is. But at least now, he has a better idea of what he's supposed to accomplish, so when he makes a second attempt, the box comes to life. Other voices fill the room as the people that appeared move around. It's the strangest thing he's ever seen — and he loves it. "Sweet shadows... and these things are regular over in Anzore? This is why Melior and Belua are trying to go there?"

"I think so. They don't really tell me much. But... when we can get there and learn how... maybe the Videre won't have to work so hard." He giggles at something a man does on the box. "Some of them are funny... this guy's a shadowhead." He sits cross legged on the ground and watches.

Azrian pays more attention to him than the box. "You've been talking to Kat— K8.0, I see." He blushes, a little indignant that Kato hasn't spoken to him in a week. "You're from Edros, right?"

"Yes... to both of those, but I haven't seen Kato in a while." He looks up to meet his eyes. "He asked me to call him Kato, and he calls me Rone now. They're nicknames."

Yeah, a nickname I gave him, he thinks a little bitterly. The fact that the kid hasn't seen Kato in so long is concerning, but maybe Kato just decided Videre are too much trouble for him. "That's cool that you guys have nicknames for each other." He sits down next to Ronan and focuses on keeping the box on. It had taken days to get Ronan to open up to him, and Azrian has questions he can't put off anymore. "So... were you taken, too?"

"Taken?" He tilts his head and sits up. "They saved me. The day I found out I was a Videre, my mom tossed me out. She said she wouldn't raise some Praediti." Ronan looks sad for a second but blinks it away. "They found me on the streets and they fed me."

That seems strange given everything Azrian has come to know about the Venandi, and Praediti as a whole. His heart breaks all the same for the boy... he can't imagine ever being thrown out by his family like that. "I was ripped away from my mom. They didn't give me a choice... I don't even know if she's still alive."

"They took you from her? Why wouldn't she be alive? They wouldn't hurt her."

Azrian nearly tells him about the fire and the circumstances leading up to him coming to Deadrun. About the blood red eyes and the menacing voice he'd heard right before he'd passed out. But he can't, he can't bring himself to do that to Ronan. "Never mind. I'm just glad you're safe." He reaches over to ruffle Ronan's short hair and the box goes dark again abruptly. "Shadows, sorry. I'm still not very good at keeping my energy in certain places once I've stopped paying attention."

"It's okay. You'll get there." Ronan stands up again and then forms a ball of energy in his hand. "Want to see me blast something?"

Grateful for the change in subject, Azrian nods with a grin. "Absolutely."

Ronan waves his other hand to make it bigger and aims at a wall singed with streaks of black, then launches the ball at it with a force that surprises Az. He grins after the impact and then turns to Azrian. "I just learned how to make it bigger."

Selfishly, Azrian realizes that Ronan would be an asset in any escape attempts. He's too young though, and Az would never forgive himself for putting him in danger. Not to mention, if he's remembering the maps correctly, Deadrun is an island north of Edros... he's going to have to cross the Wasted Waters if he wants to go home, and he doesn't think he's capable of protecting a child in the process.

He coaxes Ronan to show him again and then tries himself. It's admittedly not as impressive, but Az still manages to add a pretty sizable dent to the wall. "Eh, maybe one day I'll be as good as you," he says as he smiles.

"Definitely! You just started and you hit the wall! My first one didn't even go all the way!" Ronan's eyes light up with excitement.

Frowning slightly, Az tilts his head. "Melior's had me trying to hit targets for a week. Aiming isn't really the problem for me."

"Then what is it? Does the power make you nervous?"

"You can say that," he concedes. "I just... always thought I was human. Aiming and firing happens so fast I don't have to think much about it but keeping my power in a fixed spot once my attention shifts is hard. I keep getting distracted by it all, like I stop thinking it's real... it shouldn't *be* real."

"Why not? I think we have the coolest power out of all of them. Kato's sucks... he's always in pain. Rikard's an Itinerae and every time he teleports, he gets a bloody nose. Meka's a Tactare, but she gets headaches, too. We don't have pain. Sebbie is a Videre like us, and she's never felt pain, either."

Everything about that seems odd. "I've never known Praediti to have pain. My old boss, Rhix? He's a Viribus, and he never had any problems. I've never met Tactare or Itinerae with pain issues, either. It's only this place."

Ronan shrugs. "Maybe it just takes time. Were they young?"

"No, none of them were. Most were older than me. Rhix is at least forty. Maybe... it just depends on the person."

"Probably. Want to try again?" he asks excitedly.

Truthfully, Azrian is tired. He wants nothing more than a bath, a hot meal, and a chance to sleep, but he can't deny Ronan. Especially not now. He steps back with an eager expression, gesturing to the wall. "You first, then."

"Okay." He forms another, this time curving it to show off and then making a *woo!* sound. "Beat that."

Azrian huffs and places his hands on his hips. "Not possible, that was unbelievably cool." He doesn't even try — in the event that he could pull it off, he didn't want to take away the pride Ronan felt. Instead, he sends another blast at the same spot he'd hit the first time.

It's enough to make him even more tired, so he says goodbye to Ronan and heads to the showers. That's another thing Azrian is having a hard time understanding — somehow, they've made it so he could bathe standing up, and instead of the water pooling around him, it rains down on his head when he tells it to. But they have real soap, and something Ronan told him a few days ago was called shampoo. It smells amazing... even if it reminds him mostly of Kato.

As he cleans himself off, he thinks of the man with scars on his head. Where has he been? Why isn't he talking to Ronan? And why, all of a sudden, does Azrian even care?

He shuts the shower down when he finishes and gratefully gets dressed. Thoughts of Kato disappear as he fills his stomach, and by the time he's lying in bed that night with a blanket wrapped around him, he's starting to wonder if maybe he's been overreacting.

The Venandi saved Ronan. They're feeding Azrian, keeping him warm, keeping him clean. He doesn't have to be afraid of the dark here, because... well, it's never dark. His cheeks are already fuller than they were before he was taken, and for the first time in his life, he has a friend.

Things could decidedly be worse, and if Anzore really has all of the wonderful things he keeps being told, then maybe their mission isn't so bad. A world that doesn't need Praediti is a world he's very interested in, whether he happens to be one of them or not. The tides in Athoze would turn for the better if Praediti weren't necessary for so many things. Humans could be necessary, too... even useful.

But something in Azrian's chest won't quite let go of the circumstances of his arrival. He misses his mother so much it's almost painful, and the story of his father's life and death is weighing heavily. *Maybe I don't know if all of this is a good thing or not... but I guess I'll find out one way or the other. And if it ends up being a good thing, then maybe my parents can be proud of me for being a part of it... even if I am Praediti.*

~ V ~

THE FUEL

Kato hasn't heard from Azrian in a while but occasionally, he finds himself watching him in security. He's getting better with his powers, and he looks like he's actually starting to have fun with Ronan.

When Kato finally sees Ronan again, he looks happy, even on the grainy screen. He and Az are in the training room throwing their energy around, and now that Kato is watching them in action, he has a feeling Az might be holding back, but Kato can't think of a reason he'd do that.

Unless, of course, he just doesn't want the Venandi to know what he's capable of. The last time he reached into Azrian's mind, he had to lie about what he saw. He really doesn't want to do *that* again, but deep down... he knows if the same situation arises, he will.

He finds he actually misses Azrian. Aside from Ronan, he's the only person he's ever had an extended conversation with, and he simply enjoys his company when he's not being rude. He might be a little rough around the edges, but he's still better than most people Kato has met.

When lunch time comes, he rushes to bring the newer residents their food and then makes his way to the cafeteria in hopes of running into Az and Ronan. He's stopped on the way by Belua, who lets him know they will be getting someone new today. It makes him nervous. He hopes it's just another kid looking for a place in the world, and not another person like Az... taken from their home.

By the time he walks into the cafeteria, Azrian and Ronan are almost done eating. He fills up his tray and goes to sit with them anyway. "Um... hi," he mumbles awkwardly, busying himself with his food.

"Hi!" Ronan replies excitedly. "Are you okay? Where have you been? I haven't seen you around in forever! Why?"

Az snorts a laugh at Ronan's many questions and picks at his meat. "Yeah, what he said."

"I was in surgery again. I am okay, thank you... and they're trying to fix my migraines." His eyes flick to Azrian. "How are you guys doing?"

He shrugs as he takes a bite and chews slowly. "Good. Homesick, but... I'm getting better at this whole Videre thing."

Rone launches into an explanation of the things they've tried together, things that Kato has already seen through his observations.

"That's awesome. I knew you'd be a good teacher. Is he a good student, or a shadowhead?" Kato smiles playfully and meets Azrian's gray eyes.

"Ahh, you know me, *K8.0*. I'm always a shadowhead, I don't care for authority... not even tiny authority." He winks at Ronan to take the bite off the words, but there's an underlying level of truth there that Kato doesn't miss.

He can't help but frown. Not even at the authority part, that doesn't surprise him. What surprises him is the use of his assigned name. He pointedly looks down at his plate, trying to see where he went wrong. *I lied for him... I could have been punished... as a matter of fact... I **was** punished,* he thinks to himself, forcing down bits of food while he misses the short conversation between Rone and Az... rian. *Azrian,* since they decided to go back to given names.

"Yeah. Definitely a shadowhead," Rone agrees with a grin. "But he's gonna be stronger than me soon, so I have to be nice."

Azrian reaches over to ruffle Ronan's hair. "Eh, I meet the others later today. You won't have to deal with me for long, little guy."

"Good for you. I know how Videre love to stick together." Kato shoves some more food in his mouth and stands. "You'll fit right in, they're all shadowheads. See you, Rone, I have to go back." He stands up and takes his tray to return the food he can't bring himself to eat.

As he walks past the table on his way out, he catches a glimpse of the glare on Azrian's face. He doesn't want to know the thoughts behind it, so he doesn't try, but he also doesn't understand where it's coming from.

The walk back to security feels lonely, lonelier than normal. He thought he had another friend, but it seems Ronan is still the only one he's got. Kato has a cursory thought that the new person could possibly be a friend, but it passes as quickly as it comes. He knows better now. It doesn't matter how nice Kato is, he'll always just be a Cogitare.

The day goes by slowly. When it's time to get the residents their dinner, he makes sure to save the new guy for last. He doesn't plan on sticking around too long, but sometimes new residents have trouble eating and he'd rather have his rounds done before dealing with that.

Kato knocks on the door as a warning and pulls it open, walking in to see a guy just a couple of years younger than himself. "Hello, Callisto," he greets him, trying a new tactic with this one.

Callisto stares at him a few seconds before his eyes flick down to the tray of food. To make it easier on him, Kato walks closer to set it on his bed — but when he takes a step forward, the new resident flinches back.

Stopping in his tracks, Kato holds up a hand. "Are you okay?" He notices the bruises on his face for the first time, and although he was going to try not to, he reaches into his mind to see who hurt him. *Belua... but why?* "I'm not going to hurt you, I promise." He stays at a distance and sets his food on the bed for him, backing away with the tray. "Eat. If you don't, they'll come get the food back... we can't waste it and you need your strength."

Callisto grabs a piece of bread and takes a bite, quickly devouring the entire thing in seconds. Kato feels bad for him, but he has no idea how to help. He's still getting his strength back himself and he's in no condition to question Belua. He has to play this smart.

After he eats nearly everything that was on the tray, he meets Kato's eyes again. "What happened to your head? Did that Igneme hurt you, too?"

Kato shakes his head. "No. I had surgery."

"Why?"

"Because I get migraines. They think they're close to a solution. What happened to you?" Kato once again tries to move closer but stops when he looks uncomfortable again.

"My house burned down and they took me here. They won't even tell me if my family is okay."

It sounds so familiar Kato feels a chill travel up his spine. "Did your powers just manifest?"

Callisto shakes his head a little, suddenly very interested in the ground. "No," he says quietly. "I guess they've always been there, but I never really used them. I mostly tried to ignore them... but I hurt someone. It was an accident; I was defending myself. All I really remember is wishing the person attacking me would drown, and it... it was like the river *heard* me. The water... it..." Callisto shakes his head, his brows furrowed so intensely it's a miracle he can still see. "It came up like a wave, or an arm, or... *something*. I don't know how to explain it, but the next thing I knew, they were being pulled into the river."

"That isn't your fault, Cal." He offers him a small smile, hoping the nickname will make him feel better.

"It is. It *is*, I did it... and that... that Igneme burned my house down because of it. Told me that I had to come with him, that he was saving me from being arrested for murder. *Murder*. I..." The anguish coming off of Callisto is nearly too much. "I didn't want to hurt him. I just wanted to go home."

"Belua is... he's not very nice, but... he isn't all there is here. I believe it's manslaughter... not murder. You didn't mean to." Callisto's pain has Kato gripping the wall with one hand and his forehead with the other. "Stop torturing yourself. It was an accident."

Shaking his head, Cal draws his knees up to his chest and wraps his arms around them. "If that's true, why am I a prisoner?"

"It's for your protection. All new residents come here until they can be evaluated. When they come in here, do you speak to them the way you speak to me?"

"Evaluated?" Cal sits forward, completely ignoring everything else. "What does that even mean? Evaluated for what?"

"To make sure you won't hurt yourself. I have to report to them after this. I have to tell them your mental state and... thoughts." He blushes, feeling guilty for admitting he's reading his mind.

Cal just nods. "Thought you were a Cogitare. You're not like the rest, though. Most don't even bother to speak; they just take what they need and go." He stares down at the palms of his hands and heaves a breath. "My mental state is shit. Yesterday, I was masquerading as a human just trying to survive. Now, I don't know where I am or what's going to happen to me. Or even *what* I am. I mean, I'm an Undare, right? But apparently, I'm not a good one, or I'd have been able to put the fire out that destroyed my house."

"Not necessarily. Since the drowning happened first... I think you were too afraid to truly try again. You *are* an Undare, and a powerful one... I can see it."

The mere mention of drowning has Callisto retreating into himself — including his thoughts. They become muffled, hard to read, and Kato knows he won't get much else out of him. "Okay," Cal says quietly. "Then just tell me what I'm supposed to do."

Kato backs away, the weight of someone else's pain is too much. *What's the point if I can't take their pain away for them? I can only share it;* he thinks bitterly to himself. "Just... don't be scared. Once you're out of here... I'll introduce you to a friend. He's having trouble here too, but he's getting better. You're not alone."

"Right."

Kato can see he's shut down, so he doesn't push and takes his leave. He feels bad for him, just like he felt for Azrian. *Shadowhead.* He frowns as he walks, still annoyed with Az for unknown reasons but he doesn't dwell on that. He's much more focused on the similarities between him and Cal.

Azrian didn't hurt anyone, but why would both of their houses burn? Belua being an Igneme is no coincidence. *Is this what they've been doing? Making people feel completely helpless so they feel this place is the only option?* The thought makes Kato extremely angry, but he has to keep his emotions in check... no matter how hard that is for him. He has to. He *has* to figure out the truth.

~

Az lays in his bed, tossing a ball of energy up into the air and catching it again. It still feels strange, but at least it's a way to pass the time — the days never seem to end at Deadrun. He still wants to go home more than he can ever express, but that goal is becoming less reachable by the day. He hasn't found any sort of an exit, and even if he did, there would be no way for him to get past the guards.

Not on his own, anyway.

Finally, after days of no communication at all, he breaks down and reaches out to Kato. *"You still alive?"*

"Yes." Kato responds quickly. *"Did you think I was dead?"*

"I don't know what to think anymore. I don't trust anyone here except for you, and I know you kind of hate me, but I don't want anything bad happening to you." He throws the energy ball up again and watches it splay across the floor, sending light beams throughout the small room before disappearing entirely. *"And after the whole surgery thing..."*

"I don't hate you. Why would I ever hate you? I thought you hated me." His voice sounds so confused, Azrian can practically hear the head tilt.

He smiles to himself as he stands up and starts to pace. *"You think I'm a shadowhead."*

"You are." He pauses, but Az is sure he's smiling, too. *"Plus, you called me K8.0, and you told me that name was stupid."*

Reason tells Azrian to leave it there, to refrain from provoking the extremely powerful, extremely easily swayed Cogitare. Nothing good can come of him continuing to tease — especially since it doesn't seem like Kato knows the difference between seriousness and sarcasm.

For once, he listens to reason. *"It's after 1800, you're free, right? Any chance you wanna come say that to my face?"*

"Um... sure. Are you... in your room?"

"Yeah," Az says before he can stop himself. He'd been thinking the courtyard, but there's little privacy there. *"Stop by."*

"Okay." He's quiet for a while and when he finally communicates again, it sounds louder in his mind. *"Open up, shadowhead."*

Grinning, Azrian lets him in. "What, the Venandi didn't teach you how to knock?"

"They didn't actually." Kato walks in and sits down on his bed. "How is training?"

He hesitates, then closes the door and leans against it. "I still don't like it, or any of this, but I'm getting better at it. Watch." Concentrating, Az shows Kato the things he's learned since the last time they saw each other. When he's finished, the truth of how long that's actually been sets in, and he takes a step closer to check out Kato's scars. They're now white where they once were pink and inflamed. "Looks good."

"Thanks. They don't itch anymore. I have someone you should meet tomorrow. His name is Callisto... he has a—" Kato frowns and looks down at his large hands — "his story sounds similar to yours. You know... how he got here."

"Oh." Azrian's mood tanks and he leans against the wall with his arms crossed, trying to remember his earlier warning to himself. Pushing Kato wouldn't do any good. "Look, I'm not gonna freak out about it, but you might not want me to be the one to talk to him. You're not going to like what I tell him."

"What will you tell him?" Kato meets his eyes and Azrian isn't sure if he's reading his mind, but he hopes he isn't.

He tells as much of the truth as he can. "That it doesn't get easier. That missing home, missing family, and freedom... it never goes away. It never dulls. It just sits there, all the time. You can't look directly at it, cause if you do, you'll die. But you can't ever quite look away, either. I've been here for months now... so long that I barely remember what Cettia looks like in the night. And it just doesn't get easier."

"I can try to make it easier for you." Kato stands up and moves closer. "I could share your pain... if you wanted."

Azrian stares into those dual-colored eyes and squints. "What? How... and why in the shadows would you want to?"

"So, you don't have to carry it alone," Kato states as if it's obvious. "Shadowhead."

The offer doesn't sit right with Azrian for a lot of reasons. Praediti aren't supposed to be selfless or kind — or any of the things Kato is. He's also apparently a masochist because he *has* to know how deep that well runs. "I wouldn't wish this on anyone, Kato. Except maybe Belua. I can't let you do that."

"Okay." Kato takes a few steps back to give him space. "If you change your mind, you know how to reach me. I know you don't trust me... because I trust them... but I'm my own person. Regardless of my *stupid* given name."

Az flinches. He deserves that and then some, but still... Kato keeps repeatedly landing on the wrong side of things. "I don't trust anyone here. Not even Ronan. It's nothing personal, *Kato*." That time, he accentuates the nickname gently. The one thing he's learned is that life at Deadrun without Kato is... well, he'd rather be stuck back in the forests of Embermeadow at night. "So, when do I meet this Callisto? I promise I'll be on my best behavior."

"Best behavior? That doesn't sound like you," he teases. "Tomorrow? What time will you be training?"

Maybe he is learning sarcasm, Az thinks to himself as he smirks a little. "Same time as always. I'd say either lunch would be best, or just meet me here after 1800 again."

"Okay." Kato stands there a moment and stares at Az since he's blocking the door. "Want to talk more? I wasn't busy."

He does, but if he's being truthful, he has no idea what to say. "Nah, I... should probably get some sleep. I'll see you tomorrow though, right?"

"Right." Kato walks to the door and meets his eyes. "Goodnight, Az." He reaches for the handle but doesn't look away, and Azrian realizes yet again that he's still blocking the door.

For some reason, he can't bring himself to move. "I uh... should probably get out of your way, huh?"

"If you want to." Kato smiles and stays standing close. "Is your secret plan to keep me hostage?"

As fun as that sounds — potentially in more ways than one — something tells him that kidnapping Melior's pet won't do him any favors. "Sorry, bud. Can't tie you down just yet. I'm sure you understand." He forces himself to sidestep and drop his eyes to break the trance.

Azrian can tell Kato wants to ask a question, but he doesn't. "See you tomorrow."

He salutes the Cogitare and sighs once the door closes behind him. Maybe he's just been at Deadrun too long, but Kato looks... good. Really good. *Stop it. You're just happy he's alive and wasn't punished anymore for affiliating with you,* he tells himself. *That's why you pulled away to begin with... Kato doesn't deserve to be cut open just for knowing you.*

Shaking the thoughts off, Azrian paces for a while more before finally going to sleep. When he wakes, the day drags on; he finds himself curious about Callisto, and because of that, he's both eager for *and* dreading their meeting. If he truly came to Deadrun under the same circumstances, he might finally have a true ally — but at what cost?

His duties end too soon, and suddenly, he hears Kato's voice in his head again telling him to open the door. Az lets them both in quickly, taking in Callisto's messy brown hair and blue eyes. He's younger than them both, but not by much. "Hi."

"Hi." Kato says and sits on the bed again. "This is Callisto. Cal, this is Azrian. Remember I told you about how his house burned, too?"

Cal nods and looks at Azrian. "You didn't say he was hot."

Kato stands and walks over to feel Az's forehead. "His temperature is normal."

"Stoppit," Az says, swatting Kato's hand away. "He means he thinks I'm attractive, not that I have a fever." Chuckling, he sticks his hand out to shake Cal's. "But you're not so bad yourself."

"Attractive," Kato repeats, staring at Azrian in a way that makes him squirm. "Yes, he is. Is that something I'm supposed to mention?"

Cal takes his hand and huffs a laugh at Kato. "Is he always this way?"

The compliments have Azrian standing a little straighter. "Yeah, he is. You get used to it." He stops the handshake to point at Kato. "But listen, be careful who you say that to. Some people get weird about it."

"They do? Why?" Kato asks curiously. "Isn't it a good thing?"

Cal scratches the back of his head and eyes them. "You two close?"

Kato breaks their gaze and looks over at Callisto. "Close? Sometimes. We were close last night," he states matter-of-factly.

What in the... Azrian sighs and runs a hand over his beard. "Okay. This... isn't going well. Kato, sit. Cal... the short answer is no, not the way you're asking. Kato means we were literally, physically standing close to each other last night. We haven't... you know." He clears his throat and abruptly changes the subject before he can start daydreaming about doing exactly that. "Anyway, what's your deal? You a Videre, too?"

Cal hesitates. It looks like he wants to continue the former conversation, but thankfully, he moves on. "Um... I'm an Undare, despite years of trying to shove it down."

"Water, huh? That's kinda cool." Az tries to keep his thoughts scrambled — Kato is sitting as he was told to do and seems to be just watching, but Az has no idea if the guy is rooting around in his brain or not... and now, all Az can think about is how helpful someone like Cal would be in an escape. "Where you from?"

"Coldhallow," he responds.

Az grins, nodding as he picks at his fingernails. "I'm from Embermeadow. Barely a day and a half walk away from each other."

"I've been there. Only once but... my dad took me." Cal looks down, worry etched into his face. "I just want to know they're okay."

They're not, I can almost guarantee it, Az thinks to himself. He knows better than to say it out loud, and also knows how desperate he is to talk about his own mother — to keep her alive, even if it's only in memory. "Tell me about your family. You have any siblings?"

Cal smiles at that. "Yes, two younger siblings. Twins. Last I saw them, they were running home... before the incident." Callisto's eyes flick to Kato and he nods encouragingly. "They said I killed someone... in the water."

"Were they Praediti?" Azrian asks. When Cal nods, Az snorts. "Good for you. Bet they thought it was going to be easy. What were they doing, trying to rob you? Something worse?"

"I was being attacked. I willed the water around me to drown him, but I didn't mean to kill him, I just wanted to get away. Then Belua was there and my home was burning, but he wouldn't let me go to it to see for myself. He said he'd protect me from going to prison."

Az scoffs. "To the shadows with him, honestly. I hate that guy. But seriously — you didn't do anything wrong, Cal. I know what that's like. It's their own fault for coming after you in the first place... and it's about time someone actually fought back." He straightens up a little, glancing at Kato. "You're not gonna turn me in for saying that, right?"

Kato frowns and shakes his head, but Cal doesn't look so sure. "Maybe we should have this conversation alone, Azrian."

"Look," Az says, "Kato stuck up for me. He lied for me... if he says he won't tell, he won't tell. Even still, I can't tell you who to talk in front of — so yeah, if you wanna talk alone, we can."

Kato looks between them both and stands up. "I'll just..." He points at the door and makes his way out.

Cal looks like he feels a little bad but doesn't speak until the door closes. "Sorry about that. I don't like Cogitare. They can't be trusted. Even if they're nice."

"I get that. And trust me, I feel the same way about every single one of them — except for Kato." Az sits on his bed and leans against the wall, extending one leg out. "I didn't trust him at first, either. But he's come through for me more than once. He lied to Melior's face for me."

Cal sits on the other end awkwardly and puts his knee up. "I get that. He's a nice guy, just sucks he's a mind reader. He'll probably never have real friends because of it. Anyway, are you looking for a way out?"

Something about that makes Azrian feel terrible. Kato really has been good to him since his first day at Deadrun, and all Az has done is keep him at arm's length. He knows what it's like to not have friends, and yet he's been blaming Kato for something that isn't even his fault. He didn't ask to be Cogitare any more than Azrian asked to be a Videre. "Yeah," he says quietly. "Haven't had any luck so far, I can't even find the exit. I think it's through the area by the holding cells, but it's all alarmed. We'd never make it."

"Doesn't that guy work security? Maybe he can get us through? I may not trust him yet, but if you do... he might help. Why doesn't he just mind control Melior, though?"

"He was born here," Az explains. "I don't think he's ready to leave, *or* to screw over the people that raised him. He doesn't like me *that* much. But trust me... it's a thought I've considered a *lot*."

"We don't need him, then. We just need a plan. Is anyone else on board?" Callisto looks excited, like he'd go right now if he could. It's almost endearing.

Az doesn't want to let him down, but knows he has to. "No, the only other kid I've gotten close to is a thirteen-year-old that thinks the Venandi saved him. I think we *do* need Kato unless you're willing to die in an escape attempt."

"It's better than this... right? I mean, how long have you been here?"

He's not even sure anymore, he'd stopped keeping track a long time ago. "Months. I don't know. A long time." He watches Cal out of the corner of his eyes. "Maybe it won't be so bad now."

Cal's eyes meet his and he grins. "Oh yeah? So, you mean it, you and him never... you know. Anything?"

"Nah," Az says quietly. "He never showed any interest, and I'm not even sure he knows what *that* is, anyway. Doesn't seem to be a lot of that going around, you know? I don't think I've even seen anyone kissing."

"Really? And they're young like us? That seems weird. Maybe it isn't allowed... more of a reason to get the hell out of here."

Az chuckles. "Eh, you find you don't miss it that much, not compared to other things, anyway. Forests... rivers. You're from Cold-hallow, right? Bet you'll miss those mountains more than you miss locking lips. Not to say I don't think about it, cause I do..." He shakes his head, knowing it's useless to go down that road.

"I don't know. I stared at those mountains my whole life. Locking lips? Still a new adventure for me. I wasn't quite done traveling that road... if you know what I mean."

"You're a virgin," Az clarifies with a smirk. "I seem to be surrounded by those. But alright, you win. Keep your mouth shut and your eyes open... and maybe you and me find a way out of here. I'm a Videre. Maybe I can figure out how to do the opposite of what I've been doing and *take* energy instead of produce it."

"That's a good plan! I imagine they wouldn't do well without their precious power. And for the record... I'm not a *virgin*, I've... done... things." He blushes and picks at his hangnail.

Az is near desperate to stop having this conversation before he does something stupid like pounce on him. "Hey, I don't judge. I'm not exactly *overly* experienced. Anyway, you might wanna clear out of here... if they think we're getting too close, they won't let us see each other anymore. That'll make escaping a little hard."

"Yeah... right." Cal hops up and turns to look at him again. "Maybe when we get out of here, we can pick that conversation back up." He bites his lip and turns to leave, giving him one last look back before he closes the door.

A shiver runs down Azrian's spine, but he's not sure if it's a good one or a bad one. He takes a moment to pull his long hair up and then flops onto his bed, and for some reason, his mind wanders back to Kato. *"That was... interesting. You okay?"*

Kato takes a moment to respond but when he does, Az is happy he doesn't sound upset. *"Yes. Are you?"*

"Yeah, just feel bad about kicking you out. I didn't want that to happen. But we've got a lot in common, me and Cal... I think he needed that." Az closes his eyes and pulls his blanket up a little higher. *"Maybe I did, too."*

"Did you... never mind. I'm glad you guys are friends. I saw inside his mind... it was probably best he kicked me out so he could be more comfortable. I didn't mean to... his thoughts were... loud."

Huffing a quiet, nervous laugh, Azrian licks his lips. *"Do I even want to know what he was thinking?"*

"I assumed he told you. He wants to break out... and also do sex to you."

Even though the wording makes him cringe, it also makes him smile. *"Yeah, he... mentioned both of those things. Neither happened though, so... I guess you're stuck with me for a little."* Azrian's not sure when things shifted, but they absolutely have. Sex sounds great, but he has other needs, more important needs. He wants to go home, to stop hurting... to make sure his mom found some way to take care of herself. Taking the time to have sex — with *anyone* — seems like an insult to her when he *should* be planning that escape they'd talked about. It apparently just took the offer of both for Az to realize which one he wants the most.

"Are you okay? I can feel your sadness." Kato's voice is soft, probably too soft for his giant body, but it's nice.

"Sorry, big guy. Just... same old stuff. Sometimes I forget you can feel it. I'll catch you tomorrow, okay? Get some sleep." Az rolls over and buries his face in his pillow. If he can't get Kato fully on their side, he's going to end up screwing everything up by tipping his hand. While a big part of him wants Kato with them when they break out, he knows if it comes to it, he won't hesitate to leave him — or anyone else — behind.

He *has* to get home.

~

After Azrian stops communicating, Kato continues to stare at the ceiling with his brow furrowed. Although he won't turn them in, knowing they both still want to escape is worrisome. If they're caught, who knows how long they will have to be in the holding cells again, and the fact that he has an amicable friendship with them both will mean he won't be the one serving their food or checking on them.

He doesn't understand why the idea of Cal and Azrian together makes his chest tighten — and not in a good way. He knows what sex *is* in a technical sense, but it's impossible for him to know anything beyond a biological level. He's never been taught how or what to do, he just knows how children are made and he knows that occasionally... he gets urges. Yet, the thought of Cal having sex with Az upsets him. *That isn't why I introduced them;* he thinks to himself. *I just wanted to help them make friends.* He forces the thoughts away, because Azrian is much more focused on being free than having sex with Callisto, and that realization helps more than it should.

Melior is still refusing to speak with him about anything other than security, and it's starting to seem like he doesn't even want to be in the same wing as Kato anymore, especially alone. His thoughts are so jumbled it's a miracle he can even form a full sentence, and it finally makes Kato realize just how badly Melior *doesn't* want him fishing around in his head. He still tries, but every time he's able to focus in on any particular thought, the headaches begin. It's almost as if he has some protective barrier around his mind to cause Kato pain. But if he wanted Kato to hurt, why wouldn't he just hurt him? Why does he continue to treat Kato like an asset if he wants him to be wary of his powers? It just doesn't make sense.

The following day, Kato goes about his business as usual. By lunchtime, he finds himself wandering to the cafeteria to see if any of his friends are there. *Friends.* The word still feels foreign in his mind, but when he enters and sees Az, Rone, and Cal, he can't help but smile.

"Hello. Can I sit with you guys?" he asks awkwardly, feeling as if he's interrupting a conversation.

"Duh," Ronan says quickly with a huge smile. It fades so quickly Kato turns his head to see why. *Melior... and of course, Adeinde.* They all quiet down as the boss approaches, and the look he gives Kato sends a chill up his spine. He doesn't approve of his company.

"K8.0. I didn't expect to see you here with the trainees, don't you normally have lunch alone?" he asks, his hands clasped behind his back.

"Yes... I was jus—" He's cut off abruptly by a sharp pain in his temples. "Ah! I have to... excuse me." Kato walks toward the exit, unable to even use the words to explain what is wrong.

Before he leaves, he hears Melior address the group. "Eat up boys, I will be sitting in on your training after lunch. Don't mind K8.0, he gets those often."

Kato barely makes it to the bathroom in time before he's hurling his breakfast into the toilet. He's so incredibly frustrated with his own head that he wonders if it would be easier to give up, but deep down, he knows he doesn't have to. If he doesn't find some relief for these migraines soon, he just might die.

~ VI ~

THE BETRAYAL

A deep sense of discomfort spreads through Azrian as he watches Kato dash out of the cafeteria. Melior's staring at him and Cal like he's won some sort of prize, but Adeinde... *she's* the one Azrian's interested in. Right before Kato's headache started, her face changed. It wasn't overly obvious, but it was there, and Az isn't sure what to make of it. *Could she be the cause of Kato's migraines? If that's the case... oh, sweet shadows we need to get out of here.*

He fixes his eyes on Melior and tries to adopt a flirty grin. "I don't mind if you wanna come watch. I've learned a few new tricks, and I bet my boy Cal over here has, too."

Cal gives Azrian a curious look before playing along. "Yeah, absolutely. You should bring Belua and Adeinde, too."

The request has Melior looking suspicious, but it doesn't matter. If all goes as planned — granted, the "plan" is still coming together in Azrian's mind, like some sort of puzzle being haphazardly shoved together — taking them all out of commission is the best way to do this. But now, he has to try to find a way to get to Kato.

He tunes back into the conversation just in time for Melior to excuse himself. The second he's gone, Az drags Callisto out of his seat and toward the holding cells. He's determined to at least confirm his theory that there's a door somewhere in the area he was told to stay away from.

Cal keeps hissing in his ear that he wants to know what's going on, but Az doesn't answer. He shushes him as they make it across the other side of the courtyard and stand in the lobby. To their right is security, but it looks empty. Straight ahead are the holding cells... and to the left, the giant metal door with the alarm.

"Shadows," Az whispers quietly. "I still can't see a damned thing, but this *has* to be the exit, right? That's the only thing that makes sense."

Shrugging, Cal grabs Azrian's arm and stands close. "I don't know, I think that's where they keep the more powerful weapons. The ones they can't just store in the training area. I never heard anything about a way out or a door or anything."

"Think about it, Cal. There *has* to be a door. We got in here somehow, right? I don't see many Itinerae around here except that Rikard guy, and I *highly* doubt he's teleporting everyone in and out. Ronan says he gets nosebleeds just from trying to jump *himself*." Az's eyes fill with excitement as he walks closer to the door. The alarm has to work from some sort of power source, so if Az can control *that*, he can control the alarm.

Cal's soft hand grabs his arm and pulls him back. "Wait," he hisses. "It's the middle of the day, everyone's awake. We can't do this right now."

"What?" Az hears him, he does, but the words seem disconnected from what they're trying to do. Maybe it's desperation, or maybe it's just fear... but either way, Azrian wants to go *now*.

"We need food, water... blankets. We can't run out just us, we'll die," he says sharply. "Even *if* we make it through that door, Deadrun is an island, right? How do you expect us to get back to Edros?"

Az pulls him up against the wall to stay out of sight. "They're close. It shouldn't take that much to get across, and you're an Undare for Cettia's sake! All we need is something to keep us afloat and you can just... whoosh us across the water."

The look Cal gives him is comical. "I've never *whooshed* anything, and the last time I tried to manipulate a body of water that big, someone *died!*"

"Yeah, but you said yourself you'd rather die than stay here," Az argues. "We don't have time for this. Let's just... fine. Let's go play with Melior and that crazy lady — who, by the way, is the one hurting Kato, I'm pretty sure — and then get what we need and meet back here tonight."

Cal's eyes flick to the security room. "This is dangerous."

"So is staying here. You know what, I'm not going to argue with you. Come with me, don't come with me, I don't care. I'm leaving... *tonight.*"

~

Keeping a low profile for the rest of the day is harder than he thought it would be. He's antsy, nearly jumping out of his skin with anticipation — and everyone seems to be noticing. Even little Ronan pulls him aside after training to make sure he's okay.

"Yeah," he tells him. "I'm fine. But hey, you wanna hang out for a little bit?" Azrian asks. He wants Ronan to come with them, but even if he doesn't, he would like to see him one more time.

The boy agrees, and once they're safely back in Azrian's room, he sits him down. "What would you say if I told you that I could take you home?"

Ronan frowns. "But this *is* my home, Az. I'm already here."

A pained expression blooms on Azrian's face. "Not this home, your *real* home. Back in Edros, where I'm from, too. Remember? Home?"

"They didn't want me," Ronan says in a small voice. "They threw me out when they realized what I was, remember *that?*"

Azrian feels a nearly overwhelming urge to hug him. He's so small, so sweet... how anyone could do such a thing to someone like Ronan is beyond him. "I'm sorry, I didn't mean to make you sad.

But... what if you could make a new family? With me, Callisto, and maybe even Kato? We could be each other's family. Would that be okay?"

"Yeah," Ronan replies quickly with a smile. "I'd like that a lot. Like brothers, right?"

Thanks to the sexual connotations involved with the three older ones, Az has to laugh. "Something like that, anyway. But what if the only way we could do that would be to leave? To go back to Edros? We wouldn't need to go near your family, you could stay with me and my mom. She'll love you; I know she will."

All the happiness drains from Ronan's face and he deflates, his shoulders slumping. "I don't want to leave, Az. I like it here, it's warm and they feed me. Melior and Belua... I know you don't like them, but they're nice to me. And Adeinde brings me candy sometimes when I'm sad."

No matter what, Azrian knows he can't compete with that. Even back in Edros, they'll be pariahs until they can prove they really are Praediti. And even once they do, or if they *can*, Azrian isn't sure he wants to stick around there. He just wants to get his mom and figure out a way to take out Melior and Belua for good. No one should ever have to live in fear of being kidnapped or their homes burning down. "Oh. Okay, I understand. I won't make you come. But Rone —" he tries the nickname Kato gave him — "you have to keep this a secret for me, okay? Please don't tell anyone we had this conversation, okay?"

"I won't, but... don't leave," he pleads quietly. It's almost enough to make Azrian change his mind, but this is bigger than them, bigger than Ronan.

"I have to, little buddy. You'll be okay. I know you will. Stick close to the other Videre, okay? They'll look after you." He finally does pull Ronan in, kissing the top of his head and squeezing him tightly. "And don't ever forget that *you* are more powerful than you think you are, okay?"

All Ronan does is nod, and his tiny nose rubs against Azrian's chest as he does. "I'm gonna miss you."

"Yeah, bud. I'm gonna miss you, too."

~

During dinner, Az flashes a few charming smiles and manages to sneak himself some extra food. It's not much, but it should be enough to feed him and Cal for a couple of days if they're careful. He knows he can't risk taking more than that without drawing attention, anyway.

Back in his room, he layers up as much as he can. Two tunics, a pair of softpants — which he's come to know as *sweatpants* since arriving — and his regular uniform pants, plus two pairs each of socks and boxers. He's not sure what happened to the clothes he arrived in, but he hasn't seen them since that first day.

This will have to do.

He's been around long enough now that he notices the slight change in the overhead light to signify the end of the day. If he wasn't Videre himself, he may never have caught on.

The whole day, he's been going back and forth in his mind about whether or not to invite Kato. He wants to, if for no other reason than convenience. They don't have enough food to feed him, but Azrian would be an idiot not to admit how helpful he'd be. With his help, they could virtually just walk right out of there. But with their relationship as rocky as it has been, he's honestly not sure if Kato would join them... or simply tell on them.

Still, he has to try. *"Hey Kato, you still up?"*

"Yes. Are you having trouble sleeping?"

Az grimaces. *"Not... exactly. Can I ask you something? Are you happy here?"*

"Happy?" he asks in a confused tone. *"I... don't know."*

That isn't a no, and despite Azrian's suspicion that Kato doesn't understand the meaning of the word, it's not a strong enough answer for Az to tip his hand. "*I need a better answer than that, bud. Do you still believe the Venandi want what's best for you?*"

"*Um... yes. They help me with my migraines. Melior says I would have died years ago.*"

Azrian sighs, taking a moment to lean against the door and wish things were different. "*I get it. But just be careful, okay? You might trust them, but I don't. Keep your eyes open, that's all I ask.*"

"*Okay.*" Kato pauses a few moments. "*I have to close my eyes for a little bit every day for sleep.*"

The smile that draws is unexpected. He's going to miss Kato's innocence... and maybe he can at least admit that to himself. "*You're right. Get lots of sleep... you need to take care of yourself, Kato.*"

"*See you tomorrow, Az.*"

Instead of answering, he lets the connection fade out. He can't bring himself to tell Kato that he's wrong, and that with any luck, Az will be gone... and they'll never see each other again.

Having to do this without him is a blow, but he gets it. Some part of him always knew he'd be leaving Kato behind. At least he still has Cal, and as long as *one* of them gets out, there's hope. *Unless Melior or Belua kill one of us,* he thinks bitterly. *Or both of us.*

The thought of dying *should* be a deterrent, but it's not. He wasn't initially on board with Cal's viewpoint on this, but he absolutely is now. This isn't a life. It's not *living*. Being away from his mom, the sun, and Cettia has him feeling restless, empty, incomplete.

He needs out.

With a deep breath, he slowly pushes open his door and peeks out into the hallway. As predicted, it's deserted. He tiptoes out slowly and glances down the long corridor to the other doors, where the other Videre are probably trying to coax themselves to sleep. *I'll be back for you guys one day, I promise.*

He sets his jaw and keeps to the wall as he heads out into the pathway that connects the dorms to the courtyard. From here, the choice is easy. Skirt down that hallway instead of going directly into the courtyard, despite the ease of access if he'd have gone that way. Cal's dorms are on the other side, near Kato's, and it would've been easiest to meet in the middle — but nothing about this is going to be easy.

Once he rounds the corner at the end, he has to double back. Belua is there talking to Adeinde and another woman he's only seen a couple of times. His heart rate kicks up with fear, but he holds steady. *Just wait them out.*

Another careful glance happens to be timed just right, and he sees Cal's bright blues staring back at him from the opposite end of the room. He grins to himself for just a moment, happy that they've made it this far and pleased beyond reason that Cal hasn't changed his mind in the hours they've been apart. He can't see much else, but after a few, agonizing moments... Belua and his posse turn to leave.

Several seconds pass as Azrian stays put. He wants to make sure they've gone back to Belua's office near the training room on the other side of the compound. The problem is... he has no idea where Melior's office is, so there's no way to check and make sure he'll be out of the way.

Undeterred, Azrian sneaks around until he's face-to-face with Callisto. They don't say a word. They simply nod to each other in confirmation before turning to face the alarmed door fully.

This is where it gets tricky. *This* is where they succeed or fail, and it's entirely on Azrian's shoulders. "Cover me," he mouths silently, then closes his eyes as he feels a thrum of energy ebb and flow under his skin. It's his, and he has control.

Slowly, the lights click out around them until they're shrouded in darkness. Azrian ignores the fear blossoming from that long-forgotten danger and reminds himself that things are different now. *He* is different now.

"Keep going," Cal whispers. "I don't hear anything yet."

Emboldened, Azrian reaches out to the alarm and sucks in a breath, envisioning himself drawing all the power from it into himself. It's a strange feeling, but as he feels his own power swell, he knows it's working. Cal jumps up and down next to him in glee as the red dots coating the passcode pad fade out entirely, and they know they've done it.

Az clamps his hand over Cal's mouth and drags him forward. They don't have time to waste — he's sure there's some sort of fail-safe built in that will alert Belua or Melior that something is wrong, and they certainly can't risk making any unnecessary noise. With a level of excitement Azrian thought was impossible, he pushes open the locked door and dashes in... but runs smack into Melior.

Dread like he's never known it fills his bones, and all he can hear are the sounds of Cal's shoes hitting the concrete as he runs away. *Coward.* He blinks, knowing Melior's ugly face will be the last thing he ever sees. "Hi," he says. "I was... looking for you."

Melior looks angry, if not a little amused. "That was impressive. I wondered if you'd be able to do it or not... and you did. Your powers are growing, Azrian. We're doing good work with you."

He bites back the retort on his tongue and forces himself to nod. "Yes, you are. I'm definitely feeling stronger." The exit is right there — he was *right*, there is one... and all that's standing between him and freedom is Melior. "I should... go back to my room now," he says quickly.

"So soon? You said you were looking for me. Well... you've found me." The venom in Melior's voice is intense enough that for a moment, Az just wishes he'd kill him and be done with it. If his theory about Adeinde causing the migraines and nosebleeds is correct, he doesn't want to think about what she's capable of doing to someone that tries to escape.

"I forgot what I wanted," he lies with a dimpled grin. "Guess the energy surge addled my brain a little bit."

Melior takes a step forward. "Well then, perhaps we should run some *tests*... see exactly how addled that brain of yours is. An unstable Videre is a danger to us all, don't you think? You don't want to be a danger, *do you, Azrian?*"

"No," he squeaks, hating the fear finally seeping through in his voice. He backs up, but his body smacks into something — no, someone else. Rough hands grab him, and he pivots his head just enough to see Belua's red eyes.

"Take him back to the cells," Melior says in a bored tone. "I think we can make an example out of this one."

Azrian kicks and screams, but it doesn't do any good. For the second time, he's being taken against his will, and there's nothing he can do to stop it. In his mounting terror, the globes above their heads fill with light and burst, raining down hot, potent energy on all of them and stinging their skin. He gasps from the pain his own power is causing as it leaves angry, red welts on his exposed arms. It's enough that he stops fighting *just* long enough that Belua strengthens his hold, and there's nothing Azrian can do but writhe and twist as he's dragged toward the cells and bodily thrown back into the same one he'd woken up in originally.

He failed.

He's not going home, he won't see his mother... and eventually, they'll figure out it was Cal that was with him if they haven't already. Sadness washes over him in waves, sending him to his knees and making his body shake with loss.

He should've seen this coming, and now since he didn't... they're all going to pay for it.

~

A loud, thundering knock rouses Kato from his bed. He wasn't sleeping, not really... he could hear yelling, and when he'd tried to reach out to Azrian, all he'd gotten in return was a wall of unrelenting, crippling sadness. Reluctantly, he opens the door to find Melior.

"K8.0," he says coldly. "I'm sorry to wake you, but this cannot wait. I have a job for you, and it must be done now."

He frowns, looking around and noticing that Melior is actually alone this time. "What happened?"

Melior grins slyly. "We've foiled an escape attempt if you can believe that. I'm not sure who would ever want to leave our beautiful home, but... alas. The Videre Azrian was caught trying to sneak out, and I know he had an accomplice. You have two tasks, actually. First, find out the name of his accomplice. And second... you *will* convince Azrian to comply with us by whatever means necessary. We've tried doing this the polite way, but the boy is... he's broken, K8.0. He lived too long in the outside world and it has broken his mind, he's not thinking clearly. So, you will... simply help him along. You have considerable talents. It is time we put those to their proper use."

Azrian. A sense of sadness overtakes him and he grips the door tighter, wondering why Az didn't feel like he could trust him enough to tell him. *Because I'm a Cogitare,* he admits to himself, but that doesn't lessen the sting in the slightest. Regardless, he still won't force Azrian into anything. He can't. He can't be the monster he views him as. The monster Melior wants him to be.

For once, Melior's mind isn't blocked. It's not some muddled stream of incoherent thought, causing Kato to jump idly from one to the other without gleaning much of anything. No, this time, he can see *everything.* The look of sheer terror on Azrian's beautiful face as he realized he was in Belua's arms. The other world, Anzore, and the wondrous machines they have... but it's more than that now. He sees humans, other humans, bending and bowing to Melior as if he's their king. Praediti with multi-colored eyes like Kato's. He sees fires and lightning storms and monsoons... just a few of the tricks Melior has up his sleeve to take over. *Take over,* not learn from. Azrian was right all along... the Venandi aren't peaceful at all. Melior had lied.

He snaps back to the present as Melior barks, "Well? Whose side are you on, K8.0? This is your time to prove it. If you don't comply, I'll be forced to assume that Azrian has poisoned your mind... and you know how we fix that." His long, spindly fingers brush against one of Kato's scars and he flinches away from the contact.

"What exactly do you want me to do? Completely take over his mind?" he asks, already knowing the answer.

"Yes." There's no hesitation in Melior's voice. "It's for his own good, you must understand that. He may end up hurting himself or someone else if you don't."

Or maybe he'll be the one to finally bring **you** *to your knees.* "Okay. I still don't feel well, so it might take some digging. He's learned how to jumble his thoughts from me." *Kind of like you and Belua.* "Can I go inside his cell alone? I won't be able to focus with any other thoughts around, Sir."

Whatever Melior sees in his eyes, he obviously believes him. "Of course. Just see to it that this gets done tonight... and the moment you know who tried to escape with him, come to my office." He turns on his heels and heads in the opposite direction, toward Belua's office.

Kato watches him go and slides on some shoes before walking down the cold hallway. As he nears the cells, he can see the singes on the wall from the energy Azrian released while being dragged against his will. The image has his fists clenching at his sides and he pauses at his door to breathe.

When he finally convinces himself to go inside, Azrian looks completely deflated. "Hello, Azrian."

Those gray eyes are a lot colder than Kato remembers. "So that's what he meant, huh? He said he was gonna make an example out of me. So, he sent the Cogitare in to... what, wipe my memories? Control me? Take away anything and everything that makes me... *me?*" He stands, crossing the room until he's so close to Kato they're nearly touching. "Do it, then. I can't live like this."

"Shut up." Kato touches Azrian's face and shows him everything he was able to gather from Melior's mind, and when he finishes, he doesn't speak out loud. *"You were right. I'm... sorry I didn't see it before. Please... you have to play along."*

Azrian's face goes from horrified to relieved to angry all in a span of a few seconds. He grips Kato's shirt to steady himself, undoubtedly unbalanced from the sudden influx of someone else's thoughts. *"Whoa. What do you need me to do?"*

Kato isn't sure what to say, let alone what to do, but he knows they can't stay there any longer. He can see for himself Cal was the one trying to escape with Azrian, so he reaches out to him for the first time. *"Callisto... it's Kato. Don't freak out. I'm on your side, we have to go. Walk to the holding cells and I'll make sure no one bothers you."*

Azrian is silently watching, confusion etched across his face, but Kato can literally *feel* his trust — probably for the first time.

Cal takes a second to respond and when he does, he sounds nervous. *"Is this a joke?"*

"Joke? Why would I joke about this?" Kato asks impatiently. He meets Azrian's eyes and waves a hand. "You tell him."

Azrian's eyebrows raise drastically. "Tell who what?"

"Cal." Kato blinks at him and then huffs a laugh. "Oh, sorry. Cal thinks I'm playing a joke. Here..." he focuses on Azrian and Callisto to bring all of their minds together. *"Cal? Azrian is with me. If you don't trust me... trust him."*

"I already tried that, and—"

"Yeah, you ran away. Look, point is we're leaving now. Either get on board and get down here or stay behind."

After a tense moment, Kato can feel Cal's resolve shifting. *"I'll be right there."*

Kato breaks the connection and realizes just how close he and Az are standing. "W-we should go. Should we grab anything in here? Also... where *are* we going?"

A grin breaks out across Azrian's face. "Home, Kato. We're going home." He snatches the blanket off his bed, and only then does Kato notice the burn marks covering his arms. "This won't be big enough for three of us, but we'll figure it out. Is he close?" he asks eagerly, stepping back into Kato's space.

Kato tilts his head to search for Cal and then shrugs. "I don't know. I do—" he pauses, finally picking something up. "Yes, he's here. Let's go." Kato turns and pushes the door open, his heart sinking the second his eyes land on Belua and Callisto.

"Hey!" Azrian yells, barreling around Kato and launching himself at Belua right as a fireball appears in his hand. They make contact with an audible grunt and go flying into the opposite wall, giving Cal just enough time to duck past them and get to Kato.

"If you were serious, Cogitare... you need to do something, *now,*" Cal says quickly. "We need to go, he called for Melior and Adeinde."

Kato stays frozen in panic for a few seconds longer and then snaps out of it. He yells "stop!" at Belua to freeze him in place. "Tell them everything is clear and open the door."

Slowly, Belua straightens up like he's in a daze. His fingers fly over the passcode pad and the red lights flick off. Cal looks a little dumbfounded as Azrian struggles to his feet, and the next thing they know, Belua is pushing open the door.

"Come on," Az hisses, grabbing Kato by the shirt and pulling him forward. They follow Belua to another door — one that Kato's never seen before — and he looks to Kato for instructions. Az continues, "Tell him to open this one, too. And a boat! We need a boat."

"Boat?" He turns to Belua and can see he wants to fight it, but Kato has completely taken control. "Open the door and help us get a boat."

As Belua works on the keypad, Kato whispers, "Why do we need a boat?" to Azrian. He doesn't have time to answer before the door opens and they're following Belua outside. Kato's eyes widen in fear. "Is that... water? Where's the land?!"

"The land is that way," Az says unhelpfully. "Come on!" He drags Kato the rest of the way and the three board the small sailboat as Belua watches from the doorway. "Cal, *do* something!" Az commands.

Nodding dumbly, Cal reaches into the water as Azrian lets out the sail. All Kato can do is hold on as the boat rocks unsteadily in the water, and when it lurches forward, Kato sends one last command to Belua. *"You saw nothing. Remember nothing."* He watches as they move further and further away from the shore. "I don't... like this."

Az takes his hand and tips his head back to look straight up, his features softening in awe and wonder. He tugs lightly. "Hey, Kato... look."

Kato follows his gaze and stares at a bright ball of light in the sky. "What's that, Az?" He squeezes his hand tighter.

"That's Cettia. Sweet shadows, I was starting to think I'd never see it again... that's how we're gonna find our way to Edros. To home."

"Home..." Kato looks away sadly, realizing he doesn't have a home at all. "Your home."

All of a sudden, Azrian's mood shifts and he backs away. "Cal's home first. Coldhallow is closer, and it'll be a miracle if we survive long enough, anyway. I didn't bring enough food for three."

"I have some," Cal yells from his position bent over the side of the boat. "My pockets!"

Chuckling, Az walks up behind him and slides his hands in Cal's pockets, pulling the food out as he shakes his head. "You're gonna fall overboard, Cal. What are you even doing?"

"I'm new at this! Don't judge me," he snaps.

Kato watches them curiously, noting how their friendship has grown since he last saw them together.

A strong wave comes out of nowhere, rocking the boat so hard Kato grips the side with a whimper and closes his eyes. "I feel sick."

"How sick?" Azrian asks with concern as he hurriedly moves their things to the middle of the deck. "You're not gonna throw up, are you? Please tell me you're not gonna throw up."

"Yes." Kato sits up and leans over the side, every wave making him puke more and more until there's nothing left. He spits one last time with a grunt and palms his sweaty forehead. "Are we there yet?"

A sympathetic smile finds Cal's face. "Not even close. If we're lucky, it'll only take us five days to get back to Edros. But I don't know anything about sailing, and Az—" he flicks his eyes to Azrian — "well, I don't think he does, either. We didn't really think this through all that well."

"We're going to die. We're going to die surrounded by water with no land in sight!" Kato runs his hands through his hair in a panic, squeezing at his temples.

The air around him tightens... no, that's not the air. It's Azrian's arms, wrapping around him from behind. "Hey, breathe. Steady, Kato. In."

It feels... nice. No one has ever touched him in this way, and he likes how it settles his stomach and makes him feel warmer. He nods, not sure of what to say out loud, but he hopes Az can feel how thankful he is.

"Good, you're doing great." Az holds him for a moment longer until Cal looks over with raised eyebrows.

"Okay, we're on the water. It's dark, it's freezing, we have not-enough-food and one blanket between the three of us, and Kato's basically a giant. None of us know how to sail *or* how to make it to Edros... so what exactly *are* we supposed to do besides panic?"

Az steps to the side but stays close to Kato, then offers a half-smile as he glances up. "You're wrong about one thing. We know how to get home. We follow Cettia."

~ VII ~

THE WASTED WATERS

Kato hugs his knees to his chest and asks, "Am I really a giant? How tall are people where you're from?"

Az licks his lips as he considers his response. "I don't know. I used to think it was just the Praediti that were tall like you, but Cal and I are both a little shorter and we're both apparently Praediti. Either way, yeah... you're pretty tall. It's kind of cool, though."

"That's an understatement. Az is shorter than me, but still... I wish I had your reach," Cal says.

"I just thought Az was short." Kato meets his eyes and offers a small, weak smile just as Cal sits down to take a break.

"I just need a few minutes. I'll start again." Cal looks between them both like he's trying to understand their friendship, and Azrian has to laugh. He doesn't understand it either... if it even *is* a friendship.

He doesn't say anything, just maneuvers his way unsteadily toward the back of the boat. If he can create enough energy to blast a hole in a wall or burn himself, it stands to reason he can generate enough to move a boat. It takes him a few tries, but eventually, it happens. The water glows with the evidence of his power and the boat moves a little faster, a little straighter. "We'll swap off, Cal," Az yells over the sound of the water. "Hopefully neither of us will get too tired this way. Faster we get to Edros, the better off we'll be!"

"Definitely." Kato agrees quickly, his face still pale. "Did we bring water?"

Cal scoffs from across from him. "We have to be scarce with all of our supplies. You can't just have stuff because you don't feel good."

Kato frowns and gazes out on the water, looking completely out of his element. The whole thing makes Azrian uncomfortable — mainly because he's pretty sure they *didn't* bring water. He glances to his left and bites his lip as the options weigh themselves in his mind. "Uh... Cal? Swing that sail a little, we need to head for the Wasted Waters."

"You're kidding, right?" Cal asks, incredulous. "You're insane."

There's a definite possibility that he's absolutely correct, but Az doesn't see another way around it. "Look. We're in the Aswel Sea. Saltwater. We can't drink it, we'll die. The Wasted Waters are ironically *fresh*water, so... sea dragons or no sea dragons, we have to go. I don't suppose we have a bucket anywhere?"

Kato sits up to try and help, only finding one small bucket that looked clean enough to drink out of. "The other one looked... not for water. What are sea dragons?"

"You don't want to know," Cal grunts, moving the tiller to the left. Az nearly falls over, expecting to be moving the opposite direction, and curses loudly.

"We need to go that way!" he yells, flinging his arm out to his left. He's facing the back of the boat, toward Deadrun, and isn't sure where the disconnect is coming from — but maybe it's him.

"I turned it to the left!"

"No, you have to — sweet shadows, Cal." Az stops the flow of energy from his hands and sits up, carefully making his way back to Cal. He drapes himself over his back to steady himself and puts both hands on the tiller. "Opposite. Turn it to the right to get the boat to go left and vice versa. Got it?"

"How the hell was I supposed to know that?" he says with a chuckle, taking an opportunity to touch Azrian's hand softly. "Got it now."

Kato walks over to see what they're doing, but as always, he seems clueless. "How can I help?"

"Make sure he doesn't screw that up again, that's how." Az excuses himself from that potentially dangerous position and breathes deeply, shuddering from the first real taste of fresh air he's gotten in six months. "If the rumors are true, we should know when we cross over into the Wasted Waters. We can't screw around once we're there, we need to just get as much fresh water as we can and head back to the Aswel Sea to sail the rest of the way. Honestly, we *should* wait till dawn to do this, but if I remember the map right, Deadrun is pretty close to the Wastes and if we sail too far off course in the opposite direction, we might not make it back. Better to just do it now and be quiet about it."

Kato nods, looking at the sea surrounding them like it had answers. Cal looks like he wants to argue but doesn't. "You're right. The sooner we get water, the better."

Az falls silent as he sends a tiny ball of energy up to hover above them. It doesn't do much to slice through the unrelenting dark of the night, but it makes him feel a little better about where they're heading. When he was a boy, he thought the rumors of sea dragons were lies — but now that he's older, more seasoned in the ways of the world and the horrors out there, he's not so sure.

The wind catches just right, and they lurch a little as the boat picks up speed. Az does his best to stay steady as he watches the water for any sign of change, and despite the rumors, there's no obvious visual sign that they've crossed over. It's the smell that tips him off. It's sweet, almost alluring, something Az can see himself getting lost in for days. Gone is the salty stench of Aswel. "We're here," he whispers, then turns to find Kato. "Bucket?"

Kato grabs the bucket and walks closer. "How should I do it?"

Cal chuckles. "Maybe let someone with experience take bucket duty? That goes over, we may as well give up now."

"You ran away," Az snaps in a harsh whisper, irritated that he's being mean to Kato. He's mad at Kato for his own reasons, but

Cal doesn't have a right to be... not in Azrian's mind. "Maybe we should've chosen to escape with someone that wasn't a complete shadowhead." Nevertheless, he gently takes the bucket from Kato. "He's kinda right, though. Just... maybe sit, so you don't throw up again?"

Kato eyes him a moment before nodding and taking a seat. "Shadowhead, huh? Seems like I'm rubbing off on you."

No argument comes from Callisto, so Az takes a deep breath and spreads his legs out to lower his center of gravity. The boat isn't that big, so he *shouldn't* fall over, but it never hurts to be safe. Carefully, he swipes the bucket through the water and brings it back up, guiding their little lantern down toward the water so he can get a closer look. It appears clear, smells amazing, and at his first, tentative taste, seems saltless. "Okay, each of you take this and drink as much as you can, but slowly. When you're done, I'll fill it up again before we turn back."

Kato grabs it and rinses his mouth out before chugging a little too much. "Here, shadowhead." He carries it to Cal, who rolls his eyes but takes the bucket to drink some for himself.

When it makes its way back to Az, he sips a little at a time, then leans over again to fill it up. Once he's satisfied it's as full as it's going to get, he gingerly sets it down in the middle of the boat. "Okay. No one make any sudden movements. We're gonna lose some to natural movements, but we *need* to make sure we don't spill it. We should also tread the line between the two bodies of water as long as we can. I doubt one bucket will last the three of us five days."

"That sounds smart. This water isn't so bad. It's... calmer." Kato takes a deep breath. "Smells better, too."

Cal takes a seat and wipes his forehead. "K8.0 is just worried he'll get sick again," he teases.

"I think we're all worried about that," Az adds with a grin. "Just keep to the sides of the boat, okay? Can't have us capsizing because you two can't keep your hands off each other." He blinks, not sure why he said that — from what he's seen, they hadn't touched each other at all. He shakes his head, feeling a little strange. "It's gonna take two of us to keep this boat going at pretty much all times, so... maybe one of us should sleep."

Kato stands up and walks near the sail. "Let me help. Callisto can sleep first."

"Thanks for that... and for getting us out," Cal says with a nod.

Smiling softly, Kato scratches his head. "I just did what was right."

As Cal moves to the other side of the boat and lays down, Az retreats into his own head. If Kato would've listened to begin with, he'd already be back with his mom — and the last six months wouldn't have happened. While he's grateful to Kato and doesn't want Cal being mean to him, he can't seem to get past the truth of it all.

He slowly lowers his hand back into the water and sends a pulsing burst of energy through the depths. The boat steadily moves forward, and from the dim light the ball overhead is giving off, Az can just make out Kato's silhouette.

Neither speak for what feels like almost an hour, but by then, Azrian feels *truly* strange. Lightheaded and a little out of sorts, like nothing in the world was real at all. They're not on a boat in the Wasted Waters, the ones no sailor has ever come back from. They're somewhere warm, maybe sleeping, and all of this is some sort of nightmare. "Kato?" he asks suddenly. "Do you feel..."

Kato jumps up like he was in a trance and looks around, taking in their surroundings. "Why do I feel like I'm floating above my body, Azrian?"

Wasted Waters. Az huffs, then barks a clipped laugh, then outright cackles. "Sweet shadows, it's *literal.* Oh, for Cettia's sake... we're *high.*" He suddenly realizes why people think they see sea dragons out here — they're probably hallucinating or something, and if they never make it far enough to see what's on the other side, it's likely because they're still floating aimlessly somewhere. On some level, Azrian knows they have to be careful so *they* don't end up like that.

To add to everything else, now they'll have to take shifts when it comes to drinking water, as well. "Shadows. Did it at least make your belly feel better?"

"Yes." Kato giggles and for the first time ever, Azrian gets to see him with a carefree smile. "I like your face better than everyone else's face."

Az sticks out his tongue. "Of course you do, it's a good face." He blames the weird flutter in his stomach on the water, then goes back to staring up at the sky. "You're free, Kato. We're free. Even if we die out here... we're not captives anymore."

"I don't even know how to be free. It feels... strange." Kato looks up at the stars, leaning his head against the mast.

"It won't last. Life on land is usually a life on the run, but then again... you're a Cogitare. You don't really have to worry about anyone or anything, so... maybe it'll be different for you."

"Except my headaches... and the fact that I have nothing. I don't want to use my powers to use people. I just want to be me." He pauses, like he's nervous to ask something, but he speaks again before Azrian can tell him to spit it out. "Are you going to leave me when we find land?"

The question catches him off guard. "Honestly, Kato... I hadn't really factored you into the plan. When I reached out to you, it sounded like you didn't wanna come. I figured I'd drop Cal off in Coldhallow then head home by myself." He adjusts the tiller and heads back toward the Aswel side of things. "I guess it's up to you. You can probably stay with Cal, or you can come with me."

Kato glances over at Cal and then back at Azrian. "I'd rather go with you. I want to help you get to your mother... if you don't mind."

His chest swells a little at the thought. "Yeah, that'd be okay. My mom, she's not really a fan of Cogitare, though. I don't know how we're gonna navigate that, but if she gets to know you... it might be okay." The words feel inadequate, but he's not at a place where he can say much else yet. He still blames Kato a little, and his head is still swimming. It's taking most of his concentration to keep the boat moving in the right direction... or at least, what he hopes is the right direction. "We'll figure it out, Kato. Together."

~

Callisto waits until Azrian's asleep to start a conversation with Kato. He really is thankful for him; he'd gone against everything he knew for them to be free. But at the same time, he's a Cogitare. That makes it hard to trust him regardless of how likeable the guy is. "Did you guys feel weird from that water?"

"Yes, actually," Kato says with a laugh. "Azrian said we should take turns drinking it so we don't run too far off course. I'm glad he is getting some sleep, he's exhausted."

He watches the way Kato looks at Az. "You like him," he states simply. It's as clear as day, he'd be a fool not to see it.

Kato, on the other hand, obviously doesn't. He looks over and tilts his head. "Of course. Don't you? He's rude, but... he's a good person. It's hard not to like someone who is just genuinely... good."

That really isn't what he meant, but he also isn't in a position to push. Especially if the guy *is* that clueless. "Yeah, guess you're right. And me? You like me?"

Kato thinks about it for a moment as he stares at Cal in that way that makes him uncomfortable. "Yes. Again, you're kind of rude. But... I can tell you're a good person, too."

He nods, wishing he could say the same back. He could... and based on everything Kato has shown him, he would be correct, but he can't bring himself to say it. "You ever try to... *not* read minds?"

The Cogitare looks away again, and Cal doesn't miss the way his eyes naturally find Az's sleeping silhouette. "Yes. Sometimes I can," Kato admits. "Like right now, I don't hear either of you... all I hear is the wind and water. It's... peaceful."

"Yeah... it is. Maybe try and keep it off until you need to use it?" Cal asks in a hopeful tone.

"I'm trying. I don't want to read your minds; I want to give you that privacy. Some thoughts are louder than others and I can't help it, but most of the time, I try and focus on the words coming out of your mouth, not your head. Was it weird when I spoke to you?"

"*Shadows*, yes. It kind of freaked me out, but... it's kinda cool. Not like... having it done *to* me, or *with* me or whatever, but just the fact that you *can* do that. And seeing you control Belua was awesome. Should have made him punch himself."

Kato chuckles at the thought. "I should have. I didn't think of that."

The mood is lighter, but Cal can see how exhausted Kato is becoming. They keep the conversation light after that, and soon it's time for Kato and Az to switch places. Callisto almost envies Kato for how fast he falls asleep, but he's looking forward to talking with Azrian, so he doesn't dwell too much on it. "Sleep okay?"

Az shakes his head and stretches out, popping his back and letting out a quiet grunt. "No. Did you?"

"Nah," Cal says, shaking his head. "Not exactly a lot of room here. Where are we now, do you think?"

He glances around and adjusts the sail. The sun is starting to come up, but all they can see for miles around is water. "Smells like we're back on the Aswel, so... I don't know. Without Cettia, it's going to be hard for me to figure out how far we drifted off course while I was asleep."

Cal studies the lines of his face and the strong jaw half-hidden by a beard. "I tried to keep it straight. I'm not exactly a sailor."

"Neither am I," Az says. "I've never been on a boat in my life, I just got really used to adapting. My father used to tell me stories sometimes, he liked to sail... but he never took me with him."

While they've talked a lot since Cal was brought to Deadrun, they haven't talked about Azrian's family too much. He's curious, he can't deny it — he's curious about everything involving Az, but something about the way he said "father" is warning Cal not to ask questions. "Well, you're good at it. I didn't think we'd even make it this far."

"Me either." Azrian slides his hand in the water and sends a pulse of energy out to speed them up, then stares at the bucket. "Did Kato tell you? We need to be careful with that stuff. Don't drink too much at once."

He nods. "Yeah, he told me. I had some really weird dreams, what happened with you guys?" Az just laughs and shrugs a little, so Cal changes the subject. "What are we going to do once we hit land?"

With a sigh, Az strips off one of his shirts. "Drop you off, then Kato and I are gonna head back to Embermeadow to find my mom... if she's even still alive."

"So, we probably won't see each other again after we get to Cold-hallow, huh?" The thought makes Cal kind of sad, but his desire to get back to his family supersedes just about everything else. Nothing else matters.

"Nah, probably not."

Cal isn't exactly sure what to say to that. He busies himself manipulating the water around them to give Az a break, and between the two of them, they manage to cover quite a bit of ground before Kato finally wakes up.

Blinking up at them, Kato rubs his eyes and attempts to flatten his messy hair with a groan. "I thought this was a bad dream."

"Psh, how can it be a bad dream with me and Cal's adorable faces in it?" Az asks with a grin. He digs around in his pocket and jerks his chin up. "You like meat?"

Kato nods, slowly making his way by Azrian. Cal watches as he sits next to him, looking *way* too big on this small sailboat to be comfortable. "You know he likes meat," Callisto jokes.

"Don't we all?" Az raises his eyebrow at Cal as he hands Kato some dried meat. "Eat up, sunshine."

"Of course. It's good for our bodies... I suppose some people don't like it, but they should supplement with other proteins. Thank you." He takes a bite and closes his eyes, chewing like he was starved.

Cal snorts a laugh and goes to take a drink of their water. "You guys got my back with this damn water, right?"

Azrian looks more amused than Cal has ever seen him. "Yep, absolutely. Go for it." He nudges Kato after and leans in. "Slow down, you don't wanna choke on it."

He nods, licking some salt from his lips. "I put too much in my mouth at one time. I'll go slower."

The fact that Kato wasn't getting any of the innuendos had Cal snorting and struggling to swallow the drink he'd taken, and Az howls, doubling over for a moment and then sitting back up to ruffle Kato's hair.

"You're so innocent it's almost painful, you know that?"

Cal relaxes as whatever is in the water works its way through his system. "Maybe you should teach him, then."

"Teach me?" He runs a hand through his hair to fix it and tilts his head at Azrian. "I like to learn things." Kato takes another bite and looks between them both with narrowed eyes as they laugh even harder. "You're making fun of me."

"No!" Az says quickly, his chest heaving as he tries to catch his breath. "No, we're not making fun of you. It's more... situational humor. It's not your fault you don't know, but it's still cute."

The words confirm what Cal had already suspected, and all he does is smile softly. "Yeah, what he said."

"Cute." Kato repeats with a grin, reaching out to mess up Azrian's hair in retaliation.

The boat rocks as Azrian tries to duck, and Cal yells out as he nearly tips backward. "Okay! Enough teaching, save it for land!"

"Shadows, Cal... calm down." Az rights himself and stares down at the bottom of the boat, no longer looking all that amused. "You're right. We should be more careful, or else none of us will make it out of here alive."

Cal falls silent and eats a little bit of the food he'd brought. The mood is shifting drastically, and so much in his life has changed recently that it's hard to land on any particular emotion. Maybe it's the circumstances, or maybe it's the water... but the only thing he knows for sure is that *nothing* is certain. He'll just have to make the most of whatever time he has left. With Az, with Kato... with life itself.

~

It doesn't take long for the playful banter to subside. Kato still gets sick at least once a day, and he's sure he looks as miserable as he feels, so he tries to keep to himself. He only does what he's told to do to help.

By day four, his face is scruffier than he's ever had it, and he already misses being able to take a shower. He misses a lot of things about home — or *not* home — but he can't help it. It's all he knows. "Four days... are we still going in the right direction?"

"I don't know," Cal says quietly. Az is sleeping, but barely, and they're trying not to wake him. "I don't think it matters. I still can't see land and we're out of water. I don't see us making it much further." He rubs his chapped lips and draws his arms tighter around himself. "Maybe we shouldn't have left."

Kato rolls his eyes and chuckles a humorless laugh. "We shouldn't have left? Little late for that, Callisto. This was what you two wanted. At least you'll die free, right?"

"This was Azrian's idea! Blame him," he says sharply. "Your precious little Videre cooked this one up all on his own, I tried to tell him it was stupid and dangerous."

"Yeah? Was that why you ran when things got tough?" Kato knows he's being harsh, but he can't help it. He doesn't want him blaming Azrian. They *all* chose this.

Cal scowls. "Yes, it is. I didn't want to die there, *or* out here on the damn ocean." He pushes himself to his feet and makes his way to the tiller, tugging on the sheet to let the sail out a little more and turns the boat to the right. "We need to go back to the Wasted Waters."

Kato looks over at Az and can see he's not sleeping well, so he grabs their blanket and tosses it over his legs. "We do. I'll do the sails and you do your water thing." He's much too drained to continue an argument, but at least this way they have a goal in mind.

It's rocky, but eventually Kato starts to smell the change in the water. Cal must too, because he slumps against the edge of the boat coated in sweat. "We're here. Fill up the bucket."

Kato does as he's told and it's much easier for him to reach over the side than it was for either of them. When he comes back up, he goes straight to Azrian and taps his arm. "Here, drink a little and then go back to sleep."

"Are you kidding?" Cal asks in a whiny voice. "I just... *all* that... and you... *shadows.*"

Azrian stirs and blinks open his gray eyes, then shields them against the beating sun. "What?"

"Drink." Kato sits him up with his other hand and holds out the bucket for him to drink. He ignores Cal completely, only heading over to him when Az is finished. "Here, shadowhead."

Coughing, Az pushes himself to a sitting position and looks around. "We're back in the Wastes. *Shadows,* guys... I don't know if we're ever gonna make it to Edros. How you holding up, Kato?"

"Fine." He watches Cal drink and then takes some for himself, shivering when a few drops drips down his shirt. "We'll get there... we have to." Instead of waiting for a response, he leans back over to refill the bucket.

Something large upsets the water off in the distance, and all three of them turn to stare at it. The tail disappears under the water as quickly as it appeared and Az blinks. "Um... okay. Hold on to the sides, I'm gonna... yeah. We need to go. Cal, let out the sail a little more — the wind is with us for once."

The moment he complies, Az drapes himself over the back of the boat and grunts as he uses his powers to propel them forward. It's too much too fast and the bucket nearly spills, but Kato manages to keep it upright despite the rolling nausea in his stomach.

He's happy he doesn't see anything beyond the tail, but he watches the waters around them intently, relieved when the stench of saltwater assaults his nose. "Was that..." he meets Cal's wide eyes.

"Yeah... that was. Sweet shadows. They're real. Az... do you think this water will last us so we don't have to go back?"

He shrugs, but the fear he's feeling isn't lost on Kato. Azrian keeps his head bowed and power flowing as he says, "It's going to have to. We shouldn't be *that* far away... we've stayed relatively straight... I think if Cal and I keep swapping off like this, we might make it to Edros by sunrise tomorrow. We just have to push."

"I wish I could help more. I feel like dead weight." Kato continues to hold the bucket upright and frowns when Callisto gallic shrugs.

"You're not," Az says as he finally sits up. "We wouldn't have gotten this far without you, you know that. No one here is dead weight, and you're right... we'll make it."

Kato nods, wishing it were true. He knows they wouldn't have escaped without him, but since then? All he's done is literally rock their boat. He didn't bring food to help, he didn't even bring his own extra clothes. All he can do is hope he can make it up later. "I just realized we all drank that water at the same time."

Cal snorts. "Won't be the first time. Let's just hope we don't have another night of confessions."

"If we do, I'm going to end up gagging both of you," Az threatens.

"I liked the confessions. I have another one, actually. I've never been around people for this extent of time, so I didn't really know how to block out thoughts very well, but now... I can turn you both off easily." He smiles proudly at himself, glad to finally have some silence — especially when he's trying to sleep.

"Thank the gods," Cal says. "It's about time—"

"I'm proud of you, Kato." Azrian nods encouragingly and hands him the last of their food. "Eat. I have a feeling that once we hit land, you're going to have to carry us both over your giant, broad shoulders."

The look he gives Kato after is weird, like he has a second head or something. "Both of you? I'm not that strong." Kato smiles, because he actually caught the joke that time, but he isn't sure if he joked back properly or if he was too literal again. Either way, he doesn't get much of a response.

After a while, Azrian yawns then shivers a little as he glances at the darkening sky, and his arms glow with the evidence of his power as he compensates. "Cettia will take us the rest of the way. We just have to follow her."

"You put way too much stock in that star, Az," Cal says in a bored tone. "It's the gods that will get us home."

"I don't believe in the gods."

"If gods are real... where are they, Cal?" Kato asks curiously, he always thought the gods were fictional, but then again, he doesn't know much of the real world.

Cal's mouth opens dumbly and he huffs, trying more than once to speak, but failing.

"He can't answer you because he doesn't know, and he doesn't know because there *is* no answer," Azrian says. "Supposedly the gods are in the ether. The soil, the sky, this blasted sea we're dying on. But in my experience, if the gods *are* real... they're sadistic, vicious bastards that don't care about us at all."

"Whatever, Azrian. You got to believe in something, not just the damn star. We wouldn't even *have* a world without the gods."

Kato looks between them and can see this is something they both feel strongly about. "Maybe they were here... but now they're gone?"

"Doesn't matter, the point is that no one is going to help us but us, and that star tells me *how* to navigate home. Can your gods say the same, Callisto?"

Cal looks away, crossing his arms across his chest. "I have to keep my faith. Otherwise, what in the shadows are we even doing?"

Azrian doesn't answer. They fall into silence, and once Kato finishes eating, he takes another small sip of water. "Cal, would you like to nap?"

"Yeah, *Cal*," Az mocks. "Take a nap, maybe when you wake up, you'll actually be thinking rationally."

"I'm only going to do it because I know I'll have to take over for Az soon, but screw you both. Suddenly I'm not all that sad we'll be parting ways soon."

Kato tilts his head and turns to Az as Cal settles for some sleep. "What does 'screw you' mean?"

"Uh... well, it's not nice. Can we just leave it at that?"

"Okay." Kato shrugs and goes back by the mast to lean against it. "Should we keep the fact that I'm Cogitare a secret when we get to land?"

Az pauses, shuddering hard as he pulls his hand out of the water. "Yeah, unless we need you to do something. I'm probably gonna be hiding, too."

"So... humans? Do you think I can blend in with humans?" Kato asks doubtfully.

His face drops instantly as he takes in the scars on Kato's head, his general stature, and unusual eyes. "Just... maybe keep quiet and stick close to me. We'll tell them you... fell. And then got stuck in one of those torture rack things. Or... shadows. No."

Kato doesn't know how to respond to that, but he thankfully doesn't have to. "Az! Look!" He points at the small piece of land in the distance. "Is that home?"

He has to stand on his tiptoes and grip Kato's shoulder for support, but an exhausted, happy look settles on his face. "I think so. Unless we're still high and that's just a hallucination... I think that's Coldhallow Crest. We gotta go just around the mountain to get to the pier." Az drops back down to his normal height and sucks in a breath. "Okay, only a few more hours and we'll be there. Just... let Cal sleep, I've got this."

With a flick of Azrian's wrist, the silver energy around the boat swells. It's easy to see how much that small sliver of hope has helped Azrian find his spark again. His eyes dance with anticipation and his new, profound sense of direction has him shining brighter than any star Kato has seen since coming outside. It makes him feel hopeful, even as he stares at the home that's never been *his* home. If a place could make someone like Azrian smile that widely, it must be a great place.

~ VIII ~

THE FALSE HOPE

By the time the boat gets close enough for Cal to jump off onto the pier, Azrian is exhausted. Of course, Cal stayed asleep until the last possible moment, leaving Az to handle all the heavy lifting that last stretch of the way. He nearly collapses with relief and soul-splintering tiredness — and now he knows for sure his father didn't work himself to death on purpose, not unless he thought it was the only way to survive. *How backward is that?* he thinks bitterly, but it's fleeting... just a passing thought accentuating the strangeness of the whole situation. "Kato," he says, his voice rasped with thirst and overuse. "Can you... help me? Tie off the boat so it's steady."

He points to the edge of the pier, and Kato instantly jumps up to help. It looks like he's hardly holding it together, and once the boat is secure, he makes it a few more steps before he falls to his knees. "I never want to go on that boat again... or any boat."

Cal rolls his eyes, but the relief is written all over his face and Az doesn't have it in him to argue. He wobbles off the boat himself and drops down next to Kato, putting a hand on his back and leaning in. "Hey, Jellycrai, you okay? You're okay. It's fine, we're fine, it's all... fine." *Keep telling yourself that, Az.*

"Jelly... what?" he asks, tilting his head with a soft smile as he leans into Az slightly. "I do feel like jelly, actually."

Azrian doesn't have time to unpack the fact that Kato doesn't seem to know what craivil are. How anyone could grow into adulthood and never hear of the creatures that swim in the sea is beyond him... especially since they just spent so much time *on* the sea. "Cal! How far is your house? People are staring at us, and I've got about one and a half greetings in me before I pass out."

"Not far at all. If there's any of it left... I told you it was burning... I saw the smoke through the trees." They grab the couple things they have to their name and start walking into town. Kato keeps his gaze down, clearly trying his hardest to blend when everything about him makes that impossible.

Cal stops abruptly in the middle of nowhere and reaches out to grip both of their arms. Az whips his head around, concerned they're about to walk into a trap or something — but there's nothing and no one around. "Was this..."

"No, no... it's over there." He points off to the right and turns scared, blue eyes on Azrian. "It's just around the corner, or... it should be."

"Okay. I'll go look." Az tries to smile reassuringly as he steps forward, forcing his feet to keep moving even as he braces for the worst. But when he rounds the corner, the only house around is still standing — and there are a handful of people sitting out on the porch. "Cal, there are people here!" he yells back.

Cal rushes around and stops, staring up at the house in awe. "They lied. Thank the gods." He takes off running without a look back.

Kato peeks around nervously, trying to flatten his messy hair to block his scars. "Everyone is looking at me like they're scared of me."

"Well, they're stupid," Az says, gently taking Kato's hand like Kato had once done for him. "Come on... we're just a few minutes from a bath and a nap."

He nods, keeping a loose but sure grip as they approach the house. Cal is wiping his eyes and turns to introduce everyone.

"Mom, Dad. This is Azrian and Kato, I wouldn't be alive if it weren't for them. This is my mother, Cora, and my father, Galen."

Kato offers a quick smile just as two younger kids run up and wrap their arms around their brother, making Kato tilt his head in confusion. "Oh, these are the twins, Blue and Bash," Cal laughs.

Azrian bows his head as he pulls Kato a little closer. "Hi. We um... we'd love to chat, but... it's been a *really* long trip. Do you —" he pauses, hating having to ask for help — "maybe have somewhere we can sleep?"

Cora nods quickly. "Yes, yes of course." She grabs Azrian for an unexpected tight hug. "Thank you for bringing my boy home."

Kato tenses and pulls on Az's arm. "What are you doing to him?"

A nervous laugh escapes Az as he leans back. "Don't mind him, we had to drink the Wasted Waters to survive, and I think it messed with him." He smiles disarmingly — at least he *hopes* it is — then stares at Kato and attempts to communicate silently. "*It's a hug, she hugged me. Just relax, I'll tell you if something isn't right. Shut up and blend in.*"

"Oh," she says with a strange look. "Well, come on. We don't have a lot of space, but you two can nap in the twins' room." Cora eyes Kato's considerable height and then shakes her head. "You're a big one, aren't you? Maybe you two had better just sleep in our bed."

Kato relaxes when he realizes there is no threat and releases Azrian's arm. "Um... thank you, ma'am. Do you have showers here?"

Cal snorts at him and meets Az's eyes. "So much for blending. There's no showers buddy. Those are only in Deadrun."

The look on Cora's face sends another wave of exhaustion through Azrian. He doesn't have the time nor the strength to explain all of that to the four confused people standing in front of him, and all he can do is hope they understand. "Cal, I'm sure you can handle telling the tale? I'm pretty sure if I don't drink some nontoxic water and get at least a couple of hours of sleep soon, I'm going to die."

"Bit dramatic, Az, but yeah. I got it." Cal stands, holding a hand up to stop his mother's budding question. "Come with me, guys." He leads them to a modest kitchen and gets them all glasses of water, then points off to the side. "Bedroom is in there. Don't touch anything... including each other."

"I'll get you some blankets," Galen says. He disappears for a moment and returns with an armful of them — more than Azrian's ever seen in one place other than Deadrun. He takes them gratefully, and once they close the door to the bedroom, his shoulders slump a little.

"Sweet shadows, Kato. When I tell you not to talk, I mean *don't talk*." He kicks off his soggy shoes and strips down to just his boxers. "You should do the same if your clothes are as permanently wet as mine. We'll lay them out, hopefully they'll be dry when we wake up."

Kato nods with a small frown, but he doesn't speak as he begins stripping off his clothes. By the time he's in his boxers, he loops his thumbs in the waistband and meets Az's eyes. "Can I talk now?"

There's a moment where Az can't really speak. His eyes are glued to Kato's body, on the last piece of clothing covering him. "Uh... yeah, just leave... leave those on." He carefully lays their clothes out and turns his back to hide his blush, but it doesn't do much good. The entire upper half of his body flushes red. "Talk."

"Never mind. I was going to ask if I could take these off." Kato walks closer and whispers, "What do you use if not a shower?"

A shiver runs down Azrian's spine. "Listen, I'm gonna need you to take a step back. We bathe in the river, mostly... sometimes we bring water inside and heat it up first, though. We'll deal with that once we sleep."

Kato stands up straighter and takes one step back as asked. "Okay." He turns to look at the bed and then scratches his head before climbing inside and patting the other side. "Sleep, shadow-head."

A vague question of what part of this Cora got wrong runs through his mind. He's not as tall as Kato, he'd have fit perfectly in one of the twin's beds — but maybe she just didn't want to have to wash two sets of sheets. Sighing, Az tosses the extra blankets on the bed and climbs in, sticking to his own side. "You know we can't stay here long, right? If Cal's family is alive, my mom is, too. And if they come looking for us..."

"I know. We should go tomorrow, after a river cleaning." Kato rolls onto his side and curls into himself with a sated sigh, and Az doesn't even have it in him to comment on his choice of words.

Sleep comes easier than it has in months, and when he wakes up flattened out against Kato's body, he blames it on nothing but a subconscious search for comfort. He's warm, softer than he looks, and — *What?* Az's eyes widen as he realizes what he's doing, and he slowly tries to pull away.

Mumbling something under his breath, Kato rolls onto his back, his eyes dancing around under his eyelids.

Az watches him for a moment, mostly just happy that he can keep all of... *that* a secret. He slowly climbs out of bed and stretches, then checks their clothes and smiles when he finds them dry. They're not clean, but he'll take whatever victories he can get.

When he makes his way out of the room, Cal is playing with the twins as Cora and Galen look on with happy smiles. His chest tightens a little with jealousy. "Hey, thanks for the uh—" he points back to the room — "that. I feel a lot better already."

Cora jumps up with a smile. "It's the least we can do. Here, have some water." She brings him a wooden cup and nods encouragingly. "I'm going to make you two some eggs. Will your friend be joining us?"

"Yeah, he's still sleeping, but I'm sure he'll wake up when he smells food."

Galen walks over and puts a hand behind her back, smiling at Azrian. "We really cannot thank you enough for getting our boy home. I do have some questions about the people who took you all. Can we speak outside?"

"Sure." Az follows him out a little apprehensively. He doesn't know what Cal wants them to know or not know, and he certainly can't tell anyone the truth about Kato. When they're safely out of earshot, Azrian nods to Galen and crosses his arms. "What did you want to know?"

"I was wondering who they are. Cal said they are called the Venandi, except I've never heard of them. I'm worried they will come back for him."

Az relaxes a little. "Yeah, that's them. Just your regular bunch of evil masterminds, nothing crazy." He grimaces at the look on Galen's face and tries again. "They're evil, Sir. I don't know how else to put it. And yeah, they'll probably come after him again... but only if they think he's not wanted. So... want him. Don't shun him for what he is."

"He didn't want to tell me what he was yet, but we don't care. We love him no matter what, we'll leave to protect him if we have to." He looks around them. "Are you all Praediti?" he whispers.

And there it is — the question he *most* didn't want to answer. "Your son is an Undare. I *thought* I was human... but I'm not. I'm a Videre, which... before you even ask, yes, it's a real thing. Apparently, I'm some sort of conduit for energy, it's a whole thing." He pauses, then glances toward the house. He thought Kato's eyes would have given him away, but if Galen is still questioning it, Az won't be the one to oust him. "I'm not quite sure what Kato is, but I can tell you... Cal and I would both be dead if it wasn't for him."

Galen nods. "You are both welcome here for as long as you need. Do you have a family to go home to, son?"

"I hope so," he says simply. "My mom... I... think she might still be alive. Seeing you all makes me think she might be, but our house burned down the night I was taken. We live in Embermeadow."

"We don't have much, but we have a carriage. Will you accept a ride to Embermeadow as a thank you?"

Az nearly falls over with surprise and relief. "What? You're serious? Galen... Sir, thank you!" He laughs, running a hand through his hair. "I thought we were gonna have to walk, and after that whole boat thing... yeah. Thank you."

"No, thank *you*. Enjoy a warm breakfast and a bath. Then we'll be on our way. We have more family in the area, I will send word for them to come protect Cal."

Grinning, Az agrees and heads back into the house. The food is already on the table, and Kato is awake and sitting down. "Morning, Jellycrai," Az teases. Kato rolls his eyes, and Azrian chuckles as he remembers the way he used to say it was a Praediti trait. He vaguely wonders if he's acquired that skill in the last six months, but kind of hopes he hasn't.

They eat in silence, and after, Az taps Kato's knee. "Come on, big guy. Gotta go get that river cleaning, and then we're hitching a ride back to Embermeadow."

He nods and stands, letting Az lead the way down to the river after Cora gives them a small bar of soap. "Can I get naked this time, or should I keep these on again?"

"You can get naked, you're gonna wanna wash those, too. Just maybe stay down river a little and wait to take them off until you're in the water." He strips again himself, then tests the temperature of the river before wading in. "You can have first shift with the soap, just don't use it all. Bring it here when you're done."

He notices Kato's eyes on him as he follows suit, leaving a little distance between them before he pulls off his underwear and then bends slightly to wet his top half. He looks nervous as he starts to clean his body, almost as if he were back on the boat.

Az turns his back to Kato to stop himself from watching too closely. "You're not on a boat, Kato. This is a river, you're steady. You can stand. Just try and relax, okay?" He runs the water up each of his arms and over his chest, then through his hair. It feels amazing compared to the rough water of the Aswel Sea.

"I don't like the water. Are there dragons in this one?"

He smiles. "No, no dragons. Just me and a few little craivil, but they won't hurt you."

"Okay, good... I felt one on my leg. They're slimy." Azrian can hear the water move and then Kato's voice is much closer. "I'm done with the soap. Here."

Turning slowly, Az tries to cover himself with one hand as he reaches out with the other. "Thanks. You can uh... dry out on the bank, I'll turn around again. Okay?"

"Okay. I see what you mean now... about the sun. The *real* sun."

Facing away, Az starts scrubbing the last few days from his skin. "I told you. Whatever fake sky they have there... it's nothing compared to the real thing. This world is scary, but you can't deny it's beautiful."

"I agree. It all feels... free. I can see why this was important to you, Azrian." The water sloshes once more as Kato gets out, and the urge to look is a lot stronger than Az thought it would be.

Don't be a shadowhead, Az, he tells himself. *The poor guy wouldn't even know what you're doing... and that isn't fair.*

When he feels sufficiently clean, he wrings the water out of his hair and yells for Kato to look elsewhere. He steps out of the river slowly and grabs his clothes, closing his eyes when he feels the sun heating up his skin. He really has missed it — on the boat, he couldn't enjoy much of anything... but here, on land, back in Edros? The sun is just about the best thing he's ever felt.

~

When Callisto's extended family arrives, they help Galen pack up the carriage and say their goodbyes. The twins are sad to see Kato go; they keep saying how funny he is when he speaks, but he doesn't understand why. They laugh at everything he says, leaving him more clueless than when the conversation began. Cora packs them some road food that is surely going to be gone before they arrive in Embermeadow, but the boys are grateful for her hospitality.

It's obvious Az is ready to go. He's eager to check on his mother, and when it comes time to say goodbye to Cal, Kato actually feels a little sad. "Take care, Callisto. Hopefully, your family doesn't have to fight the Venandi."

Cal snorts. "Hopefully, Az can teach you how to be a person," he says, and again, Kato doesn't understand. "Take care of him, okay? And yourself."

Kato nods and says, "of course," but while Azrian walks over to say bye, he thinks about what Cal said. He thought he was doing well with blending, but the way everyone looks at him says otherwise. He has to do better. Kato turns his attention to Az and watches the way he moves and talks, wondering if he should try to mirror him. Out of all the people he's met, he looks up to Azrian the most.

"C'mon, big guy," Az says, reaching out a hand to help pull him into the back of the carriage. "Unless you changed your mind and would rather stay here with Callisto."

"No." Kato accepts his hand and settles inside as he looks back at the house one last time. "I'm staying with you until we find your mother, Azrian. I gave my word."

He nods, rubbing his palms on his pants as the carriage starts moving. "Then hang on tight. It's gonna be a long ride."

It *isn't* long before Kato is over the rough carriage seats and bumpy roads, but it's still immensely better than the boat, so he makes sure not to complain too much. Once they reach a place to camp for the night, they set up as quickly as they can and scarf down a quick dinner before settling under the stars. "Get some rest, boys. We'll leave at first light, and hopefully we'll make it to Embermeadow before lunch."

Az nods but stays sitting up with his elbows on his knees. He closes his eyes, and even after learning how to block him out, Kato can still hear his thoughts. He's thinking of home, which isn't surprising. What *is* surprising are the underlying thoughts about Kato. He doesn't want him to leave even after they find Roe, but he's having a hard time figuring out how to make that happen.

Like Azrian did for him when he was nervous, Kato takes his hand, hoping it would help calm him, too. He doesn't want to tell him he heard those thoughts, but he also doesn't want him to worry that he'll leave. He truly has nowhere else to go and knowing Az doesn't want him gone settles something in his chest. Instead of talking out loud, Kato opts for telepathy. *"Hi."*

"Hi," Az replies with the ghost of a smile as he glances down at their hands. *"You should sleep while you can, I noticed you weren't really that fond of the carriage, either."*

Kato huffs a laugh and lays back with a grin. *"My entire backside is sore. Traveling isn't very fun, but hopefully when we get to Embermeadow, we'll be done... right?"*

"Hopefully. But they're not wrong, Kato. If the Venandi come looking... maybe it's better we stay in Cettia's shadow."

"We?" he asks, turning his face toward him. *"Will your mom hate me?"*

The answer doesn't come right away, but Az ultimately shakes his head. *"You saved me, there's no other way around it. She's not going to be your biggest fan, but she won't turn you away. She's not built like that. She'll take you in and treat you like you're her own son."*

Kato smiles at that even though he has no idea what that means. *"What's it like... having a mother?"*

"It's hard to explain. Have you ever heard of unconditional love?"

"No."

Az lets out a breath and runs a hand over his beard. *"Uh... okay. It's when you love someone no matter what. Nothing else matters. Most mothers love their kids almost to a fault. That feeling... knowing they will always love you... it can't be explained with words."*

Kato nods and tries to understand but knows he probably never will. *"My mother never held me,"* he admits quietly. *"I wonder if that was by choice, or..."*

"What?" Azrian's head snaps toward him. *"So... when you asked me what Cora was doing, you genuinely don't know what a hug is? She never showed you any affection at all?"*

"No. She had ten children, and I was number eight. She disappeared after she had K10.0, but I never met them, either. They kept me separate, they said I was the only one to survive. But now... I don't think I believe them."

Sadness floods Azrian to a point that Kato can feel it, too. *"I'm so sorry, Kato. To have a family that big but not even know what a hug is... shadows, I can't even imagine. Stand up."* He pushes himself to his feet, watching carefully to make sure he's not disturbing Galen.

Kato tilts his head and then slowly stands, his back straightening with uncertainty as he awaits further instructions.

An awkward moment passes where neither man does anything, then Azrian steps forward and wraps his arms around Kato's middle. *"This is a hug. You just... put your arms around me, too."*

He tenses, but it passes quickly when he hugs Azrian back. It feels... better than anything he's ever felt before, and he holds on a little tighter, his face dropping into Azrian's hair as he searches for more contact. *"Wow... I..."* he can't even finish that sentence; no words would suffice.

Azrian's fingers curl against his back and he nods slightly. *"Yeah, so... this is a hug,"* he repeats. Kato suddenly gets a vision of them doing something similar back at Callisto's house, and also on the boat, but he's not sure if it's from his own imagination, or Azrian's memory.

"I like it. Can we do this sometimes?" Kato isn't ready to let go, but he can feel Azrian shift in his arms. He pulls back, and Az stares right at the ground as his face flushes pink.

"Uh... yeah, sure. Just... yeah. We should get some sleep now, though," he adds as he lays back down. He turns his back to Kato almost instantly, and he can tell the moment is over. He faces the opposite way and closes off Azrian's thoughts to give him privacy. Once it's quiet, he easily drifts off to sleep.

Several hours pass before he's being shaken awake. "Kato, get up. Come on, we gotta go," Az says quickly. "It's time to go find my mom."

"I'm up." Kato sits up and looks around, trying to orient himself to the strange surroundings. "Can I help with anything?"

Galen shakes his head and points to the carriage. "Just get yourself in there, I'm almost done."

By the time they're on the road again, Az is nearly bouncing with anticipation and nervousness. Kato can feel all of it, and while he's not sure exactly how to distract him, he tries. "Is your town similar to the one we just passed?"

He nods a little in confirmation. "Sort of? Coldhallow is at the base of a mountain *and* on the shoreline, so they're a little different than we are. Embermeadow is pretty much in the middle of nowhere... well, the middle of Edros, anyway. They're more... Undare and Caelim, while we're more Terrare and everything else."

"Got it. Should I pretend to just not have any powers? Would that be for the best?"

Looking almost apologetic, Az dips his head again. "Yeah. If it makes you feel any better, I'm going to, too. It's nothing personal, it's just... my mom doesn't like Praediti."

"Because of the man that attacked her," he states because he doesn't need to ask. "Some Praediti are bad, but not all. Not you."

Az squirms in his seat. "I wasn't always Praediti. I mean, I didn't grow up like that. I don't know what I would be like if I did. But you're right," he adds quickly. "They're not all bad."

"I try not to be bad." Kato looks down at his fingernails. "Do you think I'm bad?"

"I *did*," he answers honestly. "But not anymore. You're not intentionally bad, anyway... and I think that's what matters most."

Kato nods, looking ahead at the upcoming town. "Is this Embermeadow?" he asks excitedly, but the look on Az's face tells him it isn't. He still looks eager, like he knows they're on the right path, but he also looks impatient and ready to be home.

"No, this is Oxhaven. We're still a few hours from home, but if you two are hungry, we could stop here to eat," Galen calls back.

Azrian's stomach rumbles almost on cue. "Yeah, that'd be great... we didn't exactly leave Deadrun with any coins, though. Would I be able to pay you back when we get to town?"

"Don't mention it, son. It's my treat." Galen offers a smile as he finds somewhere to park the carriage. "Here's some coins. Grab me something too, I'll stay with the carriage."

Kato grabs them and hands them straight to Azrian. "I don't know how to use these."

"Seriously? Right, of course you don't... okay. Come on." Az drops down out of the carriage and waits for Kato, then straightens his tunic and leads him into town. "It doesn't look like this place has much, I think you'll be a lot happier with Embermeadow's food. Let's just grab some bread and cheese and head back. Follow my lead, okay? Don't say anything."

"I'll be quiet." Kato says, feeling like that's something he just needs to keep promising. It's hard, staying quiet in a new world when all you have are questions. But knowing how humans feel about Praediti — and vice versa — he knows it's for the best.

Az makes a show of loudly asking a plump old man how much for the bread and cheese, so Kato does his best to pay attention and watch how many coins he hands over. He's not sure why they're worth anything at all, but the man seems to accept them happily and even throws in a flagon of something called ale. Azrian is almost giddy by this turn of events, and quickly pulls Kato back toward the carriage. "I'm proud of you. You didn't talk."

"It was harder than it looked. What's ale? Can I drink some?" he asks, looking down at it in his hands.

"Yeah, but you might want to save it. It'll help you sleep once we get back home." Az gives him a pointed look as they make their way to Galen. They eat hungrily after that, scarfing down the bread and cheese like *none* of them have eaten in days. "For Oxhaven, it's not bad."

"It has more flavor than Deadrun cheese," Kato states, eating happily as Galen prepares to get back on the trail.

"How long were you there for, Kato?" he asks curiously, but Kato freezes in fear that he'll answer incorrectly.

Az nudges him. "It's okay. You don't have to hide from Galen. Just... everyone else, I think."

With a nod, Kato turns back to him. "I was born there. This is my first time... *not* there."

"Oh," Galen says, and even Kato can tell he's surprised. "This has to be quite a shock for you, then. Are you handling it okay? Do you have any questions?"

"Yes, actually. Thank you. Do you love your children unconditionally, too? Or just the mothers?" Kato watches his face and can see the answer before he speaks.

"Of course I do. My kids are my world, just like they're Cora's. I would do anything for them. Why do you ask, son? Did you leave your parents behind at Deadrun or something?"

"I don't have parents. Well, my father was a tube and my mother had me and then left me. I don't know anything about her... except her name was K."

Az reaches over to squeeze his knee as Galen says quietly, "I'm sorry to hear that. I hope you find your place in this world. If you ever need anything, you just come back to Coldhallow. We'll see to it you have what you need."

"Thank you. Would you still feel that way if you found out I was a —" Kato looks to Az again, but since he just told him not to hide, he doesn't — "Cogitare?"

Without missing a beat, Galen laughs. "I've known since the moment you arrived, son. You're not exactly subtle when it comes to digging around in people's heads. If you're going to try and hide, you need to shut that down."

"I'll just take that as a yes," Az cuts in. "We appreciate it, Sir."

"I wasn't..." Kato pointedly looks away with a blush after meeting Azrian's eyes. "I tried not to." He's happy Galen doesn't seem to be offended, but he's right — he needs to learn to control himself better.

They talk some more in passing about the other territories in Athoze. Etria is half intense heat, half bitter cold, and while neither of those words mean much to Kato, they send a noticeable chill up Azrian's spine. Sastrya is apparently huge, and its neighbor Rostya is home to a ruined city sprawling at the feet of a deadly volcano.

Just as more questions spring to his mind, Az starts smacking his arm. "Kato, Kato! We're here!"

Kato sits up straighter, glad their journey is finally coming to an end. "Home?" He meets Azrian's eyes with a smile, loving how excited he is.

"Yeah, we're home. Come on, my house isn't far from here!" Az says, directing Galen to stop. After a quick goodbye, they wave him off and Azrian takes off at a run toward the woods. Confused, Kato hurries to keep up.

After a few minutes, Az slows and starts spinning in a circle. It becomes increasingly clear that something is wrong, and Kato is just about to reach out to stop him from spinning when Azrian falls to his knees.

A wave of anguish comes off his friend. "I'm an idiot," he says quietly. "I was *in* my house when it burned... why did I think it would still be here? She couldn't have fixed it on her own."

What "it" Az is talking about, Kato isn't sure. There's nothing but smooth grass and dark forest in front of them and extending out on both sides — as far as he can tell, there was never a house there at all.

Kato drops down next to him, not sure what the correct social response is in this situation. "Are you sure it was right *here*, Azrian?"

"Look for yourself!" he yells, reaching over to grip the front of Kato's shirt. His gray eyes are a little wild, a little desperate. "Look. In my memories, look! It was here. She was here."

With a nod, Kato closes his eyes to see. He sees the house... the mother... the chickens... and lastly, the fire. "*Belua*," he spits. "But... Azrian, if she's not here... where *is* she?"

~ IX ~

THE BLAME

Azrian stares blankly at the plot of land that used to feature his home. It's gone, of *course* it's gone... he was an idiot to think it wouldn't be. He steps forward and looks down at where he thinks his living room used to be. The grass has grown back already, so the indents in the ground from their fireplace are obscured, if they're even still there at all. "How did this happen? I wasn't gone that long; it was only a few months... how..."

Grief wells inside of him as terror for his mother is renewed. If the house is gone, Kato's right — there's only one real question. *Where is she?*

Kato walks away and looks around the land like it might hold some kind of clue, but Az knows he will find nothing. The Venandi cover their tracks well; how else do they get away with... whatever they want? How else do they stay so far under the radar that no one has heard of them?

"We need to go find Rhix," Az says suddenly. He pushes himself to his feet, knowing his former employer might know something — and even if he doesn't, he's still the only friend he's got in Embermeadow.

As Azrian starts walking away, Kato follows silently. His eyes dart around like he's trying to take everything in all at once, but once they reach a more populated area, he moves in closer to Az. "I shouldn't talk... right?"

"No, Kato," he whispers. "Don't talk, don't read minds, don't do anything but follow me. Keep your eyes down. Once we get to Rhix, you can speak." They hurry through the thickening crowd and Az does his best to tug Kato along. It's a lot easier for someone of Azrian's size to navigate, but the people seem to shy away from Kato all on their own and Az would be an idiot not to see the benefits.

Rhix's shop is open, thankfully, and Az ducks inside as quickly as he can without drawing attention to them. The main room is empty, but the coal is still burning in the forge. "Rhix?" he yells out.

His old boss walks out with a shocked expression. He doesn't speak for a few seconds and then his eyes flick to Kato, making him stand straighter. "Azrian. I thought — who's this?"

"I'm Kato," he says plainly as he walks closer with open arms. "Do we hug?"

Az nearly stops him but decides it would be far funnier to let it play out — and he *desperately* needs a laugh. Rhix looks at Kato like he's from another world and holds out a thick, meaty arm to stop him in his tracks.

"No," he grunts. "We don't hug. Go back over there." Rhix's orange eyes travel back to Azrian and he lets out a breath. "You're dead."

"Nope. Almost, though... couple of times. Can we talk —" he jerks his head toward the door — "in private, maybe?"

Rhix nods toward Kato. "Private include him?"

Kato turns to Azrian with a tilt of his head. "We've had lots of private time."

With a heavy sigh, Azrian rubs his beard. "Rhix, this is Kato. He's... never been out in the real world before. He's a little different, and he doesn't know what he just said. It's not like that."

"Right," Rhix agrees sarcastically. He heads over to shut the door, then wipes his palms on his apron. "I'm sure it's not. What can

I do for you, Azrian? If you're not dead, it means you left me high and dry for no reason."

"I didn't. I was kidnapped. An Igneme burnt my house down and took me to Deadrun."

Rhix frowns, standing up straighter. "I went by your house. Did they also kidnap Roe?"

Kato remains quiet, his head tilting as if he might be searching Rhix's mind, but he doesn't speak.

"I don't know. They told me she was still here and safe from harm, I thought... maybe somehow she rebuilt the house, or they did it for her." He shifts his weight and tries to keep the tears from his eyes. "I don't know where she is, Rhix. Or if she's even alive at this point. They lie about everything."

Rhix nods and looks down at Azrian's state. "You should go to my home and rest, Azrian. I have to finish up here, but we will continue this conversation tonight. He won't touch anything right?" Rhix nods toward Kato and he snaps his hand back from an axe when he realizes they're watching him.

"He's probably going to touch just about everything, but I'll try to keep it under control as much as I can. Thank you, Rhix. Seriously. You're the first friendly face I've seen in half a year, and *I'm* tempted to hug you." Az knows he's allowed to say it, because Rhix knows there's no way under Cettia he'd ever do it. "We'll get out of your hair."

When his stomach growls, he remembers with a jolt that he should still have money in the back. Az ducks out of sight as Kato says something probably embarrassing to Rhix, then snatches the small satchel from its hiding place. Every tip he's ever gotten is in this bag, and while he *had* been saving up to buy Roe a better house... he has a feeling they'll need the money just to survive the coming months.

He finds himself grateful that Rhix never found it and shoves it down into the waistband of his pants before heading back out to the others. "Come on, Kato. Let's go before you end up getting your ass kicked."

～

Kato notices a bulge in Azrian's pants. He isn't sure if this is one of those things they shouldn't talk about, but he also can't stop looking at it, so he has to say *something*. "Wow... you've... grown... have you tried your hand? I can wait for you out here."

He doesn't get a response from Azrian, just a flush of his cheeks and a shove out the door, but Az isn't the only one blushing over this. Kato thinks about the times he's had to use his own hand and leans in to whisper, "Did you get excited over something?"

"Sweet *shadows*, K8.0, this is *not* the time!" Azrian keeps pushing him until they're stumbling back out onto the street together. When he straightens up, he reaches into his pants and pulls out a small cloth bag. "Coins. So we can eat. I'm not... I didn't... just shut up."

Kato bites back a smile to keep from laughing out loud. Azrian flustered is quite adorable, but he's quickly distracted by the world around him. There are more people here than he's ever been around at one time, and he tenses at Az's side.

"Hey, hey... you gotta relax," Az says quietly. "I know this is overwhelming, but it's no different than Coldhallow or Oxhaven. Just a little busier." When Kato doesn't relax, Azrian grips the front of Kato's t-shirt and turns him so they're facing each other. "I'm right here."

He meets his grounding gaze and nods slowly, knowing Az wouldn't let anything happen to him. It's hard not to remember the stories he's been told his entire life — angry mobs of humans taking out Praediti for simply being different. "Okay... I'll relax. I'm sorry."

"Don't apologize. You're not doing anything wrong; I'm just reminding you that it's still just us and you don't need to worry. Okay?

We're gonna go buy some food and clean clothes, then go back to Rhix's house and try to rest. We're safe for now."

"Okay... okay. Show me your hometown, Az. I want to see it." He figures if he focuses on Az and the town itself, maybe he won't stress about the humans all around them. It's a long shot, but he has to be strong. They've made it this far and really... he doesn't feel threatened. Not right now.

Azrian huffs a laugh and takes a step back, but still stays close. "Honestly, I hate it here. Always have... but it's better than Deadrun, and it's home." He leads Kato through the streets until they come to a small shop with a delicious scent emanating from it. "Hungry, big guy?"

"Yes, very." Kato walks up to the food to grab it with his bare hands, but Az grabs his arm to hold him back. "Do we ask first?"

"We *pay* for it first. Just taking it is a good way to get your hand chopped off." Azrian flashes a dimpled smile to the woman staring at them, then fishes a couple of coins out of his pocket. "Do you have cloth we could use to take this to go?" She nods, wrapping up two strange-looking loaves of bread. They're oozing something, but Kato bites back then urge to ask what it is. Once the exchange is made, Az jerks his head back toward the street. "We should find somewhere to eat this in private."

"Private but together, right?" Kato asks as he follows Az down a narrow road. "What's on the bread?" he whispers.

Az doesn't answer until they're sitting down by a huge tree just outside of town. He hands Kato his food, then takes a deep breath. "Yes, private but together. It just means no one else is around. And the gooey stuff is cheese — just melted, not solid like you're used to. Try it but be careful... it's hot."

Kato takes a bite, his eyes widening at how amazing it tastes. "Wow!"

"See?" Az smiles a little, but it fades as he picks off pieces of his own to eat. "I never thought I'd see this place again. Thought I'd die in Deadrun, and if not there... definitely on the ocean."

"I also thought we'd die on the ocean." Kato takes another bite, this one much larger, and hums. "I like it here."

Az watches him but doesn't say much else as they finish eating. Once they're full, he reaches over to wipe some crumbs from Kato's pants. "We need to get some clothes; we can't walk around in Deadrun uniforms forever. We stick out too much."

"Do they have clothes that fit me?" Kato asks in a hopeful tone.

"Of course they do, this place is crawling with big, strapping Praediti like you," he says quietly. "Let's go, come on."

They stand to make their way back to the busy road, but before they make it there, Kato stops in his tracks. He tilts his head at a couple with their mouths together. "What are they doing?"

Az looks closer and huffs a laugh. "They're kissing, Kato."

"Kissing?" The man slides his hands down the woman's frame, and the thoughts he's having have Kato taking a step toward them, only stopping when Az grips his arm.

"What are you doing?"

"I want to try it," he states, thinking that was obvious.

Az pulls him further away and chuckles at him. "Try it? With them? Both of them?"

Kato looks over again and then shrugs. "Do I have to pick one?"

Az stands straighter like he's much too curious not to answer. "Yeah, actually. You do. Which one?"

He doesn't have to think twice about it. "Him."

"Him? Th—the guy? Why the guy?"

Kato thinks about it a moment as he watches the couple again. "Because he enjoys it more."

Az is too intrigued, regardless of the fact that they need to get moving again. "Does he? What's he thinking?"

"He wants to go to bed with her and have sex. He's thinking about sex... very vividly." Kato stares, watching his thoughts as he's thinking them.

Az snaps his fingers to get his attention. "And what is she thinking?"

"She... not sex. She likes him enough... she feels secure with him but... he isn't her favorite person to kiss."

"He isn't, huh? Who is then? Milkman?" Az jokes.

"Milkman? No... it's her friend. A woman."

Suddenly, Azrian laughs *loudly.* "Hah! Oh, that's... that's good. It wasn't that Morella didn't want me because she thought I was human, it's because she's thinking about her *friend."*

Pulling his eyes away, Kato notices for the first time that Azrian recognizes the woman. He remembers seeing her in Azrian's mind, back when he cut his finger. "She was mean to you, right?"

"Yeah, you could say that." He rubs his chest absentmindedly and then scoffs, shaking his head. "That's not passion, Kato. Don't pay them any mind, let's just go."

"Have you ever kissed anyone, Azrian?" Kato asks, not wanting to search his mind but wanting to know the answer.

He snorts. "Yeah, few times. Not as many as I would've liked to, but... again, not many people around here want humans."

"Why not? That shouldn't matter. They should like people for who they are inside."

"That's the point, Kato. Humans aren't much on the inside, not compared to Praediti, anyway. But never mind all that, pick out some clothes." He pushes open a door to another shop filled with all sorts of different fabrics. Some are plain, others are colorful, but almost all of them look strange compared to what he's used to wearing.

He picks up something long with ties down the back, and it seems long enough for his height. It has full-length white sleeves and a burgundy bottom that looks open. "How does this work?"

"It's a dress, Kato. And while I'd never judge whatever it is you choose to wear... okay, that's a little bit of a lie, but seriously. You can't wear a dress, it isn't practical... not where we're going." He leads Kato a few tables over and picks out some trousers, a dark tunic, and a belted coat for him. "How do your shoes feel? Do you need boots?"

Kato looks down at his shoes, frowning at the disheveled state of them. "They used to be white. How much are boots?"

"Don't worry about it," Az mutters. He points over to the far wall. "Go find some that'll fit you, I'll get... the rest of it."

Kato nods and goes to check out the row of boots. After trying on four pairs, he finally finds some that feel perfect, and he puts his old shoes in their spot then goes to find Azrian. "I found some."

The look on Azrian's face is comical. "You... don't leave your old ones behind, just..." he sighs, loading up the socks and undergarments into Kato's arms. "I'll get them."

Ten minutes later, they're walking back out once again, this time heading toward Rhix's house. "We can bathe before we sleep, and hopefully after a nap, Rhix will be back."

"Is the bath in the river again?" Kato asks, his eyes still looking around curiously.

"Nah, Rhix has a tub. We just have to fill it, but... I think I can heat up water now. We'll just have to take turns."

Kato tries to picture what a tub would look like but doesn't ask any other questions until they reach Rhix's house. "Does he live alone?"

"Yeah, as far as I remember." Az opens the door and lets them in, then sets down everything they bought. "You heard him, don't touch anything. I'll go get the bath settled, you can go first."

Kato thanks him, but he's already in a different room. He starts looking around at things, wondering how he accumulated all of his stuff, but he keeps his hands at his sides. He finds a toy and thinks it's a curious thing for someone like Rhix to have in his home. Once again, he fights the urge to touch... he doesn't want to get in trouble.

"Okay," Az says from behind him. "It's ready, and I think the water is warm enough. There's a towel for you and I laid your new clothes out, so when you're done, just bring me the clothes you've got on right now."

"Thank you," he repeats, walking past Azrian and into the bathing area. He takes in the room as he strips, shivering when he steps on bricks with bare feet. He groans as he sinks into the water and reaches out to Az soon after. "*Shadows, this feels good.*"

"*I figured you'd like that. Take your time, we can probably get away with staying here for a couple of days. You've earned the break.*"

"*As have you,*" he states, and then closes his eyes to enjoy the warmth. It takes him a few moments to remember that Az needs a bath too, and he cleans himself, not wanting to use all the hot water.

His hair is still dripping when he walks out, his new clothes clinging to his damp body. "Your turn."

Azrian's jaw hangs open a little as he stares at Kato. "It's my what?"

"Bath turn. I'm done." Kato tilts his head and walks closer. "Are you okay?"

He glances up and nods a little ridiculously. "Yeah, yeah... great, just... great. Thanks for the bath, I'll be back." Ducking under Kato's arm, Az dashes toward the bathroom.

Kato walks over by some chairs and stands awkwardly, wondering if sitting on one counts as him touching something. Technically, his butt would be touching it, but does that count? Chairs are meant to be sat on, right? He stands the entire time, trying to decide if it counts, and by the time Azrian returns he still doesn't have a clue. "Am I allowed to sit?" he asks, letting his eyes travel down Azrian's new outfit. "You look better this way."

"Right, so... do you. Why are you just standing here, though? Rhix has a guest bed— shadows, I forgot to show you, didn't I? Sorry. C'mon." He leads Kato down a hallway into a smaller room, and the bed inside of it looks like it's barely big enough for one person. "Take a nap."

Kato climbs onto the bed and wishes there were enough room for both of them. It's much warmer when Azrian is with him. "Are you going to come to bed, too?"

Az shakes his head. "Not right now, I have to talk to Rhix when he gets home."

Kato nods and shimmies under the small blanket. His feet hang out of the bottom, so he rolls onto his side and curls in on himself, then closes his eyes before Azrian makes his exit. As always, it doesn't take long for sleep to come, only this time, he actually has sweet dreams.

~

By the time Rhix comes back home, Azrian is pacing and agitated. He's not sure how long Kato has been asleep and he's been waiting alone, but he knows it's been a while, and he can't shake the fear still bubbling up inside of him. "Hey," he says, virtually the moment Rhix sets a large bag down.

"Hey yourself. Why aren't you resting?" he asks curiously, pulling out some ale. "Drink?"

"Please." He waits patiently as Rhix pours him some, then takes a long drink. The bitterness makes him shudder. "Couldn't really rest, the bed isn't exactly big enough for two people, and I didn't want to take yours."

"Kind of you. He's—" Rhix nods toward the hallway — "a big one. You sure you can trust him?"

Az glances at the floor and rubs his thumb over the rim of his glass. "I think so. He got me out of Deadrun, so... that has to count for something, right? I just wish he'd have done it sooner. It took me months to get him on my side, and now my mom's missing."

"She's been missing the entire time, Azrian. I haven't seen her once, and when I went to your home, everything was gone." He frowns as he walks to a side table, pulling out an old hair clip — but not just any clip. It's his mother's. The golden leaf is chipped and singed from the fire, and Azrian can't breathe for a moment when he thinks about what she must have gone through.

He stares at the clip like somehow it will change shape and take the form of his mom. "She's dead, isn't she. She died in the fire, or... or Belua killed her somewhere else." The grief nearly chokes him as it rises to the surface, clawing its way above the fear, exhaustion, and hunger that had previously been winning out. He's not sure how or why he knows it, but he does. "They killed my mom."

"I'm sorry, Azrian. I don't know. I didn't see a body, or anything for that matter. Just this... in the dirt." Rhix looks like he might hug him for once but refrains, despite this being the one time Azrian could actually use one.

He shifts on his feet to distract himself from the urges — the urge to run, the urge to hide, the urge to hurl himself off a cliff so when he lands, he'll wake up from the nightmare he's found himself in. "Right. Well... thanks for stopping by to check on us. I uh... I'm gonna head out, I think."

"What? Where would you go?" he asks, a frown forming on his face. "Shouldn't you rest... plan?"

I could've stopped it. Could've helped her if I'd have gotten here sooner. She died because I took too long... because **Kato** *took too long.* The thoughts threaten to swallow him whole, and all he can do is shake his head. "I can't stay. I'll... I'll head west... somewhere they can't find me."

"Can you wait until the morning sun? I got you some supplies, but you need to rest," Rhix pleads, gesturing to the bag. "And what of your friend?"

"He's not my friend. He may have saved me, but it was too damn late. If he'd have let me go when I asked the first time, I might've been able to save her." He hurries forward and grabs the bag, knowing if he doesn't leave soon, he'll lose his nerve — or at the very least, the anger that's driving him. "Just... let him get some sleep, then kick him out in the morning or something. Here." Az digs a handful of coins out of his pocket and shoves them at Rhix. "Take what you need for the supplies and give the rest to Kato so he can make it back to Deadrun where he belongs."

Rhix takes the coins and grabs Azrian's arm. He stares into his eyes with a frown, and then releases him with a nod. "If you need any help, you know where to find me."

"Thanks, Rhix. For everything. I..." Az trails off, knowing that neither one of them are very good with emotions. The bag's strap sits awkwardly on his shoulder as he pushes his way out the door, and he barely registers Rhix's muttered "may Cettia guide you" before it swings closed and separates them.

Okay. Now... just go. He takes one last look at the house, then forces his feet to do his bidding despite their utter insistence to stay put. He can do this. He can be free, he can escape the pain... and maybe, if he's lucky, he can get a little revenge.

For years, Azrian has heard stories about the Regnum. Made up of each type of Praediti and a human, they rule over all of Athoze to keep the peace. If anyone can help him stop the Venandi from hurting anyone else, it's them. All he has to do is find a way to get to Redhaven.

It's with that goal in mind that he stops on the southern edge of town. If he heads east, he'll hit the Sutson Sea. Favorable winds and a knowledgeable sailor could have him landing on Sastrian shores within the month, and while he'd still have to make it to the heart of Sastrya, he knows he can do it. He's survived this long, after all... but if the Venandi *are* looking for their escapees, chartering a ship would be a sure-fire way to tip them off. And without Kato around to manipulate those they come across to keep their mouths shut, his chances of reaching his goal are immeasurably low. They'd find him, and this time... he won't go quietly. He'd rather die than get taken captive again.

"Cettia, tell me what to do," he whispers as he looks at the star. "Show me the way like you always have." When not even a twinkle answers him, he shucks the bag up a little higher on his back and looks to the west. Unending, unrelenting darkness awaits him if he goes the long way. He'll have to travel alone through the Simbian Forest, down across the vast desert of Etria, and loop back up through Sastrya to finally make it to Redhaven. The journey will take months... and that's *if* he manages to survive the elements.

Maybe I'm overreacting, he thinks to himself. *Maybe they decided they don't need us, and they'll leave us alone. I can take a ship across the Sutson and tell the Regnum what's happening... pass the burden to them. That's what they're there for. The Venandi probably aren't even thinking about us anymore. Maybe this isn't my problem at all... maybe I should just go back to Rhix, try to get my job back, and forget all of this ever happened.*

Visions of the flames devouring his home fill his mind, and his hand finds its way to his pocket. He doesn't even remember placing the hair clip there, but when his fingers close around it, he sets his jaw. *I can't forget. I can't forget, and I can't forgive... they need to be brought to justice. Ronan, Cal, all the others I saw there in cells... they deserve justice. The ones we left behind deserve freedom. And if all it takes for me to help them get it is a few months of discomfort, well... maybe I'll make my mom proud.*

All he knows for sure is that standing still won't help anyone, and each second that he wastes puts another family, another newly presented Praediti in danger. He may not have asked for this task, but it's fallen squarely on his shoulders, nonetheless.

With shaky, hesitant steps, he heads toward the forest. It's slow at first, but the tightness in his chest doesn't ease quickly enough and he finds himself moving faster to try and outrun it. One step. Two, three... he's running now, running away from the town he so desperately tried to return to. The bag of supplies weighs heavily on his back and clinks around awkwardly, sending jolts down his spine each time something in the bag smacks against him. He finds he doesn't mind; the pain keeps him awake, alert... ready for whatever the night throws at him.

He makes it about a mile before he has to slow down. Deadrun didn't exactly present him with opportunities for physical labor, which has left him out of shape and tiring quicker than he'd anticipated. Things change, though. Now that his thoughts are no longer drowned out by the screaming of his lungs or the pounding of his heart, new ones creep in. Quieter ones, ones that threaten to derail his plan entirely before he even officially gets it off the ground. *Kato didn't know. It's not his fault, and you forced him to leave with you and then abandoned him in a strange place with nothing but coins he barely knows how to use. Does that make you better, somehow?*

Attempting to push them away only makes it worse. He remembers the scars on Kato's head and the awkwardness of their first meeting, and a forceful reminder of all that Kato endured at the hands of the Venandi stops him dead in his tracks. *He was brainwashed, it's a miracle I got through to him at all. He didn't take my mom... they did. The same people that treated him like an experiment. What am I doing?*

Truthfully, he isn't sure if he's going back because Kato doesn't deserve to be left behind, if it's because Kato will be a help, or if he's just afraid of being lonely, but he has a sneaking suspicion it's all of the above. With a groan, he turns on his heel and stares back at the barely visible silhouette of Embermeadow. *He's a wreck, he barely understands the most basic of human interactions... and now I've gone and abandoned him. I should... yeah. Okay.*

He heads back the way he came and tries not to let the fear of the dark overcome him. Cettia seems to be shining just a little brighter now to light up his path, and maybe a tiny bit of him thinks she's rewarding him for making the right decision... even though he's not quite sure he is.

Rhix is waiting for him on the porch with another glass of ale when he finally makes it back, and Az stands there with a shocked expression for a moment. "How did you know?"

"I didn't know. I hoped. That will help you sleep." Rhix stands and polishes his drink down, patting Azrian's shoulder roughly.

"I couldn't leave him." He drinks it before he can stop himself, then follows Rhix back inside the house. "I'll uh... see you in the morning. Can you keep this between us? I don't think he'd understand even though I came back."

"My loyalty lies with you, Azrian. I wouldn't tell him a thing. Sleep well." Rhix nods and walks back to his room, leaving Az to stand there looking around for a couch to sleep on. The only one his eyes land on looks more uncomfortable than the ground, and he realizes with no small amount of irritation that his only blanket is likely in the bag... which is completely stuffed full.

He's much too tired to dig it out, so instead, he sucks in a breath and heads for the room where Kato's sleeping. His giant body takes up most of the space, but Az manages to carve out a small spot near the edge where he fits okay. The blanket feels good on his cold skin, and he thinks he'll fall asleep quickly — until Kato's voice rings out in his mind. *"Where were you?"*

Az jerks so hard he nearly falls off the bed. "Shadows, Kato. I thought you were asleep," he whispers, wondering how much he actually heard. "I... I went to the market."

"I *was* asleep. But then... I don't know why I woke. What'd you get?"

"Nothing, they were out."

"Out of what?" Kato asks curiously.

Shadows. "Everything, they were out of everything. Just go back to sleep." He wiggles a little to get more comfortable, then winces when he rubs up against Kato. "Sorry."

"It's okay. You're warm. Night, Azrian."

"Yeah, g'night." His stomach twists uncomfortably, but he relaxes all the same as it hits him just how warm *Kato* is. He has a feeling the blanket won't be necessary come morning, but as he drifts off, he thinks about what a gift that'll be once they reach Etria and the desert temperature drops below freezing overnight.

Maybe, just maybe... he actually *did* make the right decision.

~ X ~

THE POISON

When Kato wakes, he feels Azrian's body against his and the warmth of it makes him consider staying in bed. Unfortunately, nature calls, and he slips from the bed without disturbing him. It's not an easy task, seeing as Az's body is curled against his, but he manages... and when he stares down at the relaxed lines on Azrian's face, he smiles, regardless of the fact that he tried to leave him last night.

He won't tell Az he knows — he doesn't see how that admission would help them right now — and he came *back*. That counts for something. Kato knows there are certain things Az may never be able to forgive him for, and he believes he will carry that guilt for the rest of his days. He should have listened to Azrian when he first told him; he'd *seen* the truth in his mind on that very first day — he just hadn't wanted to believe it. He was a coward. Apologizing won't bring his mother back, but he *will* help Az in every way that he can for as long as he will let him.

The morning air is crisp when he walks outside, and he finds himself naturally looking up to the sky for Cettia. He knows he won't see her in the sunlight, but in this time with Az, the star has brought him comfort. After relieving himself, he makes his way up to the porch to get a better look at the bushes and flowers. One stands out, and it's... fluffier than any flower he's ever seen. Reaching out, he plucks one and brings it up to his nose. It smells sweet, and he wonders if it is something he could eat, but Rhix walks out and his eyes widen in fear before he can attempt to taste it. "No! *Shadows*, what is wrong with you?" he yells.

His tone has Kato dropping the flower and then staring at Rhix with a confused expression. "Why are you yelling?"

"That's Mors Byssum, Kato. Poison."

Kato stares down at the fluffy traitor in shock, and then looks at his hand. "Am I going to die? Why do you have poison here?"

Rhix huffs a humorless laugh and orders Kato inside to clean his hands. "Wash them well. I have poison because it has other uses, but shadows... you don't *eat* it."

He takes his time and makes sure to scrub his hands thoroughly before drying off. "It smelled sweet."

"Of course it did. Sweet Cettia, how have you survived all this time?" he asks, this time with more curiosity than anger.

Kato thinks about that. Supposedly, he's alive because of Melior. He's been told all his life he would be dead without him. But now that Kato is free, he doesn't believe it. Since leaving the island, he's felt stronger than ever before, and the biggest confirmation for him is the fact that he hasn't had one single migraine since he stepped foot on that boat. They were doing something to him back there, they had to have been. He decides to share this information with Rhix, because if Azrian trusts him this much, he believes he can too. When he gets to the end of his story, he concludes that the only reason he *is* alive... is Azrian. "I might still be alive if I stayed, but not for long. But out here? In the world... I would have died instantly without Az."

"That's my boy," Rhix says proudly. "He hated Praediti growing up, but that little shit stormed into my shop anyway when his father left and made me fire my best Igneme. He had his *own* fire... one I haven't seen in many humans. I know he can be a little rough sometimes, but he's had to fight for everything he's ever had."

Kato listens, happy to learn more about Azrian from an outside source. "He's very hard-headed. It's... admirable. Do you think he will ever forgive me? I know he believes if we left sooner, we could have done more for Roe... and that's my fault. I was scared to leave the only place I've ever known."

"Forgiveness isn't something Azrian has a lot of experience with, so it's hard to say. I think he will, though. He knows he'd have never made it out of there without you, and in my experience, he's not one to forget his debts." Rhix begins separating what looks like random items into two satchels. "He's scared to death of the dark, though. Just be prepared for that."

"I'll protect him," Kato says without hesitation. "What are you doing? Are these for us?" He tilts his head, picking up a strange, metal thing and examining it. "What does this do?"

Chuckling, Rhix sits back. "It's a spile. If you hammer it into a tree, you'll be able to draw fresh water from virtually anywhere. They're extremely handy if your path will take you through the Simbian Forest or Etria... and my guess is you'll be heading through both. And yes, these things are for you. Some food, a list of edible plants... a Hokrine knife that Azrian actually forged himself." He flips through some more of the items and points them out as he speaks. "Blankets, extra clothing, first-aid supplies... a water canteen, and some other weapons. Have you ever shot a bow before?"

"No. I wasn't allowed to handle weapons. Can I try it?" he asks excitedly, reaching for the bow.

Rhix regards him with skepticism and shakes his head a little bit. "You should probably take the spear, leave the bow to Az. You guys only have about a half-dozen arrows, though. You should consider sticking around here until we can make more."

"That's up to Azrian," Kato states, picking up the spear to see how it feels in his hands. "I go where he tells me to go... I mean... where else am I gonna go?"

"Listen. If there's one thing I know about Azrian... it's that he's planning to do something stupid. You don't *have* to go with him.

You can stay here with me until you get on your feet, I can teach you how to work. You'd have a life, and you'd be safe."

Setting the spear down, Kato stands straighter. "No. I'd never abandon him. If he's going to do something stupid, we're doing it together."

He regards him with a grunt. "Then you're both idiots, but there's nothing I can do about that." After packing both bags and tying them off, he points with a meaty finger toward the table. "Eat some breakfast. Your comrade is likely to eat the entire spread if you don't get to it first."

Kato eats quickly and leaves Az a good amount of food. When he finally does walk out, his hair is a mess and he looks completely exhausted, but Kato can't help but smile. "Nice hair."

Az pauses, reaching up to the mess on his head. "Yeah... it was kind of a long night." The scent of the food must reach him then because he lifts his nose into their air as he heads for the table. "Oh, Cettia... yes."

Kato huffs a small laugh and starts reading the list of edible plants. He hopes Az knows what they all look like, but the descriptions Rhix has put will help if he doesn't. "I almost ate poison today," he says in a tone much too upbeat for the news he's passing on.

With a mouthful of meat, Azrian yells something incoherent at him. It takes him several seconds to chew and swallow. "We've been here a day and you're already trying to kill yourself? This is going to be a disaster."

"It wasn't on purpose. It was fluffy and smelled sweet," he argues, as if it makes a difference.

Rhix snorts. "Is that what it takes to get you going? No wonder there's nothing going on between you and Azrian."

Suddenly, Azrian's face turns bright red. "Shadows, Rhix. I don't know which of those many insults I'm more... insulted over," he finishes lamely.

Kato tilts his head with a small frown. "Azrian does smell sweet. But I wouldn't eat a human."

"That's not..." Az purses his lips and walks over as he shoves some more food in his mouth. He pats Kato's chest and does a double take, staring at his hand for a moment. "Uh... that's not what he meant, but it's probably better you don't know." His fingers curl against his palm as he lowers his arm, then takes what looks like a hesitant step back.

"See?" Rhix says, offering no further explanation. "Anyway, I was just telling Kato here that you two should stay for a few days. Get your strength back up, prepare a little more thoroughly."

Kato watches Az, wondering why he had a reaction to touching his chest, but he doesn't root around his mind for the answer. He's getting better at learning that Azrian's thoughts should be his own, even if he does slip sometimes. "What do you think, Az? Rhix says preparation is important."

"Shadows," he whispers, rubbing his chin. "Um... it is, most of the time... y'know, with most things." Rhix howls with laughter, and Azrian flips him off. "Shut up, it's not funny. This isn't funny." He turns back to Kato as his cheeks flush yet again. "We can stay, but only for a couple of days. The sooner we leave, the better chance we have of getting out before those shadowheads find us again."

Kato hopes that he can understand the hidden messages one day and wonders how long that will take. People out here talk in a code he can't seem to decipher, but they always seem to be enjoying themselves. "What does this mean?" he asks, flipping Azrian off.

"It means you don't like them, it's basically a non-verbal 'screw you'. So... use it sparingly, and most of the time, people won't take kindly to it," Rhix explains. "Azrian's lucky I actually deserved that one."

"Oh." Kato puts his finger down, walking over to take a drink of water. He's not sure if he'll ever pick up on the social cues without having to ask Azrian, but he isn't embarrassed. This is how he learns.

Az offers him a tiny, dimpled smile. "You'll get there, Jellycrai. As long as you don't eat poison or something first."

Kato chuckles and realizes how much lighter Az seems. It's obvious Azrian feels at home here in Embermeadow, but even the comfort of home isn't enough to deter him from his goals. He's hard-headed and determined, but Kato knows he wouldn't want to be on this journey with anyone else. Whatever comes across their path, they'll handle it. Together.

~

Two days later, Az is feeling better than he has in a long time. He can eat without fear that someone will take it away, sleep without worrying about getting kidnapped — like Rhix would *ever* let that happen — and more or less has a comfortable place to sleep. It's almost enough that he changes his mind. Almost.

"Okay," he says with a sigh. "I think we've got everything we need... so maybe we should head out at the end of the week."

Kato looks up from the sweet bread he's eating and meets his eyes. "Okay. Can we take some of this sweet stuff? I really like it."

"It's sugar, and yes. I think we can take some... it'll fit." He has serious doubts that it will, but he can't bear to see the look of disappointment on Kato's face. He'll make it work. "Eat up while you can, though. A couple more days and our meals will be a lot fewer and farther between."

He nods and shoves a big piece in his mouth. "I think I've eaten the entire time we've been here. Rhix makes very good food. Will we have to kill animals ourselves out there?"

"Yeah, but I can do it if you don't want to. I get it, it's not for everyone. I'm used to having to trap my own food... it's not new for me." Az eats a little himself and licks his lip slowly. "We'll make it work."

"I'll help... are some of them poisonous, too?" he asks with a tilt of his head.

He explains as much as he can about the poisonous creatures they might come across, and how most of them won't harm them once they're cooked. "How are you with making fire?"

"Um..." Kato looks down with that same, sad turn of his lips. "Will you teach me now? So, I can know before we head out? I want to learn. I want to help with everything I can."

"Uhh, actually..." Az is well aware of what a risk this will be, but he can't deny how beneficial it'll be if he doesn't have to keep explaining things to him. "I'm gonna let you dig around my brain for a minute. Just... try to stay on topic, yeah? Don't go crazy."

"Okay." Kato moves closer. Azrian knows he doesn't need to be closer, but he opts not to ask why he does it.

Instead, he does his very best to focus on basic survival skills — building fires, trapping animals, skinning and cooking those animals, craiviling, finding water. Building a shelter, how to battle the heat... and how to battle the cold. When his mind drifts to cuddling close to share body heat, he abruptly opens his eyes and clears his throat. "Okay, that's enough."

Kato takes a step back, a small blush on his cheeks. "I... we can do all those things. I can make fires for us at night and... hug you when we're cold."

Swallowing, Az crosses his arms over his chest. "I don't know how that got in there."

"It's functional. Because we will probably get cold, and I like when our bodies are close at night." Kato shrugs and walks toward the door. "I have to use the bathroom. I'm still not used to there not actually being a bathroom, but I can't hold it any longer." He pushes down the bulge in his pants and walks outside.

"Right," Az mutters quietly to himself as he stays rooted to the spot. "This isn't going to end horribly for me at *all*." He remembers a little forcefully what happened the last time he became curious in this manner about a Praediti and shoves the feelings down as far as he can. He doesn't particularly want to get blasted across another room for being attracted to someone else out of his league.

By the time Kato comes back in, Az is silent and busying himself with sharpening blades. "Feel better?"

"Yes. Thank you." Kato grabs another slice of sweet bread and sits near Azrian. "Are you sure you want to leave?"

Azrian shifts to face him, an unreadable expression on his face. "Are *you* okay with leaving all the others trapped at Deadrun?"

The thought makes him angry, causing his brows to furrow together and his jaw to clench. He slowly shakes his head. "Absolutely not."

"Then we have to, Kato. All we have to do is reach the Regnum, okay? They'll handle it. Or, if we happen to find an Itinerae that's willing to deliver the message... we might not even need to go all the way. And you don't —" the thought of Kato not coming with him makes him pause, but he knows he has to offer — "have to come with me. I can come back for you."

"No. I'm coming. Together, remember?"

"Together." He tries to give him a reassuring nod, but it falls flat. Even with Kato having more knowledge now than what he started with, there are still a lot of things that can go wrong.

He just hopes they're ready for it.

~

"Thanks again, Rhix. Seriously. I don't think we'd be half as well prepared for this if it weren't for you."

"Of course you wouldn't," Rhix says, clasping his shoulder like he has so many times before. "You take care of each other, and if you ever make your way back here, you come on over. Alright, Azrian? Your giant, too."

Az smiles as genuinely as he's capable of in the moment. "We'll be back. For better or worse, Embermeadow is my home. And I'll need you to give me my job back when this is all over," he adds.

"Yeah, right," Rhix jokes. "Of course it's yours, kid. We'll find something for this guy, too. Just be safe."

Kato walks up and shakes his hand. "Thank you for your help, Rhix. We appreciate it."

All Azrian can do is stare. Maybe Kato digging around in his brain did more good than he thought — he's finally getting the hang of at least *some* social cues, and that has to count for something. He pats Kato's back as they turn to walk away, and he offers Rhix a simple salute before adjusting his satchel and taking off down the porch steps again.

It feels a little like the beginning of a very long day, which simultaneously seems like an understatement and the absolute truth. It *will* be a long day, but more than that... it's going to be a long couple of months. "I hope you know what you're doing, Kato," he says as they get on the road. "You're gonna be stuck with me for a while."

"Are you sure you aren't stuck with me?" he teases, pushing Az slightly with his elbow. "I don't have anywhere else to be. I want to be here."

"Oh, I'm stuck with you, alright. But you're useful... I mean... just look. The sun is ridiculously bright and it's not bothering me at all, you're so tall you block it out." Az grins widely, letting out a laugh that's nearly a cackle.

Kato actually laughs with him and pushes him with his elbow again. "Ha-ha," he fakes, running a hand through the hair tickling his forehead.

His spirits are lighter than he thought they'd be as they make their way out of town. There's a lot ahead of them, and the hair pin in his pocket serves as a reminder of that with every step, but he has hope. He's not alone... Kato's had plenty of chances to change his mind, and yet... he's here. They're together, and if they could make it out of Deadrun... they can do anything.

~

The optimism fades by the end of the second day. Azrian can tell Kato is tired — he's not used to being exposed to the elements like this, and their experience on the boat doesn't seem to have done a whole lot to condition him. Az hands him the water canteen as they pick a place to camp for the night. "Drink."

Kato takes it and drinks, stopping when some spills out of the sides of his mouth. "When we need to refill it, do we need to find a specific tree for the spile?" He drops down onto his bottom roughly, his eyes closing in exhaustion.

"Not necessarily. Some trees will yield more than others, but where we're heading, pretty much any of them should work. Same with the river, most of the rivers we'll come across are freshwater and pretty clean. I don't foresee water being an issue for us... food, on the other hand, might be a different story."

Kato nods and pulls out the jerky Rhix made them, then hands a piece to Azrian. "Eat some. You need it."

"Nah, I'm okay. We won't see many animals between here and the edge of the forest, and we need to conserve the dried stuff. It lasts longer." He puts the finishing touches on their shelter for the evening and deems a fire unnecessary. It's warm enough they should be okay with just a blanket, and the less attention they draw to themselves, the better. "Get comfy, Jellycrai."

Kato lays down and watches Az, those piercing eyes following his every move. "You need to rest too, shadowhead."

"I know that. I will, I was just trying to let you get settled." He waits a few extra moments and glances around them. It's not completely dark yet, but it's getting there, and he'd honestly prefer to be asleep before the last remaining light leaves them to fend for themselves. He lays down quickly, sneaking under the blanket. "Budge up, make room."

Kato scoots over and curled around Az's back when he faces away from him. "I won't go anywhere. The dark doesn't mean you're alone," he whispers. "Goodnight, Azrian."

It's so unexpected that Az nearly moves away. He shouldn't do this, shouldn't encourage it... but Kato's strong arm feels good, and he's too weak to push him away. "Goodnight, Jellycrai," he says. The word doesn't hold nearly as much sarcasm as it usually does, and he's not sure if it's the genuine fear of being stuck outside all night or a growing fondness for the man he almost left behind.

Either way... he's pretty sure he's screwed.

~

The next day passes a lot like the first two. They keep out of sight as much as possible, stop to rest only when they absolutely need to, and eat sparingly — but at least today, they finally find a patch of river that Az thinks it's safe to bathe in.

He hides their things just out of sight and strips down to his boxers. "The water's probably cold, Kato. Get in and get out as quickly as you can, here's your half of the soap."

Kato catches the bar as he tosses it and hurries into the cool water. The chill makes him shiver, and he pulls off his boxers to clean them as well. He doesn't look over at Az even though he realizes for the first time it's actually hard not to, but he chalks it up to curiosity. He continues cleaning his body, then rushes out to dry off. "It was cold, but it felt good to clean."

"I agree," Az says, but his visible skin is bumpy and pink. He shakes slightly as he puts on some warmer clothes. "Okay, we need to get moving again so we can warm up. How are we on water? Should we head upstream and fill up?"

"Yes, probably a good idea." Just then, a capus runs by, making Kato draw a sharp intake of breath as he jumps back. "What was that?!"

Az stares after the small, floppy-eared thing and huffs a laugh. "Dinner, if we'd have caught it. They're quick little suckers." He walks back the way they came and Kato follows, still glancing back to see where the creature ran off to. Once they're far enough to escape any of the suds or dirt they washed off, Az drops down to drink directly from the source as Kato fills up the canteen.

Once the canteen is full, he copies Azrian, cupping his hands in the water and sipping slowly until he gets his fill. "Should we set up a trap? Like the one you showed me in your mind... or not until we stop for the night?"

"We won't catch anything out here. We'll have to make do with what we've got until we hit the forest. If we're lucky, and push ourselves, we'll be there by nightfall." Az stands and flicks his hands in the air to dry them off, then nods back the other direction. "How are your legs? You good to walk for another few hours?"

"Yes." Kato stands. The truth is they hurt, but he knows that won't go away regardless, and the last thing he wants is to make Az feel bad, so he wipes his hands on his pants and follows him.

It's hard for Kato to watch where he's stepping. He feels clumsy, tripping over rocks and sticks — but he can't stop staring up at the world around him. He finds he enjoys the smells filling his nose and the sounds filling his ears, and despite being more physically exhausted than he's ever been in his life, he's excited to see the forest.

They don't make it more than halfway before Az stops abruptly and holds out his arm. He puts a single finger to his lips, and while Kato isn't exactly sure what he means, it's clear he shouldn't speak unless spoken to. A couple of moments later, a twig snaps to their left and Azrian draws his blade.

Three people almost as tall as Kato himself walk out of the only building they've passed in hours. When they see Kato and Az hauling two clunky satchels, their interest shifts immediately from whatever it was on before to them. "Well, well... not often we see anyone out here. How lucky are we, boys?" the tallest one asks.

Kato may still be learning social cues, but he instantly feels defensive. His fists tighten at his sides and he takes a stance in front of Azrian without thinking. He isn't sure if he should speak yet, so he reaches inside their minds... and all he sees is greed.

"What, does the human already belong to you?" he asks Kato, nodding behind him to where Azrian has his blade held out. "You can share, right? We're sharers around here."

Az takes a step forward. "I'm *not* a human."

"Could've fooled me. Sure *look* human."

"Screw you." Kato hopes he used that correctly, but he doesn't dwell too much on it. "Walk away or you *will* regret it... shadowhead."

"*Shadows*, Kato," Azrian whispers as the three laugh loudly. One of them flicks his wrist and sends Kato flying back with a gust of air, and he hits the ground hard enough that he can't breathe for a moment. He hears Azrian yelling something incoherent and manages to push himself to his feet just in time to see him hurl a ball of energy at the one that attacked Kato. He's not fast enough though, and the tallest grabs Azrian's satchel and starts to run away.

"Stop!" Kato yells, completely taking over all three of their minds at once. They freeze, looking around with confused and frightened faces as he walks up, taking the satchel back and leaving them frozen while he checks on Az. "Are you okay?"

Azrian looks irritated more than anything and walks right over to the one that stole from him. "This is for every single human that people like you have ever preyed upon." He hauls back, and — with a sickening *thwap* — punches him right in the nose. It gushes blood and Az jumps backward quickly to avoid it. "Have a nice day, *shadowhead.*"

Quickly, he comes back to Kato with wild, scared eyes. "We have to go *now*. How long can you hold them like that?"

"I don't know. I imagine I can have them stand here until they starve." He tilts his head, taking a step closer to look at their faces. "How would you guys feel about that?"

None of them can speak because he isn't letting them, but the mumbles they make tell him they wouldn't care for it too much. "Are there cells out here in the world?"

"Not for Praediti. Only humans." Az comes up next to him but isn't looking at their attackers — he's staring straight at Kato. "Where have you been all my life?"

"At Deadrun. But you might have been born first," Kato states, then turns toward the thugs. "Stand here for three days, then you may move. Good luck." He pivots and nods to the tree line off in the distance. "Let's go."

Az slings his bag over his shoulder again and sticks his tongue out at the three captives. When Kato gives him a look, he shrugs. "Yeah, yeah. I'm a child. But a few months ago, I'd have either walked away from that completely naked with nothing to my name but a new scar... or I wouldn't have walked away at all. I'm feeling a little springy."

"I like it." He attempts to copy him, sticking his tongue out and smiling at Azrian. "Was that okay? I want them to think about who they try to prey on."

Nodding, Az takes one final look back at them before they walk too far to really see them. "You did awesome, Kato. Yet again... you saved me. I'm beginning to think I'm going to have to be your servant when we finally make it back home."

"Servant? I don't want that. I just want a friend." Kato looks down, wondering if things like this help Az forgive him, but that isn't why he did it. He did it because he truly believed it was right.

"Friend. Right," Az says quietly. "I was mostly kidding about the servant thing... just never mind." He takes a swig from the canteen and shuffles slowly along. "Are you okay though? I know firsthand that getting tossed around like that isn't always as fun as it could be. Any injuries?"

"No. I landed on my tailbone and it hurts... want to massage it for me?" Kato teases, once again not sure if he's joking correctly.

Judging by Azrian's laugh, he is. "Very funny, Kato. If the pain gets worse, make sure you tell me. The last thing we need is for you to have broken your ass."

"Is that possible?" Kato asks, never having heard of that. "How would I sit down? And is that the qualification for an *ass* rub?" he jokes again, trying out yet another new word.

Azrian's dimples make an appearance as he scoffs playfully. "Where to start... uh... yeah, sitting *and* walking would be pretty difficult, I'd think. It's funny to hear you swear... and if I didn't know any better, I'd think you were just trying to get me to rub your butt."

"Maybe." Kato chuckles. "What are other swear words? I know 'shit' and 'screw you' and 'ass'... oh, and the finger thing. Is 'shadows' a bad word, or 'hell'?"

"Neither really. They're both just... concepts. Different words for the same place... well, shadows can be used a lot of different ways. You're already catching on." He snickers suddenly, nudging Kato. "You're supposed to be the innocent one here and I'm corrupting you... I'm not telling you any more, especially the worse ones. Come on, maybe your *rear* will hurt less if we walk in silence."

"Rear? I don't like that one." Kato lightly jabs him back and looks up at the sky, noticing that the trees are slowly starting to thicken.

Az must notice too — he seems to become even more alert than he already has been, and once they reach a long, seemingly endless line of thick trees... he stops. All sorts of weird sounds can be heard from deep within, and Kato swears he catches sight of some sort of animal swinging through the higher branches. With a deep breath, Az glances up. "Well, Kato... hope you're ready. We're here. Welcome to the Simbian Forest."

~ XI ~

THE SIMBIAN FOREST

The first few steps into the forest aren't quite as bad as Azrian had feared. Based on the stories he'd heard as a child of bizarre creatures and strange happenings, he was more or less expecting something... bigger.

Maybe bigger isn't the right word. The forest itself seems huge and a touch overwhelming — but each step that they take without a massive, flying avisim swinging down on them or volucrae swarming them leads him to relax. That is, of course, until his lumbering, overly obvious companion decides to ruin it.

"It's getting dark, Azrian."

Sure enough, he realizes how badly his eyes are straining to see in the dark. He doesn't understand... just a few minutes ago, they'd been out in broad daylight. It shouldn't be nightfall yet. "Great," he mutters sarcastically. "A forest of eternal darkness... this is *exactly* what I wanted. Funny how the stories never mentioned that."

He steps carefully over a fallen tree and creates a small ball of light to accompany them. Once again, he feels his straining, tense muscles loosen up. The fear fades, if only a little. He can breathe.

"Okay," Az says, helping Kato cross over a small stream. "That map Rhix gave us doesn't exactly help here. We know that we have to go deep and curve to our left, then basically pivot and head up. By our estimations, it's going to take about three weeks to get through... and that's *if* we don't get lost or eaten first."

"Eaten! What might eat us?" Kato asks, his golden eyes darting around them nervously.

Grinning a little, Az stands up straighter. "A valianis, maybe. They're giant, as big as you... but furry with huge paws and razor-sharp teeth. I don't *think* they eat humans... but I've never seen one, or met anyone that's seen one, either."

"Hopefully, we don't see one. I wonder if I could control them," he muses, seemingly to himself. Az has to hope he can, because if he can't... well, he doesn't want to think about that.

The change in conversation is welcome. "Have you tried before? Controlling animals, I mean. I didn't see any at Deadrun, but I guess the meat had to come from somewhere."

"No. I didn't see animals until we got to Edros, and the ones I've seen have run away before I could even think to try. It would be useful... I could make them freeze so we can eat them and not even bother with traps... but I would have to get close enough for that, huh?" Kato scratches his head, letting Az know after all these years, he still doesn't know the extent of his own powers. "I don't have migraines anymore... why do you think that is?"

He stops walking and steps in front of him, wanting Kato to know how absolutely serious he is. "I don't know how, but it was Adeinde. It had to be... I saw her face. They were hurting you, Kato. They have been your whole life."

Kato stares at him with displeasure, his lips parted in shock as he takes that in. "It was always worse when she was around. How did I not know?!" He runs a hand through his hair in frustration. "She was like a black hole, every time I attempted to read her mind... all I got was vast emptiness and pain."

Az's face scrunches up in confusion at the analogy, but that's not what he chooses to focus on. "Maybe she's a Contego? A... shield, I guess. I've heard about them, but I didn't honestly think they existed. I thought it was just something Praediti parents made up to get their heathen, shadowhead kids to behave. You can normally get an idea of what kind of Praediti people are by the color of their eyes, but with her I could never tell."

"I've never heard of a Contego, but... it makes sense they wouldn't ever tell me. And since I was so blind, I wouldn't see it for what it was, anyway." Kato moves around Az to start walking again, the crunching of leaves under his feet filling the silence.

Great. Somehow, I pissed him off... again. Az sighs as he follows. The one positive of the new situation seems to be that Kato is clearing his path — before, they were trying to wade through the thickening brush together, but now, he simply sticks close to Kato's back and lets him do it. *For once, being so much smaller comes in handy.*

They walk like that until the darkness settles fully. Az tries not to be upset that from where they are, Cettia isn't visible. "Stupid trees," he mutters as they finally stop. His bones are aching, and he's sure Kato's aren't much better. "We should stop here."

Kato faces him and nods. "Okay... I can start a fire for us. Should we try to catch —" he looks up in the trees and frowns, but he looks more confused than angry— "I thought I heard something."

Fear spreads through Azrian's body, but he doesn't show it. "I'm sure you did. And yeah, go ahead and build a fire. I'll work on catching us something to eat." He drops his bag so Kato can build them a small shelter, then grabs his bow and a single arrow. They can't afford to waste them. "Wish me luck."

"Good luck," he states as he crouches down to work on a fire, but as Azrian walks away, he sees Kato stop and look up at the trees again.

He lets out a slow, quiet breath as he scans the area around him. The light has long since gone out, so there's nothing between him and the crippling darkness but one, single arrow. *Okay. Breathe. Kato's right there, he's not far, and clearly, he won't let anything happen to me. It's just some trees and a few creepy animals... nothing to be so afraid of.*

The sounds erupting around him have him distracted, though. He can't seem to pick any out individually which will make hunting harder, but all he needs is one. Just one.

Time passes slowly as he picks his spot and waits. From this particular vantage point, he can *just* make out the glow of the fire and the silhouette of a giant moving around, and he takes comfort in the fact that Kato's still okay. *"How's it going over there?"* he reaches out, if for no other reason than to distract himself.

"It's going okay. Fire looks good. Just a little hungry. How are you doing? Any furry shadowheads around?"

He smiles to himself in spite of everything. *"I sure hope so. I don't want to listen to your stomach growl all night. Speaking of which, eat the rest of that sweet bread. It won't be any good come tomorrow."* Movement catches his eye and he notches his arrow, squinting through the dark to try and pinpoint it.

"You don't want any? I can save you some."

A small, furry something darts out from behind the trees. *"Nah, you can have it. I know how much you like it."* He lets the arrow fly and sends up a silent apology to Cettia as it pierces the creature's heart. *"Coming back, hope the fire's hot."*

Az moves as silently as he can through the trees and picks up his prize by the tail, then heads back toward the fire. Once he gets to the clearing, he holds up the animal to get a better look at it as Kato joins him. "It's a raccanis," he says. "See the black marks around his eyes? That's how you know. It's a fat one, too. If we play our cards right, this little guy will last us for a few —" claws suddenly rake at the back of his neck, and his body jerks with fear and adrenaline as he drops the other animal and fails wildly.

"Shadows!" Kato yells, jumping up to assist. The raccanis chitters aggressively, but before Azrian can even digest what is happening, Kato speaks again: "You — Azrian, you killed his cousin. He's upset... try apologizing."

Slack-jawed, Azrian just stares at him. The dumbfounded, confused trance is broken only by the creature jumping straight at his face with enough force to knock him flat on his back. Az kicks out uselessly as he yells at the thing to get off of him, but it doesn't let up its relentless, sharp attack until he finally gives in and forces out, "Okay! Okay! I'm sorry, I shouldn't have killed your —" he pushes the thing off of him finally and scrambles back to his feet, his hand flying to his bleeding face — "your cousin? Animals have cousins? What? *Ow*."

"Stoppit!" Kato snaps his fingers to get the creature's attention. "He said sorry. Can we be civil? We had no idea animals had cousins, and even if we did... we have to eat, too." The small beast screeches at him and waves his little arms. "O— okay... okay, but that means you ate someone's cousin today, too."

Azrian's jaw goes slack again, and he mutters, "Guess that answers our question about whether or not you can control animals." He scratches the back of his head, watching as Kato continues to try and reason with the raccanis. "Uh... Kato? You might wanna tell the nutjob over here that he should leave. I'm apparently about to perform an autopsy on his kin."

"Azrian!" Kato whispers sharply, then turns back to the angry animal. "What did you expect? We're hungry. Do you want some?" A high-pitched scream comes out of his tiny body and Kato looks like he genuinely feels bad. "I'm sorry. I wasn't thinking. Here... what about sweet bread?" He picks a piece off of his bread and sits down next to the creature, smiling when his little hands snatch the food and he begins to nibble on it. "What's your name?"

More intense, confused staring. Azrian is starting to think he's losing his mind.

"Okay, Leiko. My name is Kato. That's Azrian, and we're sorry. But we need food or we'll die... we have to eat yo— okay, we have to eat *Razzil* so his death isn't in vain." More screeches signal the raccanis isn't happy about it, but he reaches a short arm out for more bread and Kato hands it over seconds before the animal darts off into a bush. "He'll get over it. I don't get the vibe they were very close cousins."

What in the shadows? "Not very close... yet he tried to rip my face off?" He shakes his head, then puts the dead raccanis down to prepare it. "I don't even know where to start with all that. I'm just glad he's gone... though I'm pretty sure giving it sugar was a bad idea."

"Oh, he's coming back in the morning," Kato states, as if that's no big deal. "He likes the bread, but I couldn't bring myself to tell him that was the last of it."

The absurdity of the situation isn't lost on Az, but he doesn't have it in him to argue. "Fine, just don't give him any more food... we'll never get rid of him then." Bit by bit, he sections off the meat and gets it cooking, and only then does he stop to dig out their first-aid kit and clean up his face. "But I guess if he *does* come back, I can just shoot him, too."

"No." Kato frowns. "You can't shoot him; I've spoken to him..."

"I'm really not sure what that has to do with anything," Azrian argues. He flips the meat, then points the knife at Kato to accentuate the words. "We're not keeping him, Kato. It's going to be hard enough to fill the mouths we have without picking up *actual* strays."

"Okay but what if he can help? With berries and high-up fruit," he argues, and Az doesn't exactly have an answer to that.

It doesn't stop him from trying. "I can climb, and we've got Rhix's list. We know what berries we can eat... unless you're talking about using him as a poison tester, in which case.... sure, the nutjob can come along for a while. But *only* until we can do it for ourselves."

"His name is Leiko, and I was meaning so we won't have to climb. We can help each other." Kato walks over and studies his face. "You missed a few cuts, let me help."

Az just nods and tips his chin back so Kato can see better. "Your little friend did this to me, just remember that."

"He was mourning. I don't know what that is like, but I can imagine." Kato grabs a colwort leaf and squeezes some of the gel from inside it onto his hand, then dabs Azrian's cut. "He won this fight you know," Kato teases.

The urge to flip Kato off is strong, but the colwort feels so good he can't bring himself to argue. "Very funny." He sighs quietly at the relief and reaches up to hold on to Kato's shoulders. "He scratched by back up too, if you're offering to help."

"Of course, take off your shirt so I can get a better look. We still have a few moments before the meat is cooked." Kato turns him slowly and starts to help lift his shirt, but Az pulls away to do it himself. The fire provides enough light that he knows Kato will see, and he also knows it's nothing Kato hasn't seen before... but he's still a little nervous. The scars on his torso tell a story his mouth will not.

Kato waits, but he watches Azrian pull it off a little too intently. Az doesn't have time to think about it much further though, because when Kato notices a certain scar, he frowns. "What happened here?"

"Nothing," he says quietly. His shoulders scrunch a little in protest of someone else touching him, but he forces himself to relax. "It was a long time ago."

"Okay," Kato says simply as he begins applying the gel to his wounds. Neither of them speak until after he's finished and walking over to rinse his hands. "How's the meat?"

He keeps his head low to hide his face. "It's fine, probably ready to eat... it'll be hot though. Blow on it before you put it in your mouth." While normally, he'd laugh at his own innuendo, he can't bring himself to do it now. Despite his initial reaction, he can't deny that having Kato's strong, gentle hands ghosting over his skin felt good. He doubts it has anything to do with Kato himself, but rather the months he's spent without that kind of contact with someone else. Years, if he's being honest.

Sure enough, as Azrian pulls the meat from the fire, it looks like it's ready to eat. They don't have much in the way of plates, but thankfully, they're in no shortage of leaves the size of Kato's head. He plucks one from the forest floor and wipes it off as best as he can, then loads it up and passes it over.

"Thanks." Kato takes it and sits down, blowing on it before he takes a bite. Based on his face, it isn't great, and Az sighs quietly as he gets some for himself.

"Sorry, Jellycrai. I tried."

～

Surprisingly, Kato sleeps well that night. He wakes to Azrian shoving his arm, telling him they overslept thanks to the trees blocking the bright sun's rays. Jumping up, he looks around to take in his surroundings. If he has to guess, they didn't oversleep too badly, but Az seems flustered and when he sees the bags under his eyes, it's apparent he didn't sleep as well as Kato did.

The nearby bush begins to shake, and it has him grabbing for his spear, knowing anything could come jumping out at them — but when Leiko walks out, he sets it aside with a small smile. "Good morning, Leiko. I wasn't sure you'd return."

They ignore Az's scoff and the raccanis speaks to him as best he can. "Said would return."

"I know, but... you were also very upset."

"Because cousin. Bread help."

"I'm sorry, we're... out of the bread. I gave you the last of it." Kato looks around for something else that *isn't* the poor animal's family member. "Maybe we have something else..."

Az snaps his fingers to get his attention. "Listen, tell Nut that if he's going to stick around, he needs to get his own food. And I can't promise I won't be feeding you his great-aunt a couple nights from now."

Kato gives Azrian a pointed look and Leiko actually laughs. "You liked that nickname? Okay, Nut."

Nut says he doesn't actually care for the nickname, but he also doesn't care much about what he's called regardless, so Kato fibbed just a little to appease Azrian. If they can make some kind of food arrangement, Nut will stick around, and Kato's not in a position to be turning down extra company at the moment. He listens to Nut's terms and then turns to Azrian to bargain, expecting an uphill battle. "Okay, Nut says Cettia won't be visible at all for weeks. His deal is he sticks around and we protect him, help him find food, and he will help guide us."

Sadness crosses Azrian's face and he nods, deflating a little bit. "Of course it won't. Whatever, just keep him away from me... and if he scratches me again, we're eating *him*."

"*Play nice?*" Nut asks, and Kato nods.

"Yes, he will play nice if you do, too. We all will. If you're going to tag along, you two can't fight the whole time. Deal, Azrian?"

"Yeah, sure." He tears down the tarp they were using as shelter and folds it up, then continues packing. "Ask him if he knows where a stream or something is."

Kato looks at Nut — knowing he heard Az for himself — and he tells him he knows of one. "He says he'll lead us there when we're packed. He says it cuts through the forest a few times and we'll come across it often if we stay on course."

"Finally, some good news in this stupid forest." Az continues on for several moments, cursing everything from the ground to Cettia using words Kato has never heard before. When his rant is finally over, he points at Nut. "Lead the way, the faster we get out of this place, the better."

Kato adjusts his satchel and follows with Nut close behind. He isn't sure if he should bring up Azrian's anger, so he doesn't. He has a feeling it would just make it worse.

By the time Nut runs out in front, he knows they are coming up on the stream and the sound of flowing water fills his ears. Az carefully sets down the bag he's been hauling and wades quickly in, throwing himself forward until he's completely submerged... clothes and all.

Nut chitters a little and turns inquisitive eyes on Kato. "*Does it swim?*"

"Yes. *It* does," he jokes, smiling over at Az. "I think the cool water will help him stop being a shadowhead." Kato sets his stuff down and starts to strip for a bath.

"I heard that," Az says, apparently back above water. "I'm not being a shadowhead. I'm just... tired, and I miss being able to see." He hums as he draws his energy, but nothing happens. Kato stands in just his boxers as over and over, Azrian tries to spread light around them and nothing happens at all. "What in the *shadows* is happening?" Az yells, scrambling back out of the water and trying again. "Nut, you little shit... what's in this stream!"

"*Not stream,*" Nut says to Kato as he hides behind him.

"He said it's not the stream. It's just clean water, Az. I think you're just exhausted." Kato wafts into the water and waits until he's chest-height to take his boxers off, but no one is paying any attention to him at all. Azrian's on his knees and staring at his hands like they've betrayed him... and maybe they have.

After a moment, Az gets up and wrings out his drenched hair, then removes most of his soaked clothes. "I don't know how we're supposed to get anywhere without light," he snaps to the sky.

"Fire sticks!" Kato states excitedly. "The ones I saw in your mind all those months ago." He finishes with the soap and makes his way to Azrian, whose eyes widen as he approaches.

"You... um... Ka— um..."

Nut covers his eyes with both paws and shakes his head.

"I brought you the soap." Kato looks at Nut and then back at Azrian with a confused frown.

"*Penis out,*" Nut states, but all it does is confuse Kato more.

"Well..." he looks down at himself. "I'm bathing. Of course my penis is out."

Azrian sighs and snatches the soap from his hand, then stomps back toward the water. "Makes all the *giant* comments a lot less funny," he mutters to himself. "Of course he is, why wouldn't he be? Sweet shadows... I want out of this forest."

Nut makes a sound a lot like a laugh and falls to the ground, rolling on his back.

"I don't— the animal is laughing at me. Did you even know they laughed?" Kato pulls up his boxers and rolls his eyes. "And I don't know why you think my penis is giant right now, the water was cold."

"The water was cold," Az mocks. "Great, so I'll have to come up with a word more giant-y than giant. Excellent." He scrubs his skin quickly then gathers the suds to wash his hair. "You can't use fire st— *torches* — in forest this dense. It isn't safe. That's why we need to find those little clearings for fires."

"That makes sense." Kato goes a little upstream to drink some water and refill both of their canteens. "Do you want to rest today? So, you can try to use your powers after?"

Az shakes his head. "We don't have time to take unnecessary breaks. I'll be fine, I'm sure it was just... anxiety or something." He gets out to dry off and notices Nut still laughing, but while Kato tenses, nothing happens.

They silently pack up, and like the twins, Nut tells Kato he's a funny human. Instead of correcting him — telling him that he *isn't* a human — he ignores it. Part of him wishes he were for the simple fact that it would be easier, but the scars on Azrian's body remind him that isn't true.

No matter what you are, it's a cruel world.

~

"How about we settle here?" Kato asks, drained from another long day of traveling. Nut has definitely come in handy; he's kept them fed on fresh fruit from deep in the trees and he's the only one completely adapted to life in Cettia's shadow.

As he stares at the small beast, he listens to him yammer on about the ground and the trees. "*Why do I have to hear your complaining?*" he asks with a small smirk. Azrian is also complaining about the tree cover and how they can't see Cettia, and instead of commenting about hearing everyone's complaints all day, he decides to have a little fun.

Connecting minds isn't easy. He was able to do it with Cal in that moment because his adrenaline was pumping and it was a life-or-death situation, but that was only the third time he'd ever tried it in his life. He imagines connecting Az and Nut will be difficult, but the thought has him giggling before he even attempts it. He avoids looking into Az's mind in the process and focuses on Nut's thoughts, almost shoving them into Az's mind one word at a time. *"Tree."*

Azrian stands taller and looks over at Kato. "What?"

"What?" Kato bites back his smile and tilts his head.

"I thought I— never mind." He goes back to their packs, and Kato connects them again.

"Grouchy human."

Kato snorts at what he picked up that time and he bends over to busy himself and hide his expression.

"Who's grouchy?" Az asks, turning to face Kato again with pinched eyebrows. "Look, I'm sorry if I've been a little on edge, but it's not like I asked to be here. And why'd you say it in such a weird voice?"

"What are you talking about?" Kato manages to rush out, still avoiding his gaze.

"Scratch grouchy human." Nut jumps up on Az's leg and launches off of him into the tree, and the screech Azrian lets out is confirmation enough that Nut succeeded.

"Sweet *shadows*," he curses, lightly touching the spot that's already bleeding. "What just happened?" He scrambles to his feet and searches for Nut in the branches. "Get back here, you little..."

Kato's unable to fight his giggle this time, and he lets Az hear Nut's squeaky laughter as he ascends higher in the tree. *"Azrian slow."*

Barking a laugh, Kato finally meets Az's eyes but tries to play innocent. "What's wrong?"

"Did he just call me slow? Did I just *hear* him call me slow?" He glances from the raccanis back to Kato and rubs the back of his neck, loudly wondering if he's going crazy. Kato can tell the exact moment Az works it out but doesn't react fast enough — Azrian's face snaps toward his and the next thing Kato knows, he's being tackled to the forest floor.

Kato's fully laughing now and lets him believe he can win this match for a few moments. "What's wrong? He just wanted to say hi."

Az adjusts his grip in an attempt to pin him, but Kato can see the amusement finally budding in his expression. "I barely want him around, I certainly don't wanna listen to him insulting me," Az says.

"I have to listen to him all day." Kato finally bucks into the air and flips them, pinning Az to the dirt with his body weight. "I thought you might be curious."

"Cur—" Az exhales sharply, his body going limp under Kato. "What?"

He stays and tries to figure out why Az gave up so quickly. "What?" Kato's eyes travel his face and he suddenly has the urge to kiss him, but Nut chitters next to them and they can both clearly hear his thoughts: *No sex. No want see that.*

A deep blush graces Azrian's cheeks and he coughs as he pushes Kato's chest. "Make it stop."

Kato instantly recognizes the dismissal and gets off of Azrian, disconnecting them in seconds. "There. All gone."

"Giant squish him."

"Shut up, Nut. Are you okay, Az? I didn't squish you, right?" Kato holds out a hand to help him stand, and Az brushes himself off afterward.

"No, I'm— that was... it was fine. I'm fine." He's still blushing but goes back to what he was doing beforehand, keeping his back to Kato and ignoring Nut's chitters. One single thought slips through before Kato can manage to block him out again: *Gods, I hope he doesn't judge me for liking that.*

It makes him smile because he feels the same. Pinning Az was... *Stop, these are dangerous thoughts.* He pushes them all aside and gets back to work, and once their campsite is set, they lay down and stare up at the trees. In his time outside, he's grown so fond of Cettia that he actually understands why Az is so drawn to it. "What was that animal we saw today? It had a bushy tail and pink, round ears... it darted up the tree."

"Uh... it was a dorscuir. They're pesky little things but not bad to eat if you can catch them."

"It was kind of cute. Its thoughts were even harder to hear than Nut's." Kato looks over to see Az's silhouette. "And I haven't eaten poison... so that's a plus."

The soft sound of laughter fills the night as Azrian rolls a little closer. "A very big plus, Jellycrai. Can't have you checking out on me now, I need you."

"I know." He doesn't mean to sound cocky, but Azrian's thoughts about that are loud sometimes. "I need you too, Azzy."

"Good." Az pushes himself up and sighs as he fumbles through the darkness, nearly tripping on Nut as he makes his way toward the small pile of wood they'd gathered. "It's getting colder tonight than normal; I'm going to start a fire. Are you hungry?"

"Yeah. But if we need to conserve, I can wait until morning." Kato's truly starving, but he doesn't want Az to worry about it. "Maybe we can move... closer tonight? For warmth."

Az smiles as he squats down to light the fire. "Cuddling with you isn't the *worst* thing," he jokes. "But I don't want another night where your stomach keeps me awake, so you're eating. Just have to wait for the flames to get hot enough."

Kato smiles back and hugs his knees, watching Az move around. "Only if you eat, too."

"Yes, Sir," Az says with a playful tilt of his head, but his expression changes quickly when one of the burning logs falls off the pile and lands at Azrian's feet. He tries to stand but loses his balance and falls backward, giving the log just enough time to ignite the dry leaves around them. He moves fast — grabbing one of the thick capus-skin blankets Rhix gave them and falling on top of the log, yelling senselessly about Kato needing to run when the problem is completely contained.

Kato rushes to help, unable to even remember what they were talking about prior to the fire. "Az. It's okay, it's out." He pulls him in for a hug, hoping to calm him. He doesn't have to look into his mind to know why he's so spooked. "You're okay. We're okay. Breathe. Fire is gone. We'll cuddle for warmth and we have some berries from Nut. We're okay. Can I keep holding you for a little bit?"

He buries his face in Kato's chest and lets out a shaky breath, nodding and wrapping his arms tightly around his waist. "We can still cook on the main fire, it's lit anyway. I just... thought it was going to get out of control, that's all."

"You were too fast. Much faster than I was." Kato rests his face in Az's hair, inhaling the only scent he finds comforting in this forest. "You did good, Az. We're safe because of you."

"Yeah, I put out a fire *I* started. Good for me," he says quietly, then pulls back from Kato and holds his hand for a moment. "You can tell Nut it's safe to come back, I think I heard him run off when the log fell."

"Nut's fine. I can hear him up there." Kato squeezes his hand and meets his gaze. "Stop being so hard on yourself all the time, Az. I'd be dead without you."

~

The next day is quiet. Az doesn't speak much, Nut keeps his distance, and Kato is left wondering what other traumas will be coming their way... and if there will ever be a time that he can play around with Azrian without something or someone reminding them of what they've been through. He doubts it, but that doesn't stop the prospect from being something he looks forward to.

They settle down for the night; Nut between Kato's legs and Az on the other side of the fire staring up at a sky he can't see. He opts for telepathy — not wanting to disrupt the song coming from the forest around them — and reaches out to Az. *"I've really grown fond of the sounds out here... especially at night."*

"I've... heard worse," Az admits. *"Hey, I'm sorry I've been so hard to deal with. I think a big part of me regrets leaving Rhix's house."*

"It's okay. I'd still choose to be here if that helps at all," he offers. *"We'll make it through... any... progress tonight?"*

"Nah," Az says. *"Still nothing at all. I don't get it, Kato. I mean... why now? Why is it that the moment I need them the most, they're gone? I don't understand. But... thank you for saying that. Humans aren't worth a whole lot."*

"Why would you say that? Praediti are no better than humans, Azrian. If the world were less divided, maybe it would be a better world." He can't help but frown, knowing Az feels that way because of circumstances. But what if it's possible to change those circumstances? What if the Regnum actually do something good, like work on equality? It seems like it's their job to keep the peace, and peace includes humans. He doesn't understand why they haven't done something before now.

It takes so long for Azrian to answer him that Kato thinks he might have fallen asleep. But just as Kato himself is about to drift off, Azrian's voice fills his mind. *"Maybe you growing up in Deadrun wasn't all bad. You've got a purer heart than anyone else I've ever met, Jellycrai. Get some rest, we're halfway there."*

Kato smiles to himself at the nickname. He tries to think of one for Azrian, but before he can, sleep pulls him under, and he dreams of a different world. A better one, where humans and Praediti work together. Even his subconscious knows it's a dream, but he has to have hope that it's possible. If Azrian has taught him anything, it's that settling is not an option, and even if it takes his whole life to convince a small handful of people that peace is possible... he has to try.

~

After a few more days of the same routine, all three of them are completely exhausted and to Kato's surprise, Nut is the first to take a stand. "*Break*," he commands, sitting down on the ground with a plop. "*Water*."

Kato looks back and sighs to himself. "Azrian, Nut needs a break. He's thirsty. We've been walking for five hours; can we take a bit? My feet hurt and I'm hungry."

"Yeah," Azrian replies. "I can hear the stream, just sit down. I'll be back." He grabs their canteen and heads off through the dimly lit trees on his own as Nut flops over onto his back with a squeak.

He looks comfortable enough to copy, and soon, both of them are sprawled out and staring up at the trees above them. "Do the trees ever end?"

Nut replies a simple "*no*" but then says something that brings Kato some hope. "*Four days to Etria. Trees never end.*"

"Well, I didn't mean literally. I actually like trees, but four days... we can do four days." *At least there is an end in sight.*

When Az comes back with water, Kato and Nut stay where they were, only lifting their heads to ensure it's him. "Nut said four more days."

"Right," Az says quietly. He hands Kato the canteen and then glares at Nut as he sinks down onto his butt. "We can rest here, but we're too exposed. We can't stay long."

"I kn—" Kato pauses, trying to understand what he just heard. "The — what?" He turns toward the brush seconds before a gigantic valianis walks out. His paws are nearly as big as Nut's entire body and the markings on his face became clearer with every step. "Stop." Kato stands, holding out his hands to take the creature in. He doesn't feel threatened, but his ice blue eyes have Kato frozen in place.

Az notches an arrow instantly. "Kato, move!"

"No, wait!" Kato moves in front of the arrow and faces the valianis. "Hello, I'm Kato. This is Azrian and Nut. Can you repeat what you said? I couldn't make it out."

The animal's eyes dart between them, and his voice is much clearer in his mind this time. *"I'm called Axis. There's no time. The avisim are coming."*

"What's avisim?"

Instantly, Az tilts his bow higher. "Remember those giant things we saw when we got here? That we're swinging through the trees *and* flying?" he asks quickly. "Those are avisim."

"He says they're coming. Like... now." A branch snaps from up above and no one moves.

"They're here. I will help you."

Kato doesn't speak out loud — he can feel them watching, but he has to let Azrian know. *"They're here and Axis is going to help us fight. Axis is the valianis' name."*

Axis slowly stalks forward, eyeing Nut and taking a protective stance in front of them all. *"Is this dinner?"*

"No. That's Nut. He's... family," Kato says, because after the things they've survived together, "friend" doesn't seem to suffice.

When the first avisim drops to the forest floor, Az fires his arrow and strikes it between the eyes. With a high-pitched grunt, it falls, but three more quickly take its place. From somewhere behind him, Azrian screams for Kato to run, but there's nowhere *to* run. Their path is completely blocked, so Kato swiftly grabs his spear and prepares for a fight.

Nut is screeching loudly, making the avisim hesitate in their charge, and Axis' snarl could be heard for miles. Kato tosses his spear and hits the chest of one on the ground just as another drops from the trees and lands on his head. The wails coming from the creature are deafening, and he falls to his knees as the beast carves up his face.

The *thwack* of Azrian's arrow hitting home is the most welcome sound he's ever heard. The avisim's weight leaves Kato's body as it falls limp, and Az is there a moment later to help him back to his feet. "Up, Kato! Here!" He shoves a bloody spear back into his hand and whirls at the sound of tearing flesh — and Kato follows just in time to watch Axis rip the throat out of the largest one they've seen yet.

The forest around them grows deadly silent as the remaining avisim stare. Az sidesteps slowly toward Kato and makes eye contact, so Kato listens: *"What are they thinking? Do I keep shooting?"*

"They —" Kato listens as they argue. "We killed their leader... Axis did. They're scared." The avisim back away, launching off the floor and into the trees. "They said our scraps aren't worth another life." He falls to his knees, his face aching from the assault. "Ass."

"Wait, they got your ass, too?" Azrian kneels next to him and puts a hand on his shoulder.

"What?" He looks up confused. No, my ass is fine. Is *your* ass okay?" Kato asks, trying to look around at his backside.

Az turns to block him and holds out a hand. "But you — wait a minute, were you trying to cuss? Shadows, Kato. I'm beginning to think you need to take *that* from my head, too. But come on... let me see if we have any colwort left." He digs around through their trashed rest site and comes up short. "Okay, it's okay. Here." He pulls off his shirt and turns it inside out, then uses one of the few clean patches left to dab up the blood. "We'll make do until we can find some more. Maybe Axis or Nut can help?"

Just then, Nut comes up with a fresh leaf, handing it to Azrian and then checking on Kato himself. *"Kato, okay?"*

He nods with a small smile. "Yes, Nut. Kato is okay." The fact that Nut cares so much has him feeling a tightness in his chest, and Az cleaning his wounds makes it even tighter. Axis is still close by and Kato hopes he sticks around. "Axis... thank you."

"You are welcome, Kato. Is Azrian alright?"

"Axis wants to know you're alright, Az. Talk to him."

The look he gets in return is confusing, but then again, there's a good deal of that radiating off of Azrian. "Um... I hate to break this

to you, Jellycrai, but I can't talk to animals. I mean... I *am* okay—"
he turns to face Axis — "I'm okay, but... wow, you're big. Okay, let's
just—" Axis moves forward slowly, and they're practically eye-level
— "let's just take it easy." Az stumbles back and falls with a grunt,
then throws his arm up in defense. "Kato! Why is he looking at me
like I'm dinner? Tell him to eat one of the avisim!"

"He isn't. He wants to know you're okay. He... likes you." Kato
chuckles.

Axis nudges his arm gently and sits in front of him, but it barely
seems to make a difference in his height. "*I'm here to help.*"

"He said he's here to help. Axis, you can eat that big one, you
earned him."

"*Thank you.*" Axis nods but doesn't move. He sticks by Azrian despite the uneasiness written all over his face.

"Can we keep him, too?" Kato asks, crawling closer to them as
Nut screams something at him in a language he doesn't understand.

Az slowly reaches a hand out to touch Axis' nose. "I'm certainly
not going to tell him he has to leave, are *you?*" he asks skeptically.
"Will you shut yours up though? I think my ears are bleeding."

"Nut is scared. They're sort of arguing right now, but Nut just
wants to know he won't eat him. Axis *did* ask if he was dinner earlier. Come here, Nut." The raccanis climbs into his lap and glares at
Axis, but quiets down soon after. "There. He's quiet. They agreed to
stick to their own humans... whatever that means."

"Yeah," Az agrees, clearly still nervous. "Whatever that means.
Can you walk? We should get going... the faster we get out of this
forest, the better."

"Yeah, I'm fine." Kato touches a deep cut on his cheek and
stands. "The colwort felt good. Thank you for grabbing that, Nut."

~

Like Nut, Axis is an extremely useful traveling companion. He
may not be able to climb trees, but tonight he brought them a few

dorscuirs, and for the first time ever, all of them have their own animal to eat. Kato hums happily as he takes a bite and stares at the
giant beast fondly. "Thank you for dinner. With your hunting skills
and Az's cooking skills, we'll never go hungry again."

"You're welcome," Axis' deep voice sounds in Kato's mind. *"The
forest will thicken soon, and wildlife will be scarce. Eat your fill while you
can."*

He nods and looks over at Azrian, watching him stare into their
campfire as if it might combust any moment. *He needs a distraction.*
"Hey, Az? Do you know of any games we can play? They played
some at Deadrun, but I wasn't allowed to play."

The sudden interaction seems to startle him, and he jumps
slightly as he looks over. "What? Oh, um... yeah. I know the feeling,
the Praediti kids in Embermeadow didn't usually let the humans
play with them, but we had a few games of our own." He licks his
lips and looks around. "Okay, we played this game called Occy. It
originally started when we were making fun of the Oculare, but
kinda stuck. What you do is describe something, anything at all. It
could be something you've seen or something you want, but you
can't say what it is. The other person has to guess what it is, and
then if they can guess if you've seen it or want it, they get more
points. Usually, we just played until we got bored or ran out of
ideas, we never really had a winner or anything."

Kato's smiling as he sits up more and thinks of one to say. "I want
to play! Okay I got one... it's something I want."

"You're not supposed to tell me," Az laughs. "But okay, go
ahead."

"Okay... it's sweet... and made of bread." He bites his lip in excitement as he waits for Az to guess.

He smiles slowly. "Um... sweet bread?"

"You're good! Shadows I want some sweet bread right now...
Okay, your turn." Kato makes sure to completely block off Az's
mind, he doesn't want to cheat.

"Jellycrai... you have to be less obvious about it than that. Like... hmm. The thing I'm thinking of is wet, it feels good, it's only found one place and it only works with certain people around."

Kato frowns at him and tries to figure it out. *It's wet and feels good... well I doubt he means what I automatically thought of.* He almost blushes at his thoughts. *Only found in one place and only works with certain people around... shadows... what is he talking about?* "Um... is this a sex thing?"

"No," Az says quickly, clearing his throat and squirming where he's sitting. "It's not."

Kato scratches his head and thinks harder. "Wet... I don't know, Az. I was thinking... wait, a shower?"

His body relaxes. "Yes, the showers at Deadrun. Can you guess if it's something I want or just something I've seen?"

"I think you want it. I want one too, Az... but baths aren't so bad." Kato takes another bite and thinks of his next one as Az tells him he's right, but falls silent after like there's something else he doesn't want to say. Instead of peeking, he focuses on the game. "Okay... I have one. I'm thinking of something that looks fluffy and sweet, but you don't want to cuddle it... or eat it."

This time, Az looks truly stumped. He fidgets with his food and eats slowly with his brows pinched until it finally licks — "Mors Byssum?"

"Dammit! I should just quit." Kato laughs at how bad he sucks at this game and then waves a hand. "Your turn."

"Hey, you got the last one of mine right. I'm going to say that's just something you've seen, not something you want... and for mine—" he bites his lip and looks around the forest, then snaps his fingers — "It's really bright, guides me home, and I'm utterly lost without it."

"Cettia. Seen *and* want." Kato hugs his knees and tries to think of something that might stump Az. Instead of focusing on things they've seen or tried together, he digs deeper down to the thing he longs for the most — a family. "There's a man and a woman. They're standing over a crib and staring down at a little boy... the woman is humming something to him. What are they doing? And why am I thinking it?"

Az stares at him like he's trying to read between the lines, then pushes himself up to walk over and kneel in front of him. "They're comforting their son, and... my guess is you're thinking about it because it's not something you had. It's something you want. A mom and dad that love you."

The sadness that washes over him is unexpected, but he feels better with Az closer. "Yeah... even just one of them." The scene he'd just described came from Ronan's memory, not his own, and he finds himself wondering what it feels like to be loved.

"Kato, I'm so sorry." Az climbs into his lap and wraps his arms around his neck, squeezing tightly. "You should've had that."

The hug makes him smile and he holds Az close for a while as the fire slowly dwindles. "Thank you. This feels nice."

"We should get comfortable, but if you want me to lay with you tonight, I will. I didn't mean to make you sad... it was just supposed to be a game." He rubs Kato's back and climbs off of him to finish his cold food and set up their makeshift bed, and when they settle in together, Az ends up almost on top of him. "Is this okay?"

"More than okay." Kato smiles against the messy mop of Azrian's hair and sighs. "And you didn't make me sad earlier... I'm sorry I made the game sad."

Soft fingers trail down Kato's side as Azrian shakes his head. "It's not your fault. It happens sometimes, especially when we don't have everything we want. I can't promise it'll sound any good, but if you want... I can hum to you. I think I remember the song my mom used to sing me."

"Really?" Kato's eyes widen slightly in disbelief. "I'd... yeah. I'd like that, Azzy."

The first few notes are almost too quiet to hear — so much so that Kato wouldn't know he's humming at all if not for the vibrations coming from his chest. But as he gains confidence and hums a little louder, the forest around them seems to still for the first time since their arrival, like not even the creatures around them want to disturb the sound.

It isn't until Az finishes that the trees begin to move again, and even then, it's a while longer before the silence is disturbed by Axis reaching into Kato's mind. *"The trees are more alive in this part of the forest. They hear him, just as we do."*

Kato smiles, rubbing Az's back in slow circles. "The forest likes your voice almost as much as I do," he whispers.

"Shhh." Az mumbles something under his breath and buries his face in Kato's armpit, then laughs at himself and lifts back up. "Yeah, we should try to take baths before we get going tomorrow. We're getting smelly."

But despite his words, Az only cuddles closer, and Kato knows it really doesn't bother him. He doesn't have to look into his mind to know that Az finds his smell comforting, especially because he feels the exact same. The scent of Az reminds Kato every single day that he isn't alone, and smelly or not, it's the only thing they have that feels like home.

~

Traveling on Axis' back isn't the most comfortable. Kato imagines it isn't too bad for one person alone, but two people and an overweight raccanis leaves little wiggle room. The trees are so thick up ahead that Kato's convinced it's impossible to get through, but Axis insists he can. If Nut is correct, this should be their last challenge in the Simbian Forest, and right on the other side of this is the beginning of Etria.

"That's really thick, Ax. How are you gonna get through there at all, let alone with us on your back?"

The valianis takes a few steps forward, and just as Kato and Az begin to lean down to seek shelter in his fur, the trees begin to slowly part to make a pathway just large enough for their bodies. *"I told you. The trees are more alive here, they'll make way for me."*

Kato stares slack-jawed at the trees and updates Az in a whisper when he tenses in front of him. "He believes they're more alive here at the edge... maybe so the forest can protect itself from those who come to destroy." He feels them around him, and the buzz of the forest has his hair standing on edge. It's absolutely breathtaking. "Thank you, trees."

If they're capable of communicating the way animals do, they don't show it, but Kato takes comfort in their silence. They bend and bow, twisting around themselves and moving Athoze itself to let them through. He knows in that moment that no matter how many times he'll try, he'll never quite be able to capture it on parchment... and somehow, that brings him comfort, too.

When they finally break through and reach the forest's edge, Kato fears the animals will leave them. It makes him *almost* sad to say goodbye to the forest behind them. *"Will you guys... stay? With us?"* he asks, stopping just before the clearing.

"Me stay with Kato," Nut says quickly, sitting on his back legs.

Axis looks to a confused Azrian and nods. *"I'm staying, too."*

Kato has learned over the last few days that Axis is nearly seven hundred years old, and his full sentences make him much easier to talk to than other animals. "They said they're coming with us, Azrian. All the way."

"Oh," he says with a small nod. "That's good, but you're going to have to put yours on a diet." He steps closer to Axis and fists a hand in his long, black fur. "Nut eats more than the rest of us combined... he's getting chubby."

Nut screeches at Azrian. *"You skinny. Not my fault."*

"Azrian, you hurt his feelings and now he's defensive." Kato speaks into his mind to keep Nut from listening. *"I don't know how to put him on a diet. He doesn't listen well."*

Chuckling, Az moves a branch out of his way to get to Kato. *"Tell him no when he tries to eat fourth helpings at dinner, maybe,"* he says with a smirk. "Hey, your cuts are... wow. They're gone, how did that...?" He reaches up to brush his fingers along Kato's cheek, his brows pinched.

Kato shrugs. He doesn't have a mirror, but the soreness had stopped the day after, so he had a feeling they'd healed. "I've always healed quickly. We should get going, who knows if we'll find somewhere to rest tonight."

"Course," Azrian agrees as he drops his hand. "You're right, as always." They walk a few more paces to the edge of the trees, and Azrian sucks in a deep breath. "Okay. One forest down, one terrible desert left to go. We can do this, we just... have to..."

~ XII ~

THE ETRIAN DESERT

The sight of Cettia nearly brings Azrian to his knees. He hadn't realized how much he truly needed that star until it was gone — not just as a guide home, but as a beacon of hope. As something to believe in when everything else in the world falls flat. Cettia won't betray him. It'll always be there, bright and shining through the clouds to let him know he's not alone... and that there's more to the night than darkness.

"Hi," he whispers to the sky. Axis provides solidity behind him as Kato and Nut snore to his left, but he's not worried. He won't wake any of them... and he needs this, no matter how ridiculous it seems. "I'm uh... sorry for my behavior in the forest. I was scared... though, I won't admit that to anyone but you. I don't know what happened to my powers, but they're gone. And with Axis around for protection and Nut here to tell Kato what berries to avoid... I feel... useless. Like a zipper without a track, or a sheath without a blade. I should be happy... I never wanted to be a Praediti... or shadows, maybe I did." Azrian tips his head back and feels Axis sigh. "Maybe I hated them so much because they were everything I never could be. Maybe I rebelled against the powers because I couldn't understand why they waited so long to show themselves, and I was kidnapped because of them. Or maybe I just... maybe I just suck."

When Axis snorts, Az gently elbows him. "Shush. Go to sleep, you great big fluff ball. Don't judge me. And don't tell Kato, either." When all he gets in response is an absolutely judgmental stare, Az curls up against him and finally falls silent. Cettia won't answer — *can't* answer — and all Azrian's doing is making himself feel worse.

It's definitely smarter to sleep.

~

The days are so hot that Az isn't sure how they keep moving. The layers don't help as much as he was told they would, and he can't decide if it's worth risking the sunburn to take them off, or if he should just stop complaining and suffocate under them.

Kato hasn't said much in a while. Not out loud, anyway. But from the way Nut is chittering incessantly and Axis keeps tipping his head in question, Az can tell that there's a conversation happening, alright — he's just not a part of it.

Instead of interrupting, he soldiers on. Talking takes energy, and energy happens to be something they're all running particularly low on. Their water supply is low, and while they'd reach Hollowater soon, he's not sure how much longer he can keep walking without taking a break.

"Can we stop? Just for a minute?" he asks, but Kato doesn't seem to hear him. He clears his throat. "Hello?"

Silence.

Rolling his eyes, Az changes course and heads to the right, toward one of the huge Eodren trees that provide shade. If the others follow, they follow... and if not...

He slams the spile into the bark with a muttered apology. The shade feels incredible, and he strips down to almost nothing without thinking twice about it as he waits for the liquid salvation to flow. As it begins to trickle out, he drinks his fill greedily and then lets the cool water soothe his cracked skin.

The footsteps of the others are muffled thanks to the sand, but he hears them all the same. "Oh, you finally noticed," he says lightly.

"Why are you being such an ass?" Kato walks over and begins to strip down too. "We were in the middle of a conversation."

"A conversation I can't even hear," he mutters under his breath. "Sorry to disturb you." The bitterness makes him wince, but he doesn't take it back. He simply moves out of Kato's way and spreads the blanket out to lay on.

Kato goes under the water, drinking and practically moaning when it hits his skin. "Shadows... how can you still be a grouch under this water?"

Oh, I don't know, he thinks to himself. *Maybe because my bones hurt, my skin hurts, I wish we wouldn't have done this, and now my only companion spends all his time talking to animals I can't hear.* Az can't bring himself to say it out loud, so he just clears his throat and answers simply, "Sorry. I guess I'm just eager to get to a bed. We're only a day or so out from Hollowater."

"A bed..." Kato sighs, as if it's the best word he's heard in his life. "I'd starve for a day just to sleep in a bed for a night."

Not for the first time, Az feels bad for dragging Kato along. He could be back at a Deadrun, cool and dry, with a comfortable bed and three meals a day. *But he'd be a prisoner,* he reminds himself. *And at Melior's mercy... Adeinde's mercy.* His voice softens. "We'll get there. And I promise, we'll take a day to eat our fill, take actual baths, and sleep in our own beds."

Kato drinks some water, and then cups his hands under the stream to give Axis and Nut some as well. "Our own bed sounds amazing, but if there's only one, that's fine. I've grown used to your body next to mine."

Azrian's stomach flips. They've only cuddled a few times since leaving Embermeadow, but each of those times is seared into his brain. "We might only be able to afford one," he says with a blush. "I'm glad you don't mind."

"Not at all. Even though you're a shadowhead," Kato jokes. He pulls out the spile and walks over to sit much too close. "This unforgiving sun makes you miss the forest, huh?"

"I'm not sure anything will make me miss that forest. Scorching sun is better than never-ending darkness." He rubs some colwort over the worst cracks in his own skin and nods to Kato. "Come here, your shoulders look pretty burnt. You're too close to the sky," he teases quietly.

"Is that a tall joke? Why are you burnt too then?" he retorts with a grin, turning around for Az to get the back of his neck.

Az takes his time rubbing the gel into Kato's skin in soothing circles. "I don't really have an excuse." As he steps back to get dressed again, it hits him how hard he's been on Kato lately. "You wanna ride Axis the rest of the way?"

"Would he let me... and Nut?" He has a silent conversation with Axis and sighs. "He said not Nut." Nut chitters and walks up to Az, sitting on his back legs and holding his arms up as his fingers flex. "He wants to know if you'll carry him."

Blinking, Azrian takes in the chubby raccanis' form. "He gained a lot of weight in the forest, Kato. I *can't* carry him, at least not very far." But when Nut looks devastated and Kato eyes soften in disappointment, Az knows he doesn't have a choice. "I suppose this is what I get," he mutters, leaning down to scoop up the not-so-small creature. Nut squirms in his arms and is heavier than Azrian thought he'd be, but when Kato breathes a sigh of relief atop Axis, Az bites back any potential complaint.

"We can switch in a few hours. You need to rest too; I just need to rest my... everything for a bit." Kato cuddles into the beast's soft fur, his eyes fluttering a little. "How many times have you done sex?" he asks randomly.

"Had, Kato. It's how many times have you *had* sex. It's something you have, not something you do... though, now that I say it out loud like that, it seems backward. Whatever." Az shifts the raccanis in his arms and struggles to keep up on his short legs. "And to answer your question... not enough."

"I've never had it... or done it? Whatever. Is it better than your hands?"

Az swallows thickly. "Did you just say *hands*? As in... plural? Both? More than one at a time?"

"Yes. I use both so I can hold the whole thing. You didn't answer the question. Is it better?" Kato sits up on Axis to stare at Az, a curious expression on his face.

Poor Nut nearly falls to the ground, but Az fumbles quickly to regain his grip after he trips. "Shadows... you — okay. Uh—" his thoughts get a little fuzzy — "Yeah, uh... yes. It's better. A lot better. Like... not even in the same league, I don't care how many hands you use."

Kato eyes him a few seconds longer and then lays his head back against Axis. "Can I look in your mind and see?"

"Wh—" Az stops walking entirely, hissing and dropping Nut when he bites him for it. "Walk then, I tried." He coughs, jogging to catch up again, and pointedly ignores his heated cheeks. "Um... yeah. Just... don't judge me, I only need *one* hand, if you know what I mean."

"Okay." Kato closes his eyes and peeks into Azrian's mind. He can't help but picture his alone time back at home, but he quickly tries to think of one of the few sexual encounters he's actually had. Though he's attracted to men and women just like everyone else, he definitely has a preference, so there's no way of hiding that. Azrian does his best to focus more on how it feels than how it looks — he blames that on lingering self-consciousness — but it's been so long since he's been bent over something that it's hard not to let his mind wander to the details.

"Oh..." he hears Kato whisper, and when Az looks over at him, he squirms on top of Axis. Kato sits up soon after that, clearing his throat and looking wide awake. "Um... yeah... that looks like it feels... there's probably not words."

Azrian is so overheated now that he wishes the desert would just swallow him whole. "I... don't know how it feels from the other side, but... probably a lot better than your hands."

"Yeah, I think so. Maybe—" Kato bites his lip, his hands gripping Axis' fur so tightly the wolf snorts at him. "Sorry, Axis."

They're quiet for a while after that, but Azrian can tell it's still on Kato's mind just like it's on his. "They didn't allow that at Deadrun," Kato explains. "Not that anyone wanted to try those things with me anyway, but... I'd catch glimpses of things in people's minds. Whether it was fantasy or a memory, I couldn't tell."

"Did you... ever have fantasies? I mean, I know you didn't know anything about it, but surely you had... y'know. Desires?" Az asks carefully. He tries to keep the hope from his voice, particularly because he's not sure if that hope is coming from circumstance or something deeper.

"Yeah, of course I did. I normally imagined being on the other end... if you know what I mean. Your position seems... painful."

Az swallows again, trying to stifle the whine in his throat — but the desert is so damn silent that he's sure it didn't work. "It's not painful. I mean, it can be... but... you just have to be careful. Work up to it, especially if you need two hands just to hold yours." He notices then that Nut is nowhere to be found, so he takes the opportunity to jog back and scoop him up. "Climb on my back." Once he's settled, Az joins the others again, sneaking a glance at Kato's giant form. "So..."

"I don't *need* two hands. It's just less work if I use two. I can show you what I mean," Kato offers, as if it's not a big deal. "I saw how you do it in your thoughts, and it's similar, but when I use two, I can cover most of it and I can move my hands less. It's just... I knew they were watching... and they used to tease me in security."

A shiver runs down Azrian's spine. "Kato... Jellycrai, please don't take this the wrong way... but if you show me, I'm going to die right here. So maybe... I'll just take your word for it. Sorry they teased you, though... probably just jealous."

Kato nods, falling silent after that. He lays back down after a while and before Az realizes how much time has passed, Kato is hopping off of Axis. "It's your turn. Axis wants you to rest until we find somewhere to camp."

By that point, Az can't feel his legs anymore, and it's all he can do to hand Nut over to Kato. His lips are chapped and he's beyond ready to rest, but he tries and fails twice to get up onto Axis' back. Frustrated, he mumbles quietly, "I'll just keep walking."

~

The only thing worse than the heat of Etria's days is the cold of Etria's nights, and the only thing worse than the cold of the night is the heat of the day. It's a sick, never-ending cycle that has Azrian wishing he couldn't feel anything at all — especially the way the scorching sun and unforgiving wind have destroyed his soft skin.

By the time they stumble upon another Eodren tree, Azrian is shaking from the chill, exhaustion, and constant pain from his shirt rubbing his shoulders. "We gotta stop, Kato," he says through clattering teeth. "How far ahead did A-Axis get?"

Kato's jaw is quivering as he reaches out and holds Az close, rubbing his arm for warmth. It doesn't work as well as Kato probably hoped it would, but Az isn't sure if the gesture was for him at all, or for Kato himself. "Not far. He-he's... on the way back now."

"Right," he whispers, curling against Kato's giant body and using him as a shield against the wind. He immediately feels bad about it and pulls back, carefully dropping the pack off his shoulder with a wince when the strap tears against his raw skin. "I'll start a fire and get us some w-water. Will you get the-the blankets out? All of them?"

He shudders almost violently as he reaches for the spile and hammers it into the tree, but for once, the fresh water doesn't seem to help. By the time they've got the fire crackling and the blankets wrapped tightly around them, Axis' silhouette is visible in the light

Cettia provides and Azrian nearly breaks something trying to flag him down for extra warmth.

Kato and Axis meet each other's eyes for a long moment before Kato looks back at Az. "He said we're safe here. He wants you close to him tonight, Az."

"For once, I won't argue with him being weird." Az shifts and pats the ground behind him and Kato. "Tell him to come back here, he gets both of us or neither of us."

Kato snorts at something Axis says as he walks over and meets Azrian's gray eyes. "He said I have Nut... as if that little thing could keep anyone warm." Nut throws an actual nut at his head and squeaks out a laugh when he has to fish it out of his hair. "Sorry... I shouldn't have said little thing... I should have said chubby thing," Kato jokes with a huge grin as they both cuddle into Axis' fur.

The smile on Kato's face soothes something inside of Az. They might be miserable most of the time, but the fact that someone like Kato can still find humor and joy in their situation fills him with warmth — and it's a warmth that eventually manifests physically as he shifts closer. "You're something else, Jellycrai. Don't change."

The look in Kato's eyes is one he's never seen before, but before he asks what he's thinking, Kato tells him. "No one's ever told me that before. Even deep in their minds, they all wanted me to be what *they* wanted. Thank you."

"You can look this time. I want you to know I mean it." Az takes a slow breath and prepares for that strange feeling, then puts a hand on Kato's chest when it doesn't immediately come. "I'm serious. Go ahead, look. I want you to know that there's not one part of me that wishes you weren't exactly who you are."

Azrian feels Kato peek, but it's so small and reluctant he wonders if he actually felt it at all. "Thank you, Azzy. That makes me happier than sweet bread. And you know how happy that makes me." His smile is contagious as they stare into each other's eyes, and for a moment the discomfort of the desert disappears around them. Az watches Kato's tongue slide across his lips and nearly forgets to breathe as the urge to kiss him reaches an all-time high — but just as he's about to ask permission to do exactly that, Nut's fat, irritating body drops down on them from Axis' back and thoroughly kills the moment.

"Sweet *shadows,* Nut!" Az hisses, trying to shove the squirming creature off. "Get out of here!"

Kato looks at the animal and then at Az again, his eyes dancing with amusement. "He said no." The smirk makes Az think Nut said more than that, but Kato doesn't elaborate further.

It's a losing battle and Azrian knows it, so when Nut settles between them and sighs happily, Az doesn't try again to make him leave. He simply reaches out to pet his head and relaxes against Axis.

There will be another moment to kiss Kato or to crash and burn trying, so for now... he's just happy to have him around.

~

"Kato? Can you just... right here —" Az points between his own shoulder blades, to that spot that's cracked and raw that he just can't reach — "I need help."

"Of course." He walks up behind him, so close that Az can feel the heat radiating off his skin. Soft hands slide over Az's dry skin and he wonders briefly how in the shadows Kato's hands are still soft. "I wish we could take you to a Sana... it looks painful."

That's the understatement of the year, but Azrian's trying to complain less and internalize more.

Trying.

"We're almost out of colwort already, so go easy on it. Just... put some on the worst parts. Please," he adds quickly, realizing how sour his voice sounds. Kato still manages to touch every sore part of his skin, and Az actually feels better when Kato steps back. "I wonder if the colwort leaves are stronger in the Simbian Forest than they are everywhere else? That's not the first time they've seemed to work better... and faster, too."

"Probably. That forest was pretty magical. Sometimes I felt like I could hear whispering in the trees at night." Kato hands Az his shirt and watches him put it on with intrigued eyes. "Maybe it's also different depending on the person? Like — some heal better than others?"

Az considers that as they grab the bags again and start moving. "Yeah, maybe. I guess that makes sense, I mean... people have different reactions to all sorts of things."

"Exactly. My body reacts to certain things you do in a way it's never reacted to anyone else before. Maybe the forest's colwort likes you more too." Kato adjusts his bag and looks up at the sky with a small smile on his lips, but for the life of him, Azrian can't think of a single thing to say back to that without sounding lame or needy.

The next couple of hours involve Az walking in silence and attempting to work out how to get whatever's going on between him and Kato from an "almost" to a "definite," but he's not getting anywhere fast. It seems like every time they get close to taking a step further something or some*one* — Az shoots a glare at Nut — gets in the way, and he just ends up convincing himself that the timing is all wrong and he's stupid for even thinking about something like that when they have such a big job to do.

With that in mind, Azrian tries in vain to call his powers when night finally falls. He's so tired of the darkness and the fires they're forced to build because of it that it sets him off, and he lets the frustration he's been shoving down boil over. "For *Cettia's* sake!" he curses, causing Nut to jump. "What in the shadows was the point of having powers if they were just going to disappear!"

"They haven't disappeared," a strange voice says. *"You simply don't currently have access to them."*

Azrian whirls around and draws his blade as terror spikes through him. They were alone two minutes ago — and they're still alone now. "What? Who's there? Show yourself!"

Kato jumps up, his eyes darting around their camp in fear. "Who? Where?!"

"That voice!" he says sharply. "Didn't you—"

"*They can't hear me because I don't want them to hear me. Sit down, Azrian Mihr, son of Embermeadow.*"

His ass hits the desert sand before he can process the command. When he tries to stand, he's knocked back down. "Kato!" he shrieks. "Tell her to let me go!"

"Stop! Whoever you are? Azrian, I don't see or hear anyone. Did it work? Stop, you... voice!!"

"*He has no power over me. If you wish to know who I am, simply look up.*"

Az flicks his eyes to the sky and sees nothing but the last dregs of twilight and — "Cettia?!"

"*Ah, you **can** be taught. Relax, you're not in danger... at the moment. You want answers, do you not?*"

Kato looks as though he's seen a ghost — or like he's genuinely concerned for Azrian and when he whispers sharply it makes Az flinch. "What's happening? Did the voice stop?"

"I don't know, just shhh." He fists his hand in Kato's tunic and holds on for dear life as he tries to ground himself. "Okay, so the star is talking to me. I've gone insane... just kill me, Kato. Put me out of my misery."

"*I am not a star, though that is how you perceive me. I'm a god. Your power is mine to give and take... and mine alone.*"

Azrian's heart beats wildly in his chest as he attempts to digest that. "You're... but wait, Praediti don't lose their powers, so—"

Again, she doesn't let him finish. "*You are speaking about things you do not understand. You have been chosen, Azrian Mihr. Chosen to carry a burden... and so far, you have been... disappointing.*"

Shame radiates through him and he pushes Kato's attempt at comfort away. Of course he's been disappointing. All he's done since that first day is whine and complain about everything — his powers, his circumstances. "You should've chosen someone else, then."

"*I did. Your father failed me. You were not my first, fourth, or even tenth choice, but you were the first to escape Deadrun and truly put things in motion. The powers I have granted you are simply a means to an end. You needed to be taken to the Venandi — needed to meet K8.0 and Callisto, to see what the others there have suffered. You needed to see their plan. Right now, you have no use for my power... nor do you deserve it. I hear all, Azrian. Even your curses deep in the heart of the Forest.*"

"Shadows," he mutters. He sees flashes in his mind of the ones who came before — Ender, Ronan, the other Videre still left behind at Deadrun. Part of Azrian wants to question Cettia, to demand to know why she allows them to keep her powers when they're being used for such cruelty by the Venandi, but he can't bring himself to do it. "I'm sorry. What am I supposed to do?"

"*Stay the course. Keep Axis close to you... I am not the only one meant to guide you.*"

Confusion pulses through him as he feels his connection to Cettia break off. He looks at Axis and blinks, now suddenly understanding that the beast wasn't drawn to him at all — he was sent to him. "So not even you chose me, huh?" *Great, Az. Again, you're being whiny and selfish. So much for trying to be better. Knock it off,* he silently scolds himself. "Never mind. Do you know where we're going?"

Axis nods, and Azrian lets out a breath as he looks at Kato. "You might want to sit. Things just got... complicated."

~

"That's— wow." Kato eyes Azrian. He feels bad for him; he knows Az didn't want this, and yet he's been completely uprooted from his home — his entire life — and thrown into this world he wanted no part of. "So, you aren't Praediti? Does that mean none of the Videre are? Were they all 'chosen'?"

Azrian shrugs, letting sand run through his fingers. "Sure sounds like it. Not sure if it matters, I mean... all I know is that she doesn't think I deserve the powers right now, which is why I don't have them anymore. Guess she'll give them back if I can be useful."

"But you are useful, Azzy." Kato takes his hand with a small frown. "I'd be dead without you."

The nickname makes him look up, but he stares at their hands a moment later. "No, you wouldn't. You were happy in Deadrun, Kato. You'd have stayed like that if it weren't for me. I know they were using you, but look at you. You're starving, your skin is—" he cuts off suddenly, like he's seeing Kato for the first time. "Fine. Your skin is fine... how...?"

Kato doesn't mean to, but the following thought running through Azrian's mind is so loud that *any* Cogitare within a three-mile radius would've heard it: *"Guess I'm even weaker than I thought."*

Kato pulls his hand away and grabs them a piece of bread to share, handing Az the other half. "Eat. You aren't weak, and I wasn't happy. I was content because I didn't know any better. I was lied to... used... quite frankly, I was tortured. I haven't had a headache since we left, and you have no idea how— they were *so* taxing. I mean some days I couldn't get out of bed. You saw. They were doing it to me. You saved me."

"I'm sorry, Jellycrai." Az chews quietly for a moment and then watches the sleeping animals. "What a pair we make, huh? One sheltered and tortured, one hunted his whole life. I just want this to be over... whatever it even is. I'm tired of fighting already."

"The only way for the fighting to end is to fight to the end." Kato takes his hand again. "And I think we make a good pair. No one's stopped us yet."

Az nods a little and laces their fingers, leaning against Kato's shoulder. "Keep that optimism. We're gonna need it."

"Okay. I'll try." He keeps their hands together, loving how it feels even though Az's hands are dry and callused. "Axis is worried about you," Kato whispers, not wanting to wake the beast. "He called me lazy earlier when I rode him too long because it was your turn."

Az scoffs. "I couldn't even get up on his giant body... but he doesn't care about me, Kato. Cettia said he was sent to find us. He's just doing his job."

"Will you... shut up?" Kato meets his eyes, chuckling at the look he receives. "She told you to stop being a shadowhead. He does care about you. Maybe he was sent here, but that doesn't matter. You're his destiny. I can see in his mind, and yes... it works differently than ours, but... he's waited a long time for you, Azrian. He cares more about you than anyone before... than himself... so do I."

His expression gives away the fact that Azrian doesn't believe him, and the moment he shuts down is as clear as day. "You're right. She did tell me that, I'm sorry." He pulls his hand back, folding his arms over his chest. "You should get some sleep. I'll take watch."

"Fine." Kato rolls away and curls into himself. He's embarrassed by what he just admitted to Az, and the rejection hurts. He's never told anyone he's cared about them before — probably because he never has — and he thinks that maybe he's done it wrong. *Maybe those aren't things you say out loud?*

Either way, he falls asleep soon, exhaustion beating at his running mind, and he dreams of a bed floating out in the middle of the Wasted Waters. The sea dragon lifts his head out of the depths, and his mind is easy to read when he tells Kato he's all alone and that nothing will help him just before he knocks the bed over and throws Kato into the water. He jerks up from his sleep, gasping for air and looking around him, thankful he isn't alone. *You're wrong, dragon.*

Azrian is looking at him and Kato wipes his eyes, sitting up properly with a grunt. The hard ground is unforgiving, but he's grown used to it. "Your turn."

"Kato, I..." Az blushes, clearly wanting to say something else, but ultimately lays down. "Wake me in a couple of hours. We should try to make it to Hollowater by nightfall."

As he falls silent, Axis nudges Kato with his snout. *"He is troubled, do not let that dampen your spirits. If you do not believe he cares for you too, look into his mind."*

"No." Kato hugs his knees, watching Az's body as his breathing becomes more even by the second. *"He doesn't want me in his mind. I don't have his permission, and when he gives it, I stick to the thoughts I'm supposed to stick to. I don't want to lose him because I'm nosey."*

Nut peeks at them with narrowed little eyes. *"Sleep."*

*"You're nosey too. **You** go to sleep,"* Kato teases, a small smile on his face. *"We already slept, cover your little ears."*

The raccanis chitters, but rolls over onto his back, his tiny arms looking ridiculous sticking out from his fat belly. Axis' wise eyes twinkle playfully as he watches. *"In all my hundreds of years, I've never seen a raccanis that fat."*

"He's one of a kind... kinda like all of us." Kato smiles over at Axis and then searches for some water to share. *"You think Az is going to leave me? You know... after it's all done."* He can't help how small his voice is, even in their minds.

Axis breathes out heavily through his nose, resting his head on his massive paws. *"No, I do not. I cannot read his mind as you can, but as we've discussed... I've been waiting for him for a very, very long time. I know his story, and I know his heart. I know his future. You will play a bigger part in it than you know, K8.0."*

"Can you tell me more? Or is this some 'figure it out as we go' type of thing?" Kato tilts his head, turning back to look at Az.

"I can tell you some," his deep voice answers. *"There are things in your path... things that will test you both. It will be exceedingly important in the coming weeks that you do not give up on him, no matter what happens. Without you... Azrian will fail. And if he fails... the fate of an entire world will be sealed."*

"I wouldn't give up on him. Nothing could make me," Kato says with all the confidence in the world. *"Thanks, Axe. Get some more rest, we have a very long day tomorrow."*

The valianis shakes his mighty head. *"I need far less sleep than humans. You should sleep, I can keep watch until first light."*

"Really? Thank you. I slept like damn a little bit ago." Kato lays down, using Axis as a pillow and closes his eyes. *"See you in the morning sun."* It doesn't take long for him to fall back to sleep, and this time, his dreams are peaceful.

He wakes to the sun beaming in his eyes and blinks away his sleep as he sits up. "Good morning," Kato mumbles to Az, who looks as if he's been awake for a while.

"Hi." Az passes him some food and a little bit of water. "Axis has been glaring at me for the last half an hour, can you ask him what I did wrong?"

The great beast looks away in an attempt to feign innocence. *"I haven't done any such thing... but if I had, it would be because he's not using his words."*

Kato takes the food and listens to Axis — not sure of how to relay that information — and takes a small drink before taking a bite. "Um... he said no, he isn't."

Nut chitters at him to tell Az exactly what Axis said, and Kato frowns at him. "Oh, and since when are you two friends?"

Azrian sighs. "Never mind. Eat quickly, we need to go. It's finally starting to warm up."

"Fine, don't. Kato be sad no reason."

"I'm not s—" Kato realizes he's speaking out loud and then blushes slightly. "Nut is in an arguing mood." He nudges him softly with his foot, making him screech at him. "Axis wants you to use your words. Do you want me to ask him to elaborate?"

The flush on Azrian's face says he gets it without further explanation. "Oh, I... um... I care about you too, Kato. Should've told you last night."

"It's fine. I didn't mean to upset you with that. I thought it was something that would make you smile. It's so rare that you smile. I just wanted to see it again, but... it did the opposite, and I'm sorry. We can care about each other and not talk about it if that's better." Kato scratches his head. "It's all very confusing," he admits.

Axis snorts and repeats that they should use their words, but Kato doesn't comment back. He's too busy watching Azrian, not sure if he just said too much again.

All Azrian does is start to gather their things up, his shoulders tense and movements stiff as he shoves the last of their food and water back in the pack. He doesn't say anything at all until Kato finally stands, and then Azrian whirls around to face him. "Look. We can talk about it. You don't — you don't have to be weird about it, I'm pretty sure I'm doing that well enough for both of us. It's just... no one... 'cept my mom and maybe Rhix, but... *shadows*, why is this so hard?" he mutters, reaching up to brush sand out of his hair.

Without thinking, Kato reaches out and helps him, seeing there is actually quite a bit of sand in there. "Turn around. Let me help."

Slowly, Az turns and drops his hands back to his sides. The air around them seems to shift a little as Kato unties his hair and lets it fall. He runs his giant fingers through it, letting the sand cascade to the ground and he smiles when the tangles loosen up under his touch.

Once his hair is clean, Kato's disappointed that he has to stop, but he walks around to face Azrian with a smile. "All clean. Here." He hands him the hair tie. "I like your hair."

There's something new in Azrian's eyes as he takes it, and instead of putting it back up, he slides the tie onto his wrist. "It mostly just gets in the way... it's better when I can actually use soap," he says quietly. "That felt... really nice, though. Thank you."

"Of course. I'd ask you to help with mine, but..." Kato rubs the top of Az's head with a grin. "You're kinda short."

Az finally grins, stepping in closer and reaching up. He has to extend his arm almost all the way, but he manages, though their bodies press together for him to pull it off. "See? You're not... *that* tall," he says, but the lie is immediately evident in Kato's bones.

Kato grips Az's hips when he falls into him, all four of them enjoying a real laugh for the first time in days — but when he realizes how much of their bodies are touching, he feels something strange in his stomach, almost like a fluttering.

"Oh, um..." Az swallows, tilting his head back to meet Kato's eyes without pulling away. "I... think I missed some, but... I tried."

"It's okay. I can't see it, either." He hasn't moved his hands yet, but he finds he really doesn't want to. He loses himself in those gray eyes a moment before Nut screeches something at Axis, but Kato isn't listening.

Az slowly shifts on his feet. "Hey, Jellycrai... you remember what we saw Morella and that guy doing back in Embermeadow? They were... kissing?"

"Mmhm." Kato nods quickly, licking his lips without realizing. "Can we? I— I want to try... with you."

"Yeah," Az whispers, right before rocking up and his toes. He falls short of Kato's mouth, laughing to himself as his heels hit the sand again. "Shadows. You gotta meet me halfway, here."

"Okay." Kato leans in and presses their lips together for the first time, his giant hands curling at Azrian's sides with a whimper. It feels so good that the fluttering in his stomach feels more like somersaults and the sensation travels further down, waking up parts of him that have never woken up in front of someone else. Before he realizes what he's doing, he's picking Az up and backing him against a tree, deepening the kiss with a growl.

Azrian's instantly putty, tugging on Kato's hair, sliding his tongue into his mouth and letting out a low moan. Suddenly, there's a second growing mass between their bodies and Az breaks the kiss as he sucks in air desperately. "Sweet Cettia, Kato. How'd you... get so damn good at that?"

"Am I?" The gold in his eyes lights up and he grins widely. "I — I don't know. I just... did it. Was it okay? Can I do it again?" Kato doesn't want to stop, he doesn't want to leave this place at all, but Axis interrupts his thoughts and he reminds them they're burning daylight.

"Yeah, you can do that whenever you want, *whenever* you want," Az says, right before kissing him again.

Axis gets a little more insistent, so Kato pulls back and adjusts his pants.

"Um... Axis. He said we should do this when we reach Hollowater. And that we're burning daylight." He looks down, blushing when he sees the effect the kissing had on him. "Um..."

Azrian's pupils expand as he catches on but he quickly looks away and grabs his pack. "He's right, we can continue this once we've reached town. I want to be done with this desert... and I promise, the kisses will be better when my lips aren't so chapped. I'm sorry."

"It was the best thing that's ever happened to me. They can be better?" Kato picks up his bag and puts it on his shoulder, still annoyed at the heavy nuisance between his legs.

The grin on Azrian's face makes him look lighter than he's seemed... maybe ever. "Yes, they can be better... particularly when we're not interrupted. Give me a few days in Hollowater to kick the dehydration and treat the blistering sunburn and you'll learn."

Kato nods, biting his lip and wishing they were already there, but he'll take the promise for more later as a blessing. He looks toward the direction they're supposed to go and sucks in a breath. "Let's get there then, Azzy."

~ XIII ~

THE SHIFT

Reaching Hollowater's outer limit is such a relief that Azrian falls to his knees. He truly isn't sure he'd have been able to walk another step as it is — they'd run into a group of bandits and the detour it forced them to take had them walking well into the night, long after the sun stopped providing warmth.

But now, they're here. After weeks of traveling through a dangerous forest and unforgiving terrain, they've arrived back in civilization. Kato helps him back to his feet and urges him on until they're saying a temporary goodbye to their animal companions and paying an innkeeper for a bed.

Just *one* bed.

Though they have enough money for two, Azrian isn't sure either one of them actually want to sleep alone — and even if they did, they use the extra money to pay one of the attendants to fetch them hot water for a bath.

"You can go first, Jellycrai. I'm used to bathing in river water, so I won't mind as much when it cools down."

"We won't fit together?" Kato asks, looking over at the metal basin with his brow furrowed. "I guess not. Maybe if I wasn't so large. Thank you, Azrian." He starts stripping the dirty layers, shivering when the air touches his bare skin.

Azrian swallows. The truth is that they *will* both fit, but he isn't sure if either one of them are ready for that. Still, he can't take his eyes off of Kato as he strips and doesn't look away until the last possible moment. "Um... I'll go see about cooking some actual food. Did you... need help before I go?"

"No. I have the soap and towel. I'll come get you as soon as I'm done so you can have some warm water." Azrian hears the water move as Kato steps in, and when he submerges his body, he groans. "Oh, Azzy... it feels so good. I'll hurry for you."

The sound has Azrian jerking and darting out of the room. There's no way Kato actually sounds that good... no way. He tries to shove the thoughts from his mind as he looks around for a restaurant nearby, but of course, none are open that late. He gives up after ten minutes and heads back to the inn with his stomach growling and head bowed, and it's only then that he realizes he went out after dark at all.

It stops him dead in his tracks and he smiles proudly as he ducks back inside. *Either I'm getting braver... or dumber.*

Kato is out of the bath with the small towel wrapped around his waist as he stares down at his dirty clothes. He's shivering, but not as much as Azrian is, and nods to the bath. "It's still warm. Get in."

"Just put on... the cleanest underwear you've got and get under the blanket," Az instructs as he starts to shuck his own clothes off. "We'll do laundry in the morning when it's not freezing out."

"Okay." Kato pulls out a pair and slides them on, then uses a towel to dry his hair and climbs into the bed as told. He's visibly still shivering as Azrian climbs into the bath, and if it weren't for the insanely good feeling that washes over him in that moment, he'd have been hurrying to join him.

Getting weeks' worth of nature out of his hair feels incredible, and he doesn't even want to think about the noises he's making as the water soothes his cracked, irritated skin. Once he's cleaned up as best as he can get in the relative dark, he covers his body with colwort and follows his own instructions when dressing again.

"You still awake, Jellycrai?" he whispers, grabbing an extra blanket for them.

"Yes. I was waiting for you." Kato opens the blanket and scoots over for Azrian, tapping the spot next to him. "I warmed it for us a little, but your body heat will help us more. Can I— can we— our bodies touch?"

"It's called cuddling," Az says. It's not sarcastic or anything of the sort... this is one thing that he doesn't find amusing at all. "And yes, we can... should've been doing it the whole time, not just occasionally." He climbs in, taking a deep breath and scooting closer to Kato until they're touching in just a couple of spots.

It takes Kato a second to move in more and wrap an arm around Az, a small smile on his face. "I think so too. You fit perfectly with me."

It's undeniable. As Azrian relaxes against him, he realizes how well they truly slot together... and how nice it feels to be held like this. "Thanks, Kato," he says quietly. "For this... for all of it. You keep saying I saved you, but you saved me, too. I'd still be cowering in the Simbian Forest somewhere if it weren't for you."

Kato hums, nuzzling his face a little further. "We saved each other, Azzy. Get some sleep. I'd like to kiss you more tomorrow."

I'd like to kiss you more right now, Az thinks, but chooses not to say it out loud. Kato's right... they've had an exhausting... life, and right now, all they truly need is sleep.

Hours later, Azrian wakes to the glaring sunlight coming through the window. He blinks furiously, then buries his face in Kato's broad chest to avoid it as long as possible. The scent of soap and something uniquely Kato fills his nose, and he hums happily. "You awake?" he whispers again.

"Hmm?" Kato stirs, moving in closer so his face is in Azrian's hair. "Good morning, Az. You sleep as good as I did?"

He nods a little, curling his fingers against Kato's back. "Yeah. We should get moving though, we need to do laundry and maybe try to find a Sana. And eat... definitely eat."

"Yeah... I had a dream about food." Kato chuckles and then moves a little so he can see Azrian's face. "Can I... kiss you again first? I can't stop thinking about it."

All the butterflies in Az's stomach scatter, and he's leaning in to bring their lips together before he can even answer. Kato whimpers into his mouth and rolls Az onto his back, then slides his tongue into his mouth experimentally. He tastes better than he had the night before and Az loses himself right there in that kiss, certain he doesn't ever want to leave it.

But eventually, nature calls in more ways than one. He promises himself in that moment that before they leave Hollowater, he'll teach Kato everything he needs to know about the things he saw in his mind... but for now, they need to move.

Breakfast comes in the form of actual meat and hot stew, which was always more of a dinner food back home, but Etrians seem to have their own way of doing things. He's not sure if they reserve certain types of food for specific meals at all, or if it's tough meat and brothy, burnt vegetables all the time... but either way, it makes him homesick for Edros.

The search for a Sana is a little more difficult than scrounging up food. It takes them most of the afternoon to find one that's reasonably priced, but despite the painful process and the coins it takes to accomplish it, he feels better when his aching bones and stretched, cracked skin are mended.

He notices a bit of hesitation on Kato's part and reaches over to take his hand. "It's okay, Jellycrai. We're not... *there* anymore. She won't hurt you."

The Sana looks at him curiously, checking him for injuries that aren't immediately noticeable. "You don't look like you need my services, Cogitare."

Az opens his mouth to protest, but a closer glance at his companion confirms what the Sana said. His skin looks virtually flawless, which sends a surge of jealousy through him — but the Sana works her magic anyway and Kato sighs quietly.

"Thank you," he nearly whispers, still unsure of their surroundings.

"See?" Az smiles. "All better. Now we just need to get some warmer blankets, some more rations, and spend another night in that bed and then we can go."

"Okay, Az." Kato follows him closely to the next shop. It's louder than the others, and small children run around their feet. One small girl stops in front of Kato and points up at him. "Wow... he's a giant."

Kato blushes, holding their new blankets close to his chest and looking to Az, reaching into his mind. *"Can I talk to her?"*

"Of course. Just... speak softly. She's right, you're absolutely a giant." He smiles warmly, watching as Kato kneels down for the girl, still much taller than her.

"Hi. You're not too short yourself," he jokes, smiling at her softly. "You're going to be taller than my friend here soon." She giggles and reaches out to touch his scar, making him flinch. It scares her enough that she runs away, leaving Kato looking sad. "I didn't mean to frighten her."

Az takes his hand and laces their fingers, the movement now almost automatic. "It doesn't take a lot to scare children, Jellycrai. It's okay, you didn't do anything wrong."

Kato nods and squeezes his hand tighter. "Let's go back to our room now. It's very loud in here." It isn't too bad, but Az realizes Kato probably hears thoughts all around them and he quickly leads him out.

"I'm sorry, I don't always remember you're a Cogitare. Especially now that I... don't have any powers of my own." He keeps him close until they get to the final shop, and Az goes in alone to get some more jerky and other foods that will keep for their next long journey.

After that, there's nothing left for them to do but try and rest. They pay for another night at the inn, some better soap, and another tub full of hot water, and this time... Az doesn't want to waste it.

"Were you serious when you asked if we'd fit in it together?"

"Yes." Kato's eyes light up. "Can we? I mean... we'll be—" he leans in to whisper, even though they're alone — "naked?"

Az blushes and licks his lip slowly. "It's okay with me if it's okay with you. We don't have to, Kato. I don't want you to think I'm... taking advantage of you or anything."

"No. I want to. I... really want to." He leans in and kisses Az, his hands moving to help him take off his shirt. "Just tell me if I touch something I'm not supposed to."

This time, the shiver that races up Azrian's spine has nothing to do with the cold, and everything to do with what's to come. "Nothing is off limits, Kato. Promise."

~

"Wow," Kato states, laying on his back with Azrian at his side. "That was—" He hopes Azrian can see how happy he is, because he truly cannot find the words to express it. "I hope we do that again... every night?" he asks excitedly, knowing that probably isn't possible.

Azrian just laughs and brings a hand up to Kato's face to cover it. "It's going to be kind of hard once we're back in the desert, especially with an animal audience. Unfortunately, we may not be able to do that again until we get to Wildpeak."

Kato sighs, because that makes sense and he really doesn't want the animals watching them, but it still makes him deflate slightly. "Understandable. Was I— did I do okay?"

Chuckling almost awkwardly, Az just nods. "Put it this way... you're already better at it than I am." He curls against Kato's chest and closes his eyes, planting a soft kiss to his skin. "So good that I'm exhausted now, and we're leaving at first light. We should sleep."

"Okay. Sleep good, Azzy." Kato kisses the top of his head, closing his eyes with a smile. "See you in the morning sun."

~

Kato wakes first, blinking away the sunlight peeking in the window. He can already tell they're slightly behind schedule, but when he looks at Azrian and sees how beautiful he looks, that fluttering returns to his stomach. It's rare to see Az look so peaceful. He leans over, kissing his cheek softly and rolls out of bed, startling him in the process. "Sorry, I didn't mean to wake you."

"It's okay." He groans as he sits up and scratches the back of his head. "We're late, huh? I hope Axis isn't worried."

"He probably is." Kato starts to dress, smiling over at Az. "Did you sleep good? I sure did." He pulls on his tunic which messes up his hair, but he's still grinning widely.

Azrian nods as he gets dressed himself, then slings his pack over his shoulder. "Okay, Jellycrai. Next stop, Wildpeak."

"Wildpeak... can we cuddle out there? It's cold... and I know Axis is warmer than me, but if I wrap my arms around you... I can keep you warm, too."

"Of course," Az says with a blush. "We just have to be careful we don't both fall asleep if one of us is supposed to be on watch."

"Axis has been really helpful with watch. We can sleep a little together," Kato says hopefully, bumping Az playfully with his arm.

They scarf down a quick breakfast as they walk, and as they near their friends, they hear Nut's chittering a moment before he jumps straight on Kato's back.

"*Food,*" the furball commands.

"He wants food already. Did you guys not eat out here?" Kato asks out loud, wanting Azrian to know what was being said.

"*We did. He's always hungry,*" Axis snorts. "*You're late.*"

Kato blushes and looks at Az with a smile. "We overslept. Let's go."

~

Kato definitely didn't miss the scorching sunlight and having to walk through the sand. His feet hurt — his entire body hurts — and yet, they keep on moving. The smiles and random kisses slow as the day goes on, replaced with exhaustion and grouchiness. "Can we take a break soon? I'm so damn hungry and Nut won't stop complaining."

"Did you just swear?" Az asks, a soft, dimpled smile on his face. "I guess we better stop then." He calls their ragtag group to a halt and seeks shelter under a nearby Eodren tree. How the huge, leafy things manage to exist out here in the desert, Kato will never know — but he's thankful they do.

Nut lets out a tiny, exhausted squeak and collapses onto his back again while Axis sits close to the trunk of the tree. Once the water is flowing freely from the spile, they refill their canteens and drink their fill.

Kato slides his head under the water, bracing his arms on the tree as it soaks his hair. "Shadows... how is the water cool?"

"That's the magic of Eodren trees. I don't know how it works, exactly... but they can grow anywhere, no matter the climate. Like a little oasis." Az pulls out a bit of food and hands some to Kato. "Eat up."

"Thanks, Azzy." Kato smiles and takes it, sitting down closer than before. Now that they've cooled down, he can't help but gravitate toward Az. He just feels better when they're close.

Their break is too short. It's always too short, but Axis gently reminds Kato that there are larger things at work, and they need to keep moving. Az and Kato take turns carrying Nut and riding Axis until the sun finally begins to set over the sand dunes in the distance.

"*There is danger ahead,*" Axis warns him. He stops walking with Azrian asleep on his back, and paws at the ground. Kato studies the intricate side of the valianis' face and the way the patterns in his fur look like his own scars as the great beast continues: *"If we continue forward, we will not be able to avoid it. Going around will add extra days to the journey... days I do not think you can afford. What should we do?"*

"What kind of danger?" Kato asks in a concerned tone, but when he glances at Az's silhouette and meets Axis' eyes, he knows what they have to do. *"He's tired, Axe. I'll use my powers if I have to. I'll protect us. We have to keep going."*

Axis dips his head in acknowledgment and carries on, his ears pinned back. They make it another two miles before Kato sees a group ahead. Before he can even ask, Axis says, *"Venandi and a pack of coyanis."*

Kato tenses and looks up at Azrian with a worried expression. *"Azzy... wake up."*

Quickly, Az jerks awake and nearly falls off of Axis as he tries to grab an arrow. *"Where?"*

"Ahead. Just be ready." Kato tries to focus on their thoughts but they're still pretty far away. He can only pick up some of the coyanis' thoughts and they're all starving. The only real thought they have is *"food."*

They stop just long enough for Azrian to slide off of Axis' back and rub his eyes, then properly notch an arrow. Kato's grateful for the time Azrian spent hunting before this, because he trusts his aim to be true... no matter what.

Kato makes a point not to look into his mind, but it doesn't matter — the fear is strong enough that he can sense it whether he intends to or not. But Az keeps going, keeps his feet moving forward with those gray eyes fixed on the horizon until the blurred shapes become clearer. *"What do we do?"* Az asks. *"Do we fight, or... just try and pass them and hope they don't attack?"*

"We'll try to just pass and if I have to... I'll get in their minds. There's five of them... I've never tried to control that many at the same time, but I think I can do it. I just need to focus." Kato reaches out as they approach the small group and can hear they aren't paying attention to them.

He takes that as a good sign and tries to walk like they belong there — out in the middle of the desert with a beast that has likely never been seen in those parts.

Azrian stays close to Kato as they walk, his fingers twitching around the arrow he's trying to shield from view. *"They're looking. They're— Kato..."*

They're nearly past them completely when one of them recognizes Kato's scars. *"Shadows."*

"Hey, you! With the scars."

Kato turns to face them, his eyes dropping to the four leashed coyani as another man begins to untie them.

The man sneers. "Not every day you come across scars like those... *K8.0.*"

The mention of the misnomer still tattooed on his knuckles has anger bubbling in his chest. "That's not my name." He alerts Axis to be ready and then turns back to the men. "We don't want trouble, just... go back to your past sex stories and ignore us."

"*Cogitare?*" another man says, his hand tightening around his weapon.

"Yeah, but he's harmless. Huh? He was Melior's toy."

"If he's Melior's toy, what in the shadows is he doin' out here? Don't seem harmless to me."

Kato focuses on their minds and sees all of the horrible things they've done, then closes his eyes, forcing all five men to collapse and fall asleep. His nose begins to bleed as the coyani attack, but before he has to do anything about them, Axis jumps in front with a snarl.

An arrow whizzes past and hits one in the neck but doesn't kill him. Azrian swears loudly and tries to notch another, but Axis lunges forward and rips the throat out of the one closest to them, then swings his mighty tail and sends a second flying. The injured coyanis backs up with a whimper as Az ditches his bow and whips one of the Hokrine knives Rhix gifted, and it hits home.

"*Come, now,*" Axis commands, and Kato relays the message to the others. Azrian hastily grabs the bag he dropped and his bow, then climbs up on Axis' back with Nut clutching onto his shoulders.

Kato jumps on last, wrapping his arms around Az tightly. "Hang on," Kato grunts out as Axis takes off. He moves faster than any of them have ever seen him, and Kato's never been on something that moved so quickly — he nuzzles into Az's neck, his eyes closed tightly as Nut screeches in fear.

He can feel the raccanis squirming around on Azrian's head as they barrel through the hot desert, and Axis doesn't stop running for several miles, until long after holding on becomes difficult due to the sweat. Finally, Azrian yells for Axis to stop.

When they climb off, Azrian's face is covered in blood and he's glaring at Nut like he's going to kill him. "Stay away from me."

"Nut!" Kato tugs off his backpack and pulls out the colwort. "Come here, Az." He squeezes the leaf to squirt the gel onto his finger and starts dabbing Az's wounds. "He was just scared, Azrian. We all were."

Nut mumbles something about meaning to hold onto Azrian's hair, but Kato decides not to tell Az about that. It doesn't seem like it would help.

Az sucks in a sharp breath as Kato's fingers move over the worst of the scratches. "I know that. I know. I'm sorry."

"Don't be sorry. He's a little shit." Kato grins when Nut screeches at him, but he doesn't turn his way — he keeps his eyes locked with Azrian's. "Do they feel better?"

"Yeah," he says quietly, taking a step closer to Kato. "A... a little bit, anyway. Thanks."

"Good." Kato gives in to his urge and places a kiss to Azrian's lips, then steps back to pack away their first-aid kit. "We're almost to Wildpeak, right? I think we should get moving again before those Venandi wake."

Axis snorts, and Az takes a swig of water. "We won't be safe until we get there. Honestly, we might not be safe then, either. They recognized you. If Melior and Belua are looking for us, it's only a matter of time before word gets back to them. We didn't get far enough fast enough."

Kato deflates, feeling as if it's all his fault. He wonders if they would be better off without him, but he can't find the words to suggest it. "I know... let's keep moving."

"Hey, Jellycrai," Az says gently. He takes his hand, smiling up at him as they start walking again. "I can't read minds or anything, but I know you well enough now to know when you're punishing yourself. Don't. This is no one's fault but Melior's."

It makes Kato smile and squeeze his hand a little tighter. "I guess I just hoped we were free... you deserve to be free."

"If Cettia was telling the truth, we won't be free until Melior is stopped. We've still got a long way to go to get to Redhaven, but I'm hoping the government in Wildpeak will help. They're not the Regnum, but they might be close enough."

"Do you think we'll get to Wildpeak by dark?" Kato asks, looking up at the sun with his brow furrowed.

Az grumbles under his breath and pulls out his map, then follows Kato's gaze until he places the sun. "With the time we gained thanks to Axis' sprint, yeah. We should actually make it a little before dark if we don't stop to rest. Do you think you can keep going for another four hours or so?"

"Yes. Can you?" Kato touches his face softly to look at the cuts. "I'll carry Nut first."

"I have to," he says as he picks up the raccanis and hands him over. "We don't have a choice."

~

Sure enough, they make it before nightfall — but every single one of them feel like they're dead on their feet. Az knows they can't afford to wait until morning to talk to the sect about what's happening in Deadrun, so he convinces Kato to just hang on a little longer.

Axis and Nut once more take refuge in the woods just outside of town, and after Kato and Az find a place to drop their things and stay for the night, Az tugs him along until they find what looks like the government headquarters in Wildpeak. Still, he's on his guard. "Okay, we're going to have to tell them who we are. Kato, I know you don't like using your gifts, but we're going to need them. Just keep your ears open, yeah?"

"I know. I can do this... *we* can do this." Kato pulls open the door for Az and follows closely behind — close enough to touch.

The purple eyes of the receptionist give her away as a Tactare, and Az is immediately reminded that without his powers, she's going to think he's human. He nearly lets Kato talk, but given his inexperience, he's not sure that's the best idea and decides to give it a shot. "We'd like an audience with... well, whoever will see us, honestly," he says truthfully. "We have some information about a potential threat and need help."

"Oh?" She barely looks up. "They're not in session right now, you'll need to file a formal request and wait to be contacted."

Az shifts on his feet. "And how long will that take? We can't wait."

"The request will be reviewed in the order it was received, and then scheduled based on how important the Praefectus deem it to be." She glances up at Kato and takes a half-step back, suddenly clearing her throat. "You have a Cogitare with you. You should've said."

Anger flashes through him, but he does his best to bite it back. "Right, because humans are nothing compared to Praediti. Listen, we *need* to speak with them. It's about Deadrun."

Her expression instantly changes, and she nods once. "You should've led with that. Please follow me."

Kato reaches out to Azrian as they walk down a long corridor. "*Sorry. She's like you said... she thinks she's better than humans her thoughts make me want to trip her."* He grabs Azrian's hand proudly and walks with his head held high, and the gesture would make Azrian smile if he weren't so scared of what might happen next.

They're led directly into what looks like a courtroom. Az never had a reason to visit the sect in Edros — like here, they'd never have given him the time of day on his own even if he'd been brave enough to try and seek justice for any of the various things Praediti did to him back then — so he isn't sure what he was expecting, but it isn't this.

Four of the seven seats are filled as the Tactare leads them closer, and the pit of foreboding in Azrian's stomach only grows more pronounced with each step. He clocks the dark blue eyes of an Undare, the deep, brown eyes of a Terrare, and the orange eyes of a Viribus. Those make him miss Rhix, and he'd get lost in memories of his former boss if it weren't for the Igneme sitting on the end. Azrian tenses and considers lying right then — he knows it's not fair to presume that all fire-starters are evil, but in his experience, he's never met one that wasn't. He tells himself that he wouldn't be allowed to sit on Etria's governing body if he was evil, then addresses the question that's now been asked of him twice since he began trying to see what they're dealing with.

"There's a threat in the north," he says, knowing exactly how dramatic it sounds. "In Deadrun, to be exact. We... we escaped with one other, but there are dozens of other prisoners still there. They need your help — the help of the Regnum, too, but we've come a long way. I don't know that we'll reach Redhaven in time to deliver the message ourselves."

The Igneme stares them down. "That's insane. Deadrun has been empty for over two hundred years, there's nothing up there."

"There *is*," Azrian insists. "He was born there. The Venandi bred him, they're trying to—"

Kato laughs loudly, making everyone shut up and look at him. "You should see your faces. Sorry, we were playing a prank... but this is too much. Have a nice night." He grips Azrian's arm tightly and pulls him back the way they came, not saying anything until they're a few yards from the building. "They're working with them. They're going to tell them we came... they'll tell them everything."

Fear grips Azrian in a way that it hasn't since they left the Simbian Forest. "What? And we just... *shadows*, I knew I should've had you look first." He takes off at a run, pulling Kato back toward the inn they were supposed to be staying at, not stopping until they're inside the room. "We can't stay here. We'll have to go stay with Axis in the woods or something... or maybe try to find an outlying village."

Kato runs a hand through his hair and groans. "Dammit!" He kicks the bed frame and leans against the wall, taking long, deep breaths. "They won't make it here in time... they have to send an Avisim, and *he* even cursed how slow they travel because they're so hard to train. I think we have tonight."

"And what if they have an Itinerae? There were three empty seats, Kato..." Az packs their things quickly, but slows his movements when he realizes how long they've been running today. "Do you really think we'll be okay? Just for one night?"

"If they do, then... well... I'll take care of it. I'll do what I have to and keep you safe. I promise." Kato pulls him in to stare into his eyes and Azrian gets lost in how brightly the green is shining over the gold today. "I promise."

Silently, Azrian curses Cettia. He wholeheartedly believes that Kato will keep him safe at all costs, but who will keep Kato safe? What match is Azrian against the Venandi if he's still just a useless human?

He stands on his toes to kiss Kato, then pulls their pajamas back out of the pack. "Okay, Jellycrai. One night."

~ XIV ~

THE ROSTIAN RUINS

"Kato... we need to go," Azrian says gently. "Believe me, I wish we could stay, but we have to get going."

Not one part of him wants to get up, especially with how much fun they ended up having the night before. It had taken some convincing on both ends for them to block off the world and just enjoy the night together, but since they had, Kato's finding it hard to go back to their dangerous reality.

He pulls Az in and kisses his temple, nuzzling back in with a huffed complaint. "So tired of running. I wish we could just go live on a mountain alone. Just us... and the furry ones."

"So do I." Az goes silent for a moment, letting their breathing synchronize before speaking again. "Maybe when this is all over, we can... if we're both still alive."

"We will be. You're stuck with me, Azzy." Kato tugs his hair back to look into his eyes. "We will live together... and share a bed and a bath. Nut will annoy us, but we'll be happy. I promise." He tries to smile encouragingly, letting Az see that he means every word. He won't accept anything less.

Those gorgeous eyes are darker than normal as Az nods, and the soft smile on his face looks almost disbelieving. "I hope you're right, Kato. We've got targets on our backs; it's going to be almost impossible to travel without being recognized now."

"I know." A passing thought of separating crosses his mind, but he isn't sure he can do that so he can't bring himself to suggest it.

It only takes Az about an hour to suggest it himself. They're barely at the edge of the town before he's stopping dead in his tracks and breathing raggedly, his hands shaking at his sides. "You need to go, Jellycrai. I know you know that."

"We *are* going." Kato knows exactly what he means, but that doesn't make it any easier on him. He walks a few more steps before rounding back. "Stone it! You're safer without me, Az. We both know that. But I don't want to be apart. How am I supposed to protect you if we aren't together?"

"You're not. You're supposed to protect yourself. One of us has to make it to Redhaven, and we have a better chance of doing that if we're on our own. I'll blend in, and you'll have an easier time manipulating anyone that recognizes you if you're on your own and not worried about me." Az digs around in the bag and holds out the only map they have. "Axis knows the way. He and I will head north through Brinecoast and cross the Sutson Sea to Grimrock, then cut east over to Redhaven. All you have to do is keep going east now, skirt around the Vodter Bay and loop up through Dawndrift. Then it's just straight north. If you get to the Tizor Mountains you went too far."

Kato stares down at the map but it all blurs together. He wipes his eyes and looks over to Axis, taking slow steps toward him. *"Promise me you will take care of him."*

"I will do what I can, but you must understand that this story is already written. We are simply bringing the events to life, and as such... there are things that not even I can prevent."

"No!" he yells out loud, pointing a finger at him. *"I don't give a stone what's written, Axis."* Kato once again feels helpless, and of all the things, that feels the worst. *"Keep him safe."*

A soft hand lands on his arm. "Kato?" Az asks. "Why are you yelling at him?"

"Nothing." Kato deflates, running his hands through his hair. "You're both right. This is much bigger than me and my needs. You're strong, Azrian." He cups Az's face. "You don't need me. You'll make it there and so will I, and we'll never separate again."

Az exhales hard and dips his head in a nod. "Okay. It shouldn't take either of us longer than two weeks to get there, so... two weeks. I'll call out for you when we're close, hopefully you'll be able to hear my thoughts."

Two weeks seems like a lifetime when one of them can die at any moment, but it also gives Kato perspective. He has to make it two weeks without Az but knowing Az will be there at the end not only gives him drive to make it, but it also makes him feel unstoppable. He nods, kissing Az's cheek and turning to Nut. "You're with me." After a solemn nod to Axis, he takes one last longing look at Azrian. "See you soon, Azzy."

"Yeah," he says quietly. Az shifts on his feet once and then climbs up on Axis' back. "See you on the other side, Jellycrai."

Kato watches them go until they're completely out of sight before he starts walking the way Azrian told him to. Nut chitters on by his side, but he doesn't really listen. It's too hard to hear him over his own thoughts.

~

Walking away from Kato is harder than he thought it would be. Not just because they've become so much closer, but because he truly does feel safer with him. His hands curl a little tighter in Axis' fur as they dash toward Brinecoast at a speed that shouldn't be possible, but it doesn't do much to help the uneasiness in his gut. Something is wrong... this is wrong.

"This is a mistake, Ax," Azrian whispers, knowing the valianis won't respond. "We shouldn't be splitting up, we shouldn't..."

The abrupt visual of a group about a half mile off has Az shutting up and ducking down as low as he can, but if they notice him as Axis guides them through the shadows, they don't show it.

Brinecoast proves to be scary, lonely, and cold, even with Axis to keep him warm. Az decides not to waste money on an inn and opts instead to stay with Axis in the forest, but all that does is remind him of their time deep in the Simbian. He pushes those thoughts aside to feed them both, but he notices Axis seems a little more high-strung than normal. "I never thought I'd miss having a Cogitare around," Az says quietly. "Are you okay?"

Axis pushes Az with his nose and stands, sniffing the air around them and then zeroing in toward the north with a growl. His hair stands on end as he nudges Azrian again, snorting at his weapon and then taking a step forward.

Panic spikes through Azrian as he fumbles for the bow and arrow. He's only got a couple left and the light is fading quickly, so even if he manages to pick a target, it'll be a miracle if he actually hits it. "Cettia," he hisses to the sky. "This would be a great time to help me out."

He gets no response, and the sound of a twig snapping to his rear has him whirling around and nearly dropping his notched arrow. Az doesn't think, doesn't breathe — just lets that arrow fly and scrambles to grab his bag. "Axis, run!"

The valianis nudges him hard enough to make him lose balance and lays down for him to climb on, but before he can even catch his footing to comply, they're surrounded. Panic surges until he realizes that no one is reaching for a weapon or their powers. Instinctively, Az understands they're not here to kill him. They're here to take him, which means there are only two choices available to him: fight and hope they both get free or let them take him and send Axis after Kato.

It doesn't take much for him to make up his mind. He leans in close to Axis and rushes out, "Go. Find Kato."

The giant beast huffs at him, then looks around at the intruders before taking a step back. They look nervous when he stalks forward, but without hesitation, they part to let him through. With one last look into Azrian's eyes, Axis takes off running.

"How'd you get a valianis to do your bidding, Videre?" a woman with a tight ponytail asks.

"I'm not a Videre," he corrects. *At least not right now.* "And Axis does what he wants, he's not my slave." The sound of his own heartbeat is loud enough that he's sure everyone can hear it. It thunders in his veins, giving away just how scared he really is — despite the poor attempt at keeping a calm exterior. "What do you want?"

"You," she states plainly, her dark blue eyes dance with amusement, knowing he's no threat. "Well, not *you.* But you'll do. Will you come quietly, or do we have to hurt you?"

Another man grunts and steps forward. "Choose the latter, I've been looking forward to this." His orange eyes look menacing as he cracks his knuckles. "Where is the Cogitare?"

Knowing it won't do any good, Az tries to call on his powers. When his hands stay void of light and he remains just as abysmally human as ever, he lets out a sharp breath and stands his ground. "I don't care what you do to me. I can't tell you where he is because I don't know." The words come out firmer than he expects, but it's also not technically a lie. Kato could be anywhere by now.

The woman makes a *"huh"* noise and cocks her head at a younger girl. This one doesn't have a weapon, but her golden eyes tell Azrian what her defense is. "He's telling the truth. They split up, but—" she takes another step in, like reading his mind is harder for her than it is for Kato — "the Cogitare will come. He's in love with this human."

The Viribus barks a laugh and the others join in. "You hear that, Kareen? They're in love. Boss was right."

Kareen checks Azrian out a little longer before she laughs harder than necessary. "What's so special about him, Pax?"

Still laughing, he wipes his face with a shrug, pulling out some restraints and walking forward. "Beats me. Hands behind your back, little human."

Azrian looks over at the younger girl and can see that she doesn't want to be there. *Is she also a prisoner? And if she's like Kato, where has she been all this time?* "You're wrong about one thing. Kato doesn't know what love is, and he's too smart to walk into a trap. He'll see it coming a mile away."

As the truth sinks in, Az starts to shake. He's not wrong; with Kato's powers, he'll know what's going on — and that means Az is on his own. He turns slowly, putting his hands behind his back and squeezing his eyes shut, bracing for whatever's going to happen next.

Pax grips his wrists and squeezes, yanking harder than necessary and tying him so tight his hands instantly began to ache. "Riley, is there truth behind his words?"

She frowns, staring at Az again and then nodding, but there's something else in her eyes — something she isn't telling them.

"So nice try. You'd have been better off kidnapping the raccanis," Az says bitterly. He earns a sharp tug on the restraints which pinches his shoulders, but he refuses to show any kind of pain. He thinks as hard as he can: *"You know this isn't right. I helped Kato escape, I can help you, too,"* toward the Cogitare.

Her eyes widen and she looks away, obviously trying to block her face from the others. She doesn't comment on his offer, but she does communicate back after a few moments of walking in silence. *"You're wrong, Azrian. He will come for you... and they will kill him."*

~

Axis sniffs the air for Kato, but he's still not close. Luckily, he's smart enough to read a map so he knows exactly which direction to head. It's only a matter of time before he picks up the scent. *Must find Kato. Azrian's destiny is already in motion. He needs to know the truth.*

Knowing one's destiny makes it nearly impossible to stay on track, otherwise he would have simply told them the plan — but that isn't how it works. Telling them would have caused more harm than good, and things needed to play out exactly as they have. He didn't even have to suggest them splitting up, they got there all on their own and Axis was quite proud of them both.

He stops again to sniff the air and although he doesn't smell Kato, his nose finally picks up Nut's scent. Axis darts in that direction so quickly he'd be a blur to untrained eyes, but Kato needs to know the next step.

He needs to save Azrian, and this was the only way for Azrian to regain his powers. The only way he would become worthy once more. *He is worthy, Cettia. He is worthy.*

Paws dig into the ground as he sprints even faster. He's almost to Redhaven now, and Kato is close... he can smell the anxiety seeping from his pores, and when he can finally see him, his shoulders are tense. Kato hates being separated from Azrian, but this was the only way. No one would have been able to capture Azrian if Kato were there, he would have died for him if it came to it. *No, this was the only way. Now, he must listen.*

~

Kato hears the thump of Axis' paws and swirls around quickly, coming face to face with the beast. "Axis! Where is Azrian!?" Panic bubbles in his chest as he looks around, his stomach sinking when he's nowhere in sight. "Axis?!"

"*He will be kept safe, Kato. This was written.*"

This is exactly what Kato had feared — that Axis would follow some long-foretold prophecy over keeping Azrian safe. Kato's body trembles with anger, and if he didn't feel like he needs the valianis, he'd punch him in the snout. "What happened?!" Kato manages to grunt out, his hands clenching at his sides.

"*He's been taken,*" Axis explains. "*We barely made it past Brinecoast, I ran straight here.*"

"Taken!" Kato yells out loud, his voice echoing around them. "And you just... what? Ran away?" Nut screeches at him but he ignores him, he doesn't care about any more stupid animal prophecies. "Shadows, Axe. I trusted you. You had one job."

"*And I did my job, K8.0.*" Axis stands strong, his snout angled high. "*My orders do not come from you. Azrian Mihr will be safe, but you must get to him. Now, would you like to continue yelling about it, or would you like me to tell you where he's being held? It took me over a week to reach you. He'll have reached his destination by now.*"

"Shadows!" Kato runs his hands through his hair and sighs. "Where is he? Let's go."

"*He's being held in the Rostian Ruins. There is a great chasm that separates the ruins from the mainland of Rostya, but on the other side, the Venandi have a secret stronghold at the base of the volcano. It will not be an easy journey, and you must be sure you're ready for it.*"

"I'm ready." Kato starts walking, having caught glimpses of the Ruins in enough thoughts to know it's real. "How do we cross the chasm?"

Axis snorts. "*Carefully and quietly. There are two options. We will decide what is best when we get there. I haven't been that far north in many years.*"

"Little hot for that coat. Maybe you should shed some fur," he attempts to joke, but it feels sour on his tongue. He shouldn't be making jokes without knowing Azrian is safe.

They walk in silence for a while and when they reach the edge of Redhaven, they split up. It ends up being just like all the other towns they've passed through. People stare at him as usual, but he walks with his head held high and they avoid his path. Even here, no one wants to get too close to a Cogitare, but they don't need to. He can hear their thoughts regardless.

Kato finds them some food and makes his way back out to the trees, sitting down with them to eat. "Should we try and find help?"

"*No, it is too dangerous,*" Axis warns as Nut chirps and nibbles on his food. "*The less contact you have with others, the better.*"

"Okay, so we sleep a couple hours and then we go. It will be guarded, but probably not heavily. They assume no one would dare try and go in there... who would be stupid enough to try, right?" Kato eats a little more and then continues. "I knew most of the people who worked for Melior, but not all. Sometimes, someone would come in that I didn't recognize, and I would catch glimpses of the Ruins. It's smaller than Deadrun, but just as secluded."

"*Sleep, then. Once we're on the move, you won't be able to rest very much at all.*"

Kato finishes his food and settles in, Nut cuddling into his legs like he has been since they've been alone. The familiarity of it is the only comfort he finds all night, but he really didn't expect to sleep much, anyway... not without knowing Azrian is safe.

~

Az wakes up slowly. The dim lights illuminating the cell he's in only serve to remind him of his predicament, so he's not in a hurry to open his eyes. The cuffs are now digging into his wrists so badly that he's been freely bleeding for the past couple of days, but he's long since given up looking for any sense of humanity here.

Wherever he is, whoever these people were before they became part of the Venandi... they don't have any humanity left.

A menacing laugh interrupts the silence, and Az looks over at the cell door, his blood running cold at the sight of Belua. "What happened, Azrian? Not so efficient without your Cogitare on a leash?"

"He's not on a leash... not anymore," Az says as he sits up. "He broke the one you had him on, remember? Guess you guys are pretty mad you lost him. What a shame."

Belua twitches. It's clear his anger nearly takes over, but he forces out a laugh. "Still have that mouth on you. Would have thought a little time in the world would make you more appreciative for the people who took you in."

"You mean the people that burned my house down? You mean you?" Az rights himself and leans forward on his bench. "I remember now, you know. Your eyes aren't *quite* the same shade of red as the other Igneme I've seen. It took me a minute to work it out for sure, I mean... I had my suspicions, of course, but couldn't be quite sure. But I am now. You didn't take me in, Belua. You burned my house down and killed my mom. You took me."

"Killed your mom? Now, I don't remember that part." He smiles, turning to walk away, but he stops and looks over his shoulder. "Don't worry, we couldn't give a stone about you, especially powerless. Your boyfriend is coming... and he's the one that will pay."

Fear for Kato kicks into overdrive, and not for the first time, he attempts to reach out to the Cogitare just in case he's close. *"Kato, if you can hear me, turn around. Go to Redhaven, finish what we started. Don't come here. I'm okay, and it's a trap. It's a trap. It's a trap."*

He repeats those three words until he's nearly hyperventilating, and the absolute only thing that makes him stop is the fact that all the air leaves his lungs at once. For a moment, he's sure he's dreaming — that he either fell back asleep on this cold, hard bench... or that Belua finished the job and he just didn't notice. For standing in front of his cell is one person he never expected to see again as long as he lived, looking as alive and healthy as he remembers her.

"Mom?" He's on his feet in an instant, throwing himself at the metal between them and trying to reach through. "Mom?! H-how?"

"Azrian." She grips him tightly and gasps at his wrists. "Let me help you." She pulls out the key and unlocks the door and then his cuffs, sitting on his bed to check him over. "You're skinny."

"I know," he says quietly, rubbing the raw skin as he stares at her like she isn't real. "A... raccanis keeps eating all of my food."

"That might be the strangest thing you've ever said to me." She smiles softly. "I'm so happy they found you."

Az squints, his mind finally snapping back to the real and present danger they're in. "Happy? Found me? What are you talking about? This is the second time that shadowhead has kidnapped me. And he kidnapped you... Mom, we have to go!" He stands to try and leave, but she grabs his arm a little too low and he flinches from the spike of pain.

"Azrian. They saved me from the fire. They saved you. You were supposed to be safe with them, and then that... traitor took you away." Her face tells Az she believes every word she's saying, and Az isn't even sure where to start with changing her mind.

They brainwashed her too, he realizes. "Mom, I know you believe that, but I need you to come with me. Kato isn't a traitor; I'll explain everything once we're out of here. Come on." He tries again to tug her up and out of the open cell, but she won't budge — and he can't leave her. He won't. "Please!"

"Azrian, calm down." She pulls out of his grip and blocks the cell door. "You can't. You're still confused. I'll visit you in a few days and hopefully you'll be fed and rested."

Another pang of panic races through him. "Mom, please just listen to me! Belua is the one that burned our house down, he kidnapped us both! I thought you were dead, they..." The conversation plays back in his mind, and he realizes they really hadn't been lying. She is okay, just not safe at home in Edros like he'd assumed they'd meant. "Kato saved me, he's not a traitor. We saved each other."

His mother frowns and stares at him like she's conflicted, but they're interrupted by Belua. "Roe, I don't think he's ready."

"I'll never be ready," Azrian spits. "I swear to Cettia, one day... I'll kill you myself." He stands in front of his mom and tries once more to call on powers that are no longer there, and Roe turns away without another word.

The slam of the metal closing makes Azrian flinch and Belua laughs off his threat. "You and what army?"

Anger and something a little like despair block any words from coming out, and all he can do is watch Belua lead his mother away from him again.

It's another two full days before Azrian sees another living person. He wasn't cuffed again, but the cuts the crude metal left on his wrist are starting to get infected, which feels even worse. So, when Riley approaches his cell, he's not thinking about escape or food or even water — he wants to be healed. "Is there a Sana here?" he asks quietly, knowing just from the look on her face that there isn't. When she confirms, he flicks his eyes down to the canteen in her hands. "Is that for me?"

"Yes." She hands it over and looks around, using her mind to reach out. *"Why did K8.0 want to leave?"*

Understanding, he focuses on keeping his response non-verbal. *"They were using him. Treating him like an animal. Like a slave. They were hurting him, too. Anytime he didn't do exactly what they wanted or he started to question them, they'd hurt him."* He takes a long gulp of the water his body so desperately needs, then continues as he wiped his mouth: *"Are they hurting you?"*

"No. I get migraines and they help me but they're rare. How were they hurting him?" She pulls out a wrap and ointment and starts treating his wounds, which isn't as good as a Sana's healing touch but also isn't something he's going to push away.

"They were giving him migraines, too. Then doing surgery to dig around in his brain, but they told him it was to help." He watches her hands and notices how pretty she is, then wonders idly if all Cogitare are unreasonably good looking or if it's just her and Kato. *"Are they really going to kill him?"*

"Yes." She slows her hands. *"I don't want them to. I've only met him a couple of times but... he's..."* Riley blushes and looks around them. *"I don't think he's a traitor. He can't be."*

Hope sparks against all odds. *"He's not. Kato is the best person I've ever met. He's strong and selfless and cares about doing what's right. The Venandi are the traitors, Riley."*

Riley finishes up the wraps and eyes him warily. "*I know. I've seen inside his mind. I will come later with food.*" She backs out of the cell and locks it, frowning as she turns away.

As soon as she's gone, Azrian slumps against the wall and tries again to reach out to Kato to head him off. "*Jellycrai, if you can hear me, I need you to leave. Please. They're going to kill you. You have to run, it's a trap. They don't want me, they want you.*"

He still gets no response, but he repeats the same message every few minutes until he passes out from a mix of exhaustion and dehydration.

~

"*Kato. This is the last time I'm going to try this... I'm beginning to think you aren't coming for me. Maybe Axis didn't find you, maybe you figured out on your own it's a trap... I don't know. But if you can hear me, Jellycrai, it means you're too close and you need to leave. They never wanted me; I'm just bait for you. Don't give them the satisfaction. Please. Just go to Redhaven and finish the job, then go get that little cabin. Don't come here.*"

Azrian's voice catches him off guard so badly he slips on a sharp rock. "Ouch!" He cusses as Nut's nails dig into his shoulders. "He's ridiculous if he thinks I'd ever leave him," he grunts to the animals. "*I don't want a cabin. I don't want to finish anything. Not without you, shadowhead.*"

"*Shadows, Kato! They'll kill you if you come here. Please don't die for me.*"

"Shut—" he slips again, stopping himself on a branch and splitting his hand. "*Dammit. Az... as much as I'd like to talk right now... if I fall... I'll burn. Give me a moment.*"

No answer comes as Kato takes a deep breath and tries to right himself. Nut is clawing into his neck trying to find purchase as they make their way up the far side of the chasm, Axis already near the top thanks to his agility and powerful body. It takes nearly everything Kato's got left to keep them steady, and they nearly lose it right at the top. His entire body hurts as Nut climbs off of him to safety and it seems impossible to muster the strength to lift up, but when he imagines Az in another cell, he finds it.

Kato collapses onto the ground, catching his breath a moment before reaching out to Az. "*Azzy... please tell me they haven't hurt you.*"

"*Shadows, Jellycrai, don't scare me like that. They... haven't really hurt me, no.*"

Suddenly, Kato gets flashes of other things. A bone-dry canteen, an empty plate, bleeding wrists... a girl he vaguely recognizes with eyes like his own and a woman that looks a little like Azrian himself.

"*Is that your mother?*" he asks without thinking, and then feels the need to apologize. "*I'm sorry I looked. I just had to know where you are.*"

"*Yes, she's been here the whole time. They got to her, though... she actually thinks Belua is a good person.*"

Kato's speechless for a few moments, not sure if he should celebrate Azrian's mother being alive or apologize for her being another one of their puppets. "*I'm glad she's alive. We'll just have to convince her. And the Cogitare? She looks familiar.*"

"*Her name is Riley. She knows you... she likes you. She's been helping me a little when she thinks she can get away with it. I'm pretty sure I'm alive because of her.*"

Axis nudges Kato's arm and stops him from responding right away. He turns his great big head toward the horizon and the building they can now make out in the distance, then bends down for Kato to climb on. "*Advise him to be ready,*" Axis orders.

"*Az. You gotta be ready. We won't have much time once we are seen. Please tell me you can run.*" Kato climbs up on Axis, gripping his fur tightly.

There's sheer, unfiltered panic in Azrian's tone as he responds this time. "*Kato! Please, don't do this! They're going to kill you and I can't stop it. Please, just... leave!*"

Axis takes off at breakneck speed and sticks to the shadows, which grow darker with each passing second as they approach the entrance to the stronghold. *"I'll kill them if I have to. I'll make them kill themselves. But I won't let them kill you."* He thinks about something Axis told him a few days ago and hopes it helps Az. *"You can stop it, Az. All of it. The power is inside you. You are worthy. Please... you have to believe me. Believe in yourself."*

"Kato, I don't know what that means! I've been trying, I can't! Please, ju—"

"Az! Azrian!" Kato yells into his mind until he's convinced he won't answer, and then he takes a chance. Reaching out to Riley is a risk, not only because she could turn them in, but because he doesn't know her well enough to just speak to her... it might not work. But he does it anyway. *"Riley... Riley can you hear me? It's... Kato."*

Her soft voice echoes in his mind over Axis' near-silent footfalls. *"You shouldn't be here,"* she warns.

"Yeah... I've heard. I— we need your help. The world needs your help. Look into my mind, you'll see the truth. You'll see you can trust me."

Kato flinches as she full-scale attacks his mind, but the deeper she goes, the calmer she gets. He can feel the shift as Axis comes to a stop beside the wall of the facility, and it's confirmed with her next answer. *"Stay where you are."*

Less than two minutes later, the grating of stone fills the silence, and a door opens up in the once-smooth wall next to them. All three slip inside, and Kato looks at her face closer than he could have in Az's mind. "Thank you, Riley. I remember you." Nut screeches at them and Axis snorts for them to keep moving. "Where is Azrian?"

"Belua has him. Someone tipped him off when you crossed the chasm, and he went straight to Azrian's cell. I think he's being held in Belua's private chambers." Riley turns on her heels and starts leading the way through the twisted corridors, and Kato realizes they'd have been utterly lost without her.

"I can take care of him, I have before. Why is Azrian convinced they'll kill me? Is it because they have you now and I'm just a threat? Or is it personal?"

"It's both," she rushes out, then holds a finger to her lips as she slows down and tiptoes around a corner. Within seconds, they're surrounded by Venandi as the power gets cut.

It's pitch black, but he doesn't need his eyesight to know they're close. *"Walk away."* Kato focuses on their minds, trying to manipulate all of them at once. *"We're the good guys."*

One by one, he hears the shuffling of feet as the tension in the room lifts and the thoughts of the Venandi get farther away. It stays dark though, and Axis growls quietly as he tries to shove his way through the tight corridor.

"He's this way," Riley says silently. *"Hold on to me and follow."*

Kato grips her hand and lets her lead the way, his heart pounding in his chest. *I'm almost there Azzy. Just hang on.*

He stays quiet but reaches out to Riley. *"Belua is probably with him. Can you make sure Az is okay as soon as we enter?"*

"Of course." Riley comes to a sudden stop and clenches his hand, then whistles low. It sounds like some sort of signal, and Kato's pretty convinced of that when the door swings open and he hears Belua's voice.

"Who in the shadows cut the damn power? Where are the Videre?"

Kato steps in front of Riley and reaches out with his mind, but he feels... off. It's a familiar feeling he used to get at Deadrun right before a migraine hit. *"No Videre here, Belua. Try again later,"* he tries again, this time making contact but it's like running against the wind — he can't hold it. *Shadows.*

A soft, evil chuckle fills the dark space. "K8.0. The prodigal experiment gone wrong, come home at last." Heavy footfalls echo off the walls and get a little closer with each one. "You're actually late, I figured you'd run to save your little boyfriend before we even got here."

"Kato," Az sputters from somewhere to his right. "Shadows, I told you not to!"

Kato is just happy to hear Az is alive and takes a steady breath, nudging Riley toward where he heard Az and moving slowly away to scale the wall. "My name is Kato. And I'm more than just some experiment, Belua. That's where you shadowheads went wrong." He uses his mind to cut off Belua's airway, but it only lasts a few seconds before his head starts to hurt once more.

"This is going to be fun," Belua hisses. The next thing he knows, the room erupts in flame and the heat drives them all back a step, but also illuminates their surroundings. The cause of his mental block is made clear when his eyes register Adeinde on their way to locate Azrian — Az, who's wide-eyed and cowering as a wall of fire builds in front of him.

He takes one step toward him to help and Belua screams, sending a concentrated ball of flame straight at him. Kato's able to dodge most of it with minimal damage, but he has to dive onto the floor, and the way his face scrubs the concrete hurts worse than the small burn on his arm.

"Kato!" Az screams, lunging himself at Belua's body with his hands full of silver light. They collide and careen through that building inferno, and Kato loses sight of them entirely.

Riley's hand closes around Kato's wrist and yanks him toward the window. "We have to go!"

Nut screeches and jumps on his shoulders again as Riley pulls him, but he rips his arm from her grasp. "No! I won't leave him!"

"*I have Azrian. Go Kato! Now!*" Axis' voice booms in his mind and he looks into the smoky room one last time before following Riley through.

~ XV ~

THE REGNUM

Az uses the last of his strength to cling to Axis. The rush of getting his powers back was great, but as it turns out, rage-killing someone as powerful as Belua has some lingering effects.

The valianis dashes through the halls of the burning building and makes so many sudden movements that Azrian nearly falls off, but he uses what little energy he can muster to light Axis' way through the smoke. When they break through the main door and out into the fresh air, Az barely has time to be relieved before Kato hauls him off the animal's back and into a hug.

"Ka— I'm okay," he says quietly, wrapping his arms around his large body. "I want to kill you for not listening to me, but I'm okay."

Kato squeezes and holds him there like he has all the time in the world, and then pulls back to look into his eyes. "Me? I told you I never wanted to separate." The scrape on his face has Azrian reaching out to touch it, but before his fingers even reach the skin, Kato is slamming their mouths together in a messy, desperate kiss.

It nearly knocks Azrian off his feet, but Axis is still behind him to brace him as he tries to keep up with it, and the adrenaline still coursing through him kicks into overdrive and wakes up parts of him that would be better off sleeping at the moment. "Jellycrai," he rushes out between kisses. "I'm okay."

"You better be." Kato presses their foreheads together and then peels himself away. "Alright, Axis. We have to go." He grips Az's hand and guides him along, and Riley finally looks up from the ground she's been staring at since Kato first kissed him. It's clear from the look on her face that she's got something to say, but she keeps her mouth shut and her gaze averted as they start to walk.

Eventually, Az realizes that Riley isn't the only one biting her tongue and braces himself to get yelled at. "Kato, I'm sorry, okay? I thought... I thought we could make it."

"I know. I hated every day without you, Azrian." His grip on his hand tightens and he looks around at the others, seemingly realizing that this isn't the time. "Riley... who will they send with Belua dead?"

"I'm not sure. Adeinde took Azrian's mother. We had an Itinerae here, so they're long gone by now. I'm sorry, Azrian."

Kato frowns, looking over at Az and reaching out with his mind. *"We'll get her back."*

"But she's alive? What about the others that were there, the other prisoners?" Azrian asks Riley, his voice small. The moment he'd seen those flames, he'd feared the worst, especially when he nearly lost control of the surge of energy pulsing through him. "You're sure they'll be okay?"

"The others escaped the same way we did; I can hear them. And Adeinde won't hurt your mother, not until they've..." She stops and looks at Kato with a look he recognizes. She finished her sentence, just not out loud.

Anger flashes through Azrian and he pulls his hand out of Kato's grasp. "Awesome. Yet another person that can talk like I don't exist." He conjures a small ball of silver energy and lets it float in front of him as he walks toward the chasm, fondly remembering the people like Rhix, Callisto and Ronan that *couldn't* carry on silent conversations.

Everyone is silent for a few moments before Kato speaks out himself. "I'm sorry. She didn't want to worry you. She just said they won't hurt your mom until they kill me."

"I was there, you know. Belua told me every single day that I was nothing but bait, that they were trying to get you. This isn't news to me."

"Maybe not, but do you know why? What the *real* goal is... at Deadrun *and* the Ruins? I'll give you a hint. It's not *just* universe-hopping for profit," Riley says.

Az blinks at her. He was at Deadrun, too. He heard them. He was put to use to try and accomplish that very goal... so what is she talking about? "I don't understand."

"Yeah, I get that." She sighs, scratching the back of her head and pushing her short hair up into a bun. "They're trying to make more."

Before Azrian can ask, Kato interrupts. "More Praediti?"

"Not all Praediti, why would they need another soil bender? No, they need us. And him." Riley nods at Azrian. "The surgeries, they weren't to help, they were to see if they could remake you. Hybrids, too. Imagine what an army of Cogitare that could also teleport, or... or manipulate air could do. Melior would rule the universe. All of them."

"And have they succeeded?" Kato stops walking and stares at her, seeing the answer in her mind before she speaks.

"Yeah... once. You."

Azrian shivers, stepping closer to Kato on instinct. "You mean... he wasn't supposed to be a Cogitare? He was born human?"

"Well, his mother was human. But whatever they did, it was when K8.0 was inside of her. They had tried so many times... think all the letters before the letter K, plus the seven of those that came before him. I didn't know this before, I only investigated when I met Azrian. I would have told you, Kato." She touches his arm and stares into his eyes.

"And you? Did they torture your mother, too?" Kato asks, his chest rising and falling quickly.

"No. I was born this way and they brought me here for a *better* life. My parents agreed." Despair flashes in Riley's eyes, but it's gone as quickly as it came. "We have to keep moving."

The bond that forms between Riley and Kato in that instant would've made the old Azrian jealous. But now, so close to the end, with so much lost and so many truths shattering their realities... Azrian is glad they found each other. He's glad they *all* found each other. "You're right. We should keep moving. The sooner we get to Redhaven, the sooner we can finish this."

He notices Kato is practically silent the entire journey to the chasm. Not just out loud, he seems to be trapped in his own thoughts. He doesn't speak until they're staring down the deep, gaping hole and fear overtakes all of them. "Axis... can you hold Nut this time?" Axis nods at him and Nut climbs on. "Okay, Az. Please be careful, I will jump in after you." Kato pulls him in for another kiss, this time slow and deep.

Riley squints at them. "Um... why aren't we just taking the bridge? Or the boat? Do you really think the Venandi risked their lives climbing down into that thing and back up the other side?"

Kato pulls back abruptly and frowns at her. "There's a damn bridge? I assumed they teleported in with your Itinerae."

"Most of the time, we do, but he's not always around. Melior calls him to Deadrun sometimes." She pets Axis' head and points off to the right. "It's down here, maybe a half mile or so."

Az expands his silver light a little and sends an inaudible "thank you" up to Cettia. He may not understand why his powers come and go so erratically, but he had them when he needed them most — saving Kato, and just maybe saving his mother, too.

By the time they reach the bridge, his muscles are tired again from lack of use in that cell. The wooden, rickety thing swings over the expanse of the chasm in a way that screams danger — but Az doesn't have it in him to fear it at this point. "Okay, I'll... I'll walk you guys over one by one, so we have light."

Everyone agrees, but Axis insists he and Nut go first. "He wants to make sure it's safe on the other side before we cross, Az." Kato kisses his hand and whispers, "Be safe."

Crossing with a giant beast and a fat raccanis makes him nervous. He wants to ask Riley if the bridge can bear that much weight at once, but he makes a conscious decision to stop being such a shadowhead and to just... do whatever he needs to do for once.

Axis steps onto the wood and then looks back at Az with an encouraging huff, nodding for him to lead. He fists one hand in Axis' fur and uses the other to guide the light, then takes a couple of tentative steps. They make it halfway before they come to the first missing plank, and Az actually laughs. It's so cliché that it seems almost ridiculous, and it's the humor alone that gives him the strength to actually step over and help guide the animals across, too.

The rest of the trip isn't long, and they reach the other side without issue. He rubs Axis' head and whispers, "Just howl if there's danger, okay? Be careful."

When the valianis dips his snout in acknowledgment, Az makes his way back across the bridge to get Riley. This time, the trip is easier — he feels more confident since she's so much smaller than the animals and he knows the way now, but when they reach the other side, he realizes he doesn't know what to do. Kato is on one side without light, alone, and if he goes back to get him, Riley will be over here in the same situation.

"Just sit tight until Axis comes back, okay? We'll hurry."

"It's okay. I don't hear any thoughts around here, only the raccanis' complaining." Riley takes a seat to rest, looking around with wide eyes as Az slowly makes his way back.

Kato is pacing, one hand scratching his head as Az approaches. "This might be worse than the boat. I'm heavy... what if it breaks and I kill us both?"

"Are you suddenly heavier than our chubby raccanis and a valianis the size of a small house?" Az asks, his eyebrows raised. "We're going to be okay, Kato. I need you to trust me. Come on." He holds out his hand, smiling in spite of himself and the very real danger they're in. Kato being afraid of anything is a little adorable.

Kato audibly swallows and takes Az's hand, letting him lead the way onto the wooden planks. "But what if Axis made the wood weaker?"

"Don't let him hear you say that, he'll eat you," Az jokes, expanding the light with a deep breath. They take another step forward and Azrian squeezes his hand. "See? It's sturdier than it looks. Kind of like me."

That seems to distract Kato enough to start making real progress across the bridge. "I think I forgot... maybe you should show me tonight how sturdy you really are."

"Ka—" Az almost trips, grasping onto Kato and sucking in a sharp breath when the bridge sways below them. His heart thunders in his chest and the silver light dissipates, throwing them into complete darkness. "Shadows," he whispers sharply. "Sorry!" He closes his eyes and concentrates until the light comes back, then smiles sheepishly up at Kato. "Not a good time to say something like that, Jellycrai."

"Oops." Kato chuckles as he squeezes his hand softly. "I missed you, Azzy."

Suddenly, Azrian wishes they were anywhere in Athoze *other* than this bridge spanning a chasm that could kill them. It's been too long, too many sleepless nights without Kato. "I missed you, too. Now come on, we need to get to the other side."

They move a little slower, still plastered together, and neither of them breathe freely until their feet are firmly planted on solid ground again. Riley is blushing furiously, and it doesn't take Azrian long to figure out why — the thoughts she probably overheard weren't exactly appropriate.

"Sorry, Ri," Az says, then clears his throat.

Kato laughs again, wiping his sweaty palms on his pants. "Yeah... you didn't need to see those memories."

Riley looks relieved when Axis appears again and nods to tell them it's clear. "No one is here yet; we should destroy the bridge. It'll buy us time... unless Dabbe comes back and just teleports them over, but that isn't likely. They don't want to risk him, he's the last one of his kind under their control that isn't a child."

"You're right." Az clenches his jaw as he walks to the edge of the chasm and bends down, wrapping his hands around the ropes tying the right side to the post. He sends one, quick plea up to Cettia that his mother really did get away from the Ruins, then sends a burst of energy out that frays and shreds the rope. He moves quickly to do the same to the other side, then braces himself as the whole thing falls... and falls... and falls.

A dull *thunk* echoes as the planks finally hit the other side, and Az makes his way back to the others. "Should we camp here then since we know it's safe?"

Kato looks over at Axis for a few moments and then at Az. "He said if we walk a few yards that way, the trees will cover us for the night. But... we need to leave before sunrise."

Riley pets him again and he nudges her hand with closed eyes, loving the new attention as if he *isn't* hundreds of years old. It gives Azrian an idea, and he nudges Kato to get him to follow along. "Riley, why don't you take Axis and Nut tonight? They'll keep you warm. Safe, too. Kato and I can sleep together."

"Only if you two keep your thoughts quiet in the morning." She raises an eyebrow and Axis snorts, making her and Kato laugh.

"He told her about the time he saw us." Kato grabs his hand again, smiling widely at him. Az can tell Kato is happy they're back together, but now that things have slowed a little, he sees the bags under his eyes and how slumped his shoulders are. It becomes pretty clear how hard Kato must've pushed himself to get to Azrian as quickly as he did and coupled with how grueling the journey as a whole has to have been for someone like him, Az finds himself thinking less about sex and more about simply bringing Kato some comfort.

They set up their makeshift camp quickly and eat what little they have left in Kato's pack, and Az slides behind Kato to massage his muscles as Riley and the others turn in. "Thank you for saving me, Jellycrai."

Kato turns with a grin, their lips meeting much slower than their reunion, and this time, Kato moves to kiss down his neck. "I know we stink but... you still smell good to me."

He shifts to climb onto Kato's lap, loving how well he fits there. "Shh. That's enough talking for now."

~

Walking up to Redhaven is intimidating. The trip took longer this time, but Kato blames adrenaline on how he made it to Ruins so quickly. Now that Az is safe and their group is a little bigger, it takes days to arrive and all of them are exhausted and weak. They take another night to rest and clean up on the outskirts of the city, hiding in the trees with their beasts. Nut has lost some weight, but Kato thinks it's best because he can move much faster now.

When they enter the city limits, Kato opens his mind and reaches out to see if it's safe. "*Stay close, Azzy. We'll run if we have to.*"

"*No. I'm tired of running, Kato.*" Az squeezes his arm and straightens the pack on his shoulder, looking more determined than Kato has seen him since their escape from Deadrun. "*We finish this. One way or the other.*"

As they walk the streets of Redhaven, people stare. They got as clean as they could that morning, but their clothes are still worn and dirty and make them stand out among the clean-cut citizens.

Riley walks so closely their arms brush, but Kato doesn't mind. She's just as nervous as they are, and he remembers how it feels to betray the Venandi. As much as they might believe they're doing the right thing, it's still hard not to feel guilty. She seems to take comfort in the fact that she's not the only Cogitare to stray, and Kato somehow just instinctively knows that they can count on her now no matter what... just like Azrian could count on Kato.

As they approach the building where the Regnum meet, Azrian's thoughts become loud — too loud, loud enough to get caught if the Regnum's Cogitare happens to be on the wrong side. But before he can even try to calm him down, they're approached by a woman and a man with identical features.

Neither say a word, they just... *stare* until Azrian finally clears his throat. "We're here to see the Reg—"

"I know who you are and why you've come, Azrian Mihr. You're a long way from Embermeadow. My name is Neginah," she adds as she turns her attention to Kato, answering an unspoken question. "This is my brother Hanigen. He may not be an official part of the Regnum, but we come as a package deal."

Kato can see they mean no harm, but he's still on guard and that knowledge doesn't stop him from standing in front of Az. "Oculare," he says to Az. He knows their black eyes give them away, but he doesn't want him feeling left out of anything. "They've seen the future."

Riley gasps when she sees what Kato sees, and she looks around to make sure they're still alone.

Hanigen smirks. "You Cogitare always ruin all the fun," he says playfully. "Care to ruin the punchline, too?"

"No. Tell him in your words." Kato nods to Az, his body tense as he grabs Azrian's hand. "Tell him how the Regnum is under Melior's thumb. How they will have a hand in the destruction of our universe."

The man rubs his jaw and sighs. "You said no, and yet you did it anyway. You're exactly how we saw you," he says with a laugh.

His sister smacks his arm and straightens up. "You're right. We knew you were coming, so we've been waiting for the last two weeks. You'll find nothing but betrayal within those walls, but you do have allies. People just like you that think the Venandi need to be stopped. We've seen the end—"

"And the end isn't pretty," Hanigen finishes. "So, who's up for a little rebellion?"

Azrian stiffens next to him, but he sets his jaw and dips his head in a single nod. "That's why we're here, but... if the Regnum won't help us, I don't know what to do. My powers come and go."

"We saw that too," Neginah admits. "But you have them now and from what we saw, you will have them when you need them. They will not help you here, but we will."

"Can we trust them, Kato?" Az asks silently. *"We need to be sure."*

Kato nods, looking deep into their minds for any sign of dishonesty. *"We can. They don't want Melior in power any more than we do."*

"Okay," he says out loud. "Then I only see one option. We need to go back to Deadrun and deal with him ourselves. Belua is already dead. If we get rid of or capture Melior... the rest crumbles, right?"

"Yes," Hanigen nods. "Everyone does his bidding because he has something over them. Even Belua — or he did. Their bond grew and Belua forgot what it was to love. Most of the others still have family. They don't want to be there. We guarantee you, the Venandi will crumble."

Riley asks, "So, how do we get there?"

"Boat," Az replies. "We're going to have to head to the northern coast of Sastrya and sail across the Aswel... again."

Kato's entire body stiffens so hard everyone around them notices the change. "Az..."

Riley's confused, but within seconds she's hiding a laugh behind her hand. "Boats? Really?"

"It isn't the boat part. It's the sailing part. You weren't there... you wouldn't understand."

Sighing, Az tugs him away from the group and whispers sharply, "We've traveled over chasms and-and dealt with kidnappings and burning buildings and creepy forests and tundra and you're still afraid of sailing?"

Kato nods, feeling his cheeks heat up when he realizes he's being a child. "I can't." He scratches at his scars and whispers, "Shadows... I'm sorry."

He softens, placing a firm hand on his arm. "Okay, Jellycrai. I get it, I do. But you know that means we need an Itinerae, right? And if the Regnum are compromised, the one here won't help us willingly. Are you prepared to do what needs to be done?"

That sounds so much easier to Kato, and it would save them time — weeks. "Yes. I will. Riley is willing too, but this one is on me."

"It's on all of us in one way or another." He threads their fingers together and searches his face, then guides them both back over to the others. "Change of plans. We're going to commandeer ourselves an Itinerae and cut the trip down by... a lot. We'll take tonight to prepare and get going in the morning. The sooner this is over, the better for everyone."

The twins share a long look, and Kato can practically hear the conversation they don't need to have. They decide to help with that as well and both think of a name at the same time. "Exus?" Kato asks.

"Yes," Neginah nods. "He's our Itinerae. We can get him out here at first light, but you must all be prepared to go. Your valianis as well."

Azrian's eyes turn almost silver as he nods. "We'll be ready."

~

They spend that night so far north of Redhaven they're practically at the base of the Tizor Mountains. But the distance allows them to build a fire for warmth that Azrian won't look at, and it casts a bright enough glow around their campsite that they can take stock of what they have left.

"I don't know what good actual weapons will be, but I'm taking them just in case Cettia decides to cut me off again," Az says as he sharpens his last Hokrine knife. "I don't think she will, but... it's better safe than sorry."

"I don't think she will either, Azzy." Kato sits behind him and watches him work. He's always felt protective of Azrian, but now that they're together, he never wants to leave his side. Bad things happen when they're apart.

Az continues silently for a while until the moonlight and flame are dancing off the shiny, sharp blade, then sets it aside to do the same to his final two arrowheads. When he's done, he leans back against Kato's chest and Kato embraces him, kissing his temple. "Do you think we're gonna live through this, Jellycrai?" Az asks quietly.

"Yes," Kato says quickly, not really wanting to think of the alternative. He knows Azrian wants a real answer though, so he sighs and kisses his cheek. "We will. Together... and if we don't... we'll do that together, too." As ominous as it sounds, he feels it needs to be said. He needs Az to know that he's by his side no matter the outcome.

"Then I guess we better live," he responds. "I'd like to experience what it's like to know you when we're not on the run and scared every day."

Kato smiles at that, but it slowly fades from his face as he thinks about it. He truly has no idea who he is outside of the Venandi. Even now that he's left them, his days still revolve around them. Granted, he's constantly running from them or fighting them, but outside of that... who is he? Who *is* Kato? And most troubling... will Azrian still want him?

~

The next morning, everyone is packing their things and preparing to leave when Kato rises. He jumps up, feeling bad for not helping until Axis puts him at ease. "*I told them to let you rest.*"

Kato nods. He's thankful for that, and for the fact that Riley can understand him like he can. "*Thank you.*" He stands, taking off to

search for Az and finds him by the river and filling up their canteens. "Morning, Azzy."

"Hi," he says quietly. "Big day today, huh?"

"Yeah." Kato pulls him in for a kiss and stares into his eyes. "No
matter what happens... I love you."

Azrian swallows, suddenly looking even more nervous — and a
little skeptical, too. "Will you promise to tell me that again when
this is over and we're safe?"

It's clear from thoughts too loud to block out that Azrian doesn't
think he's worthy, that a lifetime of being told he wasn't good
enough is still taking its toll. It's also clear that Azrian feels the
same way that he does, he's just too afraid to voice it out loud for
fear of having it ripped away from him. Kato just kisses him, wishing he could take away all his doubts. "Of course, Azzy."

Once all this is done, Kato will be able to show Az how worthy he
is, but for now, they have something big to take care of. There's no
room for self-doubt on either side. "Let's go kick their dicks."

"Their... what did you just say?" Azrian huffs a surprised laugh
and drops his head to Kato's shoulder. "We're going to need to work
on your battle talk, Jellycrai. Though, I'm pretty sure that method
would be effective."

Kato chuckles and interlocks their fingers, slowly making their
way back to camp with the canteens. "I'm not so sure, Melior's is really small... might not kick the right spot."

When Azrian laughs the sound that fills Kato's ears seems a lot
like magic, especially since it's been so long. "Shadows, Kato. Now
that's all I'm going to be thinking about when we get there. Should
properly confuse any Cogitare they have there, though."

He snorts and kisses Azrian's temple as they walk. "He may have
blocked most of his mind from me, but he couldn't hide his biggest
insecurity."

They join the others and Riley smirks when she hears what
they're talking about. "Yeah, some thoughts come through no matter how hard people try to hide them."

"Don't remind me," Az says sheepishly. "Sometimes I forget that I don't have any secrets from Kato whether it's my choice or not."

"I told you, I stay out of your mind unless I need to or you reach out to me, Azzy. I don't snoop... anymore," he admits with his own shy grin.

Riley smiles at them and throws her bag over her shoulder. "If we weren't walking toward sure death... I'd tell you both how adorable you are together."

"Thanks." Az elbows Kato and straps their bag to Axis' back. "It's good to know that I was cute right up until my deathday."

"Always cute." Kato helps lift another bag and straps it down too. "Axis, if you need to drop all of this, don't hesitate. It's just stuff... we need you safe."

Axis nudges him softly and then turns back to where Riley was petting him. Nut is nervous too, but he crawls up Kato's back and clings to his shoulders. After one more longing look at their small group, Kato stands tall and exhales a deep breath. "Last chance to back out, everyone." But he doesn't even need to read any of their minds to know they're all in.

For better or worse, deathday or the first day of the rest of their lives... this is it. With any luck, this journey will be over by nightfall, and they'll simply have to deal with whatever happens next.

~

Hanigen meets them outside of the courthouse with a sly smile. "I was beginning to think you wouldn't show."

"Believe me, it was a close call," Az admits. "But we're here. Where's Neginah?"

"Coming," he responds. "She's getting Exus out here as we speak... it's just proving to be a little harder than she thought it was. My twin has lost a little bit of her charm over the last few years."

Kato can see in his mind that Exus won't be persuaded to their side, so his hand tightens in Azrian's as he mentally prepares to take over another person's mind. It isn't ideal, but they don't have another choice, and Riley will be able to help when they arrive at Deadrun.

It only takes a few more moments for Neginah to come out the back door with an older man behind her, and Kato knows that's his mark. He doesn't waste time, reaching out and pushing past the natural defenses the Itinerae has built up as part of his training for the Regnum, and really, he's no match for Kato.

By the time they've joined the group, Exus' eyes are blank. "You wish to be taken to Deadrun?"

"Yes," Az answers quickly. The spike of fear he feels nearly knocks Kato's focus off, but they're transported as a group so quickly to the rocky cliffs outside of Deadrun's fortress that it doesn't matter that he almost failed.

Exus' bitter laugh sends a chill up Kato's spine. "Good luck... you're going to need it." He's gone in a blink, and Riley nearly slips off the rock she's clinging to.

"What in the shadows did that mean! I thought you had him, Kato!"

"I—" Kato feels like he failed, and he stares into Azrian's gray eyes. "I did... he..."

Riley curses and looks around them. "It's almost impossible to keep focus while being transported, it isn't his fault. But that isn't important anymore, they know we're coming. What do we do now?"

Kato tries to focus and reach out, but they're still alone on that mountain top... for now. It's much colder on the island than it was when they left, and he rubs Azrian's arms absentmindedly until Riley locates Axis and Nut and they head that direction to meet them.

When they're outside the gate itself and realize it's still sealed shut, Az kicks the concrete in frustration. "Of course he couldn't get us *inside*. Kato, you're gonna have to get Melior to open the door somehow."

"*Welcome home little K8.0. We've been waiting for you,*" Melior's voice booms in his mind, making him flinch and look around. One look at Riley tells him she heard it too. Just then, the gate alarm sounds, and it begins to slowly open for them. It sends off every red flag in all of their minds, but they don't have a choice.

They have to see this through.

~ XVI ~

THE RETURN

Azrian stares at the scared faces of his Cogitare friends and realizes *something* just happened — something he couldn't hear, but he can guess. The gate is open, which can only mean one thing: the Venandi are more prepared for them than they're prepared for the Venandi. "Kato," Azrian hisses as he hurriedly starts unstrapping the bags from Axis' back. "How bad is it?"

"Bad," Riley answers for him. "But screw this, I'm going in." She tugs her blond hair up into a tie and sprints through the flashing red alarm lights, disappearing from their view. It doesn't do anything but raise Azrian's anxiety level.

A snarl sounds above the alarm as the fur on Axis' back stands up, and for the first time, the patterns on the side of his face glow like they're magic. It would be one of the coolest things Az has ever seen if he weren't so sure they were about to die, and his feet start to move on their own in response. "C'mon!" he yells to the others, following Axis in and staying close as they move past the weapons room to Melior's office.

The door is unlocked, but Melior's nowhere to be found when Kato opens it. The office itself is almost completely empty. There's nothing but a desk and a map of a land Azrian doesn't recognize on the wall behind it, and the entrance to the weapons room is still barred off.

They don't have time to dwell — just as they're pushing their way back into the small hallway to get to the main part of the compound, they run smack into two very familiar faces.

"Callisto?!" Azrian whispers sharply. He expected to see Ronan, but not Cal. "We took you home! What happened?"

"No time for a reunion, you guys are seriously stupid. Heads full of shadows. Why would you come here?" Cal asks, grabbing Kato's arm and tugging him toward the security room. "They've already captured that girl you came here with."

Dread fills Azrian's gut as he realizes this whole thing is a trap. There are no Venandi in the immediate area. No one to capture them, no one to fight. They might not even be here at all for all they know — and as the alarm stops and the exit door swings shut loudly enough to make them all turn; he knows he's right.

They waltzed in here without much of a plan at all... and now they're stuck. "Um..."

Ronan grips his sleeve with his small hand. He looks terrible, like he's tried to resist the Venandi since the original escape and has paid dearly for it, and all it does is renew Azrian's resolve to finish this... trap or not. "Az, I know where they are."

"Tell me," he says softly. "We'll get you out this time, I promise. We're here to finish this, Ronan. We just need to find Melior. Is he here?"

The small boy nods and points to the left, toward the courtyard. "They're waiting where they do the surgeries. They want Kato."

Kato curses and closes his eyes, obviously focusing very hard, but whatever he's trying to do doesn't take. "Shadows! I can't even reach out to Ri. I hope she's okay." He runs a hand through his hair and looks into Ronan's eyes. "Would they let everyone else go safely if I turned myself in?"

"No," Ronan says quietly. "I don't think they're going to let any of us go. They want you the most, but now... Azrian likely killed Belua, and they've been running all kinds of experiments on me and Cal."

Azrian scoffs. "I think I had a good reason, and it's not like I wanted to. I didn't want any of this." What he did will haunt him forever, but if they're able to save everyone else... he tells himself it's all for the greater good. "So, what do we do now? If they're prepared for us, this isn't going to be easy. Where's Adeinde?"

"With Melior," Cal answers. "She brought your mom back here and hasn't left his side since. I think they've even been sleeping in the same room. He won't let her out of his sight."

He glances at Kato, knowing that if they don't get rid of Adeinde or find a way to separate her from Melior, all will be lost. "And where's my mom at now?"

"You know the rest area on the other side of the training room? The kinda big spot between the Sana's office and where they do surgery? They've made that into an extra holding cell because the ones by the entrance are full. They've been taking all kinds of Praediti." Cal flips on one of the monitors and points, showing them the holding cells that Azrian was kept in when he first arrived. Every single one of them is full, and every single trapped Praediti looks terrified. "They've basically given up this half of Deadrun to us, except for those cells. We can't figure out how to get the doors open so we've been doing what we can to feed them, but we have to sneak into the kitchens to pull it off and it's almost always a fight."

Ronan waves, then points at his bruised face with a satisfied grin. "I'm the smallest, so usually I go. They don't catch me for very long."

Azrian's heart sinks when he thinks of what they all must've gone through since they escaped originally. He wishes more than anything that Ronan would've come too and that Callisto would've stayed with them, but there's nothing he can do to change the past. "Okay. We need a plan. We should try to free the Praediti in the cells first. The more people we have on our side, the better... and the more chaotic this place gets, the harder it'll be for Adeinde to block our powers."

"Yeah, we've tried that, but thanks," Cal says sarcastically. "I already told you, we don't know how to get the doors open. If we enter the code wrong, the alarms will go off and all of Melior's little soldiers come running."

A slight smile crosses Azrian's face. "I'm not doubting you, Cal. But you didn't have Kato. Is there a guard down there?"

"Sometimes," Ronan says. "But not right now."

"Perfect. Kato, are you ready?" Az reaches out his hand and is surprised to find that he's not as scared as he thought he'd be. Maybe it's adrenaline, maybe it's stupidity... or maybe it's just exhaustion bubbling over to the point that he doesn't care what happens — he just wants this to be over.

~

As for Kato, he's a ball of tension and nerves, and he can't help but feel like this is his fault. Maybe if he would have helped Az escape and then stayed here for his punishment, Az would be living out in the forest instead of here knocking on death's door. He takes Azrian's hand, leading the way to the cells and like Ronan said, there isn't anyone there.

The password used to be a series of 9 numbers, and he hesitates with his fingers over the buttons. *What if they changed it? What if I give away our exact location by making a mistake?* He reminds himself that they don't have time for self-doubt, so he types in the code *462021520*, but the alarm blares the second he hits enter. "Shadows!" Kato punches the keypad and looks around, his eyes wild with fear. "They changed it... I'm sorry."

Az looks as if he's about to tell him it's okay, but before words can leave his lips, they hear a metal door clanging and all turn to see who's coming. It's Riley, and she looks shaken and terrified. "They said—" Kato touches her arm to help ground her. "They said turn yourselves in... or die."

One look at the others tells Kato all he needs to know, and regardless of their weakened state, they would rather die standing. He nods, closing his eyes and reaching out to someone — anyone in the vicinity. It takes a moment, but someone is scaling the wall outside the doors, trying to listen in on their plan.

Kato can't help but smile as he easily takes over his mind. He recognizes him before he sees him, and he remembers all the times this security guard was rude to him. "Hello, Loni. Long time no see. Show yourself."

He rounds the corner, his eyes glossed over showing everyone he's completely under Kato's spell. "Guess Melior needs his shield close, huh? Couldn't send her off with a nobody like you?" He tilts his head and nods at the keyboard. "What's the code?"

"Two. Four. Nine. One. Three. One. Five. Two. Zero," Loni states with a monotonous voice.

"Thank you." Kato types it in and the alarm stops just as they hear the cell doors slam. "Now go inside one of those cells and lock yourself in. Forget you saw us." He turns to leave and Kato follows, walking up to the group of confused Praediti. They shy away from Loni and even from Kato, but he holds out his hands. "We're here to help. Is anyone hurt?"

Several of them are, but none seem bad enough that they'd need a Sana's help. One older man steps toward the front and rolls up his tattered sleeves, revealing cuts and bruises marking his aging skin. "You'll wanna keep them two locked in," he says gruffly, pointing to two former guards. "They ticked Melior off, but old habits die real hard."

Kato nods and looks over at them. He recognizes them and they mostly stuck to themselves but still, the man is right. "Go inside the cells. We'll figure out what to do with you after." He uses his powers so they don't argue and then looks at the man's cuts. "They aren't even trying to pretend anymore, are they?"

"No, they haven't been trying to hide their true intentions since you lot escaped," he responds, then waves for some of the others to follow. "We know who we're dealin' with and what we're up against. We ain't afraid." His deep brown eyes turn molten as the ground shakes below him, but even that small effort makes him cough. "Shadows, I'm too old for this."

"I'm sorry they've done this to you. To all of you. It ends today." Kato's hands tighten at his side and then he reaches out to touch the man's arm, wishing he could give him strength.

To his surprise, the man stands taller and nods, looking just a little bit lighter, so Kato steps back. "They know we're here. The element of surprise is gone, but it changes nothing. Those who aren't ready to fight can stay here, but the rest of us... let's go." He turns, taking Az's hand and leading the way down the narrow halls he used to call home. *Here goes nothing.*

The courtyard is completely deserted as they make their way through it, and the dorms to the right side of the compound look like they haven't been used in weeks. Azrian's breathing quickens as they push through the side doors leading up to the training room and find that empty, too — too empty. "Kato," he whispers. "They can't all be in surgery. Where is everyone?"

Suddenly, pain explodes behind Kato's eyes. It's blinding and he falls to his knees with a groan, his hands squeezing his skull. He thinks he hears Riley's cry next to him, but it sounds so far away next to the pain. "My head!" Kato yells, fearing it will explode.

Nut screeches from somewhere behind them, followed closely by the unmistakable sound of Axis' growl and Kato nearly blacks out from pain. He's never felt more useless in his life.

He hates it more than anything, and he calls out for Az, needing to know he's okay before he dies. "Az! It's—" Kato struggles with words, unable to warn him that there's no way he can help in this condition — "Adeinde!"

~

Terror explodes through Azrian as he sees Kato collapse. It's not fair, they can't even see their enemy — how is he supposed to fight someone he can't see? "Kato?" he calls out, dropping down to put a hand to his chest as he convulses on the ground. His heart is beating so fast and so violently that Az fears it'll give out, and blind fury toward Melior and Adeinde overpower everything inside of Azrian except for fear of losing Kato.

"*Melior!*" he screams, spinning around as balls of wild, silver energy build around his clenched fists. He stands, pivoting and closing his eyes until he can *see* his power stretching out and disintegrating everything in its path. It weaves around his allies and wraps them in protective bubbles as the dressers, targets, and rock formations crumble to dust, and there — behind the large, magnetic board the Tactare used to practice telekinesis — is Adeinde herself. Pure, unfiltered fury flashes in Azrian's eyes, but before he can make a single move to try and take her out, he sees a giant black mass flying through the air.

Axis snarls as he knocks her to the ground, and the series of sounds Azrian hears next will haunt him for years to come: a scream cut off by the sound of tearing flesh, a gurgle, and then silence.

Kato and Riley stop almost instantly, rolling onto their backs as they catch their breath. Az kneels back down to wipe the sweat from his forehead and he still feels hot, like his entire body was just on fire, but the color is slowly returning to his skin.

"I'm fine, Azzy. We can't stop." The giant scrambles to his feet with a groan, blinking and shaking his head quickly as if he's trying to shake away the fog. "Melior!"

Chaos surrounds them now — everywhere Azrian looks, the dust created by his outburst clouds the room, but flashes of Videre light appear off to his left. Riley dashes toward it to find Ronan as two of the others they freed from the cells use their gifts to attack the door to the surgery room, but all the air leaves Azrian's lungs as one of the Caelim in Melior's employ cuts off his air supply.

He chokes, reaching out to call on his powers, but his mind is getting fuzzy. As quickly as it began, it ends. One look at Kato tells Az he's got the Caelim under control and based on the way her hands cling to her throat, he's using her own power against her. "How does it feel?" Kato yells and suddenly she's collapsing to the floor and he's working on the next. "Melior, you coward!"

Kato's face changes, and it doesn't take much for Az to realize that Melior must've answered him. He's stalking toward the now-open surgery door before Azrian can say a word to stop him, and he can't even follow because his path is now blocked by a Viribus.

If there's one thing he learned from his time with Rhix, it's that Viribus are incredibly strong, but not terribly fast. Az rushes toward him and catches him by surprise, sending a single pulse of power straight through his gut and sending him flying. He dashes after Kato and panics all over again when he gets to the door and sees him slamming his own head against the wall.

The sight is so strange that for a moment, Azrian *can't* react. He doesn't understand what's happening or why and would probably stay frozen if it weren't for Ronan's small body pushing past him and blasting Melior back. "Leave him alone!"

It clicks in Azrian's head that Melior was somehow the cause, and when he finally comes into view, he can see the change in him. His head is shaved, and along with the menacing scar down his face, he has two fresh ones almost identical to Kato's. One of his eyes is gold — yet fogged over, and the other is as black as always.

The light from Ronan must have blinded him and Kato rushes at him with blood pouring down his face. The gold in his eyes flashes as he takes hold of Melior's mind, and Melior grips his head, yelling out in pain. The screams seem to go for so long that even after they stop, they echo off the walls until the entire compound goes eerily silent.

"We did it, Kato." Azrian looks over at him with an exhausted smile, but Kato is on the floor... and he isn't moving. "Kato?" His chest tightens as Ronan rushes to Kato's side, but Az still can't seem to convince himself to move. It's like after everything, his body is refusing to take even one more step, and it couldn't have happened at a worse time.

Riley slams into him and knocks him forward with enough strength that it seems to break the spell, and Az follows her and once again drops down next to Kato. He starts screaming, first for a Sana he knows won't come and then incoherently, so loudly and fiercely that it burns his lungs.

The sound causes Kato to jerk awake and take a deep breath. "Shadows, Az." When their eyes meet, Kato's are greener than he's ever seen and the cuts on his forehead heal completely. "Why are you all staring at me?" He sits up quickly and looks around the room, ready to continue fighting.

"You — how—" Az gasps for air, shock and relief making him unable to string more than a few words together. "Jellycrai?" he finishes softly, blinking to try and make sense of what just happened.

"You've been a Sana this *whole damn time?*" Riley yells, smacking Kato in the side of the head. Az reacts on instinct, tackling her back and trying to protect the skull that should absolutely *not* be healed. Kato is a Cogitare, he knows this, he's *seen* it, felt it, heard it... so how?

"I'm not a Sana, Riley." Kato stands, looking almost normal as he helps Azrian to his feet. "I don't know what I am." His hand cups Azrian's chin and he kisses his lips, sending warmth and slight pain throughout his entire body, but when Kato pulls back, Azrian feels like he's been completely healed.

Riley butts in and holds out her hand. "My head hurts too, Kato... if it has to be a kiss, I'm okay with that, too."

Kato rolls his eyes and then touches her head, closing his eyes and focusing on her for a few seconds. "It's hard... I'm tired."

"No, it actually feels better. Thanks." She steps back and Ronan wraps his arms around Kato's legs to hug him tightly, and despite his exhaustion, he can tell Kato heals him, too.

Suddenly, little bits and pieces of their journey flash through his mind. Little injuries that seemed to disappear too quickly, even using colwort. The way the cold and heat didn't seem to affect Kato quite as much as they did Azrian, and how his skin didn't suffer the same chafing and dryness that his did from the elements and lack of proper baths. But try as he might, he can't remember if Kato's eyes had changed at all during that. He was generally too wrapped up in his own situation to pay attention, and now he regrets it.

"It makes sense," he says finally, and the dull sound of conversation dies around him. "Obviously the Venandi were trying to figure out how to make more Praediti. They must have succeeded if Melior had Cogitare abilities in addition to being an Oculare, so maybe they made Kato into a Sana during all those operations and just never told him. He's a hybrid."

Kato looks over at Az with an unreadable expression and then he slowly walks toward Melior, staring down at the man who controlled nearly his entire life. Azrian joins him taking his hand as they take in Melior's bloodshot eyes and just as Kato begins to kneel down for a closer look, one of the prisoners yells for help.

All of them dart over and see a Caelim holding out his hands, sweat pouring down his face as he uses wind to keep Melior's soldiers trapped in a corner. "What do I do?!"

"Let them go." Kato puts a hand on his shoulder and the man slumps into him, pure exhaustion etched into his features.

Cal makes his way into the room past the rubble, blood coating his face but otherwise seeming unscathed. "What should we do with them?"

And suddenly all of them, even Kato, look to Az. He blushes and shifts on his feet as the weight of such a decision falls on him, but he doesn't bother seeking out Cettia's guidance. "Freeing them could be dangerous. Melior and Belua might be gone, but someone could take their place and we'll be right back where we started."

"We weren't helping him on purpose," a man around Azrian's age says. "He threatened almost all of us. They had my grandpa here and told me if I didn't help, they'd kill him."

The older Terrare from the cells steps forward, his back hunched. "That would be me. Slait wouldn't hurt anyone, he's been takin' care of me for damn near a decade." He joins his grandson and hugs him, clapping him on the back and sighing in relief. "I'm sorry I couldn't protect you."

The scene reminds him of his own mother, who had been completely brainwashed by Belua. If it could happen to her, it could happen to anyone. "Have any of you seen my mom?" Az asks, distracted from the true goal. "I was told the Contego brought her here."

"Roe?" A young woman steps forward. "She was with Melior in the surgery room. I think she's still there."

Kato touches his cheek and smiles softly. "Go to her. I'll stay right here. I can hear her thoughts."

With a rare blossom of hope, Az kisses Kato and uses his silver light to lead the way back into the surgery room. If his mother is here... he'll find her.

~

Kato looks around at all the battered people and realizes he's out of his league. He can't heal them all. He's just now learning, and if it weren't for him being on the brink of death, he probably would have never even realized it was something he could do.

He knows he heals faster than most, but he's honestly always considered himself lucky and never looked too closely at it. The green around his pupils was always so light he chalked it up to being a result of his birth, and honestly, he's always hoped his human mother just had green eyes. Like that was one part of her he carried with him. Whether that's about her, or humanity, he isn't sure.

Now he knows the truth. He doesn't have anything of her... he's nothing more than a lab rat gone right... or wrong? He isn't sure anymore.

"Kato?" Riley touches his arm, and he realizes how loud his thoughts probably were. "You aren't a lab rat. You're Kato the Cogitare... Sana? Whatever, you're Kato, and you just helped save all these people. That's what matters."

He nods, thanking her with his mind and then looking around the rubble for something to restrain the ones that chose to help Melior of their own accord. Once that's done, he stares at them and wonders what to do. "I can read your minds. I know how you truly feel. Riley—" Kato switches to telepathy — *"Should we take them home?"*

"Yes. They only played Melior's game because he had power. Now... I think they would choose the right path... or at least most would."

Kato nods, not seeing another option unless they chose to just outright murder them, and that isn't who he wants to be, especially if they're innocent. *"How will we get everyone off this island?"*

She squints at him as she tries to think of an answer, but neither one of them have a clue. He turns and does a quick count, and if he includes Azzy and Roe, there are over thirty of them that need to find their way out of Deadrun and back to their homes... and three that need to be dealt with some other way. It's clear from their minds that they weren't just following along because they were being threatened. They believe in Melior's goal, and if given the chance... they'll pick up where he left off.

Azrian joins them again with Roe and a pregnant woman he's never seen before. Both Az and his mother look strained — not like they've had the reunion they deserve by any means — and Kato's immediately on guard. "What's wrong?"

"She's just having a hard time understanding what's happened here," Az says quietly. "She was stuck with Belua for a really long time. I think it's just going to take a bit for her to remember who the good guys are."

Roe slides her hand out of Azrian's grip and goes to join some of the others, but Az keeps his chin up and looks around. "Where are you all from?"

The answers come quickly. There are people from all over Athoze with them — from Coldhallow where Cal lives to Dawndrift in the southern corner of Sastrya and everything in between. Azrian seems most interested in the group of people that claim they're from Redhaven, and as he walks closer to them, his expression gets even more curious. "One of each. Are you guys..."

"Family members of the Regnum under Melior's control," one of them states. He's nearly as tall as Kato with brilliantly blue eyes, and Kato's actually a little jealous when Azrian stares at their shaking hands. "I'm Jasestros. Son of the Regnum's Caelim, but I'm actually an Undare. Melior told her that if she didn't behave, he'd send me back bald and missing a few appendages." He grins, ruffling Azrian's hair when he finally breaks the handshake. "Thanks for the rescue."

"Yeah," Az says in a high-pitched tone. "No problem." He scoots over to Kato and plasters himself against his chest, then keeps looking through the crowd until he spots a lady with yellow eyes. "Would you be able to go find help? I know you can't teleport everyone out of here, but maybe... you could find someone? Neginah and Hanigen maybe? They're part of the Regnum."

She nods proudly, but Az holds up a hand as he tips his head up to Kato. *"Is she okay? Will she really help?"*

Kato looks into her mind, and in it he can practically see her entire life. She's someone who wouldn't hurt a fly. He looks at Az and nods. *"Yes. She's more than okay."*

"Okay. Please hurry," Az says to her. Her face softens into a proud expression as she disappears, and Az lets out a sharp breath. "Now, we should get those three to the cells with the other guards, then maybe get everyone some food, a shower and some clean clothes. Ronan and I can handle the power needed for all of that. If there are still any other Videre here, they can help too, Cettia willing."

A few Videre step forward to offer assistance, and Kato is just glad it isn't all on Azrian and Ronan. They're all exhausted, and now that they potentially have help on the way, the battle is wearing on all of them. "I will help in the kitchens. Who knows how long it will take Neginah and her twin to get here. We have to ration food and make sure everyone is fed." He touches Azrian's face and kisses him softly. "Don't wear yourself out."

"I can help in the kitchens," a young man offers as he steps forward. His eyes are brown, but there's something different about them that catches Kato's attention: there's a splash blue in one of them. "Tague," he states, holding out a hand to Kato.

He takes it with a smile. "Thank you. Terrare?" Kato asks, unable to help himself.

"Yeah. Don't let the eye fool you, I can only use the ground."

They share a chuckle and Kato releases his hand and touches Azrian's back. "I think one or two more people would be helpful. Do you have family here?"

Tague shakes his head. "No, my father works for the Regnum. They took me when he started asking questions."

Kato nods, feeling bad for him and all the families like him. "Well... you'll see your father again soon."

"I'm... gonna go help," Az says slowly, then pulls Kato into a kiss. There's a possessive energy to it that makes Tague clear his throat, and Az blushes a little as he pulls back. "Nice to meet you, Tague."

Once they have a small team of people together, he leads them to the kitchen and starts showing them where everything is. They take a quick inventory and Kato puts Tague in charge of that while a woman named Kiran takes over the perishables with the help of her daughter Aira. A younger boy named Costi tries to take charge of the cookies, and Kato laughs, sneaking him one and then steering him towards the milk cartons. "One per person, okay?" The boy eats his cookie quickly and nods, helping without any complaints as Kato works on slicing the bread and meats. Riley joins him a while later, letting him know a good amount of people are showered and hungry, and with her help, they start getting food out to the cafeteria tables.

By the time everyone is fed and clean, it's Kato's turn to shower, and though the water is cold he can't find it in himself to care. He's so tired he nearly falls asleep standing under the water before Azrian finally joins him. Kato wraps his arms around him and sighs. "How's Roe?"

"She'll be okay, but... can we *not* talk about my mother right now?" Az asks playfully, kissing his jaw.

"Of course." Kato simpers, his hands running along his back. "I missed you."

Soft lips trail down his chest as Az sinks to his knees. "Missed you too... let me show you."

No amount of exhaustion in the world would be enough to make Kato deny Azrian, and he watches him with lust-blown eyes as the world disappears around them. For a little while... it's just them. No Venandi, no Deadrun, no trials yet to come. Just them.

Everything else can wait.

~ XVII ~

THE BEGINNING

"The Itinerae returned briefly. She took Rikard with her, but I can guarantee neither of them are a threat. They just want to go home after they help the Regnum." Kato looks around the room and he feels weird speaking as if he's in charge. He isn't... and he sure doesn't want to be. "She said Neginah and Hanigen have the support of the Regnum to rescue us all. Most of them just want their loved ones back, but I'm sure there will be some people out there that believed in what Melior was doing. We'll have to deal with those people eventually."

"Eventually might be sooner than we hope," Riley speaks up. "If they band together —" She meets Kato's eyes but doesn't finish that sentence.

Instead, Jasestros finishes it for her. "We could be right back in this situation, again."

Kato looks over to Az and can tell he's still wary of new people, but Jase and Tague have proved themselves very useful in the last couple days, and Kato's kept a close eye on their minds. They truly just want to help.

"Look, there's nothing we can do about it right now," Azrian says quietly. "We stick to the plan. We send the prisoners with Hanigen and Neginah and we take everyone else home where they belong. Beyond that, it's the Regnum's job to keep Athoze safe — we can politely suggest they utilize Deadrun as a Praediti prison, but it'll ultimately be up to them to decide whether or not to actually do it. *I certainly don't want to stand guard over it, do you?*"

"Shadows, no," Jasestros hisses. "I'd like to go back to living my life sometime soon."

Tague looks at him in a way that reminds him of the way Cal used to look at Az, and one look into his mind confirms his suspicion. Tague wants to go home too, but he doesn't want Jasestros to be far. He briefly wonders how that will work out for them when he picks up the tail end of Cal's second kidnapping story.

"— they didn't even pretend to be good guys anymore. They threatened the twins and gave me a choice. But as far as I know, my family and home are okay, and open if anyone needs a place to stay."

Kato can't help but smile at the memory of Cal's parents, and his small time with Blue and Bash. He would like to see them again. Maybe he'll understand why they find him so funny. "That's kind. I'm sure someone here will take you up on that. Riley... what do you plan on doing?"

"I'm going back with Hanigen. I still don't trust the Regnum and it's not like I have a family, so..." She shrugs, leaning back on her chair until she's balancing precariously on two wooden legs. "Someone needs to keep getting their hands dirty, might as well be me."

It's so unsurprising that Kato simply chuckles, but he admires her for it. "Well, if you ever get tired of being dirty, come visit. Ronan's grown fond of you... but don't tell him I told you that."

She salutes him with a smile. "Yeah, but he's insisting on going with you two, and I'd rather not stick around for your honeymoon phase. I'll come visit eventually. You too, Cal."

Cal snorts a laugh from his seat. "About time. Thought you two would have gray hairs by the time you stopped that dance. Especially you, giant."

"Maybe it would have happened sooner if you weren't in the way in the beginning of our journey." Kato grins, looking at Az from the corner of his eye. He may be pretty clueless sometimes, but he knows he has a bond with Az that is more profound than he's ever felt with another person. Even in the beginning.

Az blushes and takes a deep breath. "Okay, okay. So, they won't be back for a few days, do you think we can keep this place running until then?"

"Definitely. There are a few Videre that are helping with electricity and we just have to ration the food, but if it's only a few days we don't have to be scarce. They always made sure to have enough food here to last a month." Kato pushes the thoughts of a honeymoon phase out of his mind to focus on the task at hand, but the conversation that ensues after is much less entertaining.

When they're finally wrapping up with a concrete plan, Riley stops Kato from leaving with a soft touch to his arm. "Can I talk to you for a minute?"

With a nod, he goes back to his seat and watches everyone leave, then turns to her. He could look into her thoughts, but even a Cogitare deserves the privacy of their own mind. "Is everything okay?"

"Yeah, I just thought you should know that your brothers are alive. Well, most of them, anyway. I've met four, but I've heard rumors there are two living down in the southern part of Edros. I wasn't sure if that was something you wanted everyone knowing."

"Brothers?" Kato sits up straighter and looks around for Az, but he must've gone out with the others. "And... how are they? How'd they get there? Do they know who I am? Or even about me?" He nearly asks a million more questions before she holds up a hand to speak, and even then, it's hard to fall silent and let her talk.

"They know who you are, but Melior forbade them from talking to you. Maybe now that he's dead, you can get in touch with them? I don't know. I'm not good at the whole family thing, I just figured you deserved to know that you have siblings out there." She smiles awkwardly, patting his shoulder and skirting toward the door. "I'll tell them to get in touch if I see them."

"Okay. Thanks." Kato stays in his seat, staring at the table in front of him. Why would Melior make him forbidden? Did he want Kato to feel isolated and completely alone? *Of course he did*, Kato realizes all too quickly. He never wanted Kato to feel accepted, all he ever wanted was a blunt instrument... and he always hated that Kato was more.

He gets lost in those thoughts until Azrian comes back in and sits next to him. "Hey, Jellycrai. Dinner's ready and Ronan's waiting for us... you okay?"

"No," he answers honestly, pulling Az into his lap with a sigh. It isn't until they're comfortable and Azrian's touch has calmed him that he finally feels the courage to continue. "I guess Riley's met my brothers. Not all of them, but four of them and she said two others live... I don't even remember where. But they were forbidden to talk to me by Melior. I have family in this world, and he took that from me, too." Kato doesn't mean to sound as if he's whining, but he knows he can trust Az with these feelings.

Az kisses him sweetly and settles in, wrapping his arms around Kato's back and rubbing soothing circles. "So, we'll find them. We'll find all of them and we'll bring them home... to *our* home."

Kato finds that doubtful, but he can't focus on future what-ifs anymore. They have far too much to do, and he has something far too amazing right here in his lap. "I love you, Azzy. I told you before we were walking into a death trap, and I'm saying it now when we're free. I love you."

"And I still think you're nuts, but... I love you too." He lifts Kato's hand and kisses each of his tattooed knuckles. "K8.0, Kato... whoever you are. I think you're wonderful, and so does Ronan... who is still waiting for us. Are you okay to go eat?"

"You can't kiss my fingers and then bring up a teenager. You know what that does to me." Kato chuckles at Az's flush and kisses him one more time before standing and setting him down. "Yeah, let's go eat."

They walk to the cafeteria hand-in-hand, but dinner is already over by the time they arrive. Ronan has two plates ready for them though and smiles widely when they join him at the table by the window. "So, you guys are super sure I can come with you, right? I won't be any trouble? Did you like my cooking? I'll cook for you!"

"Rone," Az says with an amused expression. "We've been through this a dozen times in the last couple of days. Of course you're coming with us."

Kato ruffles his hair and realizes how long it's gotten. It makes him wonder if he's growing it out to be like Azrian. "What he said. I mean, who else is going to cook for us?" he jokes with a grin.

"Pshh, no one," Ronan beams. "You two would be lost without me."

Az leans a little closer to Kato and he doesn't have to peek to know he's thinking about all the time they survived on their own, but neither of them will say that to Ronan. "We absolutely would. Not to mention, I'll have to bring backup if I want to convince Rhix to give me my job back. You'll be pretty handy there; he won't even need coal anymore."

"You mean —" Ronan looks around and leans in to whisper — "I can use my powers?"

A familiar darkness spreads across Azrian's face as he nods. "It's encouraged. I know you were young when you were brought here, but not everyone is like your mom. You'll be better off using your powers and people will love you for it."

"Cool!" He sits up more confidently this time but when he spots Roe across the room, his smile fades. "And your mother? She seems... off."

Kato's felt the same, but regardless of her trusting Belua, she still can't seem to look him in the eyes. "Az... I know this is a lot to ask, but do you think your mother would let me look into her mind?"

"No," Az says instantly. "Not after what happened to her."

Kato nods, not wanting to push in front of Rone. "Okay." He busies himself with his food and reaches out to him with his mind. *"I think another Cogitare messed with her mind, Azrian. I only want to help."*

"What?" Azrian asks out loud, dropping his fork and staring at him. "So, you think that's why she's acting like this? Like she barely knows me, and *we* were the bad guys here?"

"Do you have a better explanation? I don't, and I haven't looked into her mind because I remember how she feels about people like me. She's your mother and I want her to... like me." Kato blushes at that and tries to get back on track. "I feel a disconnect, which is something a Cogitare is capable of. And you said she hated Praediti before this... suddenly she's convinced Belua of all of them is a good person? Something is off. But I won't look unless I have your permission." He knows he should be asking Roe for her permission, not Azrian's — but if she isn't herself, how could she ever properly consent or even understand that he's only trying to help?

Ronan quietly excuses himself as Azrian's breathing kicks up. "Um... yeah, okay. I trust you. I know you won't hurt her, and if you can help her..."

Kato rubs his back like he did for him only moments ago. "I hope I can. But not here, do you think you could get her to come to our room for a conversation? I don't want her to feel attacked here in the cafe."

"Yeah," Az says quietly. "I'll try, but she doesn't seem to want to talk to me much." He visibly braces himself and stands, then wraps an arm around his head to pull him in and kiss his hair. "Meet me there in five."

Kato nods and watches him walk away. He's nervous to be in a small space with Roe — even without her thoughts, he can feel her hostility toward him — and the hatred for his golden eyes even more. It makes him wish they were greener... or more human. He's lost in his thoughts when Tague and Jase join him at his table, but after a quick conversation he realizes he's about to be late. He jumps up and takes their trays to the back before rushing toward their room, then stops a few feet away and listens to make sure they are at least speaking civilly. The fact that he doesn't hear yelling is promising. After one more deep breath, he slips inside, instantly suffocating from the tension in the room. "Hi, Roe."

"I should've known," she says coldly. "Have you come to kill me?"

Azrian's face crumples as he reaches out to her. "Mom... it's not like that. I know you'll probably never forgive me for this, but he wants to help you. *We* want to help you."

"Help me?! By trapping me in this room with that... monster?" Roe looks at Kato with pure disgust and her words actually make him flinch.

"I know you don't have any reason to trust me... but if it means anything to you, I love your son and I want to help his mother. I can really help you. I think someone messed with your mind."

Roe's face twists into an expression of rage. "The only one messing with my mind is *you!*" she screams, but Az grabs her and holds her arms behind her back.

"Please, Kato. Just do it," Az rushes out with glossy eyes. "Hurry."

"Let me g—"

Kato shoves his hesitation aside and instantly takes over her mind. He has her sit calmly, and when he's able to focus on the depths of her mind he hits a wall that was left behind by a much older and more skilled Cogitare than he is. It's a struggle, but as soon as he pushes past with a pained grunt, he sees exactly why that wall is so strong: they've almost completely rewritten Azrian's mother. She knows her son, but they've detached her ability to love him unconditionally and it makes Kato heartbroken for him. He decides then and there to never tell him and works even harder to restore it, instead.

All of it takes much longer than he'd hoped, but he's able to finally find Azrian's mother buried under the rubble they've left behind after nearly two hours. Blood drips from his nose as he coaxes her out from behind the barriers, and when she snaps out of that daze, the look she gives him makes him nervous that it didn't work. He psychs himself up to try again right up until she catches sight of Azrian — and suddenly, it's as if she's an entirely different woman.

"Azrian?" She holds out a hand and then pulls him in so tightly Kato tenses. "My boy! Where are we? I yelled for you through the smoke and... did you hear me?"

"Sm—" Azrian struggles against her grip to get a better look at her, but his confusion is clear. Kato tells him silently that she won't remember anything that happened to her after Belua kidnapped him, and after struggling with that information for a moment, Azrian hugs her properly again. "I'm sorry, Ma. No, I... I didn't hear you."

"But you're okay! Thank Cettia." She hugs him again and looks at Kato with a frown. "Why is he here... and where are we?"

Kato meets Az's eyes and backs toward the door. "I'll give you two a moment." He doesn't want to go, but he can feel she'll handle the information better if he's nowhere in sight. Hopefully, what he just did will help her see he isn't evil. He isn't a monster.

He walks awhile around the compound before he decides to go outside. It was never an option before, but now the fake grass inside the court doesn't help him at all and he hasn't seen Axis and Nut all day since they refuse to be inside longer than a few minutes at a time.

He doesn't even have to call out to them before Nut's chitters can be heard coming closer. "Hey, buddy. I've missed you two." Axis approaches with a head nod and plops down next to him on the ground. "Will you guys ever sleep inside with us?"

Axis snorts his response, and Nut yells into his mind. *"No! Hate walls. Can't breathe in walls."*

Kato huffs and lays back on the ground, staring up at the clouds with a small smile on his lips. "You know what... I actually agree."

~

"So... that's it," Az finishes, keeping his eyes low. "It's been a really long trip, but Kato isn't the enemy, Ma. He saved you, and... well, he saved me, too. He's coming with us."

"How would you know? He could have messed with your mind, with all of our minds." Roe looks as if she wants to believe him, but old habits die hard. "Cogitare take advantage of their darkness."

Tears threaten to spill all over again as a familiar hopeless feeling washes over him. He can't — *won't* — go anywhere without Kato, but he just got Roe back. "I need you to trust me. I trust him with all of me... and you will too one day. It's not a trick." He hugs her again to stop her budding argument, then steps back and clears his throat. "Get some rest, okay? I'll bring you some food later on, or if you wake up you can just come down to the cafeteria."

She nods, seemingly too exhausted to attempt to argue and leans on him the entire walk back to her room. Roe touches his face softly and steps inside. "Be careful, Azrian. I'll see you in the morning sun."

"In the morning sun," he echoes with a small smile, then backpedals until she shuts the door. He pivots and wipes the corners of his eyes as he starts to look for Kato, and when he doesn't find him in the courtyard it becomes pretty obvious where he's at.

He heads outside and shuffles with his hands in his pockets until he's collapsing next to Kato and Axis, and for once, he doesn't even mind Nut scrambling to get between them.

Kato looks over at him and then rolls over to plop his giant leg over his waist and make Nut move. "Hi, Azzy."

"Hi," he laughs, squirming a little to get comfortable. "Thank you for what you did in there. Did your nose heal okay?"

"Yeah. I forgot it even happened." Kato kisses his cheek and lays his head down. "I'm sorry things are still difficult. I can... stay away if that helps you."

Az nudges him. "Don't think you're getting away from me that easy, Jellycrai. She'll come around eventually... I did."

"I don't want to be anywhere else." He squeezes him a little harder. "I'll keep showing her I'm not like the Cogitare she met. I wish that never happened to her and although I could have taken the memory away, I felt that was wrong."

"That's because you *aren't* like that Cogitare, or anyone else. You're a good person, Kato. And she'll see it." He snuggles in, letting the heat from the sun warm him the way it's supposed to instead of the brutal heat of the Etrian desert, and all of a sudden, he can see their future laid out. A rebuilt house on their old plot of land, Ronan going to school, the occasional vacation that allows them some much-needed alone time. Maybe a beach or a trip to Coldhallow Crest. But above all, he sees happiness in his future — and a definite lack of Videre powers. Kato is finally getting a chance to be his true self, and Az wants the same opportunity. "Can I ask you something?"

"Of course." Kato touches his face softly and moves him by his chin to look into his eyes, and the contact grounds Azrian.

He takes a steady breath. "You meant it when you said you don't mind me as a human, right? You'd still want me around if I wasn't a Videre anymore?"

"Absolutely, Az. I love you for you... you know that, right?"

"Yeah, of course." The words still solidify his choice whether he already knew it or not, and Az is more grateful than ever that he found someone like Kato. "Just making sure, that's all."

"I can see the wheels turning and I'm not even looking into your head. Whatever you do, I support you. Always." Kato lets his hand slide down Az's chest and kisses behind his ear. It's been a couple days since they had some alone time while the sun was still in the sky, and Az isn't going to waste this opportunity.

He shifts to straddle him and grins, reaching up to tie his own hair back. "I love you too, by the way... now let me show you."

~

Az sits on the edge of the cliff just outside Deadrun's main entrance and stares up at Cettia. She seems to be shining a little brighter than normal in the last remaining dregs of darkness, and it brings him comfort — so much so that he nearly stays silent in order to preserve that precious peace. But there are questions still unanswered and a favor he has yet to ask of her, and this seems to be as good of a time as any.

"Cettia...? Do you read me?"

"I wondered how long it would take you, Azrian Mihr."

The voice in his mind still unsettles him even after all of his practice with Kato. He isn't exactly sure where to start with the things he yearns to know, but it becomes clear to him quickly which question is pressing most heavily on his heart. *"Can you tell me what really happened to my dad?"*

"You already know," she responds. *"Ender was a victim of Deadrun. The first of many, as I'm sure you've gathered. He couldn't escape and it cost him his life."*

"So—" Az rubs his chest and tries to breathe, but his lungs feel like they're about to betray him — *"So he didn't want to leave us?"*

"No, he did not... but I think you knew that, too."

Az traces absentminded lines on the rocks with his finger. He knows if he focuses on that for too long, he'll break — and he's come too far to let that happen now. It's time to keep moving. *"What about the rest of the Videre? What will happen to us now that Melior and Belua are dead?"*

"That's up to you. I wasn't able to reach the Videre once they were inside of Deadrun's walls, but now that the enchantments surrounding it are broken, I have access to you all once more. Do you wish to keep your abilities, Azrian?"

And here it is — the real reason he's sitting out in the cold talking to the sky when he should be getting everyone organized to finally leave. He wants to be painfully, awfully human again with every ounce of his being, and Cettia is the only one that can make that happen. "No," he says out loud, but it's barely any louder to his own ears. "I appreciate everything you've done for me, but the thing is... I guess I was pretty great before you gave me powers. I don't need to be Praediti to be good."

"*You don't,*" she agrees, and Az can swear he hears humor in her tone. "*But as you wish, Azrian Mihr. You will no longer have access to your powers. You will be exactly as you were before.*"

No, I won't, he thinks to himself. *I'll be better.* "Thank you. That's all I ask."

"*Enjoy it while it lasts, Azrian. I'll be calling on you again soon and I expect you to be ready.*"

Azrian's jaw goes slack as the words register, but each subsequent attempt to find out what that means goes unanswered. He's ready to start screaming at the sky when he spots the ship off in the distance — the ship bringing their salvation.

The boat's horn startles him even though he's staring right at it, but it's such a welcome sound to Azrian that he sprints to the side and down to the rocky edge, beaming and waving like a madman.

He greets Neginah and Hanigen with relieved laughter and tight hugs, then leads them inside as he tries to fill them in on everything that happened — his conversation with Cettia already long forgotten.

They've just confirmed their agreement to take the prisoners back to the Regnum with them when Kato comes over, looking nervous.

"Where's the Itinerae?" he whispers sharply, tugging Azrian away from others.

Confused, Az follows. "She stayed behind to help the Regnum check the Venandi's other strongholds, remember? Apparently, this place and the Rostian Ruins weren't the only ones, and those people need rescued, too. What's wrong?"

Kato stands straighter, looking around them with a blush. "I'm not going on that boat."

"Jellycrai, you have to, unless you think Cal can somehow part the water for you so you can walk back to Edros."

"Is that possible?" Kato asks, meeting Az's eyes just a little too hopefully.

Azrian blinks. "No, no it's not." He huffs, taking Kato's hand. "Look, I know you don't like it. But I'll be right there with you, and once we hit land, we don't ever have to go on a boat again, okay?"

"Didn't we just save the world? Why a damn boat?" Kato runs his hand through his hair with an exasperated sigh. "Fine. But you're not allowed to leave my side, and if I puke..." His face twists.

"If you puke, you're on your own, so... better eat light." Az laughs to show he's kidding, then plants a few quick kisses on his face. "But don't worry, I'm sure I'll find ways to keep you distracted. We'll go straight to Edros. Just think of all the sights you'll see on the way! Maybe you could draw a few of them after we rebuild the house. You could decorate the walls with your artwork."

Kato smiles widely. It's been so long since he's gotten a chance to draw that he's nearly forgotten he has the skill, and the fact that Az likes his art enough to hang it on their walls makes his chest tighten. He kisses his nose. "Yeah... I'd like that."

"See? Then it'll be fine, we'll take the boat."

"And then never again? Promise?" Kato pulls him in and nuzzles into his neck, his body slumping in defeat. "You're lucky I want to be by you, or I'd just make *this* place home."

Az lets out an offended gasp. "Here? Deadrun?" He pulls back, feeling Kato's forehead with the back of his hand. "Are you sure you're part Sana? I think that head injury stuck."

"It did. Carry me or I'm not getting on that boat." Kato playfully leans some of his weight onto Azrian, but even some is too much, and his knees threaten to give out.

"Kato!" he laughs, shoving him off. "Come on, we need to get everyone on board. I don't want to spend another night in this place as long as I live."

Ushering everyone onto the boat is a struggle. Kato isn't the only one that shares a fear of water, but after an hour, everyone is on and staring up at Deadrun. "Yeah... I don't want to spend another night here either," Kato says from behind Az, wrapping an arm around him and resting his chin on his shoulder. "Let's go home."

CETTIA'S DAWN

Please enjoy this preview...

1 The Dream

"Push. Breathe, K. I can see the head." Melior stands near her legs with his hands clasped behind his back. Her screaming has his teeth on edge despite the Sana's calming touch, and based on the crowning head, this may be her largest baby yet. "Don't stop, it's right—" K screams as the head exits her body followed quickly by broad shoulders, and the rest of him slides out with ease as she slumps against the bed. "It's a boy, a very big boy."

K begins to cry, but the baby doesn't. His skin is turning blue as the Sana turns him over and places a firm slap to his backside, and only then does he make his first noises.

Relief floods through Melior. He's happy the baby is alive and that all those extra steps he took to ensure it was a male have worked yet again. "Good job, K. He looks healthy."

The Sana hands 8.0 over to Melior after wrapping him in a towel, and the baby is still screaming, his hands in tight fists as he jerks and kicks his long legs out of the towel. "I think he's hungry, K..." he trails off, holding out the baby to its mother — even if he knows the response she will have.

"Get it away from me!" K barks, her eyes full of rage as she glares at the wailing child.

"How many times have we been through this? He is large, a wet nurse won't have what he needs, not yet. He needs **you**." He can see she won't change her mind, and as much as he has the power to force her, he doesn't want to put 8.0 at risk. He's the largest baby to ever be born at Deadrun; he'd like to see what else is special about him.

The Venandi won't be able to start tests until he's two years old, but in the meantime, he hopes 8.0 isn't like so many of his siblings and shows his powers early on. Melior feels there is something special about this baby, he just doesn't know what yet.

If only he would stop screaming. "Talitha, take him. Get him to stop crying so I can examine him."

The Sana doesn't hesitate as she holds out her arms and exits the room. The wailing baby's screams echo throughout the halls, and it isn't until he can finally hear himself think again that he turns toward K and frowns. "What kind of mother are you? He came from your womb."

"I am not his mother, nor the other seven. **You** did this to me. He isn't natural; he isn't mine. I want nothing to do with them." She lays her head back and tears well in her eyes, showing him that regardless of her cold shoulder, she feels for him. "Kill me... please! I don't want to live like this anymore."

It's almost enough to make him want to take pity on her, but she is the only human to ever survive this long. The only human to give him seven healthy babies — eight if he counts 1.0. He isn't done with her yet. "In due time, K. Once we figure out why that child is crying, the Sana will be in to clean you and take you back to your room. Cooperate, K... we don't want to restrain you again. We're supposed to be past that, yes?"

K deflates. She obviously doesn't want to be treated like a prisoner again, but she nods all the same and pulls the rough sheet up to cover her lap. Recognizing that he won't get anything else out of the woman today, Melior leaves her be — he has more pressing matters.

As he walks down the hall toward the courtyard, he can hear the baby's cries reverberating off the cafe's walls and he rushes over to make sure he's okay. He refuses to accept another failed child, and if he is a fluke, K might just get her wish. "What is happening!"

Talitha looks flustered as she holds a bottle to his mouth, trying to get him to suck. "He needs a wet nurse; he won't take the artificial nipple."

"Of course he won't, he's at least twelve pounds. He needs real sustenance. Is L still lactating?" Melior asks, remembering she passed last month the second the question leaves his lips. "Stone it. Well, we have to restrain K and let the child take it. He is more important than her moral stance." He takes 8.0 from her arms and nods at Belua standing in the doorway. "Help me restrain K. I have a feeling she will fight this time." As always, his faithful crony bows his head without hesitation and follows him to the room.

~

Once 8.0 has finally stops crying, everyone on staff looks depleted. He'd cried for hours, drinking his fill from his mother over and over until he finally fell asleep on her chest. K refuses to look at him for longer than necessary, and the second he closes his eyes, she's begging for someone to move him. "Please... take him. I have nothing left."

This time, everyone hesitates. No one wants to wake the hairless banshee and deal with his screeching again, but K crying under him doesn't help in the slightest. 8.0 begins to squirm and whimper, and only then does Melior grab him off and hand him to Talitha. They all still again as the infant falls back to sleep and they breathe a collective sigh of relief.

"You will feed him again when he wakes. You will feed him until we manage to get the bottle to work. Do you understand?" K purses her lips and turns away without an argument, but Melior doesn't trust her not to harm herself. "Keep her restrained... and Belua... stay with her. Make sure she eats and stays hydrated; our newest member needs her for now." Belua stands guard with a nod and Melior goes to get some rest of his own.

It continues this way for days on end. He still hasn't seen the baby's irises because even when he's awake, he's screaming so loudly his eyes are tightly shut. It's infuriating, and after a week, Melior lays him down on a bed and studies him. The crying is unbearable for everyone involved, and not for the first time, Melior considers tossing him into the Aswel Sea.

Suddenly, 8.0 stops crying and Melior tentatively moves closer. He doesn't want to break whatever spell the little nuisance is under by making too much noise or any sudden movements, so he's careful about it as he sits next to him and gazes into his eyes for the first time — his very **golden** eyes. "Sweet Cettia in the sky!" Melior jumps up from the bed and gets a closer look. "A Cogitare!"

The elation and surprise he feels have him nearly yelling in celebration. Thoughts flash across his mind as he thinks of all the things he can accomplish if he can groom this Cogitare the correct way, and as his mind reels, the baby begins to fuss again. "No, no... we were making progress. Shhh... be a good lad."

He scoops up the baby and clears his mind to focus only on him, and when 8.0 settles once more, he finally realizes the problem. "It's the noise, isn't it? All the busy rooms, a million thoughts screaming in your tiny head." Melior almost laughs at how clueless he's been, and now that 8.0 is calm, he can see just how intelligent the Cogitare seems to be. 8.0 reaches out a hand and touches the scar down Melior's cheek as he gazes into his endlessly black eyes. There's a level of comprehension on his face that nearly makes Melior forget the small Praediti is only a week old.

They keep 8.0 separate from then on out. Only one person goes in at a time to feed him, and he's taking a bottle without assistance and watching whoever is feeding him with wide eyes by the time he's a month old. The green ring that appeared around his pupils is unlike anything Melior's ever seen — unlike anything **anyone** has ever seen — but Melior hopes it's a sign they've finally achieved their goal and not a weakness in the child's Cogitare powers.

8.0 rarely cries now that his little mind is quieter, and it isn't until he knocks his head with the bottle and the unforgiving glass busts his eyebrow open that he starts again. When the bleeding ceases, Melior lays him down for a nap and sighs at the new mark on the baby's face before taking his leave.

When he returns hours later, he drops the bottle he has in his hand and ignores the shatter of glass as he stares at the child in awe. His eyebrow is completely healed. Confused, Melior grabs a piece of the broken glass and brings it to 8.0's arm, sliding down just enough to break the skin. When he wakes, all he releases is a pained whimper as he pulls his arm away, but Melior has to see... has to see if he heals again.

After calling for another bottle, he begins to sing loudly in his head, and the distress it causes Kato brings Melior an almost unhealthy level of joy. "You're a Cogitare. You have to be. But how... how have you healed?"

He watches the wound with a mounting level of disappointment. A true Sana would've healed already, and while the bleeding has slowed, the skin is still visibly affected. He's about to call in Talitha to see if she somehow snuck in earlier and healed the child herself when right before his eyes, the split skin begins to mend.

Speechless, Melior lowers the glass shard to do one more test, but something stops him from getting any closer when his hand is just inches away from 8.0's arm. The small Cogitare is staring into Melior's eyes again, only this time, he has frozen the Venandi's leader in place. He remains completely unable to operate his own body until he decides he's seen enough for one day, and 8.0 finally relinquishes control after making him step back and drop the glass.

If he hadn't seen it with his own eyes, he would have never believed it — but now he knows it's possible. The dream he's been trying to realize for longer than he can remember is coming to fruition at last — and if 8.0 is this powerful as an infant, he's positive he'll be an unbelievably powerful adult. "I knew you were special. We've finally done it. K8.0... you are a success."

~

Kato jolts awake as the sound of Azrian's voice cuts through the dream. For a moment, he's disoriented and scared, but he quickly reminds himself that he's not in Deadrun anymore. He's safe in Embermeadow with Azzy and Ronan by his side. Melior is gone, and so are Belua and Adeinde. There's no one left that can hurt him.

He repeats these things in his mind as his breathing steadies and he readjusts to this reality — *his* reality. The only reality that matters now. "I'm sorry," he says quietly, running a broad hand over his face. "Did I wake you?"

"No, I was already up. You okay, Jellycrai? You were yelling in your sleep."

"I... yeah." Kato rubs his arm absentmindedly and drops his gaze to inspect a mark he knows isn't there. Scars rarely last on his flawless skin, and even if they did, that was just a dream. It had to be. "I had a strange dream."

Az gently pushes him back down and lays against him. Though his hands have gotten rougher from their journey and now his renewed apprenticeship, they still feel good on his bare skin. "I could tell. Do you want to talk about it?"

Kato slides a softer hand down Az's back and ghosts his fingertips over one of his scars. It makes him wonder how big Azrian was when he was born, but he knows he and Roe aren't in a place to ask yet. She can still hardly look at him.

He tells Azrian the details of the dream he can remember, but it's already fading from his mind. "I don't know. I don't remember much after he tried to cut me the second time, I think I was waking up. But it was just a dream, right?"

"I don't know. I guess it had to have been, you wouldn't remember your own birth... but maybe it was a memory? Melior's memory?" Az asks, goosebumps rising under Kato's fingers. "That happens sometimes, right?"

"Yeah. Sometimes I'll get a random memory from someone's mind... but why now?" He knows Az can't answer that question, so he pulls him in for a gentle kiss instead. "I don't think I can go back to sleep."

It's clear from the barely muffled sounds drifting through the door that they're not the only ones awake, which isn't surprising. Ronan needs to be up for school and Roe always starts breakfast with the morning sun unless Rhix stays over, which he didn't last night.

Az huffs and carefully bites Kato's chest. "Come on. We'll get some breakfast and take a walk before the day starts."

"I'd like that." Kato sits up and leaves all the negative thoughts of his dream behind on his pillow. "I wonder if Ri is still here? She got in late last night, we hardly got to talk."

He huffs, smiling a little as he gets up to dress. "I'd imagine. It's not like her to just crash for a night and leave without bringing us news."

"Is it not like her? She's kind of unpredictable. I never know when she's coming, but she normally has good news."

Az gives him a knowing look and motions for him to cover up, then opens the door. "I'll go find out."

It makes him laugh. It definitely isn't the first time he forgot to cover up before leaving their room, and the last time it happened, Roe gave them an earful about it.

Kato hastily pulls on some comfortable pants and a white tunic, but ends up running straight into Azzy when he follows him out. He looks up to see why he stopped so suddenly and comes face-to-face with Rhix — Rhix, who has one hand on Roe's door handle like he'd been trying to sneak out quietly.

"Uh... morning," Rhix says with fake enthusiasm. "Did you two sleep... ah, shadows. Let's just pretend neither of us saw what we saw."

"I'd like that a lot more than I care to admit." Az turns away and tugs Kato along by his tunic until they're leaving Rhix behind, but Riley greets them with a giggle that slowly grows louder.

"Rhix slept in your mom's room, didn't he?" She grins at Azrian's flush and even Kato has to bite back his laugh. He attempts to hide it as a cough, but when Az looks at him as if he's betrayed him, he knows he's failed.

Shadows... if looks could kill. "Az doesn't give a stone, right, Azzy?" he blurts out, trying to ease the tension.

"Wrong, I give several stones," he mumbles, crossing his arms over his chest. "All of the stones, actually. Whole... riverbed full of them." Az heaves a dissatisfied breath through his nose and pushes past all of them to go help with the food.

Kato and Riley exchange amused glances behind him as they follow, and Kato whispers "isn't he adorable when he's annoyed?" just a little too loudly.

With his hair pulled up, it's easy to see the way Azzy's neck flushes, but he doesn't comment further as he starts helping Roe dish up the food. "Do we have enough?"

"We'll manage," she says quietly. "Can you make sure Ronan is up for school?"

"I got him." Kato turns and heads to Ronan's couch, but he's already awake and putting on his shoes. "Did you sleep okay, Rone?"

He gazes up with tired, grumpy eyes — and for a split second, he actually looks a lot like Azrian. "There are a lot of people here," he grumbles. "Can I stay home today?"

"Nope." Kato beams widely and ruffles his bedhead. "You're going to be the smart one around here and teaching me stuff soon. Can't go missing school yet, you just started this year."

Ronan's chest rises and falls with an irritated sigh. "I don't know how I'm supposed to learn anything when I can't sleep. I feel like my brain is full of volucrae."

He dresses all the same and follows Kato back to the kitchen to get some breakfast, and sure enough, it's almost impossible to squeeze them all around the small dining table. Azrian's practically in his lap and his elbow knocks against Rhix's more than once, but the food is delicious and none of them complain outwardly about the cramped space.

Rhix offers to walk Ronan to school on his way to work and it gets a little easier to breathe once the two of them are gone. Riley helps Roe clean the dishes which leaves Kato and Az in charge of cleaning up the rest of the house.

"We need a bigger space," Az mutters. "I don't know why we didn't just build it bigger to begin with. It's not like we don't have enough land."

Kato thinks about that while he finishes up their living area. When it's as good as it's going to get, they head outside to work on the landscaping. "That would have been smart. What if we build another place? One that's... ours."

"Really?" Azrian smiles softly and leans up on his toes to kiss his jaw. "That sounds great, but we're still not even done with this one."

"That *is* true." Kato looks around and tries to form a plan, but as he's about to say more on the matter, Riley walks over as she dries her hand on a towel.

"I see you two are still just as gross."

"Gross?" he asks, his eyes darting to Azrian. "We're not gross. We bathe."

He snickers, bumping Kato with his hip. "She means gross in a good way. Like we're cute. She's just jealous though, right, Ri? You wanted Kato all to yourself."

She opens her mouth to argue, but smirks as she gives Kato a once-over. "Not my usual type but I wouldn't say no. Anyway, that's not why I came in here," she says. "Kato... the whole reason for my little intrusion? I found your brothers. The ones that live in Bridgehelm."

He's still stuck on the joke when her words seep into his brain and make him stand straighter. "Bridgehelm? You said two of them were there, right? What are their names? What are they like?" he asks excitedly.

"Yes. Teagon and Aleon. You'd probably know them as K5.0 and K7.0 if you remember them at all. Teag's a Viribus bigger than Rhix and Aleon is an Itinerae. Neither of them have dual powers like you do, though. They want to come visit."

Azrian reaches over to take Kato's hand. "That's awesome news! But sweet Cettia, where are we gonna put everyone?"

Kato wants to respond, but he's struggling with words. Most of his life he'd believed he'd never know his brothers — if they were even alive — and now the prospect of meeting two of them was almost too much. He stares at them both so long they actually start to look worried for him, and he forces out the first words that come to mind: "Um... I can sleep outside with Nut and Axis."

"That's ridiculous, Kato," Az says instantly. "Your brothers would what, then... sleep with me?"

"You? No. You'll be with me." The thought makes Kato frown even though he doesn't fully understand the emotions behind it. "We'll figure it out. Maybe we can go to Rhix's house with them? Since he's always here in your mom's room."

Azrian grimaces as Riley giggles. "Kato," Az starts with a sigh. "We'll just put them on the couches. Ronan can sleep in our room on the floor. It'll be okay."

"Okay, then. It's settled, which is good. They'll be here any day now," Riley says.

Kato grins from ear to ear. When they left Deadrun, things were a constant uphill battle and each day felt like a struggle to survive, but it's only gotten better now that they're settled and finally beginning their lives. "Will you still be here when they arrive?"

She shakes her head. "Nope, I promised Neginah I'd be back to help her and Han. We've got almost everyone back where they belong, but we're still trying to get Deadrun set up as a prison. Praediti-proofing is harder than it sounds."

"Yeah, Melior used pure fear and stealing kids when they were young enough to be manipulated. I imagine containing adult Praediti is much more difficult. There's only one exit at least." Kato ruffles her hair. "You're still the shortest Praediti I know. Rone might pass you soon."

"They put the most dangerous ones in the smallest packages, K8.0," she replies in a mocking tone. "Guess that means you're harmless."

Azzy scoffs. "Yeah right. He's about as harmless as Mors Byssum."

Kato rolls his eyes and wraps an arm around Az, slouching so his chin is resting on his shoulder. "Does that mean you shouldn't eat me even though I smell sweet?"

Riley releases a disgusted noise as she turns back to the house. "That's exactly what I meant by gross, Kato!" she calls as she ducks inside, and Kato huffs into Az' neck.

"Well, at least that'll be one less person we have to house... but I'll tell you, I'm starting to like the idea of building another house. I know it'll be a lot of work, but it'll be worth it. Especially if Rhix and my mom stay together, though I can't figure out why she doesn't just stay with him. I think he's doing it to mess with me." Az tilts his head to kiss Kato's cheek and holds there for a moment. "Shadow-head."

"I-I heard him and Roe talking about it the other day. She won't leave because she said *this* is her home — even if the foundation is new — and she's worried to be far from you. If she had it her way, you'd never leave her sight." Kato turns to pull him against his chest and kisses the top of his head. "Can you blame her? You're really cute."

"Okay, but that doesn't give her the ri—" Az yelps, wrapping his arms tightly around Kato's neck as he lifts him up by his thighs. "Sweet shadows, Kato, you can't —"

Kato kisses him to stop the rambling and can feel the second he stops struggling and turns to putty. "I can't what?" He kisses again and nips Az's bottom lip. "I can. You're mine."

"Yours," Az whispers breathlessly, but Riley's voice invades Kato's thoughts to kill the mood.

"*Oh please, for the love of Cettia, wait until I'm halfway across Edros before you continue this.*"

Kato cackles loudly at her and when Az looks at him like he's crazy, he realizes he should probably explain what's so funny. "Sorry. Ri heard all that." He sets Azrian down and grips his chin.

"We'll pick that up later when Roe runs to the market with Rhix. It's been a while since we had the house to ourselves."

"Too long," Az agrees. He lets out a shaky breath and straightens his tunic, but his face instantly falls. "I doubt she's going to go until after Ronan's back from school. I don't think we'll have it to ourselves today, either."

"Then I'll just have to take you to the woods," Kato says loudly enough for Nut and Axis to hear from the porch, and Axis's huff echoes through the air around them.

Nut runs up and sits at their feet, staring up with his hands out. "*Rhix sweet bread,*" he states as Kato lifts him up as if he hasn't gained all of his weight back and then some.

Luckily for him, Kato's craving it too. "You think Rhix can make some sweet bread? For our guests, of course."

"Yeah, it depends on how late he is. He taught me how to make it though, do you want me to try?" Az asks, reaching up to scratch behind Nut's ear. "Maybe I'll make his fat free."

"Is that possible?" Kato looks at Nut and even without being a Cogitare, he'd be able to tell he isn't pleased. The raccanis snaps at Azrian's fingers and chitters as he turns away, jumping down and walking back to the porch with an attitude. "Well, he's mad at you again." Kato chuckles and takes Az's hand, pulling him back toward the house.

The grumpiness radiated off of Azrian as they passed Nut in the doorway. "He knows this is my house too, right? I don't get why he hates me so much; I'm trying. Sort of... occasionally."

"Sort of... occasionally," Kato mimics with a grin. "He's fine. He really does love you. Trust me, he can't lie to me. He's just a furry shadowhead."

Az glares at the chubby raccanis one more time before softening. "Fine. I'll get started on that sweet bread."

~

After another few days pass, Kato begins to worry his brothers won't come. The stress of it triggers yet another nightmare — one where Kato's a toddler and Melior is yelling about a baby girl. It settles something Kato was beginning to doubt: these are just dreams. They have to be. There's never been a baby girl at Deadrun. Young children, yes. But a baby? Kato would have known.

"I'm sorry I woke you again."

Az blinks sleepily. "S'okay, Jellycrai. What happened?"

"I don't know. It's kind of fuzzy, but I was at Deadrun again and Melior was angry. I was probably younger than three." Kato scratches the back of his neck and groans. "Why do I keep dreaming of that place? I want to forget I was ever there."

There isn't anything but understanding on Azrian's face as he lays down against his chest. "Trauma's funny that way. The harder we try to forget, the more it tries to hold on. You can't forget Deadrun for the same reason I no longer allow fires inside the house. Things like that leave scars... and I'm not talking about the ones on our skin."

"Right. Internal scars. Those always seem to hurt more." Kato ghosts his fingers up his arm and stares at the ceiling, thinking of how far away Deadrun *should* be yet how close to the surface it always is.

"Tell me how to help," Az whispers.

For the first time that morning, Kato smiles. "You do help. Every single day, Azzy." His thoughts travel back to his brothers, and he wonders what they're all doing right now. Are they happy? Alive even? The mere scraps of information he's gotten the last year aren't enough. He wants answers. "Do you think they're really coming? My brothers."

"Of course. I don't think Riley would lie, but maybe they're just as nervous as you are. They'll come when they're ready."

"Yeah... maybe... I wonder if Nut will be nice. He's been trying to sneak inside now that the weather is cooling down. Does it snow in Embermeadow?"

Azrian's stubble rubs against Kato's bare chest. "Yeah, it snows like crazy here. We still have about a month before it starts, but you tell that little shit that I'll fry him if he tries to steal you from me again."

Kato laughs a little louder than he meant to, seeing as the sun hasn't even peaked over Coldhallow Crest. "He could never replace you. I like the little guy, but not the same way I like you." He's still grinning as he rests his eyes, and Azrian's breathing calms the knots threatening to return to his stomach as he thinks of Aleon and Teagon again. "What if they don't like me?"

"Then they're wrong," he says quietly, knowing exactly who Kato means. "I didn't like you at first at all, but things were different with us. You *were* sort of holding me hostage and ignored me when I tried to tell you it was wrong. Your brothers don't really have a reason not to like you."

"Technically *I* wasn't the one holding you hostage... but yeah, I can see why you blamed me. I didn't see it back then — I was pretty upset about it, actually — but now I understand. I was stupid. They shouldn't have been able to lie to me for so long. I didn't want to see the truth. Thank you for opening my eyes, Az."

Rhix swears from somewhere beyond their door, but Az simply clears his throat and tries to ignore the fact that the Viribus stayed *again.* "You helped me a lot too, Kato. I didn't trust Praediti other than Rhix before you, and definitely not Cogitare. We helped each other."

"Yeah but—" They hear another noise out there and he sits up with a curious expression, but he doesn't look into anyone's mind. Since they arrived back in Embermeadow he's been trying really hard to give everyone in his family privacy.

Family. The word is still foreign for Kato, but it also settles something in his chest that he's long grown used to feeling — emptiness. An emptiness that's finally beginning to fill. "You're right, Az. You're always right..."

Just as Kato wonders if the noises outside are loud enough to drown out what he wants to do, Rhix pushes his way into their room with a wild look in his eyes. "Azrian, it's Ronan. He never came home last night."

Check it out now to find out what happens next!

GLOSSARY

Praediti

Caelim (kay-lim) - a Praediti gifted with the power to manipulate the air around them, usually characterized by pale blue irises

Cogitare (co-gi-tar-ay) - a Praediti gifted with the ability to read and control minds. They're known by their golden irises

Contego (con-tee-go) - not much is known about these rare Praediti, but their eyes appear almost colorless

Igneme (ig-nay-may) - a Praediti gifted with the ability to create and manipulate fire, usually characterized by red irises

Itinerae (eye-tin-er-ay) - a Praediti gifted with the ability to teleport. They're most often gifted with pale yellow irises

Oculare (awk-you-lar-ay) - a Praediti gifted with the ability to see things others can't — ghosts, auras, other planets. They're typically identified by their black irises

Sana (san-ah) - a Praediti gifted with healing powers, usually characterized by green irises

Tactare (tack-tar-ay) - a Praediti gifted with telekinesis. They usually have light purple irises

Terrare (ter-rar-ay) - a Praediti gifted with the power to manipulate Athoze itself. They usually have dark brown irises

Undare (oon-dar-ay) - a Praediti gifted with the ability to manipulate and control water. They typically have dark blue eyes, but can sometimes be confused with Caelim

Videre (vih-dere-ay) - someone gifted with the ability to create and manipulate energy. They're known by their gray irises

Viribus (vih-ree-bus) - a Praediti gifted with unnatural strength, usually characterized by orange irises

Characters

Adeinde (ah-den-day) - Melior's right hand; resides mainly at Deadrun; characterized by short, dark hair and colorless eyes

Aira (ay-rah) - captive at Deadrun; the daughter of Kiran

Axis (ax-is) - the valianis that accompanies Azrian and Kato through the Simbian Forest and on the rest of their journey; nearly 700 years old

Azrian Mihr (az-ree-in Meer) - shoulder-length dark hair and deep gray eyes; Videre; 5'8

Belua (bell-oo-a) - Melior's partner-in-crime; 6'3; Igneme; he travels from Deadrun to the Rostian Ruins

Blue - young sibling of Callisto; Bash's twin sister

Bash - young sibling of Callisto; Blue's twin brother

Callisto (cal-listo) - captive of Deadrun; fellow escapee of Azrian and Kato; Undare; 5'11

Cora (core-ah) - Callisto's mother

Costi (cost-ee) - young captive at Deadrun

Dabbe (dab) - Itinerae that works for the Venandi

Ender (en-der) - Azrian's father; Videre; captive of Deadrun

Galen (gay-len) - Callisto's father

Hanigen (han-ig-en) - twin brother of the Regnum's Oculare, Neginah; also an Oculare

Jasestros (jase-strows) - captive of Deadrun; Undare

K - Kato's human mother; captive of Deadrun

Kareen (kah-reen) - member of the Venandi that assists in the kidnapping plot

Kato/K8.0 (kay-toh) - member of the Venandi and resident of Deadrun; Cogitare; his eyes are golden with a green ring around his pupils; characterized by messy auburn hair with an undercut and scars that run from his temples nearly to the back of his head; 6'5

Kiran (keer-ian) - captive at Deadrun; the mother of Aira

Loni (low-knee) - member of the Venandi; works security at Deadrun

Melior (may-lee-or) - the leader of the Venandi; primary residence is Deadrun; he's an Oculare with long, graying hair typically pulled up

Meka (mee-ka) - young captive at Deadrun; tactare

Morella (more-ella) - Caelim; resides in Embermeadow

Neginah (nehg-ee-nah) - the Regnum's Oculare, twin sister of Hanigen; assists Kato and Azrian in Deadrun

Nut - a raccanis named Leiko who meets Kato and Azrian in the Simbian Forest and accompanies them on the rest of their journey

Pax (pahx) - member of the Venandi that assists in the kidnapping plot

Razzil (razz-ill) - raccanis; kin to Nut

Rhinn (r-in) - member of the Venandi who takes over bringing Azrian his meals

Rhix (rix) - Viribus; Azrian's boss; blacksmith; 6'3

Rikard (rih-kard) - young captive at Deadrun; Itinerae

Riley (rye-lee) - member of the Venandi; Cogitare; 5'5

Roe (row) - Azrian's mother; human

Ronan (row-nin) - young captive at Deadrun; Videre; 5'1

Sebbie (seb-bee) - young captive at Deadrun; Videre

Slait (slate) - Tactare; helped the Venandi after they took his grandfather captive

Tague (tag) - Terrare; held captive at Deadrun when his father began asking too many questions

Talitha (tah-lee-tha) - Sana; works for the Venandi in Deadrun

Tuyon (toy-on) - a loyal customer of Rhix and Azrian

Wayke (wake) - Oculare from Embermeadow

Others

Anzore (an-zore-ay) - Athoze's sister planet; believed to be devoid of Praediti

Athoze (ahth-os) - the world as a whole; consists of Edros, Etria, Sastrya, Rostya, and Deadrun

Avisim (a-vee-sim) - these creatures are best described as flying monkeys; they will kill for food and supplies but after years of hard work, they can be trained to send messages and letters, even over large bodies of water

Bonefell (bone-fell) - the lone inhabited town on the Sastrian Peninsula

Bridgehelm (bridge-helm) - located in the southernmost part of Edros

Brinecoast (brine-coast) - a fishing town located on the cusp of The Sutson Sea and The Vodter Bay

Capus (cape-us) - cross between a cat and a rabbit with floppy ears and a long tail

Cettia (set-tea-ah) - the brightest star in the night sky; always in the same position, making it useful for navigation

Coldhallow (cold-hallow) - located on the northern coast of Edros, Coldhallow is a fishing town that survives off craivil from The Aswel Sea

Coldhallow Crest - the mountain range just northwest of Coldhallow; the only mountain range in Edros and one of only two in all of Athoze

Colwort (cole-wart) - aloe

Coyanis (coy-an-iss) - a coyote the size of a large dog

Craivil (cray-ville) - fish

Dawndrift (dawn-drift) - located in southern Sastrya

Deadrun (dead-run) - Presumed abandoned, Dearun lies at the most northern part of Athoze and is one of many Venandi bases

Dorscuir (door-scur) - a small creature with a long, wiry tail and large ears; a cross between a mouse and a squirrel

Edros (ed-rose) - Home to Azrian, Ronan, Cal and others, Edros boasts the most mild climate in all of Athoze; Coldhallow Crest offers snow and chilly weather, but the coastal cities are prime for beach-going year round

Embermeadow (ember-meadow) - Azrian's birthplace in central Edros

Eodren trees (ey-o-dren trees) - trees that grow all over Athoze, no matter the climate

Etria (eh-tree-ah) - Sitting in between the Simbian Forest and Sastrya, Athoze's hub, Etria's climate and landscape are as different as the Praediti found there. Freezing cold nights and scorching hot days await you if you choose to venture here, but some of the best food and finest clothing can be found in Etria's towns

Faech (faych) - the worst of all the swear words known to Athozians, it's only used in extreme circumstances

Grimrock (grim-rock) - located on the coast of The Sutson Sea in Rostya

Hazelfort (hazel-fort) - near the heart of Sastrya, Hazelfort is just south of Redhaven

Hokrine (hoh-kreen) - extremely sharp, durable metal typically used for knives, spear tips and armor

Hollowater (hollow-water) - this town is located in west Etria

Mors Byssum (mores-bees-um) - translated as death cotton, Mors Byssum is extremely poisonous but looks harmless

Oxhaven (ox-haven) - this small town is located between Coldhallow and Embermeadow in Edros

Praediti (pray-dee-tee) - humans blessed with magical abilities; easily differentiated by the color of their irises and the powers they freely display.; Praediti powers are not hereditary, though having a Praediti parent greatly increases your chances of being born with abilities

Praefectus (pray-fect-us) - the ruling government in individual territories; the authorities except in cases that need escalated or controlled by the Regnum themselves

Raccanis (rah-can-nis) - known by their black eyes and tiny hands, a raccanis is a cross between a raccoon and a small dog. They're extremely loyal and loving... as long as you keep them fed

Redhaven (red-haven) - the capital city of Athoze and home of the Regnum; located in Sastrya

Regnum (reg-num) - the governing body of Athoze; consists of one of each kind of Praediti and a human

Rostya (ross-tee-ah) - More rural than any of the other territories, Rostya's mainland is full of bustling towns and growing markets now that the Great Chasm has blocked it off from the volcano

Sastrya (sass-tree-ah) - Athoze's capital, Redhaven, lies at the foot of the Tizor Mountains in Sastrya; the ruling Regnum have their headquarters here; the southern part of Sastrya is dry, vast desert, while the northern half is more temperate with mild winters and warm summers

Softpants - also known as sweatpants, softpants are found almost exclusively in Deadrun

Sweet bread - bread found in Edros with sugar baked into it

The Aswel Sea (as-well sea) - saltwater and vast, the Aswel Sea joins Sastrya, Rostya, Edros and Deadrun; it can take months to navigate the rocky waters

The Etrian Desert (et-tree-an desert) - this desert spans most of Etria, where you face scorching temperatures in the day and below freezing at night

The Rostian Ruins (ross-tee-an ruins) - destroyed long ago by volcanic eruption, the Ruins were abandoned completely and separated from the mainland by a chasm created by Terrare; not much is known about what lies on the other side

The Simbian Forest (sim-bee-an forest) - this magical forest is home to creatures of all sorts. From the craivil that fill the rivers to the avisim that own the treetops, there is no shortage of wildlife in this forest so thick Cettia's light can't peek through the trees

The Sutson Sea (sutt-sun sea) - this is the only body of water that joins the four main territories - Edros, Etria, Sastrya and Rostya - and is often used for quick trade routes

The Tizor Mountains (tie-zor mountains) - this mountain range provides shelter and privacy for the Regnum when they're not in session in Redhaven; not much is known about the interior of the mountain beyond the occasional rumor that there's a hidden city inside

The Venandi (ven-an-dee) - a group of people run by Melior and Belua; their main goal is to reach another planet to learn and adopt electricity that can be used without Videre

The Vodter Bay (vod-ter bay) - This stretch of water joins the southern part of Sastrya to the Etrian port cities

The Wasted Waters - The only freshwater sea in all of Athoze, it's shrouded by mystery and intrigue since all those brave enough to sail the waters are never seen again

Valianis (vall-ee-an-is) - a wolf the size of a horse; they're incredibly intelligent creatures with preternatural speed and a small amount of magic

Volucrae (voll-you-cray) - insects of all kinds in Athoze

Wildpeak (wild-peak) - this town is located in southern Etria

ABOUT THE AUTHORS

Celia Oliva was born in Northern California where she still currently resides with her husband, two kids, and three dogs. She is a stay-at-home mother and a full-time student that loves living the fandom life.

Emily Wilson was born and raised in Ohio and currently resides in her hometown with her daughter and three rescue dogs, Hera, Diesel, and Frankie.

Visit them at www.celiketchpublishing.com

CPSIA information can be obtained
at www.ICGtesting.com
Printed in the USA
LVHW091952140421
684522LV00015B/210/J

9 781955 054027